Courting Pain

Book 5 of
The Courtship Saga

A.R. Kaufer

ISBN 979-8-3481-7712-6
Cover image & design by: A.R. Kaufer
Background, *Courting the Stars,* & Moon Phase on spine by Cassie Evans
Courting Books Publishing
First edition, December 17th, 2024.

To all my readers who have
taken pain over and over but still
walked through the flames with
their head held high

Falling, screaming,

Hoping, praying,

All we can do

Is hold on...

-A.R. Kaufer

Chapter 1

As Rafe walks out, he can't help but smile when he notices Ana sitting in front of the fireplace. With her hand raised, she studies her ring. He chuckles, knowing she is unaware of how often she admires it.

"Did you look inside the band?" he asks as he approaches her.

She startles at his voice before meeting his gaze. "No." Removing the ring, she raises it and rotates it in her hand. "It says *Mia Estrela* inside!"

Rafe sits beside her, taking the ring, and placing it back on her finger. "Of course. Who else would it be for?"

She giggles before kissing him softly on the lips. "Thank you for everything. Breakfast is ready, too."

He helps her stand and walks with her to their table. "How did you sleep last night?"

"After dancing all evening? Of course, I slept well. No nightmares, either."

"You really love our ottoman, don't you?"

"Of course I do. When we were forbidden, and you would scoop me up into your strong arms and carry me in there, those few minutes mean more to me than you'll ever know." She averted her eyes. "I want to tell you something, but I'm not sure how you'll react."

"Just be honest. That's all I ask for."

"If the treaty fell through, or it wasn't going to happen, and we couldn't be together, I considered asking you to take me away. I knew we couldn't go back to Earth, but I thought we could disappear to another realm. Don't get me wrong, I didn't want to abandon my kingdom, but I didn't want to rule over one where love was forbidden, either."

"You really thought about leaving?"

"Yes. I wasn't going to lose you, not after everything we'd been through. I would rather be a nobody, hiding away, than to be queen over a kingdom where love was illegal."

Rafe rakes his fingers over his stubble while absorbing her words. "I don't know what to say. I've been trained and programmed to protect the throne and kingdom, so the thought of running away scares me. However, if it was the only way I could be with you and not fear being seen together in public, I could see myself taking you from here."

"Rafe, I am grateful the treaty went through. I risked everything for us."

A knock at the door interrupts her. Rafe answers and lets Aylin in. "Everything all right?" he asks as she approaches Ana.

She holds up the book she previously borrowed. "I have a few questions, if Her Majesty will have me?"

"Of course," Ana says getting to her feet. "We only just finished our breakfast. How can I help?"

They sit on the chaise, with Rafe gathering dishes to give them privacy. Then he goes into the washroom after handing them off.

Ana helps Aylin with a few Earth objects mentioned in the book and answers questions as best she can. She tells Aylin she is impressed at how well she is doing, understanding a book from a planet she's never been to.

"Thank you, Majesty. I am enjoying it immensely."

"I'm glad to hear that," Ana says, lowering her gaze to the floor.

"Is something the matter?"

"Can I ask you a very personal question? Please, understand, you are under no obligation to answer it."

"Of course, mi'lady."

"I know Joph said he walked in on you and Roesh in the medical center at NightFall. Have you and Roesh… You know…" Aylin's eyes meet hers, and she can see the confusion etched on her face. Ana blows out a breath. "Have you had sex?"

"Yes, we have. If I may ask, why are you embarrassed to discuss this?"

"I went through a lot on Earth, which I'm still working through. Being engaged to Rafe, waiting for our wedding night, I want to be ready. I can't really talk to Kara about this, as she doesn't have experience with men. At least, not to my knowledge. Or wings. If you are uncomfortable or don't wish to discuss this, I understand."

Rafe steps out from the washroom and goes to the window, so they may continue to speak in private. He can't hide the concern on his face, but he gives Ana the space she deserves. He knows she will speak to him, if something is wrong.

Ana gives him a small smile before returning her attention to Aylin. "Mi'lady, I will happily answer any questions for you and help anyway I can."

"Oh, thank you. I can't tell you how much I appreciate this."

"What would you like to know first?"

"What is it like? Does it hurt?" Ana asks.

"It can be painful the first time, but it's different for everyone. I don't need any details, but I'm sure the two of you have… done other things, right? The night of the wedding, do those first to lead up to it. It really helps get you ready and makes everything go a lot smoother." Aylin's brow furrows at how red Ana's face is. "Your Majesty, are you all right?"

"Yes, I apologize, but I do embarrass easily. It's me, not you. I can't help it. I'm so worried, with my wings, too." She cocks her head when Aylin gives her the biggest grin. "What?"

"Mi'lady, that can be the best part. If I may be so bold, taking to the air with nothing between you while in each other's arms is absolutely incredible."

"Really?"

Aylin nods. "Oh, yes."

"Wow. Um, what about controlling my wings while we're… um…"

"Have they been an issue so far?"

"No, but I've read how intense sex can be, and how lost in the moment people are. I'm terrified they'll shoot open."

Aylin stifles the laugh, turning it into a cough. "Apologies. You are still training to use your wings, correct?"

"Yes."

"At your next training session, do this. Fly a lap or two, then land. Bring your wings in and walk a lap. Alternate, flying and walking. What this does, your wings will prepare for flight, wanting to open, and walking instead well help you control them. It took me a long time to work with my wings."

"What? Being born with them, I thought everything was natural for you?"

"No, Majesty. Some of us take right to them while others need a bit of time."

"I apologize, but that actually makes me feel a little better."

"No apology necessary."

"Aylin, will you keep this conversation in your confidence?"

"Of course, Majesty. If you wish to command me so, I will understand."

"No, it's okay. I trust you. I wouldn't have opened up to you like this if I didn't. It's hard for me to trust, but I can see how kind and genuine you are."

"High praise, thank you."

Ana glances at Rafe, who is pacing in front of the window. "Speaking of training, he's probably ready to take me to the center. I will try what you suggested. Thank you, and please know, you are always welcome to stop by."

"Yes, Your Majesty." She stands and bows. "Thank you."

Ana walks up to Rafe and takes his hand. He kisses her palm while studying her face. "Are you all right? You look a little flush."

She gives him a reassuring smile. "I'm fine."

He pulls her to him then strums one hand through her wings. "And these? How do they feel?"

"Really, I'm okay. I do need to stretch them, though. Can we go to the training center?"

"That's a good idea."

He follows her into the closet, where she pins a tiara in place, then studies her reflection in the mirror along the back wall. Rafe steps up behind her.

"Still nervous about being crowned a prince?" she asks when she notices him staring at her tiara.

"No, not at all."

She tilts her head and smiles. "Really?"

"Fine, yes, I am a little bit. What did you girls talk about?" he asks in an attempt to change the subject. "Is she liking the book?"

"She is."

He clasps her hand and leads her from their quarters and into the corridor. Two guardians Ana doesn't recognize greets them.

"I am Kellan, and this is Erick." They both bow. "We are here to serve you." Kellan is similar in height to Ana, with long blonde hair. Her wings are almost silver, contrasting against her dark uniform.

Erick is a tad shorter than Rafe, with dark brown hair and pale blue wings. Ana tries not to stare at either guardian's wings.

"We are going to the training center," Rafe explains.

"Yes, Guardian," Kellan answers.

"I have resigned my commission. Please, call me Rafe. Both of you."

"Yes, sir— uh, Rafe."

She leads the way with Erick on her heels. Rafe guides Ana through the crowd. The noise and bustle are a nice distraction from her thoughts, so she enjoys it until they arrive at the center.

Kellan inspects inside while Rafe and Erick keep watch over Ana. Once she gives the all clear, Rafe leads Ana in while they stand guard in the corridor.

Ana opens her wings and stretches them, noticing when Rafe does the same. "You need to work yours, too. Don't you?"

"They are a little stiff." Ana approaches him and kisses him while her fingers ruffle one of his wings. He gently grips her wrist and steps back. "We are here to train," he says before his lips meet hers.

"Hmm, I'm sure there are other things you could train me in."

"What has gotten into you?" he teases as he goes into the air.

She doesn't speak as she joins him, her thoughts focused on Aylin's suggestion as she completes a lap. After landing, she retracts her wings. Rafe is instantly beside her.

"Are we done already? Is something wrong?" His voice wavers with concern.

"I'm okay. It's a training exercise Ayling told me about."

He says nothing as they walk a lap, then return to the air. She repeats the process, flying then landing again. Rafe shakes his head in confusion.

"What is this technique for?"

"It helps me control my wings. She's right, flying for a bit then landing, then walking, they want to open on their own. I retract them and keep them closed."

"Are you having a problem with them? Why didn't you tell me sooner? Are they hurting? Do you—"

Ana lifts her hand to silence him. "Rafe, really, I'm okay. It's to help when we're… when, um," she stutters for a moment before collecting herself. "It's to help when we are together. Physically."

He chuckles and kisses her on her forehead. "Why now? You've done so well with them."

"Thank you. I know I have, but with our wedding this year, I want to be ready for the wedding night. I wanted to start training now so that night is as natural as anything else."

"Ana, I'm sorry."

"Whatever for?"

"I didn't think about any of this."

"It's okay."

"Thank you for opening up and sharing this with me." He kisses her softly. "I want you to be open like this, to know we can discuss anything."

"I'm trying. Can we return to our quarters now?"

Chapter 2

Ana and Rafe wait in the corridor with Erick while Kellan inspects inside. "All clear," she says as she joins them.

"Thank you," Rafe responds, taking Ana's hand and leading her into the room.

He's going towards the closet when Ana locks the latch in place. "Rafe?"

He turns and watches her walk to the middle of the room. When she faces him, he joins her. "What's wrong?"

"Nothing. I would like a little more training, with my wings," she answers as they expand from her back.

"What kind of—" Before he can finish, her mouth is on his, devouring him as she climbs into his arms. He takes off into the air.

"No, love."

"What do you mean?"

She pulls away and holds his hands. "Close your wings."

"Ana, are you sure you're ready to try this?"

"Only one way to find out."

"Hmm, okay." He does as she requested, closing his wings and clasping her hands firmly.

She holds him against her chest, and he takes one hand up her gown and to her inner thigh. Once she nods in approval, Rafe slowly lowers her undergarment.

"Ana, if you feel your wings giving out or—"

"I will tell you, I swear. Because the last thing I want to do is hurt you."

While his fingers tease between her legs, she keeps her focus on her wings. The pleasure rushes between them. Her wings go limp momentarily when she's overwhelmed, but she catches herself and keeps them in the air. Once they are finished, she slowly lowers them to the floor.

"Mia estrela, I can't believe how well you are doing with your wings!"

"That was intense," she rasps as she falls into his arms. "I need a shower now."

"We both do." He carries her into the washroom, gently places her on the vanity, and starts the water. "Go ahead and get in while I get clean clothes for both of us."

"Yes, love."

Ana strips down and steps under the hot water, letting it ease her sore muscles. Rafe joins her a few minutes later. They clean and dry off, then dress. The bell rings as they step out of the closet.

Rafe answers the door. He gestures Kara and Evren inside, along with staff who set up lunch then leave.

Ana takes a sip of tea before smiling at Kara. "Thank you for the ball last night. It was absolutely wonderful! How late did the two of you end up staying?"

"I'm glad you enjoyed it. We left around three, once everything was cleaned up."

"Kara, I'm so sorry."

"Sorry for what? You're our queen. It's not your responsibility."

"I know, but still—"

"Don't worry about it. We all enjoyed last night, and that's what matters."

"Yes, we did."

"I'm glad, because I know how self-conscious you were before we left."

"Honestly, I don't know why I let it overwhelm me like that."

"You look really happy today. And relaxed. I haven't seen you like this in a long time," Kara says before finishing her bread. "I've been worried about you."

Rafe and Evren gather dishes and leave, giving Ana and Kara some time to talk.

"I've accepted my wings, accepted who I am. It's a new year, and a new me, and I'm trying to move on from the past to focus on the future instead." Her eyes close as a shuddered breath pushes from her lips.

Kara takes her hand. "Ana, what's wrong?"

"Hmm, my wings are hurting. We tried something new, and it was really intense."

"Do you need Rafe?" Kara asks when Ana's grip tightens.

"Absolutely not. You know he will try to take it, and you know he can't."

"Then what can I do?"

"Distract me. Talk to me about your upcoming wedding."

"Oh, um. Okay. I think we have nearly everything picked out. The menu has been a sticking point, because she really wants traditional elvish food, and I like the NightFall cuisine."

"Why not have both?"

"She's worried if any elves do come, it might offend them." Kara watches Ana for a moment, relieved when her grip eases. "Are you feeling better?"

"Yes, it passed."

Rafe and Evren return. He leans down and kisses Ana on her forehead. "Everything all right?" he asks, looking at their hands clasped together.

Kara laughs as she stands. "Yes, we needed a moment for some girl talk."

"Oh, Bela and Joph should be joining us for dinner tonight," Ana reminds Evren as she joins them. "I'm not sure what time they'll arrive. We'll probably eat around five."

"You're excited about telling them, aren't you?" Kara asks.

Ana laughs in response. "Of course. You know how much they mean to me."

"To us," Rafe says, taking her hand and kissing her palm.

"I really like Joph," Evren admits quietly. "He's very smart."

"Yes, he is. I feel bad I haven't interacted much with the leader of MorningStella."

"I know we're waiting for our honeymoon to go there, but you could invite him here for a meet and greet," Rafe suggests.

"I love that idea. I'll message him."

"Hmm."

"What, Kara?"

"May I suggest you dine with him in the dining hall or set up private dining in one of the ballrooms? Since it will be your first formal meeting, it would be inappropriate to host him in your private quarters."

"That's fine. We'll set something up. Speaking of the dining hall, I guess I should have more of my meals there. I need to walk around more and meet my people, instead of hiding in here."

"Ana, you've had to keep a low profile because of assassins and Remus. Now that things seem to finally be calming down, we will do as you wish."

"Thank you, Rafe."

"Speaking of which, Evren and I are going to check on things. I'll let you know when Joph and Bela arrive."

"Thanks, sis."

Ana walks them out, then she faces Rafe. "I am exhausted after all of that. I'm taking a nap. You don't have to lay with me, if you aren't tired."

"Let me use the washroom, and I'll join you."

"All right."

She changes into a nightgown, dims the lights, and waits by the fireplace. He steps into the room and can't help but stare.

"What are you looking at?" Ana asks, worried something is wrong with her hair or gown.

"Only the most beautiful woman in the entire universe. The way the flames are illuminating you, capturing your lovely features, it took my breath away."

She blushes furiously. He steps up beside her, gently cups her face, and kisses her. His tongue teases inside her mouth as his desire for her grows, until she steps back.

"Rafe, can we get a nap?"

His brow furrows. "What's wrong?"

"I'm exhausted from our training sessions."

He lifts her up and carries her to bed before stripping out of his jacket and shoes. After climbing in, he pulls her to his chest and kisses her on top of her head.

"Get some rest."

With his shirt clutched in her hand, she falls fast asleep. Her exhaustion washes over him, and he joins her only moments later.

The bell rings, waking Rafe. Ana sleeps peacefully beside him. He answers the door to find Kara waiting for him.

"Everything all right?" he asks.

"Yes. Where's Ana?"

"Getting a nap."

"I wanted to let you know, Bela and Joph are here. They said five is perfect for dinner."

"We'll see you all then. Thanks."

Kara looks down for a moment. "Ana said she did some intense training today. Is that why she's napping?"

"Yes, but she's fine."

"All right. Thanks."

Rafe shuts the door and returns to bed. He takes Ana's hand, concentrating, and gasps softly when he feels her pain.

"What are you doing?" Ana asks, pulling away and stretching.

"Will you tell me about it?"

She yawns and shakes her head. "Tell you about what?"

"Your pain."

Her gaze lowers. "It's nothing," she says with a shrug of her shoulder.

"Don't hide from me. Why do you hurt? Where?"

"Rafe, please, I'm okay."

He takes her hand and pulls her onto his lap. "Fine, I won't ask again. Even though I am worried sick about you. If it's serious or gets worse, promise me you'll tell me."

"I will."

"All right. Oh, Bela and Joph arrived. Dinner has been arranged."

"Good." Ana turns to Rafe, leaning up and kissing him. "Now, about earlier by the fireplace…"

"No, Ana. Not until your pain is gone."

"It's not a big deal."

"Then why won't you tell me about it?"

She pulls away and walks to the washroom, where she turns on the water while stripping down. Rafe rushes to her.

"We already had a shower. Did you have an episode? Is it your wings? Talk to me, Ana!"

The anger in his voice penetrates her chest. "I would if you were asking out of concern, but I can't talk to you when you're angry like this."

"Ana, please, tell me. I am begging you," he says, clasping her hand.

She steps into the shower. He undresses and joins her a few moments later. Her gaze meets his, and he can see both her pain and anger.

"All right. If you must know, my wings are sore from earlier because I pushed myself."

"I don't understand."

"The physical exertion—"

"No, I get that. I mean, I don't understand why you didn't tell me?"

"Because I was afraid you would be angry with me for pushing myself so hard. Or angry with yourself for letting me. Or both." Her shoulders sag. "I was afraid you wouldn't let me train like that again."

"I'm not angry at either of us about it. Will you let me help you with it?"

"Not to take the pain?"

"I'll massage your back, here in the shower." He grows concerned when tears slide down her cheeks. "Is the pain that bad?"

"No, I'm grateful you aren't angry at me."

"Ana, we've talked about this. I'm working on it for you. I'm upset you're hurting, but not angry." He starts gently at first, massaging around her wings, before working harder on her shoulders. "You are very tight from this. I think next time, we'll do a little more warm-up. Let's finish in here, get dressed, and we can play some cheshire until dinner."

"Sounds good. Thank you, love."

Chapter 3

Rafe answers the door, then gestures Bela and Joph to enter. Bela approaches Ana, taking her hands, and bowing.

"Your Majesty, that gown with your wings… There are no words."

While getting dressed, Ana decided on a crimson gown covered with black lace roses. She smiles at Bela. "Thank you, Count." She opens her mouth but is interrupted when the bell rings again. Rafe lets Kara, Evren, and staff inside.

Once everything is set up, they sit together at the table. "Majesty, if I am not too bold."

"Joph, please ask whatever you'd like," Ana responds.

"Bela mentioned your wings. I know you had some trouble with them in the beginning. How are they now?" He glances over when Bela sighs loud enough for everyone to hear.

Ana chuckles softly. "Bela, he knows he can ask me anything. It's okay, really. We have started flight training. It was scary the first time. My wings gave out, and I fell, but Rafe was right there to catch me."

"I can't imagine how scary that was," Bela comments while buttering his bread.

"I almost decided I was done with it, that I didn't want to try again."

"What convinced you otherwise?" asks Joph.

"Smaug, my dragon." She laughs. "Oh, right. He lives in the woods now. The other dragons accepted him."

"How did they respond to you?" Joph inquires, his eyes brimming with curiosity.

"They let me pet them and fly around with them." She giggles when Joph's jaw drops. He slams his mouth shut while shifting in his seat. "There's no reason to be embarrassed," she assures him.

Joph turns to Bela. "Can we go see them?"

"Tomorrow. It'll be dark soon, and I'm tired from our trip."

Ana nods. "Yes, tomorrow should be fine." Her smile grows. "We have news to share."

"As do we," Bela says.

"Please, go ahead."

"Joph and I discussed it in great length, and with everything going on with Remus at the time, we decided to get married."

"Congratulations!"

"Thank you, mi'lady. We held a small ceremony last weekend."

"Oh, you're married now!" Ana exclaims. "I'm so happy for the both of you."

"We all are," Rafe adds. Kara and Evren nod.

"Thank you. I apologize that you weren't invited."

"Remus was still a threat. I understand completely. We all do. I sincerely hope you and Joph will come to ours."

Bela sits up straight. "Sorry?"

"Rafe asked me to be his wife, and I said yes. We are now betrothed."

"Ah, wonderful news indeed! Of course we will come. Wild nestles couldn't keep us from it."

"I am envious, though," Ana admits.

"Of what?" Bela asks.

"You and Joph were able to have a small, private ceremony. Kara and Evren will have that, too. Don't get me wrong, I am excited to marry Rafe, but we will have to have a huge wedding. Not what I had in mind."

Rafe faces Kara. "We have to, don't we?"

"It's tradition," she says, keeping a neutral expression. "I'm sorry. If there was any way to change it, I would."

"No," Ana says. "It's all right. At least we can get married now. I shouldn't even complain."

Rafe takes her hand. "Ana, it's one of the most important days in your life. There's nothing wrong with having a preference."

"I mean it. It's okay. We wed, then you are officially crowned as Prince. Still nervous?"

He chuckles. "No, not anymore."

Bela's eyes widen. "I never thought of that. First, a Guardian Queen. Now, a Guardian Prince! Things are changing for the better, aren't they?"

"Yes, Count." Rafe smiles at him before giving his attention to Ana. "I have a confession to make."

Her heart hammers in her chest. "What?"

"When Bela was being threatened with execution, and you left here to go and save him, I was so angry at you."

"Yes, I know this."

"You don't know why. It wasn't just because you went behind my back, but because I was jealous. You dressed up to dine with him, displayed affection to him in public, and you spoke so highly of him. I thought you had feelings for him. Romantic feelings. I thought that's why you were so adamant to save him."

"Are you serious?" Ana asks. "Rafe, of all people, you should've known better."

"I know that now, but when we were in the woods that night, and Bela introduced Joph as his partner, I nearly fainted from shame. I was angry at myself, and I took that out on you."

Ana shakes her head. "You thought I was in love with the count?" Everyone remains still, enthralled in the drama unfolding before them. The tension eases when Ana breaks into a fit of laughter. "Oh, my God. How could you possibly believe that? You know you are the only man I will ever love!"

"I know, I know. I am so sorry."

"Ana, I had no idea you thought so highly of me from the beginning."

"I did. I considered you a friend from our first meal. I have a sense about people, one that's usually right. I do apologize for staring when we first met. You were the first vampyra I'd ever seen."

He looks at Rafe. "You truly thought she had feelings for me?"

"Yes."

Ana gasps. "That's right! You were angry when he introduced himself and asked me to dine with him."

Bela chuckles. "Really?"

"Yes, he was. Rafe, you know I only have eyes for you."

"I do. I was stupid."

"You know you're forgiven. You are right, though. I do have feelings for him."

"What?" Rafe practically yells.

"Feelings of compassion and friendship."

"Ana," Rafe exclaims as the table erupts with laughter. "It's not funny," he says, losing the battle and joining in. "Fine."

When he stares intently at her, she cocks her head. "Don't you dare!" she cries out, unable to defend herself as he plants kisses along her face and neck.

"You know you deserve the punishment."

She playfully bats him away. "Bela, Joph, my apologies."

"None needed, Majesty," Bela says before taking a drink. "As I've said, I am happy your people is so open and expressive with your emotions. I wish my people were, as well. You two are a wonderful couple."

"Thank you. Will you and Joph be going on a honeymoon?"

Bela shakes his head. "I do not know this word."

"Right, my apologies. On Earth, when a couple gets married, they go on a honeymoon after. Meaning, they take a trip together, to celebrate being wed."

"I see. We haven't planned anything. Is that something you and Rafe will do?"

"He's taking me to MorningStella. It's the only quadrant I haven't been to. I'm excited to see the beach."

"It is beautiful there."

"You've been?"

"Once, a long time ago." He smiles at Joph. "Perhaps a trip would be nice."

"We could use the time away."

Ana smiles, taking Rafe's hand and squeezing it. He brings it to his lips and gently kisses between her knuckles. "I can't wait to take you there."

"Yes, with Kane and Remus dead, it's nice to think of traveling. Not that danger isn't still around, but at least it's not hovering over us like before," Bela says.

Ana's smile slips momentarily before she excuses herself. "I need to use the washroom."

Rafe and Kara exchange a concerned glance when she takes off. Rafe excuses himself as well, then he knocks on the door. After receiving no response, he opens it, only to find Ana sitting on the edge of the tub with her face buried in her hands.

"What's wrong?"

"Nothing," she says with a sniffle.

"Are you ill?" He grips her chin and raises her head, forcing her to meet his gaze.

Her eyes lower. "No."

"Then what's wrong?"

"Hearing him speak of Kane and Remus. It brought back such awful memories."

Rafe pulls her to him and holds her tightly. "They are dead and gone. You're safe now. It's all right." She cries into his chest, as his hand strokes through her hair.

She finishes and wipes her face clean. "Thank you."

"Always, for you."

They return to the table. "What time are we leaving to see the dragons in the morning?" Ana asks.

"We'll go after breakfast."

"Wonderful," Joph exclaims, causing everyone to look at him. "Apologies," he mumbles.

"We are all excited to see them," Ana says with a quiet laugh.

"Speak for yourself," Kara teases.

Ana rolls her eyes. "You know you want to see them."

"Thank you for having us for dinner. We will return in the morning for breakfast, then see the dragons."

"Yes, Bela," Rafe confirms.

"Good night," Ana says when they reach the door.

"Until the morrow," Joph offers with a bow before following Bela from the room.

Kara and Evren approach, ready to take the dishes to the kitchen then turn in. "We'll see you guys tomorrow."

"See you then, sis," Ana says with a smile.

Once they leave, Ana and Rafe sit on the chaise. After a few moments of silence, he takes her hand.

"Do you want to talk about it now?"

"About what?"

"The washroom."

Ana pulls away and goes to the window, her arms wrapped tightly around her stomach. Rafe steps up beside her.

"You don't have to tell me anything, you know that."

"Do I?"

"What do you mean?"

"If I wanted to talk about it, I would. You shouldn't have to keep asking me to open up."

"Ana, you were taken and traumatized. More than once. It's understandable you don't want to discuss it. But you need to."

"I think I want to read for a bit before bed."

Rafe forces his smile. "Anything in particular?" She shakes her head, so he goes to the bookshelf.

While he's looking, she struggles to contain her emotions. Between Remus' torture and what happened at the camp, she becomes overwhelmed.

"Rafe—"

He rushes to her and catches her as she passes out. Gently picking her up, he carries her into the closet and places her on the ottoman. He changes into pajamas, then changes her clothing as well before taking her to bed.

Despite not being tired, he climbs in with her, holding her and comforting her.

Chapter 4

"Ana, what happened last night?"

She finishes pinning in her tiara and faces him. "What do you mean?"

His jaw clenches. "You fainted."

She sits on the ottoman, refusing to meet his gaze. "Because I was back in MoonFrost, being tortured. I was back in that tent, with that man, and…" Her breath hitches. "I hid from you again."

He sits beside her. "Look, I'll say this a million more times, if it's what it takes to get through to you. I want to be here for you. I want to help you. More than anything, I want you to know, you don't have to go through this alone. Let me in. Please."

"I'll try to do better. I know you mean what you say. We're about to have company, and I just want to have a good day. We can talk this afternoon, I promise."

"All right. I'll hold you to it."

He stands and goes to his closet, removing a jacket to slip on. When she doesn't get up, he steps closer to her.

"Ana, what's wrong?"

She sighs. "Sorry, not thrilled about putting on yet another gown."

"I know you miss being comfortable. I do, too. I miss my sweatpants."

Ana giggles. "When did you wear those?"

"To sleep in."

"I can't picture you in sweats." She stands and walks to a rack of gowns. A cream-colored one catches her eye. "This is a little different from what I normally wear."

"I think it'll look great on you."

She changes into it and examines her reflection in the mirror. "I don't know."

"It looks great. Especially with your wings."

"Thank you," she says. He opens the drawer and removes her rings. She smiles as he slips them on. "Are we getting matching bands, for the wedding?"

"If you want to. I would like that."

"So would I. Could we go next week and look? I know there's no rush, but I'm going into the village to order new gowns."

"What kind of gowns?"

She looks at him. "Are you ignoring my question?"

"What? Of course not. Yes, we can go look at rings. I'm sorry. I was confused, after you said you were tired of gowns."

"I would like some that I pick out."

"Ah, I understand. Yes, we'll go into the village. Just say when you want to go, and we'll make it happen."

"Thank you, Guardian."

He bows to her. "My pleasure, always, for Your Majesty."

She runs and jumps into his arms, kissing him hard. "Jerk!" she cries out, when he flies up into the air. Her grip is tight as she looks down.

"Surprised?"

"Always!"

"I believe we have company."

He lowers them down, and they leave the closet. He walks to the door, then lets Kara and Evren in. Breakfast is set up, as Bela and Joph arrive.

Ana looks at Joph. "You're really excited to see the dragons, aren't you?"

He chuckles. "Is it that obvious?"

"It's okay. I am, too. They really like me."

"You're the only one they like," Kara exclaims with a laugh.

"Because of the prophecy?" Joph asks, looking down

when Bela shoots him a sharp look. "My apologies."

Ana approaches them, taking each of their hands. "Bela, it's okay. Joph has done so much for me, he can ask anything, any time. Really. Joph, I mean that. You know how much you both mean to me."

"Yes, Ana," Bela says.

"Thank you," Joph replies.

"Yes, because of the prophecy. Apparently, the Crimson Queen can have a calming effect on creatures. It's why they respond to me so."

Evren joins them. "I've been reading a book of our myths and legends, and it says the Crimson Queen can tame even the wildest of beasts."

"Well, that explains Rafe," Kara says.

He blushes as everyone laughs. "Kara, really?" he says with a chuckle.

Ana scowls playfully at Kara. "Sis, be nice."

"Yes, Ana. Come on. Let's eat!"

They sit at the table and begin to dine. Joph looks at Ana. "Majesty, if I may, now that you are getting married, have you discussed having children?"

Ana laughs as Bela hangs his head, having given up on ever having any control over Joph. "Not really. We're still taking things slow."

"I understand."

"Joph, I know Ana said you can ask anything, but that was a very personal question. Why would you ask that?" Bela scolds.

"It's okay. Honestly, I think as a scientist, you are curious to see what our offspring would look like. Am I wrong?"

"No. That is quite the reason why. I do apologize." His eyes meet Ana's, his concern growing at the sight of her frown. "Oh, my. I did not mean to upset you."

When she realizes everyone is staring at her, she hangs her head and continues eating. "You didn't, Joph. I'm fine."

Bela gives Joph an angry look. "Ana, we can go if you need

us to."

She looks at him. "No, I'm okay. Why would you go?"

"I want to make sure. The look on your face—"

She smiles at him. "I'm fine. I just… this isn't really the time or place to discuss that."

"I want children," Evren says. "Kara and I have talked about it."

"How would that work?" Ana asks. "Since you're both female?"

Joph speaks up. "You do not know how babies are made?" Bela nearly chokes on his food.

"I… what?" Ana asks.

"No, no," Joph tries. "I am so sorry. I mean, I know you know the natural way. I am talking about what we can do here, in our labs."

"What do you mean?"

"Well, Kara and Evren, for example. Let us say Rafe donated his… genetic material. I could then take DNA from Kara and Evren, creating an embryo which would then be implanted in whichever one of them wanted to carry the baby to term."

Ana looks at Rafe. "We could have an heir to the throne, without having to have children ourselves."

Rafe grins at the idea. "It's brilliant!"

She looks at Kara. "No rush. It could be twenty or thirty years from now, but what do you think?"

Kara smiles at her. "We actually considered asking. We wanted a guardian, to help ensure our baby would be immortal like us. They could actually take DNA from all four of us, so the offspring would be as much yours and Rafe's. We would raise them, with you two acting as Godparents. When they are old enough, we could tell them who they are and about their role in the kingdom."

"Kara, Evren, will you be okay having a child with wings?"

"Yes, Ana," Evren answers. "We discussed that."

"Wow. Something to think about, for the future. Thank you, Joph."

Joph smiles at Bela, who is beaming with pride. "What to do with you, Joph? You and your scientist mind?"

Ana turns to Kara. "Are you sure you would want me, too? We don't really know what I am, just a human guardian and a new species."

Kara reaches over to take her hand. "You are my sister, and yes, we will have all of us put in. Like you said, no rush. Evren and I want to enjoy being married and traveling before we even think of having children."

"All right." She notices the concern on Rafe's face. "What?"

"I'm worried you're going to get overwhelmed."

"I thought you would be happy I'm talking about the future."

"I am. What you said worries me, though. Ana, we know exactly what you are. Joph and Winslow have already answered that. Why are you questioning it?"

"I'm not. It slipped out. I didn't mean it," she says as she stands. "Excuse me."

She goes into the washroom. After locking the door, she splashes water on her face. *I have to stop overthinking. We are having a good morning, and I am ruining it. Ugh! Why am I like this?*

Ana opens the door, stepping back in surprise as Rafe is standing there waiting. With a gulp, she manages a smile.

He walks in, forcing her back, and closes the door. "Ana—"

"Please, don't hurt me," she whispers as tears flood her eyes.

He takes her in his arms. "Ana, I would never."

"I'm so sorry! The way you came in, shutting the door behind you… I know you would never hurt me. Please, don't be mad."

"Oh, mia estrela. Still bringing down walls. I'm not mad.

I'm sorry I scared you. That was never my intention! I wanted us to have some privacy. We've fought enough in front of Bela and Joph."

"Yes, we have. I'm not overwhelmed. I was starting to be, but I came in here and calmed myself down. You're right. I am a human guardian. I know what I am. I shouldn't be questioning that." She holds him tight. "Just stay with me."

"Always," he whispers, stroking through her hair.

"Forever," she replies. She looks up, kissing him. "I'm okay now. I was having a moment."

"All right." They return to the table. Rafe looks at Kara, seeing the worry on her face. "An Earth moment. She's okay."

Kara nods in understanding. "When are we leaving to see the dragons?"

"We can go now. Is it cold outside?" Ana asks.

"It's not bad, actually. You're fine in what you're wearing."

"Are we ready then?"

Everyone else stands up. Rafe takes Ana's hand. Kellan and Erick come to attention when they enter the corridor. "Where to?" Kellan asks.

"We're going to the woods." Rafe smiles at the confusion on Kellan's face but says nothing.

"Yes, Rafe." They lead the way.

Ana looks back, seeing the excitement on Joph's face. "Joph, can I ask? Why the fascination with dragons? Do you have them in NightFall?"

"We do, in the woods nearby."

"Had you seen them before? I mean, before seeing Smaug?"

"No, I had not. I am usually inside, working and studying."

"How do you know so much about them?"

"There is a book about them. I have had it since I was a child. I have always been intrigued by them."

"What is the technical name for them?"

"We call them anguis."

"I see. Bela, what do you think of the dragons?"

He shrugs his shoulders. "I don't really have an opinion, one way or the other."

"Oh, okay," she says, attempting to hide her disappointment.

"My apologies, Ana. I've never really seen them. I am curious to see how they interact with you."

"It's okay. I know Rafe isn't thrilled with them, either. He called them pests, saying they can be a nuisance."

"Well, that was before I saw how Smaug truly cares for you, and we saw how they interact with you. I wouldn't say that about them now."

"Thank you!" she beams, squeezing his hand. She smiles as they leave the palace, heading for the woods. She looks up at Rafe. "Maybe after lunch we could have some training?"

"How do they feel today? I know we worked them hard."

"They're a little tight, but no pain. I need to stretch and use them."

"All right. After lunch." Rafe laughs. "You'll probably use them once we find the dragons."

"You're right."

They go into the woods and listen. They hear the dragons squawking. Ana slowly makes her way towards them. Smaug runs up to her. He jumps up and down at the sight of her. She picks him up, petting him. Rafe glances around and sees the look of amusement on everyone's faces.

A small group of dragons approach her. Everyone watches in shock when Ana opens her wings, flying up with the dragons following her around. She lands in front of Rafe, and the dragons land with her.

Laughing, she kneels as they run around her and allow her to pet them. Looking up, she observes the wonder reflected on Joph's face. She lifts Smaug and brings him to Joph.

"He remembered you! I cannot believe it. It is fascinating."

Kellan steps forward. "Majesty, did a dragon bond with you?"

"Yes," she says, explaining about the rejected egg and releasing him into the woods. "We come out to visit. He remembers me every time."

"And he only acts that way with you, Majesty?" Erick asks.

"Yes. Rafe and other guardians have shown him their wings, but he only wants to see mine."

"May I?" Kellan asks.

"Please," she says, setting Smaug on the ground. She steps back. Kellan walks up to them and opens her wings. She looks at the dragons, but they pay her no attention. They look up when Ana returns to them. She opens and closes her wings, watching as they do the same.

"Oh, my! They really do only respond to you," Kellan says. "Majesty, it's incredible."

"Thanks! Joph, any questions or anything you want to see before we return to the palace?"

"Would you fly again? I want to see if they will follow you once more."

With a smile, she spreads her wings and soars upward. She laughs as the dragons are following her again. She zips through the trees before returning to the ground. They walk behind her, and she watches them.

"Um, Rafe?"

"Yes, Ana?"

"I think they are staying with me now."

He laughs. "Oh, no. We are not having pet dragons!"

She returns the laughter, then kneels down, gesturing towards the woods. "I'm returning home. You do the same. Go on." The dragons look at her once more, before turning and going deeper into the trees. She walks up to Rafe and takes his hand. "Are we going back now?"

"If you're ready."

"I am."

———————— ❦ ————————

Bela looks at Ana once they are inside the palace. "Joph and I will retire to our quarters for some rest. Shall we do lunch?"

"Yes. Dining hall or in our quarters?"

"Whatever you prefer, Ana."

"Dining hall will be nice."

"We'll see you there at noon."

"Until then, Bela. Joph." She smiles at them before walking to Rafe. She looks at Kara. "What are you and Evren going to do until lunch?"

"We're going to check the Communications Lounge and a few other things. We'll see you at noon in the dining hall."

"Okay." She looks at Rafe. "Just us until lunch. Do we want to go to our quarters or the battlement?"

He turns to Kellan. "We're going to the battlement." He sees the confusion on her face. "Flying session. I'll lead the way."

"Yes, Rafe."

They go to their battlement, where Rafe instructs Kellan and Erick to stand guard at the door. He takes Ana up the stairs. She smiles, remembering the night he proposed to her.

"Mia estrela, why are you happy?"

She looks at him, then her ring. "Good memories."

He kisses her. "Very good."

She steps out and stretches her wings. Her eyes meet Rafe's. "Light training today. After yesterday and working them in the woods, I don't want to overdo it."

"I'm glad to hear you say that." He watches her take to the sky, then joins her. "Where to?" he asks.

"Around the palace a bit. Then we'll get cleaned up for lunch."

Hand in hand, they fly through the air. He smiles, appreciating her natural ease. His fingers tighten around hers.

"What?" she asks.

"Watching how incredible you are. You were so scared, so upset, when this happened to you. I tried to picture doing this with you, but it was hard back then. I hoped you would accept your wings, would start using them, but I didn't know how long it would take for you to do that. You've done so well in such a short time."

"I lied to you that day."

"What do you mean?" he asks as they round their final lap.

"You told me I would be okay, that I would accept them. I said yes, but I didn't mean it. I was too tired and hurting to argue. At the time, I never thought I would accept them."

"Ana, it's okay. You died and grew wings. I don't blame you, for anything you said or felt that day. Or even in the days after. You had to learn to accept them on your own time. I'm grateful you have."

"Me, too," she says. "I'm sorry it took so long."

"No, don't apologize for that. It was scary and traumatic. I can't even imagine how it felt, what you went through." He lowers down to the battlement, pulling her into his arms. "I'm thankful to have you, wings and all." He kisses her as they land.

"Let's clean up and get ready for lunch."

"Did you work up an appetite?"

"Yep!"

He laughs, taking her inside the palace. He looks at Kellan. "Please escort us to our quarters."

"Yes, Rafe," she says, leading the way. She goes inside while they wait. She steps back out. "All clear."

Rafe takes Ana inside, looking at the clock. "It's only eleven. What shall we do for an hour?"

Her face lights up with a smile as she gazes at him. "Oh, I don't know. Do we need a shower?"

Ana selects a crimson dress that features gold trim. Next, she decides on a gold crown. As she approaches the mirror, she unfolds her wings. The sight makes her smile.

Rafe dons his black slacks and a crimson dress shirt. After admiring her in her gown, they leave the closet and head for the door. They step out into the hallway.

"Dining hall," Rafe says.

"Yes, Rafe," Kellan replies, leading the way.

Chapter 5

They walk into the dining hall to find Bela and Joph already seated. As they're greeting them, Kara and Evren enter. Everyone sits, as the first meal is brought out.

"Bela, how are our chefs doing with your cuisine?"

"Very good! I am impressed."

"Thank you."

They look when a man approaches them. "I am Ambassador Cabor of MoonFrost."

He bows, then slowly rises up. Rafe sees the pistol in his hand, grabbing Ana and diving on her, as Kellan jumps at the man. The pistol fires, hitting Kellan as she lands on the assassin.

Rafe and Ana fall to the ground, a scream escaping her lips as she lands on her wing. He picks her up and rushes to their quarters. Kara and Evren stay low, while Erick deals with the assassin. Two royal guards escort Bela and Joph out for their safety.

Rafe bursts through the door, rushing Ana inside and settling her on the chaise. He kneels in front of her. "Were you hit? Where are you hurt?"

"My wing," she says with tears streaming down her face.

"Did I do that?" he asks. She nods. "Ana, I'm so sorry." He closes his eyes, grasping her hand, and focusing on healing her.

"It's okay! You were protecting me. I'm okay now." As he rises, she reaches out to him, but hangs her head in dejection when he pulls away. Rafe walks to the window. "Please?" she says softly, wiping her tears.

Kara and Evren run in. Kara immediate examines Ana "Is everyone all right?"

"We're fine," Ana answers. "Is Kellan okay? Did the

assassin survive?"

"We'll go find out."

"Thank you, Kara." Ana rises to her feet and approaches Rafe. She takes his hand. "Love?" His anger penetrates her heart. "What's wrong?"

He stalks into the washroom. She sits on the chaise to wait, until she hears the shower running. Not wanting to deal with his anger, she shakes her head and rises from her seat. She leaves their quarters and heads towards her mother's library. Inside, she makes her way to the sofa in front of the fireplace, where she lies down and drifts off to sleep.

Ana wakes up and remembers where she is. Kara's presence beside her catches her off guard, causing her to sit up. "How did you find me?"

"Rafe. He's keeping watch." She nods towards the door. "Now, what were you thinking?"

"I'm sorry. I—"

"No, don't. Just don't. Armed assassins in the palace, and you decide to go off on your own! I really wonder about you sometimes."

"Kara, please—"

"It was reckless of you to run off like that!" Kara yells.

Ana gets to her feet and flees from the room. Rafe is surprised when she runs by. They get to her quarters, where he grabs her wrist. She shoots him a sharp look, causing him to release her. She stays by Kara, ignoring her while he clears the chambers. They go inside.

"What were you thinking?" Rafe demands, his anger flowing through her.

Swiftly, she pivots on her heel and dashes into the washroom, forcefully slamming and securing the door. She starts the water, her whole body still tense. Stepping into the water, she allows it to cascade over her. Her pounding heart slows, and her thoughts settle. She comes out, drying herself with a towel and putting on clothes. Before leaving, she takes a sip of refreshing water. She makes her way to the chaise and settles in. Kara joins her.

"I'm sorry. I truly am. I was so worried and scared, after what happened to you the night of the Snowflake Ball. I didn't mean to be angry with you."

"It's okay, Kara. I know you were worried. I'm sorry. Rafe was angry, because he accidentally hurt my wing when he was protecting me from the assassin. I couldn't bear to be around his anger, so I left. It was foolish, I know."

"How are you now?"

"He healed me. I'm okay." Her gaze shifts to him, and she sees he's observing them. "I don't know what's wrong with him."

Kara nods. "One minute." She approaches Rafe and begins to talk to him. Grasping his hand, she pulls him towards the chaise. "You need to talk to her!" she snaps as she walks away from him.

Ana glances up before turning back to watch the fire. She doesn't look at him when he sits beside her. Tears threaten to escape. She takes a deep breath and meets his gaze.

"Ana, I'm sorry. For everything. I was so angry at myself for hurting you. That's the last thing I ever want to do. I'm supposed to protect you, not break your wing!"

"Rafe, I'm okay. You healed me. It only hurt for a moment, and you did it to save my life. You pulling away from me hurt so much worse." His head lowers. "Look at me, love. Please?" He looks into her eyes. "Please, don't ever pull away from me like that. I was hurt and scared, I needed you."

"I'm so sorry," he says, as a tear rolls down his cheek. "How can I make this right? What can I do?"

"Kiss me?"

He leans forward, his mouth devouring hers, as he takes her hands. He brings them up, kissing them both. "I'm so sorry, mia estrela."

"I won't say it's okay, because having you leave when I needed you, really hurt. But I know you were angry at yourself and not me, so I understand." She looks at Kara. "How is everyone else?"

"Bela and Joph are fine, in their quarters. Kellan is in the Medical Center. She was hit in the chest but is expected to recover. The assassin is downstairs being interrogated. Erick was able to capture him alive."

Ana turns to Rafe. "You want to see Kellan, don't you?" He shakes his head when she nods. "All right. I'll make you a deal. Let's have lunch brought in, since we hardly ate. Then we'll go. All right?"

"Yes, love." She looks at Kara. "Where is Evren?"

"She's getting Kellan's family."

"Oh. I didn't think of that."

"Ana, it's okay."

"Yes, Kara." She looks at Rafe. "Would you see about lunch, please?" He nods and steps out. She approaches Kara. "Whatever my reasons, I'm sorry I had you scared. I never wanted to do that."

"He accidentally hurt your wing, but he was the one angry?"

"He was angry at himself for hurting me. You've seen how he is, when I've been hurt in training. He takes it very personally for some reason."

They look up when he steps in. "It will be here shortly."

"Rafe, why do you get so upset when you hurt her? We all know it was an accident. We know that in training or trying to protect each other, it can happen."

His jaw clenches. "She's been hurt enough. I absolutely hate myself when I hurt you, because that is the last thing I would ever want to do." He kneels in front of Ana and takes her hands. While looking at her, he kisses them.

"Rafe, I could understand if you hurt me in a moment of anger or heat of an argument. You have never done that. Every single time, it has been an accident. It's not your fault. Why do you take it so personally?"

"Because I see it as failure."

Pulling him up gently, Ana has him sit next to her. "How is it failure? How is training me to defend myself failure? How is saving me from being killed by a bullet failure?"

"Ana—"

"No, Rafe. Why are you like this?"

"I've blamed myself for you getting shot in that alley. I should've been there sooner! I failed you then."

"You literally saved my life. You had no idea that was going to happen! What was it you said, everything that has happened, happened for a reason. Who knows? If we had bumped into each other at the coffee shop and started talking, I might've built up my walls and walked away. I tried to even after you helped me, because I thought I was protecting myself.

"Nothing that has happened to me, from the mugger to me dying and growing wings, to what happened today in the dining hall, is your fault." She caresses his cheek. "I was the one hurt, yet I don't blame you. So, you don't have the right to blame yourself."

"Ana, it doesn't work like that."

"Yes, it does. Look at me." She gently grabs his face, leaning up and kissing him. "You have to stop blaming yourself. These walls we're bringing down? Apparently, that's one of yours."

"But I—"

"No. Just stop. Please, love. Please?" She brings his head down to her chest, holding him, as she breathes with him. "I need your comfort and love, not blame or anger. Can you do that for me?"

"I'll work on it." He sits up before kissing her again.

"Sorry, Kara."

She laughs. "No, it's okay. You're in your own chambers." She walks to the door to let staff with food in, as Evren steps inside. "How is Kellan?"

"She's fine. Resting now. Her mother and sister are with her. They'll take her back to the barracks shortly."

"Hmm. We'll see her tomorrow. I don't want to overwhelm her today."

"Good idea," Rafe says, taking her hand and walking with her to the table. They sit and eat. "We can go check on Bela and Joph when we're done."

"Yes, please." She looks at Kara. "Do we have two guardians outside?"

"You do."

"Who are they?"

"Rayan and Asuin."

She looks at Rafe, who gives her a reassuring nod. "They are good."

"All right."

"Let me warn you. Rayan has green wings, Asuin's are gold."

"What? Really?"

"Yes."

"Oh, just when I think I've seen all the different colors!"

Rafe laughs, helping her up. "Let's go see our friends." They step out into the hall. Ana tries not to stare at Rayan's and Asuin's wings. "We're going to our friend's quarters. I'll lead the way."

"Yes, Guardian."

They go to Bela and Joph's quarters, where they are welcomed inside, with their guardians standing watch outside.

"Bela, I am so sorry."

"Ana, please. Everything that happened at NightFall, this was minor in comparison. We had lunch brought in and are doing fine."

"I'm grateful because I never want to put you in any danger."

"Mi'lady, as you well know, danger is everywhere for us."

"I hate that it's true, but you're right." She looks at Joph. "How are you?"

"Fine, Majesty."

"When will you return to NightFall?"

"Tomorrow, if that's all right."

She looks at Rafe, who nods. "Yes, that should be fine. Would you like a private dinner tonight or join us?"

"We will gladly join you, if it's not imposing. Then we'll leave in the morning."

"Dear Count, you know you are never imposing on us! Dinner in our quarters will be fine."

"Thank you, Ana. You are most gracious. Say, may I take Joph to your library?"

"Of course!"

"Thank you, again. We will see you at five for dinner."

"Until then, Bela."

They return to their quarters, waiting outside as Rayan goes in. He comes out a moment later. "All clear, sir."

"Rayan, you may address me as Rafe."

"Yes, sir—Rafe. We'll be out here if you need anything."

Kara looks at Ana. "We're going to retire for a while. We'll be back at dinner. I think you and Rafe could use some time to talk."

"Thank you. We'll see you then."

She enters the closet and slips out of the gown before putting on her black pants and shirt. Her hoodie is the last thing she slips on. She sits on the ottoman, wrapping the blanket around herself. Rafe walks in, unable to his concern.

"Are you cold?"

"Yes."

He takes her into his arms. Holding her tight, they sit on the ottoman. "What's wrong?"

"Nothing, I'm just cold."

"Ana, are you sure?"

"I swear."

He feels her forehead. "You're not warm, so that's good. Maybe we'll stay in here tomorrow."

She lays her head against his chest, knowing she will not be staying in. "Yes, Rafe."

Ana pulls away and goes into the main chamber. Rafe changes into his hoodie, stepping out, as she walks in from the hallway.

"Ana?"

"Hot cocoa and snacks. Is that okay?"

"Of course." He smiles. "You wanted to see his wings again."

She laughs. "I can't help it! I've never seen green ones before! What other colors are there?"

"I know it was hard to see at the ball, since it was dim in there. We can go to the barracks tomorrow, to check on Kellan. We can walk around, see the guardians."

"That would mean a lot to me. Thank you." She steps up, kissing him. She takes his hand. "See? I'm fine. I was a little cold."

"Ana—" He turns when the bell rings.

He goes to get their snacks. He takes them to their small table in the back. Drinking her cocoa, she joins him.

"Tomorrow, I would like to try flying at the battlement again."

"Let's see how you feel, first."

"Really, Rafe?"

"What?"

"Now you're being overprotective. The assassin is in custody, no one was killed, I'm not sick. Please, love, don't do this." She squeezes his hand.

"I'm sorry."

"No, it's okay. You have every right to be worried, but like you say to me, that's why we talk."

He reaches up, gently ruffling through her feathers. "How are they?"

"They're fine. You healed the one, and they're recovered from our training session. Watch."

She stands up and goes to the middle of the room. Her wings expand, stretching, then she flies to the ceiling. She circles around once before landing at the table.

"See? I'm fine." She sits next to him, taking his hands.

"I know. I can see and feel that you're fine, but I'm still upset about what I did. I can't help how I feel. I'm working on it."

"Rafe, thank you, for what you did in the dining hall." He tries to pull away, but she grips his hands tighter. "Please, love. You saved my life."

"No, Kellan did that."

"And if she had been too late, I would've been on the floor, instead of shot. You both saved me. Please, don't pull away. Stay. Stay with me. After everything we have been through—" Her words die in her throat as his mouth is on hers, his tongue gently presses against her lips. She opens her mouth, letting him in, as she pulls closer to him. "Rafe—"

"Shower?"

"Please, I—" Before she can finish, he has her in his arms, running into the washroom. He places her on the vanity. "Rafe?" she tries again.

He hears her tone, stopping, and turning back to her. "What's wrong?"

"Nothing. I'm just a little tired. I wanted to have snacks, then take it easy before dinner." She looks down. "I'm sorry."

"Here I am, being either too overprotective of you or selfish." He picks her up and carries her to the chaise. He holds her in his lap, stroking her hair. "I'm sorry."

"Love, it's okay. I told you, we all have off days. Today has been one of those for you. Are you okay? Is something wrong?"

"I saw him standing up, the pistol in his hand. I thought about what happened in NightFall, when you dove at the assassin. I had to act quickly and get you to safety."

"You did! You moved me out of his range then brought me here. Rafe, you did your duty. You have done nothing wrong. Nothing that should make you feel like this! What is going on?"

"I saw his pistol, and I thought I was going to lose you."

"Oh, love." She wraps her arms and legs around, laying her head on his shoulder. "You didn't! I'm right here, safe and sound, because of you." She looks at him. "You had a reaction, an episode."

"What?"

"It's okay. It happens. Now we know it's something for us to work on. Like in the pharmacy, when you overreacted."

"You cried out in pain, and I saw red!"

"You told me about the process, for you to obey the king or queen's commands. What else do they do to you?"

"What do you mean?"

"Are you programmed to protect us, at any cost?"

"No. We are indoctrinated to follow your order. We have training to defend and protect. It's drilled into us."

"You… you are so overly protective, I had to ask."

"I told you, I fell in love with you the second I saw you. My instinct to protect you, coupled with my feelings for you, went into overdrive. I see now what you mean. I'm sorry."

"Love, you have nothing to apologize for. We have been hurt, protecting each other. It will happen."

"But I shouldn't be the one to hurt you!"

Ana sighs. "You have to let this go. I've already forgiven you and moved on. Now, you need to, as well. Can you do that? Can you let it go?" She squeezes him tight, focusing on her love, her happiness, her warmth, and sending it to him. She caresses his face. "For me?"

"You're right. If it had been reversed, if you jumped on me, hurting my wing, I never would've been mad at you. Because I know you would be acting out of love, like I was."

She kisses him. "I truly hope you mean that."

"I do. I really do. I'll continue to work on my anger, work on my walls, too. I didn't realize I had those."

"We all do. Some are like fences, helping to keep unpleasant memories at bay. Some are like a fortress, protecting our mind, protecting our heart, at all costs. You are storming into mine, tearing them down, and saving me. Do you know that?"

He smiles at her. "I do."

"I love hearing you say that." She laughs when he looks confused. "I'll love it even more when you say it on the first of August."

His smile grows, realizing what she is saying. "Me, too."

"Um, what do I wear to the beach? I can't exactly go swimming in my gowns."

"They have sea clothing there."

"They have what?"

He laughs. "That's what they call bathing suits."

"Sea clothing? Okay. What does it look like?"

"You'll like it. It covers well, while still affording movement for swimming. Actually, I never thought to ask you that. Do you know how to swim?"

"Yes, I took it in college."

"You can major in swimming?"

She laughs. "No. It's a PE requirement, like the fencing was. I figured, since I had to have the credits, I may as well try different things. Had no idea the fencing would come in handy."

"You are incredible with a sword."

She blushes. "Can we go back to our snacks?"

"Ana, why didn't you say something sooner?" He picks her up, carrying her over to their table.

"We were breaking down walls. I didn't want to interrupt."

He puts her in her chair, sitting beside her. "Still want a nap after?"

"No, but maybe just rest for a little while."

"Okay."

"Hmm." She leans up, kissing him. "We could make ourselves tired for a nap."

"Thank you, but we'll play some cheshire, then have dinner. After that, who knows what I may do to you?"

She smiles at him. "Anything you want," she whispers in his ear.

He peppers her face with soft kisses. "For now, let's take it easy. I'll enjoy taking your king and queen."

Chapter 6

Rafe follows Ana into the closet to change for dinner. He strips out of his pants and shirt.

She smiles, slipping the gown off and letting it fall to the floor. "Did you want dessert first?"

He shuts and locks the door before walking to her and kneeling before her. His mouth caresses along her stomach and hip. He smiles as she parts her legs. Her breath catches in her throat as he's on her. She trembles, as he continues to explore. She holds his shoulders, smiling as he reacts to his own touches.

Unable to bear it any longer, she pulls him up and kisses him. He breathes heavily as she strokes him, starting off slowly before picking up the pace. Throwing his head back, he lets out a moan. He embraces her, kissing her as he finishes. He lies beside her and holds her to his chest.

"Oh, Ana. We both needed that."

Turning to face him, she rolls over and kisses him. "You are truly remarkable."

"So are you. Hmm. We definitely worked up an appetite."

"You certainly whet mine."

"Ana!" He kisses her, passionately, holding her tight. "We need to get dressed."

"Yes, love."

Running to the washroom, she retrieves a towel for him. She picks out a pale blue gown. It has long tulle sleeves, a floor-length cut, and delicate rose embroidery on the bodice. She walks to him after getting dressed.

"Are you okay?" she asks, stifling the laugh.

"I need a moment."

Sitting at the edge of the ottoman, she watches him. "Am I too much for you?"

He laughs. "You are everything to me."

She starts to stand, when he grabs her hand and pulls her on top of him. She kisses him, caressing his face, then pulls back. "Company, love."

"Yes, Ana."

As she gets dressed, she checks herself in the mirror in the back. She spreads her wings with a smile on her face. Rafe steps up behind her, in black slacks and a shirt the same color as her gown. She retracts her wings in, turning to him.

"What?"

"I waited so long for the day you would come in here and smile, seeing yourself in this mirror. Between what happened on Earth, your wings, everything you've been through, I didn't know if it would ever happen."

"I love my wings. They are so beautiful! I love what we can do with them."

"Oh, such as?"

She leans in and kisses him. "Flying," she teases, stepping back.

"Ana! How dare you?" He holds her close, showering her face and neck with gentle kisses. "Do you submit?"

"Never!" she cries. She laughs as she falls into his arms. "Oh, Rafe. I love you, so much."

"I love you, too, mia estrela."

He goes to the drawers and retrieves her rings. As he slips them on, he takes her hand and they leave. When the bell rings, he makes his way to the door. He lets food service in. Everything is set up. Bela and Joph arrive as they are leaving, followed shortly by Kara and Evren.

"So, Joph, since you asked us. May I ask, are you and Bela talking about having children?"

Rafe nearly chokes on his drink. "Ana!"

Bela chuckles, looking at Rafe. "What are we to do?" He laughs when Rafe shakes his head.

Joph turns back to Ana. "We have discussed it. It is

something we would like to do, but like Kara and Evren, are not in a rush to do." He looks at Rafe. "She is right. I asked first, it is only fair that she gets to ask as well."

"Yes, Joph," Rafe replies.

"Bela, I was wondering. Could Rafe and I come stay next weekend?"

"Of course! Any particular reason?"

"I would like to tour your quadrant and meet more of your people."

"That would be wonderful. It would mean a lot to us."

She looks at Rafe. "I'm sorry. I didn't mean to put you on the spot."

"Oh, no. It's fine. I think a little weekend trip could do us some good. Kara can run things while we're gone." He winks at Kara, who sticks out her tongue.

Ana laughs before turning to Bela. "You're leaving in the morning?"

"Yes, I have some affairs to attend to, especially since you are coming next weekend."

"If it's too much trouble—"

"Ana, for you, it's never any trouble. I insist."

"Thank you."

Rafe directs his attention toward Bela. "Could we speak for a moment, in private?"

"Of course."

They get to their feet, stepping over to the small table and sitting. Kara looks at Ana. "Any idea what they're talking about?"

She shakes her head. "Not a clue." Curious, she glances at them. They stand up and return. "Everything okay?" she asks.

"Fine," Rafe replies, sitting back down. He sees the worry on her face. He takes her hand, kissing it. "Really."

"Yes, love." They finish eating, getting to their feet and walking Bela and Joph to the door. "Breakfast here at eight?"

"Sounds good, Ana. Until the morrow." Bela bows before

taking Joph's hand and leaving.

She smiles at Rafe. "What?" he asks.

"That's the first time I've seen them show any affection."

He laughs. "As Bela said, they aren't quite as public with their feelings."

She turns to Kara, who is collecting dishes. "Kara, can we do something together Wednesday? Just you and me?"

"Did you have something in mind?"

"Yes."

"All right."

Ana hugs her and Evren. "Get some rest. We'll see you both tomorrow morning."

"Okay." Kara and Evren leave.

Ana walks up to Rafe, kissing him. "Can we go for a little walk before turning in?"

"Anywhere particular?"

"Lead the way!" she says, taking his hand. They step out, seeing Rayan and Asuin. She looks at his wings, looking down when he catches her staring. "I apologize, Rayan. I hadn't seen wings of your color before."

He laughs. "Your Majesty, it's quite all right. Where are we going?"

"I'll lead the way," Rafe says.

They go downstairs and into a corridor she doesn't recognize. "Rafe, where are we going?"

He looks at her, smiling. "You'll see."

"Yes, love." Her brow furrows.

They continue down the corridor, going down another set of stairs. They walk through an arch, another hallway, and out a series of doors. They go into a small chapel.

"Haven't studied this, have you?"

"No," she exclaims as she admires the room. "It's beautiful! What is this?"

Dark wood walls and marble floors make up the small chapel. A few wooden pews are lined on either side of the aisle, and a small section off to her right is where pilgrims light candles for prayer.

"This is the chapel of Reyna. She was a goddess who fought in battle and brought peace to the entire galaxy. The story goes, a great war broke out between realms, as each one wanted to have all the power over the others. She went with her battalion to fight in the MoonSol Realm. After she defeated their armies, she continued to each realm, defeating every single one. A treaty was forged, ensuring peace between the realms. That was over two thousand years ago, but the peace still stands."

"War between the realms. I never thought of that. Wait, so it's a legend, right?"

"Not entirely."

"Rafe, are you telling me I have power over this galaxy, not just this realm?" she asks as she approaches him.

"Yes, Ana. I'm sorry you didn't know this. Once you've been here for a year, you will be crowned as Grand Empress of the LunarAstrea Galaxy."

"What?" she asks, nearly fainting. He guides her to a pew and has her sit down. He kneels beside her. "Why didn't you tell me this sooner?" she demands.

"I didn't want to overwhelm you. If it helps, you'll still be addressed as Queen in this realm. Only when the other monarchs visit here, would you be addressed as Empress."

She refuses to look at him, as anger and worry stir within her. "Take me back to our quarters, please."

"Ana—"

"Now."

He takes her hand, leading the way out. Their guardians follow behind. Rayan goes inside, then comes back out to signal that it's safe. Ana goes into the washroom, locking the door behind her. First, she removes her clothes, then she enters the shower. She turns on the tap. Leaning against the wall, she sits on the floor with her knees drawn to her chest. As Rafe walks in, she glances upward.

"Why do I even bother to lock the door?" she asks, hanging her head.

Rafe undresses before scooping her up and holding her in his arms. "Ana, please. I know it's a lot to take in, but why are you reacting like this? It's really just a title."

"Rafe, you told me I was a lost princess, that you were sent to restore me to the throne. You never mentioned that I would have an entire galaxy!"

"It's not a big deal. It truly isn't. Each realm has a monarch in charge to rule over their own land. You will meet once a year to continue ensuring peace. There are no additional responsibilities or anything. I'm sorry. You're right, I should have told you sooner. I was afraid you would react like this, and you were already dealing with so much, from Kane, to your wings, to bringing peace. Now that things had calmed down, I decided to tell you."

She clings to him, holding him tightly. "I can't seem to get warm!"

"Here, mia estrela." Moving closer, he holds her near the running water. He increases the temperature. "You will get warm. It's okay."

"Does Kara know any of this?"

"A little."

"Why didn't my father march on the other realms?"

"Oh, he knew better. They have all built up their armies, knowing one day the treaty could break. I can assure you, it won't, though. Everyone wants peace. Even though it was so long ago, the scars of that war cut deep. So much so, no one wants to relive that."

"Please, put me down. I'm okay now."

He puts her on her feet, kissing her. "I'm sorry I didn't tell you."

"No, you're right. It was better to do it now, than when I was so overwhelmed." She looks up at him. "Has there ever been an empress with wings?"

"No, Ana. You will be the first."

She sucks in her breath. "Oh." She turns off the water, stepping out and drying off. "Grand Empress Maeriana. Wow."

"Are you okay?"

"Yes, love." She looks at him. "When is the anniversary of my arrival? I didn't really learn the dates at first, so much I was trying to learn."

"We arrived here on the fifteenth of September. It will probably be towards the end of the month when you are crowned."

"Another coronation? Where does this one take place?"

"Here, in the palace. It will be done in the throne room, same as your last one." He leans down, kissing her. "And I promise you, I will be here for this one."

"Do you get crowned, too?"

"Oh. I hadn't thought about that."

She smiles up at him. "Well?"

"No. It's whichever royal has the highest ranking. Not that I even want to think of it, but since you asked. If something happened to you, then I would be crowned."

She laughs. "Emperor Rafe."

"Ana, don't you dare!" He kisses her passionately while holding her close.

"Why not?" she asks with a playful tone. "I think it's cute."

With a chuckle, he picks her up and carries her to bed. He gently lays her down, then leans over her to cover her in kisses on her face and neck. "Submit?"

"Only to you, my love."

He stops, looking at her. "You sure you're okay?"

"I am now. I'm sorry for how I reacted."

"It was a lot to take in. I understand. Would you like some snacks? Would that help?"

"Yes, love."

Standing up, Rafe heads out into the hall. Ana lies in bed,

replaying the conversation in her mind.

Empress? Really? It was scary enough, finding out I was a princess, knowing I would become Queen. Then becoming the Crimson Queen, and now I'm to be crowned an empress?

She can hardly breathe as the thought of it overwhelms her again. Rafe steps over, his eyes on her. He swiftly climbs into bed, enveloping her in his arms.

"Breathe with me, Ana." She matches his breaths, calming down. "Better?"

"Yes. I'm sorry. I was thinking about it and got overwhelmed again. I'm okay now, really. Was my father crowned as Emperor of the galaxy?"

"He was. That was around three hundred years ago, before… well… everything. Thankfully, he kept the treaty and kept the peace, at least for the other realms."

"Empress of the six realms," she says softly.

"Ana, please, don't get overwhelmed again."

"I won't. I'm just thinking of it."

"Are you sure?"

She laughs. "I'm not overthinking it, I promise. You said nothing will really be different though, it's only a title?"

"Really. You may host the monarchs from the other realms."

"All six realms at once?"

"No, Ana. A few here or there to check in and see how their realms are doing. That's all. They will all be here for your Empress coronation, though."

"Were you present when my father was crowned?" She sees the look on his face. "I'm not talking about him. I want to know about the ceremony itself."

"All right. Yes, I was. It's very similar to when you were crowned Queen."

"Will Audressa perform the ceremony?"

"Yes, it's the chancellor's duty." The bell rings. "I'll get our snacks." He walks out, and then returns with Kara a moment later. Ana stands up.

"Everything all right?"

"Yes, she was returning when I got our snacks. She wants to check on you. I'll take these to our table."

Kara approaches Ana. "Rafe told me he explained to you about being crowned Empress. How are you handling that?"

"I'm okay. It was really overwhelming at first, but once he explained that my duties don't really change, and that it's really more just a title, I'm okay."

"He's right."

"So much to look forward to this year, from your wedding, the Rose Ball, my birthday festival, our wedding, then a coronation!"

"You're looking forward to your birthday festival?"

"Yes. Rafe told me about it. I know it's more for my people than me, so I'll be okay. Did you know he and I have the same birthday?"

"What?"

"Different years, obviously. Um, speaking of which, what year was I born?"

"Oh, right, time difference from here and Earth. You were born in 294 of the fourth era." She looks at her. "What?"

"I keep thinking I'll get used to that. I keep wanting to tell myself it's two thousand and twenty something, not 305 of the fourth era." She takes Kara's hand. "Join us for snacks?"

"I'll stay for a minute. Evren was running an errand and will be back shortly."

"Okay." They walk to the table. Rafe pours them each a cocoa, while Ana hungrily eats some bread and cheese.

"You know you can talk to any of us, right? To continue to open up? I hated how scared you were, how much you turned inward, when we first got here. I didn't know how to get you to come out."

"I'm sorry for how I acted in the beginning."

Kara lets out a sigh. "Ana, you were literally taken from

Earth, brought to a strange, new planet, where you had an archduke attacking you, told by Rafe he didn't love you, then died and grew wings. Believe me, you handled everything as well as could be expected. You had so much put on you!"

They look up when Evren walks in. She joins them. "Rayan told me Kara was in here. I hope I'm not imposing."

"Evren, you are never imposing," Ana says with a smile. "What do you know about the role of Empress?"

"Oh, Rafe finally told you about that? He swore me to secrecy."

She turns to Rafe, laughing. "Really?"

"We all agreed, we didn't want to overwhelm you."

"You were right. Now that I know, I do have a few questions. It's getting late. If the two of you want to go on to bed, we can talk more at breakfast."

"Yes, Ana. That will be fine. You are okay to speak about it in front of Bela and Joph?"

"Of course."

"All right. Evren and I will retire for the night. Ana, I know you have Rafe, but I am telling you right now, if you need me, I'm right next door."

"Thanks, sis. I truly appreciate that." Kara and Evren leave. Rafe looks her over, studying her face. "What?" she asks, laughing.

"Making sure you are okay. Other than taking a shower, you are handling all of this surprisingly well."

"Rafe, I literally laid down, died, and grew wings. Finding out I have another title is mild compared to that." While enjoying a petit cake, she smiles. She looks at him, yawning. "I'm almost ready for bed." He flashes her a playful smile. "To sleep, love. You have worn me out today."

"I would say the same for you."

She bursts out laughing, nearly falling out of her seat. "Oh, my God!"

"What?" he asks.

She looks at him while trying to compose herself. "So, if I'm Empress of the galaxy, and I'm a human guardian, does that make me a guardian of the galaxy?"

"Ana!" Rafe exclaims, laughing. "We don't have Rocket here."

"You actually saw that?"

"Yes! I thought it was quite funny."

"I can't believe you understood the reference! That is too funny. We'll have to tell Kara tomorrow. She won't know what to make of it." She gets to her feet. "I'm using the washroom, then I'm ready for bed."

"Yes, mia estrela."

She goes in, relieving herself and washing her hands. She brushes her teeth, looking in the mirror. *Empress. I just—wow. I still can't believe that will be my next title. I thought I was done after Queen! I wonder if Rafe will let me crown him as King, since I would still have the higher title?* She chuckles at the thought, stepping out. She sits on the chaise, waiting for him. He steps out, picking her up and carrying her to bed.

"Empress," he says, laying her down.

"Yes, King Rafe?" He looks at her, confused. She smiles at him. "What? If I still have the higher title, you could be crowned King. King Rafe and Queen Ana. No?"

"No, please. I can assure you, I am fine with being crowned as Prince."

She wants to ask but doesn't want to push. "Okay. I'm sorry."

He laughs. "No worries." He climbs into bed and cradles her in his arms. "Now sleep, my little warrior."

"Yes, love." She clutches his shirt, relishing his warmth. "Hmm. I love you, so much."

"Oh, mia estrela, you know how much I love you, too."

Chapter 7

Waking up, Ana looks up at him. With a smile, she caresses his jawline and climbs on top of him, showering him with soft kisses.

"Hmm," he moans, bringing his hands up and cupping her face.

"Morning, my love," she says, lowering her head to his chest.

"Same to you. How did you sleep?"

"Very well. Woke up, forgetting I had wings." She laughs. "I sat up, and they folded around me again, nearly scaring me like my first day with them!"

"Are you okay?"

"Oh, yes. Obviously I reacted better this time. I'm glad I've accepted them, but forgetting them and then seeing them again can be a bit much sometimes."

"How do they feel this morning?"

"A little tight. Definitely look forward to working them." Sitting up, she leans over him, her gaze fixed on his. "Can I ask?"

"What?"

"Why don't you want to be King?"

"It's not necessary, is all."

"Rafe, why not?"

"What do you want from me?" he snaps.

She jumps to her feet and charges into the washroom. She slams the door and collapses against it.

A moment later, Rafe knocks. "Ana, please. I'm sorry."

"Why are you so upset? All I did was ask!" Pushing down her tears, she rests her head against the door.

"Because I'm already overwhelmed with the thought of

becoming a prince, and I hid from you. I'm so sorry."

She opens the door, and her eyes fix on him. "Why? I thought you were okay with it. Did something happen?"

"I have spent over five hundred years being threatened with punishment of death to be with a royal. I risked everything to be with you because I couldn't hide my feelings anymore. I can't simply turn off all those years."

"Love, I understand that. That's why I've tried to give you some space, to not push you. All I did was ask a question!"

"I know," he says, gently grabbing her arm and pulling her into his chest. "And I was a jerk. I'm sorry. I am okay with being a prince. The thought of becoming a king was too much."

"And I'm to be the empress! How do you think I feel? At least you knew all of these things, keeping them from me. I'm not even mad about it because I understood your reasons."

"Oh, mia estrela, forgive me?"

"Yes, love. Please, be open with me. That's what you always ask of me, and now I ask the same for you."

"I will." He leans down, kissing her. "I am truly sorry."

"I won't bring up your coronation again. I didn't realize it upset you so."

"No, Ana. It's okay. We can talk about it. It's our wedding and coronation day." He glances at her as she tenses up in his arms. "What's wrong?"

"Sorry. I was thinking about my last coronation and wedding day."

"Kane," he says softly. "Ana, it's a miracle we both survived. You know that, right?"

"I do. When Winslow told me about the poison, I was so worried about how to tell you, all of you. I knew you would be devastated. I didn't want that."

"God, Ana! You were dying but still worried about us?" He lifts her into his arms and carries her to the chaise. He sits down, with her nestled in his lap. "You always worry so much about everyone else! How do you carry all of that?"

She laughs. "I just do. You, Kara, and Evren had become my whole world. You were the only ones trying to protect me from Kane, trying to help me with my duties and accepting my role. Even if I thought you didn't love me, I still cared deeply for you and wanted you in my life. The thought of telling you I was dying was almost too much for me. I knew I had to because I knew we would say goodbye. I never imagined you would carry me into the closet and confess your love for me while saving my life!"

"I honestly didn't believe I would survive. I couldn't let you die, though. Not only because you are the queen, and it was my duty, but because I love you too much to lose you."

She holds him tight. "Thank you for always saving me. Thank you for always being here for me. My life would be so empty, so lost, without you."

"Please tell me I'm not your only reason for living?"

"No, love. If you had died that day, I would've been devastated and heartbroken. I would've grieved, but Kara and Evren would make sure I resumed my duties. It would've been more than I could bear, to even think of," she says as tears stream down, "but I would've went on. Killing myself would've dishonored your memory and made your death in vain."

"You really thought about this, didn't you?"

"Rafe, I overthink everything," she says. "It's how I am." She kisses him. "Now, are we getting ready for breakfast?"

"Yes." He stands, then takes her into the closet with him. On the ottoman, he keeps her close in his arms. "I brought you in here. You had poison ravaging your veins, but I was the one dying. Thinking of losing you was too much. I wasn't going to let it happen, no matter the cost."

"Rafe, it was a horrible day. You were kidnapped and tortured, the archduke tried to force me to marry him, I was nearly killed, then you died right here. All of my fear, my pain, everything I went through, was worth it because now I am here, in your arms, as your future wife." She turns, wrapping her arms and legs around him. "Believe me, love. I wouldn't change a single thing, if it would mean we wouldn't be here now."

"Yes, my little warrior." Rising, he helps her up. "As you said, we need to get dressed for company."

"Are you excited about going to NightFall next weekend?" She sees a look of surprise flicker on his face. "What?"

"I am. I'm curious, are you thinking of going to MoonFrost as well?"

"I don't think I can, not yet."

"Good. I was hoping you wouldn't. Let things calm down a bit, then maybe we'll travel there." He kisses her forehead. "And of course, we have MorningStella in August to look forward to."

She smiles at him. "Yes. I'm very excited about that." She goes over to her gowns, looking through them and letting out a sigh. When he laughs, she glances up. "Sorry, what was that?"

"You and your gowns. We'll go to the village tomorrow."

"That would be great. Thank you." She pulls out a forest green gown. "Hmm. I don't know about that. I think I would look like a Christmas tree."

Rafe nearly doubles over with laughter. He collects himself. "You won't, I promise. It will look fine on you."

She glances at it once more. It features long sleeves and a billowing, lace-covered skirt. Approaching the mirror, she holds it up. "I'll try it on. I swear though, if you laugh again, it's getting donated!"

"I won't. I promise."

"Hmm." After removing her pajamas, she put on her corset. Turning to the mirror, she slips into the gown. Her wings unfold, allowing her to inspect the color combination. "Okay. Not as bad as I thought." Her eyes meet his when she realizes he's standing behind her.

"Ana, you look lovely. I'm not just saying that, I mean it."

"Thank you, love. I needed something different, besides pink, blue, or crimson."

He walks to his dresser, selecting charcoal pants and a shirt, then finishes by putting on a dark green vest. He returns to her. "Well?"

"We match!" she says, turning to him and kissing him. "I don't feel as self-conscious in this color, thanks to you."

He laughs, as she grabs his head, kissing him hard.

"Thank you."

He leans down by her ear. "Always my pleasure, Your Majesty."

"Rafe," she cries out, falling into his arms, laughing. "What am I going to do with you? I swear!"

"Hmm. Marry me?"

"You bet!"

"Speaking of which." He goes to the drawer, getting out her rings, and placing them on her fingers. "There we go. Isn't that better?"

"Yes, love." She bites her lower lip.

"What?"

"When we go to the village tomorrow, I'd like to go to the jewelry vendor."

"To look at bands?"

"Yes, but also, I would like a ring to sleep in." She smiles at him. "My hand feels so empty at night without it. Is that weird that I want that?"

"Ana, what about us has ever been normal?"

She laughs. "You're absolutely right!"

"Yes, we will go there, the fabric vendor, and anywhere else you would like to go. Even in the market, if you want."

"Let's hope it's not raining."

"Oh, yes. January is rainy, but it's warming up, too."

"Is it really hot in the summer?"

"It's tolerable."

Hearing the bell, Rafe leaves. He welcomes everyone in. Once the food is set up, the staff departs. Bela and Joph arrive, followed by Kara and Evren.

"Ana, I love that gown!" Kara says.

"Do I look like a Christmas tree?" she asks timidly.

"Absolutely not. Green is a great color on you. I mean it. Especially with your eyes. Now, come eat with us."

"Yes, sis." She approaches them and takes a seat. "Evren, can I ask now? I don't want to bother you."

"Ana, you know you're not bothering me. I'll answer as best I can."

"Are there any additional duties?"

"As I'm sure Rafe told you, you will occasionally meet with the other monarchs to check in on their realms. Otherwise, no. Nothing will be different. It really is just a title."

Bela looks at Ana. "Oh, right! You are the Grand Empress."

She laughs. "Even Bela knew? Everyone knew but me?"

"My apologies," Bela says.

"Oh, no, Bela. Please, it's fine. They didn't tell me because I was already dealing with so much. Rafe took me to the chapel last night and told me."

"Told you what?" Joph asks.

"That I will be crowned as Grand Empress of the galaxy."

"Really?" Joph notices everyone is staring at him. "I am sorry. I spend so much time in my lab, doing research and medicine, I do not pay attention to much else."

"It's quite all right. It was shocking to find out, but I am okay." She looks at Kara. "So, I'm a human guardian, right?"

"Yes, Ana. Why?" Kara asks, confused.

Ana grins at her. "Will that make me a guardian of the galaxy?"

Kara nearly chokes on her food. "Ana!" She bursts out laughing. "Really? You're going to be crowned Empress, and you're making jokes?"

"Would you rather I be crying on the shower floor?"

"No, but let me guess, you already did?" She sees her eyes go down. "Oh, Ana. I'm so sorry."

"It's all right. It was a lot to deal with. I swear, I'm okay now."

"Rafe, I thought we were going to tell her together?"

"I know. I'm sorry. She wanted to walk around last night and see something new. We ended up in the chapel. I apologize."

"It's probably better it was just the two of you, given how she reacted."

Ana laughs. "Yes, I would've been embarrassed if you and Evren had seen that." She looks at Bela. "Or you. Count, I know I've said this before, but you know how much you and Joph mean to me, right?"

"Yes, Ana. We are very honored to be in such high esteem with the queen. It truly means a lot to us."

"You earned your place. I do not give my friendship nor my trust easily."

"High praise, Majesty. Thank you for being an ally from the beginning. I am so grateful we could work together to bring about peace."

"Bela, I'm going to ask you something. Please, be honest. You will not hurt my feelings. Did you read the entire treaty when it was given to you?"

"I did. I was pleased that you wanted to free the slaves. Of course, I was also pleased you wanted relationships to be open, as well."

"Thank you. I swear, I don't think anyone else read past whatever they were getting out of it."

"You were very smart, writing it that way. They never saw it coming. Captain Declan and I spoke before the meeting. I explained to him I had read through, and that I was very pleased with it."

"That's what he meant, when he said at least two of the leaders wouldn't approve a new treaty. I never knew he was referring to you."

"Oh, yes. For Joph and I to be able to be together,

publicly? I supported your treaty, completely. Honestly, even if he and I didn't have to hide, I still would have supported it. You did an excellent job."

"Thank you. Hopefully, that's the only treaty for the realm I'll ever have to write! It was stressful enough, writing that one."

"I cannot imagine." Joph takes a sip of tea. "Do you try to go out and see the dragons often?"

"Yes, Joph. They are so cute!"

Kara laughs. "Only you and Evren would think that."

"Wait, if there aren't birds, where do they get the feathers for arrows?" Ana asks, looking at Rafe. "Don't tell me—"

"Oh, no," he replies, laughing. "Really? There are birds in MorningStella. A few different kinds. You'll see them when we go."

"Okay. I was worried."

After breakfast, Ana walks Bela and Joph to the door.

"We will be leaving shortly. We look forward to seeing you Friday evening."

"Thank you, Bela. I am excited to tour your quadrant and meet more of your people."

"We are honored, Majesty," he says, bowing.

He and Joph leave. Kara and Evren gather dishes and step out.

"Thank you," Ana says when Rafe joins her on the chaise.

"For what?"

"A wonderful morning."

"Not all of it."

"Love, it's okay. You were overwhelmed." She chuckles. "If anyone can understand that, it's me. Really. Now, are you okay to discuss your coronation? If not, I won't bring it up again."

"Give me a little more time."

Her smile grows. "Like you always do for me?" She kisses him again. "Least I can do. We won't talk about it, until you are ready." She takes his hand. "Can we go for training now?"

"Sounds good, mia estrela."

As they enter their quarters, he notices the tinge of crimson on her cheeks.

"Did you overdo it in the battlement?" he asks, placing his hand on her shoulder and guiding her to the chaise.

"No," she says, lowering her head as he sits with her.

Rafe takes her hand. "Why are you embarrassed?"

"I was wondering what our first time will be like on our wedding night. I'm both excited and nervous."

"I am, too. It will be our biggest first yet."

"I hope I don't ruin it."

"You know you aren't. No matter what happens. You have endured such hell, are still enduring it to bring down your walls. You know how much I love you and how much you mean to me. I promise you whatever happens, our wedding night will not be ruined!"

"How can you say that?"

"Because it's the truth. Let's say we start to undress, touching and holding each other. You have an episode, and you are unable to continue. We'll have snacks and cocoa, sit in front of the fire, and hold each other. Then we'll have a whole week in MorningStella to try again. See? Nothing will be ruined."

"Oh, love. What did I do to deserve your patience and understanding?"

"We are made for each other."

"I know. Oh, I had an idea, for before the wedding. I'm not sure how you'll feel about it, though."

"Tell me."

"I thought maybe for a month before, we um, we didn't you know… do what we've been doing?"

"Really?"

"I think it would make the wedding night more special. If you're worried, we don't have to."

"Worried?"

"Going from not touching to going through everything together."

"I see. I think it would be okay. You can let me know how you're feeling, and we can go from there. How does that sound?"

"That sounds good. Um, can I ask?"

"What?"

"The wedding night. You said you had something planned, and I don't need to know details. I want to be surprised. I'm wondering though, can we spend it here in our quarters? Or does that mess up your plans?"

"No, it's perfect. I'm happy you want to, but I'm curious, why?"

"Because this is our home. I get it, the whole palace technically is. But this room, this bed, is ours. I want our first time to be here, where it's special to me."

He kisses the back of her head. "To us, because I feel the same way."

"Really?" she asks, looking up at him.

"Yes, mia estrela. Really."

She leans up and kisses him. "I'm so excited for our wedding day. I know, we have so much to do before then. We have Kara and Evren's wedding next. I can't wait to see them get married!" She laughs when her stomach grumbles. "Can we have lunch brought in?"

"Of course!" He steps out into the hall and returns a few moments later. "On the way."

"Thank you. Can I ask, what were you and Bela talking about?"

"Oh, it's a little something for when we stay next weekend. You'll see."

"A surprise?"

"Yes."

"Hmm. Okay. I guess I'll trust you."

He gasps, smiling. "Ana!" He steps up, planting gentle kisses on her cheeks and lips. "I love you, mia estrela."

"I love you, too." She stands up, putting her arms around his waist.

"Are you okay?"

"Yes, love. Just needing you."

He wraps his arms around her before kissing the top of her head. "I'm right here. Do you want to have a lesson while we eat?"

"Yes."

"All right. Where are we eating?"

"Can we try out the sofa you had brought in?"

"Sounds good." He carries her over to it and gently places her on the plush seat. The bell rings. "I'll be right back." He goes to the door, getting the food tray. He sets her cocoa on the small end table, and places his on the other one. He sits down with their plates in his hand. She takes her plate and picks up bread with cheese. "What do you want to know?" he asks.

"What do you want to tell me?"

"Ana—"

She laughs. "No, I don't mean like you're keeping something from me. Although, I truly hope there are no more secrets."

"We all have our secrets."

"Rafe!" she cries out, laughing. "All right then, keep your secrets. What I meant was, is there anything you want to teach me? About the realm, the palace, anything like that?"

"Well, since we are going to visit NightFall next weekend, let's talk about the vampyra."

"I thought Evren and I already did?"

"Yes, some of their history. When you first got here, we were at war with them. Now, they are your strongest ally. You and Bela made that possible. MoonFrost and NightFall have had battles and skirmishes for years, centuries even."

"Because MoonFrost doesn't like the vampyra?"

"Partly. Here's what you don't know. About twenty-five hundred years ago, a vampyra was married to a countess from MoonFrost. Keep in mind, the vampyra had only been here about five hundred years then. Both quadrants thought it was wrong and didn't want such a union."

"What happened?" she asks, taking a sip of her cocoa.

"War. They told the countess they would stop if she would agree to annul the union. That's what they call divorce here."

Ana gasps. "Did she?"

"No. She fought for her love, saying they had every right to be together. She went into battle with him, fighting alongside him. He was wounded. She rushed to him and held him in her arms. At the sight of their love, both quadrants retreated from the field."

"Rafe, did he... Did—"

"He lived. Bela is a descendant of them."

She gasps. "Really? He's part... human?"

"Only a little bit. After their union, they stayed in NightFall and their offspring only stayed with vampyra."

"That explains so much!"

"What do you mean?"

"What Bela meant, about understanding forbidden love. I thought he was referring to himself and Joph, but I see. That's a great story."

"Well, I like ours better."

She smiles at him. "Me, too. We won't tell Bela that, though."

"It'll be our secret."

She laughs. "What other secrets do you have?"

"I don't know what you mean."

"Rafe, you kept it this long, about me becoming an empress. What else do you know? What aren't you telling me?"

He leans down, kissing her. "Ana, I have five hundred

years' worth of secrets."

"Rafe, that's not fair!" she says, laughing.

"Ask me anything. I mean it. Ask, and I'll answer honestly."

She thinks back to their sword fight. "No, that's okay."

"Ana, what's wrong?"

"Sorry. I was thinking back to the training center, when you made your wager. That was a dangerous wager to make."

"What would you have asked me?"

"Rafe, if you don't know—"

"I did know."

"What? Then why offer? Unless you were sure you would defeat me."

"No, you are incredible with a sword. If you had bested me and asked me, I would've told you the truth. Like I said, it was getting harder for me to keep it in. I thought I was going to burst if I couldn't tell you. You were honest, telling me how you felt about me. But I lied, I hid, I deflected, trying to protect us both."

"You were willing to risk everything in a sword fight?"

"I was fighting *for* you. You were so angry, saying it was typical that I wouldn't even fight for you. I was trying to show you I would."

"Rafe! I'm so sorry I didn't see that. I was so obsessed with trying to free Evren and bringing peace, I didn't see. Oh, how could I have been so blind?"

"You were dealing with so much back then. Please, mia estrela, everything has worked out now."

"You tried so hard to show me you cared, without saying the words." She caresses his face as she plants a soft kiss. "Forgive me for being so blind."

"There is nothing to forgive. We are getting married and ruling our kingdom. Everything that happened, has only brought us closer." He looks at her, as she smiles at him. "What?"

"I love it when you say 'our' kingdom."

"Why?"

"I don't know. It makes me really happy."

"The thought of marrying you makes me happy."

"Rafe! Oh, love, me, too."

"Ana—"

"We're waiting until August. I promise I won't rush us."

"All right."

"Sorry."

"I'm glad you're excited because I want you to look towards the future."

"I am. You see that I am."

"Don't get too excited."

"Hmm. You know the affect you have on me."

"We are eating lunch."

"Yes, love."

"How can you have anything left?" he asks with a laugh. "I'm still recovering from our workout. Now, I mean it, ask me anything."

"What happens when two guardians marry? Do they stay in the barracks?"

"Yes and no. They are given their own quarters, which are down on the same level as the barracks. We haven't had as many weddings, nor children being born, since they were taken by NightFall. Melian said right now there are twenty-eight children and eight babies on the way. Do you want to see the guardian children?"

"At some point. I'm curious, is all."

"But you don't want any of your own?"

"I don't, but if you do—"

"No, I like what you and Joph discussed. I think it's a great idea."

"Really?"

"I mean it. As I said, never having any interest in romance or sex, I never saw myself having children. Can I ask, do you know why you don't?"

She looks down. "After what I endured as a child, I couldn't imagine having one of my own. Like you, I never thought I would be interested in romance or starting a family."

"You would be a terrific mother, and—" He stops when she stands and walks to the window. He steps up beside her and places his arm around her waist. "What's wrong?"

"Please, don't. I can't think of it."

"Ana?"

"My foster mother was the only mother I ever knew, and she was gone so suddenly. Coming here, finding out about my own mother, it's too much. I don't want to think of being one myself!"

"I'm sorry. We won't talk about it until you're ready. I didn't realize."

"No, I am the one who should be sorry. I didn't mean to snap at you."

"It's all right. Please, sit with me?"

He returns with her to the sofa, pulling her into his lap. With a soft sigh, she snuggles closer, finding comfort in the rhythm of his heartbeat. She drifts off to sleep in his embrace. They lay down together, reminiscent of their first night as a couple.

Chapter 8

Ana wakes up, realizing where they are. She rolls over onto him, kissing him gently. He opens his eyes and smiles.

"Well, this was a better way to wake up, than having Kara yell at us," he says with a hearty chuckle.

"I didn't mean to fall asleep. I didn't even realize I was tired."

"Ana, we trained, and you brought down walls. It's a wonder you stayed awake as long as you did." He sits up, pulling her with him.

She lays her head on his chest. "Yes, love."

"Now, are you ready for dinner or do you want to wait a bit?"

"We'll wait."

"Do you want to stretch your wings?"

"Yes," she says, rising to her feet. Taking his hand, she walks to the center of the room. She extends them out, furling and unfurling them. Her gaze lifts to meet his. "I won't say it's normal, but it also no longer feels weird to do this."

"That's good. How are they today?"

"A little tight. They needed the exercise," she says, rising towards the ceiling. He flies up next to her, taking her hand.

"Majesty," he says, pulling her into his arms.

"Rafe?"

He smiles at her, holding her closer and singing softly, as they dance in the air. She clings to him as he takes her around the room. They lower down to the floor.

"Another first?"

"Yes. Did you enjoy that?"

"Very much. Aylin was right about being together in the air. It is romantic!"

"Hmm. What else did you two talk about?"

"Rafe!" She blushes.

"I won't ask. All right."

"Love, would you see about dinner?"

"As you wish, Majesty." He kisses her hand, then steps back. He walks away but returns a few moments later. "On its way. Now, are you staying dressed like that or do you want to change?"

"Like this. I'd like to get a shower and change into pajamas after we eat."

"Did you say shower?"

"Rafe—"

"I'm teasing. We'll get cleaned up, then turned in. You'll need your energy for going to the village tomorrow."

"Oh, we were supposed to go check on Kellan!"

"We still can, but you'll have to change."

"I know. Can we?"

"Yes. Let's get dressed, have dinner, then we'll go down to the barracks."

"Oh, I feel awful!"

"What's wrong?" he asks, rushing to her.

"No, not like that. I'm sorry. I feel awful that I forgot about checking on her, after she risked her life for mine."

"It's all right. You hosted dignitaries today."

She takes his hand, going into the closet. "What should I wear for going into the barracks?"

"Hmm. Not that silver-blue gown."

She laughs. "You really like that one, don't you?"

"What? Of course not. What makes you say that?"

"Well, I guess I could donate it then…"

"Ana, you wouldn't!"

She smirks at him. "Maybe, maybe not. It depends on you."

"Yes, I love that gown on you. It is the sexiest I have ever seen you, in a dress. Is that what you want to hear?"

"Hmm."

"What?"

"So, if I wore it before you confessed your love—"

"That's mean to think about. I probably would've brought you in here and told you exactly how I felt."

"Yes, love, I will keep that gown."

A crimson gown, long-sleeved and trimmed in white lace at the hem, catches her eye. Removing her hoodie, she puts on the gown. She slips on silver shoes and a matching crown. She accessorizes her outfit with a bracelet and necklace from her drawer. Rafe is sitting on the ottoman, putting on his boots, as she walks up to him.

"What about this?"

His eyes rise, and he draws in a sharp breath. "Oh, you are testing me! That is gorgeous on you. Please, open your wings?"

"Hmm. Maybe I should make you beg?"

He falls to his knees in front of her, taking her hand and kissing it. "Please, mia estrela."

Pulling him up, she kisses him. "Rafe, I was teasing!" Stepping back, she spreads her wings.

"Just so you know, everyone will be staring at you."

"They would anyway, regardless of what I'm wearing."

"Ana, are you feeling self-conscious again?"

She brings her wings in. "A little, but I'm all right."

He pulls her into his arms. "We don't have to go anywhere."

"I want to. She at least deserves my gratitude, after what she did for me."

"All right."

They step out as the bell is ringing. Rafe walks to the door, getting their dinner. He sets it up at their small table.

Ana joins him. "I wonder what Bela and Joph will be like, as parents."

"Bela is a little more open, whereas Joph is so focused on his work. I'm wondering what Kara will be like. She's so protective of you, I can't imagine how she'll act around a pregnant Evren."

"Oh, I didn't even think of that. She will be a force to be reckoned with!"

"Thankfully, they aren't wanting to do any of that for a long time. Maybe she'll calm down some by then."

"Have you met Kara?"

They both laugh. "You're right."

They finish eating. She gathers dishes. "Let's return these, then go down to the barracks."

"Good idea." He leads her out, as Rayan and Asuin come to attention. "We're going to the kitchen, then the barracks."

"Yes, Rafe."

Ana looks at Rafe, surprised to see him looking a little more relaxed. She puts her hand on his arm. "Thank you."

"I'm trying this for you. We'll see how long it lasts."

They go into the kitchen, were Yeona takes the dishes and puts on the counter. "Majesty, if I may, that gown is lovely!"

"Thank you, Yeona. Have you made pizza yet?"

"We had it for lunch the other day. The staff truly enjoyed it. Thank you for sharing that with us. Are we going to cook again?"

"I would like to."

"Yes, Majesty."

With her hand in his, they depart from the kitchen. The guardians guide them towards the barracks. Melian welcomes them at the door.

"Rafe, Majesty, how can we help?"

"We'd like to check on Kellan."

"Right this way."

They go to her family's quarters, where she is now recovering. Melian knocks on the door. A guardian Ana doesn't recognize opens the door. She immediately bows at the sight of the queen.

"Your Majesty, how may we serve?"

"I apologize. What is your name?"

"I am Rienna, Kellan's mother."

"It is an honor to meet you. If Kellan is up for company, I would like to see to her myself."

"Yes, Majesty. Please, come in," she says, opening the door and gesturing them inside. "I'll get her."

"Rienna, please. If she's recovering—"

"She's fine now, Your Majesty."

"Very well."

Rienna walks out, then returns a minute later with Kellan. Kellan walks up to Ana and bows. "Majesty, how can I be of assistance?"

"Oh, no, Kellan. I came here to personally thank you for saving my life. I am in your debt."

"I was simply doing my duty."

"Please, Kellan. It was more than that, I assure you. How can I repay you?"

"Majesty, there is nothing I require. I will be returning to duty tomorrow."

"I insist you have a few more days."

"Majesty?"

"It was a serious wound, please."

"Yes, mi'lady. Thank you."

Rienna steps up, bowing. "Thank you, Your Majesty. We truly appreciate the time with her."

"She is an amazing guardian. I am lucky to have her."

"Thank you," Kellan says, bowing. "Please, call on me any time."

"For now, rest and recover."

"I will, Your Majesty."

Rafe takes Ana's hand and guides her out of the quarters. He leads her through the barracks, highlighting the separate living quarters for each rank, their armory, and the classrooms.

"You're right, Rafe. Everything here is much nicer than I would've expected. I'm sorry I was so upset before."

"Ana, you were trying to take care of your people. It's quite all right. I love how kind-hearted and passionate you are."

She looks up at Rafe, yawning. "I'm ready to turn in."

"Let's return to our quarters."

Rayan nods at Rafe, leading the way. Rafe squeezes Ana's hand.

They arrive at their quarters, waiting in the hall as Rayan checks inside. "All clear," he says, stepping out. Rafe leads her in.

"You were quiet on the way here. Are you all right?"

"Fine," she says softly.

The shift in her tone concerns him. "Ana, what is going on?"

"I guess thinking about the guardians, and…"

"And what?"

"How grateful I am to have them. They are willing to put their lives on the line for me. Kellan didn't even know me, but she risked her life for mine."

"It's our duty."

Ana sighs. "How am I supposed to just accept it? I went from being told I was no one important on Earth to being considered the most important person here."

"Why are you thinking about this now?"

"Because she took a bullet for me. For me!" She goes into the closet, with Rafe following behind.

"Any one of us would do it."

"But to take such a risk for someone you don't even know?"

"Any guard or guardian here will give their life for you. It is why we are here."

"I'm not worth it!"

He picks her up and sits with her on the ottoman. "Talk to me."

"I was getting overwhelmed. I didn't mean to. I'm all right, I promise. It's a lot to take in."

"Okay."

Standing up, he assists her in getting on her feet. While he gathers his pajamas and finishes getting dressed, she goes to the washroom. When he steps in, he hears water running. As he enters the shower, he notices Ana leaning against the back wall. He rushes to her.

"Ana, what's wrong?"

"Nothing, I'm really tired."

"It's been a long day." He guides her under the showerhead to wash her. Stepping out, he dries her off and dresses her. He brings her to the chaise and gently settles her on it. "I'll be right out. Please, stay here?"

"I promise."

He runs back in, cleaning off. After drying off and getting dressed, he exits. Ana is asleep. Lifting her from the chaise, he carries her to bed.

"Oh, mia estrela. Sleep tonight." He kisses her forehead and holds her close.

Rafe opens his eyes, looking down and seeing Ana still asleep. He checks the time on the clock. It's a few minutes past seven. His touch is gentle on her face, and he smiles when her lips part. He gives her a tender kiss. Looking up at him, she holds the back of his head and kisses him.

"Morning," she says.

"How are you?"

"Better. I did have a bad dream."

"What was it about?"

She shakes her head as she sits up. "I dreamed I died in those woods."

"You did."

"Yes, but this time, I didn't come back."

"Ana—"

"And I'm sorry about last night."

"You have nothing to apologize for. It's all right."

"Yes, love. What time are we having breakfast?"

"It will be here at eight, along with Kara and Evren. Are we going to the morning briefing?"

"Yes, then lunch. I'd like to go to the village after."

"That's fine. Are you announcing our engagement today?"

"We can at the briefing."

"Ana, can I ask, why don't you want to do it at the dining hall?"

"We will, at lunch. I only meant—"

"It's okay. I know."

"I'll get dressed."

"Can I hold you like this?"

She sits up, wrapping herself around him. "Please," she says softly. "I'm okay, but I need your comfort."

"I will always give you that."

"Forever?"

"Yes, forever."

As she holds onto him, she tries to suppress the past. She clings to him, relishing the comfort and security of his presence.

"I'm okay now. Thank you, love."

He stands up, carrying her into the closet. "Are you okay to wear a gown?"

"Yes, I am. I know it's part of my duty. I can be comfortable here on the weekends with you."

"And in the evenings."

"Yes, love. Thank you."

Ana searches through the sea of gowns. She sighs, picking out a pale pink gown. She slips it on over her corset, then she adds a necklace and bracelet. Rafe steps over to her, getting her rings out and slipping them on her.

He kisses her hands. "You look beautiful."

"Thanks."

Approaching the shelf, she selects a silver circlet. Entering the main room, she unfurls her wings. She looks at them, angry for being there. She reclines on the chaise. Rafe steps out.

"Are you in pain?"

"No, I'm fine," she replies softly.

He's walking to her when the bell rings. He lets the staff in as Kara and Evren follow behind.

Kara goes to Ana. "Sis, what's wrong?"

"Nothing. Just a little tired today."

Kara watches Rafe approach. "Ana, it's more than that. Don't turn inward. Please open up to us."

The staff leave. Ana turns to the fireplace, focusing on the flames. "I'm having a bad day."

Kara sits up. "What does that mean?" She looks at Rafe.

"Her wings."

"Oh. How can we help?"

Ana shakes her head. "You can't. Let me deal with it on my own."

"What happened?"

Ana wipes away her tears. "I had a moment last night, and it won't go away. I keep thinking maybe it would've been better if I had died in the woods instead of changing into what I am."

Kara's gaze falls on Rafe. He moves toward Ana and takes her into his arms.

He sits on the chaise, holding her with the deepest affection. "Ana, no. We are so grateful you are still here. You brought about peace and freed your people. Why do you think that?"

"I don't. I really don't. I'm so sorry. I was overwhelmed from nightmares and everything yesterday. I'll be okay. Just give me a few minutes."

"Take however long you need," Kara says. "Can I bring you a plate? Will you eat for me?"

"We'll eat together in a minute. I promise."

"Okay."

She looks up at Rafe. "I'm good now. I need to use the washroom, then we'll eat." He stands up, carrying her in. He leans against the doorway. "I'll be right out."

"Ana, I love you, but I'm not leaving you alone."

"Rafe, I promised you—"

"I know, but you're upset. Let me stay with you."

"Close the door, please."

He does, turning away to give her privacy. She finishes and washes her hands, splashing cool water on her face. She dries off, looking at him.

"I mean it. I'm okay now."

"I'm still worried. Maybe we should stay in today."

"Love, don't you think getting some fresh air and seeing the shops will help lift my spirits?"

"Yes, you're right. Are you okay to eat?"

"I am." She steps up, kissing him. "Thank you."

They go to the table, joining Kara and Evren. Kara practically stares at Ana. "Are you okay?"

"Kara, I'm fine. I had a moment this morning, but I promise you, I am."

"You have me worried. You're acting like you did when we first brought you here. I thought we were past that."

"We are. I just had a rough night."

"What was your other nightmare?" Rafe asks.

"What?"

"You said you had nightmares. I know you had the one where you laid down in the woods and died. What was your other one?"

"I only had the one," she replies while continuing to eat. "Kara, we're going into the village after lunch, and I was wondering—"

"Ana, no. Don't do that."

"Do what, Rafe?"

"Don't hide from us. Talk to us. You know how much we

all care about you. Let us help."

She looks at Kara, struggling not to cry. "As I was saying, we're going to the village to look at some shops—"

"Damn it, Ana. Talk to us!"

She closes her eyes as the tears escape. "I was doing fine! Why would you do that?" she asks, looking at him. "Why are you so angry?"

"I'm not. I'm worried sick about you."

"Why?"

"Because you just told us you wonder if it hadn't been better if you had stayed dead! Please, talk to us. Let us help you."

She sees the worry on Kara and Evren's face. "I was back in MoonFrost, chained to the floor. Only this time, Remus was… He…" She buries her face in her hands. "Why would I dream that?"

"It's a combination of what happened there and in his camp. Oh, Ana. I'm sorry! Why didn't you tell me about this?"

"I'm ashamed. I wasn't hurt like that! Why am I so scared?"

"Ana," Kara says, "you were literally kidnapped, tortured, and attacked. You have every right and every reason to be scared. These are the walls you're bringing down, right? You can't do that, if you don't let us help you. Now, is that why you said that? Because you were overcome from that nightmare?"

"Yes," she quietly replies.

Rafe lets out a small gasp. "Oh, mia estrela. How can I help? What can I do?"

"I want to put on comfortable clothes and stay in this morning, but—"

"Then that's what we'll do. Kara will run the briefing, then we'll join her and Evren in the dining hall for lunch to announce our engagement."

"Really?"

"Yes," Kara answers. "You stay here, take it easy."

"I'm sorry."

"No, no apologies, Ana. Stay with Rafe this morning. We will handle everything."

"Thank you," she says softly.

She watches them leave. Rafe stands up and carries her into the closet. He helps her into her comfy clothes, putting his hoodie on, too. Then he takes her to the chaise.

"Is this okay? The two of us, sitting here and watching the fire?"

"Yes, love. I'm sorry I hid from you and for what I said."

"Ana, you have survived so much. More than any one person should ever endure! You are so strong, so incredible. I wish you could see that."

"I'm trying to. Thank you." She clings to him. "Being with you right now is what I need more than anything."

"I'm right here, and I meant it, when I said I'm not going anywhere. I am with you, always."

"Forever," she quietly replies, kissing him. She lays her head on his chest.

"Do you want to get more sleep?"

"I'm not tired, just… I guess overwhelmed, though I am feeling better. Will you tell me about MorningStella?"

"What do you want to know?"

"How long have they been around? What's their history?"

"They were established around three thousand years ago. A group of travelers from here decided to explore the planet. Upon finding the beautiful beaches and warm, temperate climate, they established a capitol there, with the queen's blessing. It quickly grew into one of the biggest cities of the four realms."

"Really?"

"Oh, yes. But don't be fooled. The city is walled and away from the beach. With only your cottage and a few other buildings around. They wanted to protect the beach, to preserve it, so they didn't build up on it."

"I'm glad to hear that. I am excited to see it with you."

"I can feel it! We are waiting, right?"

"Rafe!"

"I'm teasing, mia estrela."

"Yes, love."

"MorningStella is known for their exotic fruits and seasonings."

"Yes! I used some in the kitchen. Everything was really good."

"What else would you like to know?"

"How do they feel about the vampyra?"

"They've traded and mostly kept the peace. It's MoonFrost that is so intent on hurting them. It's raged on for centuries. I truly believe you will bring the peace and keep it."

"I'm working towards it. With Remus dead, I hope it's simply a matter of time."

"You weren't thrilled with the MorningStella cuisine at the festival. I hope you can find something to eat while we're there."

"Oh, I'm sure they have a good variety."

"Would you like to get cleaned up and start getting ready for lunch? You can shower by yourself, if you need to."

"I'm okay. Yes, a quick shower would be nice. Then we'll change."

He gets to his feet, holding her in his arms. Nestled against his chest, he carries her inside. He seats her on the vanity, leaning down to gaze at her. "If you need to be in here alone, I trust you and will give you space. I don't want you overwhelmed or self-conscious."

She smiles at him, leaning forward and kissing him. "Thank you. Please, let's get cleaned up."

"All right."

Disrobing, she throws her clothes into the hamper. She enters and lets the water flow over her. As he joins her, she washes her hair. He helps her clean up. She steps out, drying off and slipping on her robe as he finishes washing.

As she enters the closet, she sighs upon seeing all of her gowns. Thinking of announcing their engagement, she becomes aware of the need to dress nice. Upon searching, she locates the blue gown she wore the day the treaty passed. She adds a silver crown, shoes, and smiles at her ensemble.

Rafe enters and walks to his dresser. Seeing what she is wearing, he slips on black slacks and a pale blue shirt with a silver vest.

"You like that dress, don't you?"

She smiles at him. "It's the most important gown in here."

"Because you wore it the day we could be together."

Her smile grows. "You remembered that?"

"Mia estrela, how could I ever forget? That was one of the happiest days of my life, knowing we didn't have to hide anymore." He gently runs his hand through her wings. "Now, how are these? Are you still angry?"

She looks down. "You felt that this morning?"

"I did. It's okay. Please, be honest."

"I'm not angry anymore. I love my wings, and I'm so grateful that you and I are alike. You died for me, and I repaid the favor. We are equals, we are partners, and you are the love of my life."

"Ana, is that why you want me to be crowned King?"

"Yes, love. Please, don't get upset."

"I'm the one who brought it up. I'm okay. Why?"

"Because you have earned it. You fought for and defended this kingdom over five hundred years. You risked everything to save me. If anyone is worthy of being crowned King, it is you, my love."

"Can I think on it?"

"Of course. There is no rush. I won't pressure you or bring it up, until you want to discuss it."

He escorts her to the drawers, holding her hand, and slips her rings onto her fingers. They leave the closet and enter the main chamber.

"Open your wings," he says, expanding his out.

She opens them, looking at him. "Flying?"

"Yes, Ana. You need to stretch them and use them this morning." They soar through the air, completing a few laps of the room. He lowers to the ground, holding her against his chest. "I'm glad you're feeling better."

"Like you said, there will be moments. I am okay now. Are we ready to head to lunch?"

"Excited about making another announcement?"

She laughs. "Is it that obvious?"

"Yes. That's good. It makes me very happy."

"Did you want to announce it?"

"Only if you are feeling self-conscious."

"Oh, no. I am excited."

"Then please, announce the good news."

"Yes, love," she says, stepping up and kissing him. He takes her hand, leading her out to the hallway. Rayan and Asuin come to attention. "Dining hall, please."

"Yes, Your Majesty."

Chapter 9

Rafe and Ana are surprised to walk in and see the dining hall is nearly full. They go to their table, where Kara and Evren are seated. She sees the look on Ana's face.

"I may have mentioned at this morning's briefing that you were making an announcement at lunch. I hope that's all right?"

"Yes, Kara. I didn't expect a crowd like this. I'm glad, though."

Ana looks around, seeing some familiar faces. She takes a deep breath, standing up. Kara hands her a miniature sound amplifier. "Thanks." She holds it to her mouth. "Excuse me, if I could have everyone's attention, please." The room goes silent, with all eyes on her. She swallows hard.

"Good day, everyone. I have an announcement to make, then you may resume your meal. I am very pleased to announce that Rafe, my personal guardian, has asked me to be his wife, and I said yes." She looks around as there is some scattered applause. "I know this sounds familiar, from before. Some of you were here when Kane made a similar announcement. He kidnapped my friends and threatened to kill us all if I did not agree to marry him." She sees some looks of surprise and confusion.

"We are very excited about getting married, and I am so happy to genuinely share this good news with you!" More applause and whistles. "Thank you so much. Please, resume as you were."

After sitting down, she gives the amplifier back to Kara. She looks up as Countess Anwyn approaches. She bows as Ana gestures for her to rise.

"Your Majesty, congratulations! We are very pleased with this news."

"Thank you, Countess."

"Majesty, if I may, could we have lunch together one day this week?"

"Of course. Would Thursday be fine?"

"Yes, Majesty."

"Then we will dine here at eleven on Thursday."

"I look forward to it. Thank you." She turns and walks away. Ana looks at Rafe, as confused as he is.

"I wonder what she wants?" she asks.

"Ana, she may just want to have a nice lunch with you. There may not be an ulterior motive."

"I know. I'm sorry. After Kane—"

"It's understandable to be a little suspicious." He looks at Kara. "What do you know about her?"

"Hmm. Her family is from the MoonSol Realm. She's lived here her whole life, coming with her mother when she was a baby."

"Kara, how do you know so much about everyone?" Ana asks.

She leans over, close to Ana. "We have files on everyone here."

"Are you the NSA?"

Her head rolls back as laughter erupts. "No, Ana. Nothing that sinister! We do keep tabs on everyone in the kingdom, for your protection." She takes Ana's hand, squeezing it. "How are you? You seem like you're better."

"I am much better now."

"All right. You said something about going into the village after lunch. Evren and I are meeting with the chancellor to go over some things for our wedding. We could go later if—"

"No, it's all right. Rafe and I will go. You and I are still on for Wednesday, right?"

"Yes. What are we doing?"

Ana smiles at her. "We'll meet here for lunch, then you and I are doing something special."

"You're not going to tell me?"

"Nope!"

"All right. We'll see you for breakfast tomorrow."

"Yes, that's fine."

"Then we'll see you at eight in your quarters."

"Yes, Kara. Thanks, for today."

"I told you, I'm here for anything you need." She takes Evren's hand and leaves the hall.

Ana turns to Rafe. "Are we ready to go into the village?"

"Let's go to our quarters first. We'll use the washroom and get your purse."

"Thank you."

Rayan and Asuin lead them back. Rayan steps out. "All clear, Rafe."

"Thank you, Rayan."

Taking Ana's hand, he guides her inside. Ana uses the washroom as Rafe enters the closet to get her coin for the market. He changes into his boots. As he walks out, he spots her sitting on the chaise.

"Are you all right?"

"I'm fine. I didn't know if you were—" She gestures to the washroom.

"Yes. I'll be right out."

Standing up, she walks to the window and looks out. It's a grey, cloudy day. She prays it doesn't rain while they are out. Getting sick is the last thing she wants to deal with right now. Rafe steps up beside her and takes her hand.

"What are you worried about?"

"I love the rain, but I don't want to get caught out in it."

"I think we'll be okay."

⁓⁓

They arrive at the clothing vendor. Rayan opens the door.

"Rafe, are we coming in or—"

"Stay out here. If it starts raining, you may come in."

"Yes, Rafe. Thank you."

They go inside, thankful it isn't busy. The owner comes out, happy to see Ana. "Ah, Your Majesty! Welcome. How can I help today?"

"I'm not sure. I love the gowns I have, but it seems like they are starting to look alike. I would like to have some custom made, if that's all right."

"Yes, here." She gestures to a table with books of patterns and fabric samples.

Ana looks at Rafe. "Are you sure you're okay while we're looking?"

"I'm not leaving your side."

"Thank you, love."

They sit at the table, observing her as she chooses gowns. After almost an hour, she looks at the woman. "I'm sorry. I think I've lost count! How many gowns are we up to?"

"Ten, Majesty."

"I would say that is plenty for now. Thank you."

"Yes. If you'll come with me."

She and Rafe follow her to the register, where she types everything in. Rafe pays her, wishes her a good day, then they turn and leave. Ana looks at him, blushing.

"What?" he asks, leading her out.

"Do I want to know how much all of that cost?"

He laughs. "Probably not. We can learn about coin and the money system when we return to our quarters. Now, were you still wanting to go to the jewelry vendor while we're here?"

"If that's okay?"

"Of course." They walk to the jeweler. He looks at Rayan. "Same as before."

"Yes, Rafe."

He leads Ana inside. She walks up to a counter, amazed at all of the beautiful stones. "Oh, Rafe! You were right."

"Can I help you?"

Her body tenses up at the sound of his voice. She looks over and loses her color. She grips Rafe's hand.

"Ana, what's wrong?"

The owner approaches her. "Your Majesty, I—"

"Rafe, arrest him!" she cries out.

"Ana, what—"

"Now! Please!" she yells.

He runs and binds the owner in the same magical bindings he's used before. "Ana, who is he?"

She takes a breath, her head swimming as she's fighting down the memories. "He came into the tent when Remus took me."

Rafe studies him for a moment. "Who are you?"

"Please, Majesty, as I was trying to tell you. I was acting as a spy. Kara herself asked me to when she learned of my history."

Ana rushes to the door and flings it open. "Rayan, go get Kara and bring her here. Tell her it's of the utmost importance."

"Yes, Your Majesty." He takes to the sky, flying as fast as he can.

"We'll know the truth soon enough."

"Majesty, please. I mean it. Once he left your tent, I was going to come back and free you. I looked in, but your guardian was already there."

"Please, stop talking. We will discuss this once Kara is here."

"Majesty—"

"Please!" she cries out. "Please, I can't," she adds.

Hearing her voice break, he closes his mouth as he hangs his head. Rafe glances at her occasionally, unable to hide his concern. They look up when Kara comes in. She runs up to Ana, obviously surprised at the sight before her.

"What is going on? Why is Jerrod in bindings?" Kara asks

as she takes in the scene.

"Kara, how do you know him?"

"Ana, I can't—"

"I need to know! Please, tell me everything."

"He was a spy during the great Stellar Wars, which were almost a hundred years ago. He saved many lives and risked his own, trying to bring peace. I approached him, asking if he would use his skills again. He was working for Remus, under my orders."

Rafe releases the binds. Jerrod steps up to Ana, hands up and palms out, to show he is no threat. "Your Majesty, my humblest of apologies."

"No, Jerrod. Please. I am so sorry. I saw you, and I was back in that tent. It was a horrible night, and I'm sorry I took it out on you."

"You had every reason to be suspicious."

Ana turns to Kara. "You knew we were coming to the shops! Why didn't you tell me this?"

Kara's eyes go down. "I'm sorry. I was excited about meeting with Audressa to discuss the wedding, and I let my personal life interfere with my duties."

"Kara, it's all right. I should be more involved in the affairs of the kingdom. If I had been, I would've already known about this." She turns back to Jerrod, stepping up to him and taking his hands. "Thank you for risking your life for us. I'm sorry about my reaction."

He bows to her. "Your Majesty, it's quite all right. Honestly, I probably would've reacted the same way, too. After what Romere put you through."

"Who is that?"

"He's the man who assaulted you. I was coming in, ready to free you. I saw him hurting you when your guardian killed him. I slipped back out of the tent, trying to keep my cover with Remus." His eyes go down. "I'm sorry I didn't get to you sooner."

"Jerrod, it's okay. As you said, my guardian saved me. I'm fine now."

"Yes, Majesty."

She looks at Kara then Rafe. "I need to return to my quarters, please."

"I'll take you," Rafe says as he approaches her and clasps her hand.

"Jerrod, if it's okay with you, we will return in the near future to look at rings. If you don't want to see me again, I understand completely."

"Your Majesty, you are welcome any time. I guess I'll take it as a compliment that you honestly believed I was working with him."

She smiles at him. "Thank you. Your understanding and patience is appreciated, after everything."

He bows again. "Yes, Your Majesty. Thank you as well."

She turns to Rafe and follows him outside. He looks at Rayan and Asuin. "Up for flying?"

"Yes, Rafe."

He turns to Kara. "One of them could take you."

"No, thank you." She laughs while holding up her hand. "I'll walk. I'll check on you guys in a little while."

"All right."

He pulls Ana into his arms. Neither says anything as he flies back to the palace.

"Ana, I'm so sorry for what you just went through. Are you okay?"

"Yes, Rafe," she responds in a subdued tone. "I'm tired. I'd like a nap before dinner."

"Okay."

In the closet, he sets her down on the ottoman. She takes

off her gown and corset, putting on the pajamas he gives her. She lies down and wraps herself in the blanket. Before he joins her, he locks the door and changes. He crawls up beside her, pulling her against his chest.

"Sleep, mia estrela. Everything is okay. You're safe. I'm not going anywhere."

She turns to him, clutching his shirt and relishing his warmth. "Yes, love."

"Will you tell me, how you're feeling?"

"I'm okay. I was terrified at first, hearing his voice and seeing him. I was back in that tent, chained to the cot and watching him run in to inform Remus. Having Kara explain who he is, knowing he was trying to help, makes me feel better. I had a moment."

"I know, but you are still recovering from your nightmares. I don't want this to add to it."

"It won't. Being here with you is taking care of that. I feel your love and assurance, I promise."

"Then sleep well, my little star. I'll be here when you wake up."

"Yes, love," she says, falling asleep to his heartbeat.

Rafe looks down at her, wondering on Jerrod's words. *He's sorry he didn't get there sooner. She says Romere didn't hurt her like that, but the way Jerrod said that, I truly wonder. I won't push her. I've done that enough. Still, how badly was she hurt before I got there? Did she heal herself so I wouldn't feel what had been done to her?*

His eyes close at the thought. He feels her shivering in his arms, focusing on his love for her. He smiles as she calms down.

"I'm sorry, Ana. For everything," he whispers, planting a soft kiss on her forehead. "Truly sorry."

He lays with her, falling asleep, praying she doesn't have nightmares.

Rafe wakes when he hears the bell ringing. He looks down, seeing Ana is still asleep. He gently pulls away and goes to the door. "Kara?"

"I wanted to see how she's doing."

"She's napping. What happened today wore her out."

"I'm so sorry, Rafe. How did I not think to tell her something that important? I feel awful for it."

"Kara, don't," Ana says, walking up behind Rafe. "Sis, please. Come in."

Rafe opens the door, letting Kara and Evren inside. He and Evren walk to the small table to give them privacy.

"Ana—"

"No, Kara. Yes, it's something I wish I had known before walking in there. You are running a kingdom while I nap and do nothing!"

"Ana, do I need to bring Rafe over here? Because I know how he feels when you say things like that. You nap because you are recovering from the hell you suffered protecting your people. You've stopped battalions from marching on NightFall, it was your critical intel that led us to Neven, which got us the location of the main camp, and you were tortured defending your guardians. Do I really need to go on about what you have done for your people and your kingdom?"

"You've done all the work."

"Rafe, please come here."

"Kara, no, don't." She looks up as Rafe is walking up behind her. "Rafe, please, go back to Evren. Ignore Kara."

"Normally, Ana, I would love that advice." He smiles, winking at Kara, who shakes her head. "However, I can hear it in your voice. What is going on?"

"Do you want to tell him what you said or shall I?"

"Kara! You would break my confidence?"

"In this instance, yes. Because honestly, I don't know what else to do!" When Ana doesn't respond, Kara gives her attention to Rafe. "She says I'm running the kingdom while she naps and does nothing."

"Ana!" Rafe says, walking around and kneeling in front of her. "Really?" He sees her eyes go down. "Mia estrela, please. I'm sure Kara has reminded you of everything you have done for this kingdom!"

"Yes," she replies. "But Rafe—"

"No. Listen to me, Ana. You have never sat around, doing nothing for this kingdom. Even sitting here now, being alive is important. You have fought for your people, been tortured for them, died for them. Please, do not ever say you have done nothing!"

She falls into his arms, clinging to his chest. "Rafe, please. I know that. I know what I have done. It's still not enough."

He stands, walks to the chaise with her in his arms, and settles down. "There is peace in the realm. We are getting married this year. There are no battles, no war. Why do you feel this way?"

"Because Kara knows everything going on in this kingdom, and I don't!"

"Then let her teach you. Let her show you what she knows, but don't you dare say you've done nothing."

"I'm sorry. You're right. I know you are." She looks at Kara. "Instead of a lesson, can we learn about the kingdom? Will you take me through what you know?"

"Of course. We'll start tomorrow after lunch. We'll go to my office, where my files and paperwork are. How does that sound?"

"You have an office?"

Kara laughs. "Is that okay?"

"Oh, Kara! Of course it is. I was surprised."

"Ana, now that there is peace, we will learn all of this together. So you and I can run the kingdom together, once we're married."

"Will you get upset if I ask?"

"No, mia estrela."

"Have you thought any more about it? About letting me crown you as King?"

"Ana!" Kara says. "Your treaty—"

"Yes. The treaty states the guardian would maintain the lower status. Once I am crowned Empress, he could be crowned as King."

"Oh, right. I didn't think of that," Kara admits.

"I was already worried about becoming a prince, so you could imagine my shock when she suggested I become a king. I'm thinking on it, though, trying to process it."

"A guardian king. I, for one, would like to see that." She looks over, seeing Evren. "Oh, Evren, sweetie! Please come and join us. I'm so sorry. We didn't mean to leave you out! You're so quiet."

Evren walks to Kara and takes her hand. "It's okay. You three have a special connection—"

"Please, believe me, Evren, when I tell you that you are every bit as important to me as Kara and Rafe."

"Yes, Ana. Can I ask, what's going on?"

"Kara, would you please fill her in? I don't want to relive it all right now. I'm sorry, Evren."

"Kara and I will talk later. Can I do anything for you?"

"Will you tell me how it went with the chancellor today?"

"Oh, that went well. We were discussing various marriage vows, trying to incorporate both customs into the wedding. Audressa says she is comfortable with everything we have decided so far."

"I'm glad to hear it." Ana looks at Kara. "I'm sorry I interrupted it."

"We were done. Honestly, I was scared when Rayan arrived, saying you were calling for me. I didn't know if you had been hurt or what had happened."

"I'm fine, Kara. Really. Mentally and physically. Just a little tired."

"Ana, that is perfectly acceptable. Stop pushing yourself."

"Okay. I'll try." She looks at Rafe. "Can we have dinner?"

"Evren and I will go."

"No, Kara. Please, join us," Rafe says, getting to his feet. He places Ana on the chaise, then he walks out into the hall.

"I insist," Ana says. "Please?"

"Yes, we'll join you."

"Thank you."

Rafe steps back in. "Dinner will be here shortly."

"Kara, would you help me clean up?"

"Yes." She takes Ana's hand, taking her to the washroom. Evren goes to get her clean clothes.

Rafe walks in with her. "Evren, you went in the washroom when I brought Ana back from the camp. Could you tell, was she… you know?"

"Rafe, I honestly can't say. There were no bruises or marks since you said she healed herself. The way she reacted, and the fact that it upsets her so, I truly wonder."

"I do, too. I don't want to push her."

"That's best. She needs to continue to recover from it." She sees his head go down. "Rafe, what's wrong?"

"That's why I'm so worried. I feel like if she wasn't, she would be over it by now. How can I ask her without sounding like I'm pushing or doubting her?"

"Rafe, you can't. All you can do is give her patience and time. When she's ready to tell you, she will."

"I honestly believe he hurt her, even though she adamantly denies it."

"Really?" Ana asks, walking in and wearing her robe.

She goes to the dresser to place her rings inside. Refusing to turn around, she locks it.

"Ana, please. We are worried about you. The way you react, your fear and terror. I want to know everything that happened."

"I've told you what happened," she says, spinning around. "He didn't do that! How many times, how many ways, can I say it before you'll believe it? What will it take?"

"Ana—" Rafe tries, stepping towards her.

"No! I am telling you, for the last time, that it didn't happen!" She turns away, leaning against the drawers. Rafe steps up behind her.

"I believe you. I swear I do. I will never bring it up again. I was so worried about you. We all have been." He pulls her into his chest. "Please, Ana, don't be mad at us."

She turns, holding him tight. "I'm not. I want to be, but I know you are acting out of love." She looks at Evren. "Did you think that, too?"

"I wondered, but I didn't want to ask."

"I can understand. You're right, I should be past this by now. I am working on it, trying to be."

"Ana, I never should've said that. You deal how you need to and take the time you need."

"Can we have dinner, please?"

"Yes, Ana. Hey, just think, you'll have Roesh and Aylin back tomorrow."

"Oh, yeah! I'm excited to talk to her." She turns to the drawers. "I want to look real quick." Opening them up, she looks through the jewelry and finds a plain silver band. She faces Evren. "Is there anything special or important about this?"

Evren takes it, holding it up and looking it over. "No. I don't recognize this."

Ana slips it onto her ring finger, smiling at Rafe. "It fits."

"Now you have a ring to sleep in."

"Yes, love."

Evren leaves to give them privacy. Ana goes into the washroom to clean up. Dinner is delivered, and Evren helps Rafe set the table. He considers continuing their conversation but thinks better of it. A short while later, Kara and Evren join them.

Kara looks at Ana when she pushes her food around with her fork. "Sis, is everything all right?"

"Yes. Can we just eat, please?"

"Of course. I'm sorry."

"No, Kara." A deep breath escapes her lips. Rising to her feet, she grabs Kara's hand. They go to the chaise.

Rafe looks at Evren. "What's that about?"

Evren shakes her head. "Either she's telling her what happened in the closet, the camp, or both."

Rafe continues eating, growing concerned when he sees Kara pull Ana into her arms. "Should we go to them?"

"No. Give them their privacy." Rafe can't hide the concern on his face, and Evren places her hand on his arm. "Rafe, you need to give her space. She's talking with Kara, not turning inward or pulling away from us."

"You're right." He finishes his plate, looking up when Kara and Ana return. She sits beside him, squeezing his hand.

"I'm okay," she reassures him, as she eats her dinner. She looks at Kara. "Could Rafe and I have breakfast alone tomorrow? We'll meet you in the briefing room at nine-thirty?"

"Yes, that's fine." Kara finishes eating. She gathers the dishes with Evren. "We'll see you then."

Ana stands up, hugging Evren and Kara. "See you tomorrow."

She makes her way to the sofa, sits down, and observes the rain falling outside. Rafe takes a seat next to her. She glances his way.

"You want to know what Kara and I talked about."

"I do, but it's not my business. Just the fact that you were talking to her is enough for me, whatever it was about."

"Thank you."

"Tell me, are you okay?"

"I am." She takes his hand. "Really. I know I've had a

rough couple of days. I'm much better now. I promise."

"Okay. I see you're in pajamas. Are you ready to turn in?"

"You were going to teach me the money system here."

"Oh, right."

He pulls out her purse and sets it between them. She opens it up, looking at the various coins. He explains who or what is on the coin and the monetary value of each one.

"So, how much were my dresses?"

"Do you really want to know?" Rafe asks as he places the coins into the bag. She nods. "Okay. Remember, you have personal wealth, separate from the treasury."

"Rafe?"

"About seven thousand dollars."

"What?" she exclaims. "Rafe!"

"Ana, believe me. It's more than okay. You are expected to dress a certain way. There is a budget for it."

"Rafe, I know how much is in the treasury. I read the reports, when I decided to free the slaves, once I realized how much gold there truly was. Now, dare I ask, what is my net worth?"

"Hmm. Give me a moment." He runs some figures in his head. "What you have is equivalent to roughly three million dollars. Which is more than enough to cover your expenses and anything else. You also earn a yearly salary, as Queen, which will continue to build up your worth."

"Dare I ask, as old as you are, how much are you worth? Besides being priceless to me," she adds, smiling at him.

He laughs, shaking his head. "Roughly one million."

"You're right. You are well paid."

"Well, having such a high rank and being over five hundred years old, plus my inheritance."

"Of course. I didn't think of that. I will never remember all of these," she says as she runs her fingers through the coins.

"You will. It just takes studying them. If you want, we can go to the market once a week, making small purchases so you can learn the different coins."

"Once the rain is gone?" she asks, nodding to the window.

"Of course. I need to get cleaned up. You're okay out here?"

"Yes, I'm enjoying the rain."

"Okay. I'll be out in a minute."

He heads to the closet to grab his pajamas. He gives her a look before making his way to the washroom. She stretches out on the sofa, snuggles under the blanket, and falls asleep.

Rafe cleans up, getting out and drying off. He dresses and steps out, but doesn't see her. He rushes over to find her asleep. Kneeling beside her, he lovingly caresses her face. At his touch, her lips part, and he plants a gentle kiss. With a smile on his face, he lifts her up and her arms wrap around his neck. He carries her to bed and lies down beside her. She reaches for his shirt, holding him tight.

Chapter 10

Rafe's eyes fly open when Ana is on top of him. "What's the matter?"

"Just hold me, please," she begs.

He wraps his arms around her, holding her to his chest. "What's wrong?"

"I need your comfort."

"Did you have a nightmare?"

"Please," she begs softly.

"Okay. I'm sorry." He sits up, turning on the lamp. He looks at the clock, seeing it's almost five. She clings to him as he strokes her hair. "Please, tell me what's wrong?"

She pulls back and looks at him. "I just need you now."

He studies her face, not wanting to push her. "Okay. I'm right here, when you're ready to talk to me." He caresses her jawline. She leans up and kisses him, wrapping her arms around his neck. "Ana, do you need another day?"

"No, Rafe. I'd like to get more sleep. Please?"

"Yes, mia estrela. I really hope when we wake up, you'll talk to me."

"I will."

***

At seven o'clock, Ana wakes up. She snuggles into Rafe.

"Morning, mia estrela."

"Morning, my love."

"Will you talk to me now?"

She pulls away, sitting on the edge of the bed. "Rafe, please."

"I'm sorry." He crawls to her and places her on his lap. "I'm worried about you."

"I'm fine. What do you want to know?"

"What woke you up? Did you have a nightmare? An episode?"

"No. I simply woke up, feeling afraid. No idea why it happened. I knew if I told you that, you wouldn't believe me. Really, I'm okay. I'm not hiding. Look, when I was talking with Kara, I told her what happened in the camp and about you in the closet with Evren. See? I'm not hiding!"

"All right, all right. Ana, please. I believe you."

"I'm getting dressed."

She steps into the closet. Selecting a gown, she places it on the ottoman. She takes fresh undergarments and heads to the washroom.

Rafe appears in the doorway. "You're getting a shower?"

"Yes, alone," she says, shutting the door.

While undressing, she turns on the water. She steps in, losing the battle and weeps. When Rafe walks in, she looks at him in surprise.

"I'm standing here until you tell me what you need."

She approaches him but is unable to meet his gaze. "I'm sorry."

"Talk to me, please."

"Why? You're the one who said I should be over this by now."

"Oh, mia estrela!" He grabs her, pulling her into his arms. "That is not what I meant. I'm sorry. Please don't hide because of me."

"Then what did you mean?"

"I said it because I was worried you had been… hurt worse at the camp. I let my fear take control and said something I should not have said. I am truly sorry."

"It's all right. I've had some reactions and episodes. You're right, though. I should be past it by now."

"No, Ana. I was wrong. I shouldn't have said that. You were hurt and scared, and you will take as long as you need to cope with it. Will you tell me about it? Tell me what happened this morning?"

"I had a nightmare. That's all. It's stupid," she says, trying to pull away. He takes her hand, keeping her close to him.

"Say the word, and I'll let you go. Please, talk to me."

"I was back in his camp. What do you want to know?"

"Why are you being like this right now? Why won't you talk to me?"

She pulls away, standing under the water. Rafe steps up to her.

"Ana, did he—"

"Oh, my God!" she cries out. "Why won't you believe me?"

After turning off the water, she leaves the shower. Wrapping herself in a towel, she sprints to the closet, slams the door shut, and locks it. She dries herself and puts on fresh pajamas, then lies down on the ottoman. She cries into the pillow.

Rafe picks the locks, coming in angry, until he sees her asleep. Taking deep breaths, he tries to relax. He sits on the edge of the ottoman. Gently, he picks her up and carries her to bed. He heads towards Kara and Evren's quarters.

After a moment, he knocks. Kara opens the door. "What's wrong?"

"Bad morning."

"Still? What is going on with her?"

"I think seeing that man yesterday is forcing her to deal with too many bad memories at once. Dealing with Remus and everything that happened."

"I'll take care of the briefing. We'll stop by for lunch. If she's up for it, we can start learning about the kingdom, as well."

"Thank you."

He approaches a staff member and places an order for breakfast. He returns inside. Walking towards her, he realizes that Ana is still sound asleep.

Watching her, he sits on the edge of the bed. When the bell rings, he raises his gaze, then opens the door. He graciously accepts the food tray and arranges it on the small table. Once finished, he returns to the bed and crawls into it. He lies next to her, gently stroking her face and neck.

She opens her eyes, looking up at him. "I'm sorry. Please, I—" Her breath hitches.

"What is it?"

She sits up, pulling him with her, then crawls into his lap. She takes his arm, wrapping it around her waist, as her fingers trace along his hand. "I need to tell you something. It won't be easy for me, and I need your calm and patience."

"I'm right here, ready to listen with love. Please, Ana."

She closes her eyes, thinking of the night in his camp. "I wasn't hurt in that camp. I mean I was, but not the way you were thinking. He did attack me, and he nearly killed me. I…" She lets out a sigh. "I keep having nightmares, where you don't stop him." Tears form in her eyes, and she wipes them away. "It's so stupid. You did save me. I don't know why I keep doing this."

"As you said, you were attacked and nearly killed. Your brain is trying to process everything. I wish you would stop hiding. If you would let me in, I will help, however you need me to."

"I know." She looks at the clock. "Why aren't Kara and Evren here?"

"You were still asleep. I told her to go on, to let you rest. They'll be here at lunch. I have breakfast, and I really hope you'll eat."

She crawls up to him, wrapping herself around him. "I'll eat. Just, will you hold me right now?"

"I will."

"I'm so sorry that I took out my shame and anger on you."

"Ana, I won't say it's okay, but I can understand. I'm going to ask a question, that you absolutely do not have to answer. Do you understand?"

"Yes, Rafe."

"Is that everything I need to know? I mean, I know you are still dealing with some stuff from Earth. As far as here goes, is that it?"

"You know almost everything. I promise, I will be ready by August, ready for our wedding night."

"Maeriana Rose, you listen to me. There is nothing wrong with using August as a deadline for yourself, to help you want to heal and cope. If you are not ready, we will wait until you are. Nothing will be ruined, I will not leave you, and we will take our time. Please, tell me you believe me."

"I do, Rafe. I promise I do." She pulls back, looking at him. "How can I thank you? You are too forgiving, too patient with me. More than I deserve."

"You have suffered enough."

She kisses him as tears fall. She pulls back and sees the worry on his face as he wipes them away. "Happy tears. I love you. I love you more than I could ever say."

He smiles at her, kissing her hard. "I love you, too, mia estrela."

"Can we eat?"

He stands and escorts her to their table. A smile plays on his lips as he observes her eating. He gently touches her face and neck. "My little warrior."

She laughs. "Thank you, love."

He takes her hand, kissing it. "How was it? Sleeping with this ring on?"

"I liked it. Since I'll only wear it in quarters and wedding rings aren't a thing here, I think it's okay."

"Me, too. Let me know when you're ready, and we'll go look at wedding bands."

She looks down. "It might be a little while."

"Ana, it's fine. We can look at NightFall, if you want."

"Oh! I didn't think of the shops there. Do they use the same currency?"

"Yes. All quadrants do."

"Oh, good! I always hated doing money exchanges at the bank. It didn't happen often, but it was a pain."

"I remember doing it myself, back on Earth."

"I'm looking forward to our weekend trip."

He smiles at her. "I am, too."

"I'm curious to see what you have planned."

He laughs. "Trust me, you'll like it."

"Yes, love." She looks at the clock. "Should we get ready for the briefing? It'll be starting soon."

"Kara is taking care of it. They'll bring lunch here."

"Oh, right."

"We can go, if you want."

"I do."

"Then let's get dressed." He takes her into the closet, sitting on the ottoman and holding her tight.

"Love, are you okay?"

"Yes, Ana. For now, let me hold you?"

"You will never hear me say no to that." She clings to him, kissing him. "Hmm. Maybe we can skip the briefing."

"Not today. Not while you are recovering. I don't want you to overdo it. Maybe this evening, after dinner, we can have some time?"

"Yes, love."

Standing up, he helps her to her feet. She walks to her gowns and picks out a navy-blue gown trimmed in gold with gold stars along the bodice and hem of the skirt. She slips it on, seeing Rafe in black pants with a navy-blue shirt. He smiles at her as he joins her.

"That is beautiful. I haven't seen that one before."

"Neither had I. I guess I haven't seen them all." She

laughs. "I am excited for my new gowns, though."

"I understand. Honestly, I should probably get some new clothes, as well. I wore my uniform so much, I rarely wore anything else. Only having a few nice outfits for when I did have to dress up." He gently runs his fingers through her wings. "Do you need to stretch these?"

"We can, after lunch. Then we'll join Kara to learn about our kingdom."

"All right." He slips off her band, taking it to the drawers. He gets out her rings, putting them on her and kissing her hands. "Shall we?"

"Yes, Guardian."

He laughs as he leads her from the closet. They go to the door, where Ana smiles at the sight of Aylin and Roesh. "Morning!" she exclaims.

"Morning, Majesty," Aylin says back, bowing. "Where to?"

"Morning briefing, please," Rafe says.

"Yes, Rafe." Aylin and Roesh lead the way.

"Did you two have a good couple of days off?" Ana asks.

Roesh smiles at Aylin, nodding. She looks at Ana. "We did. Roesh and I are now betrothed."

"Aylin!" She grabs her, pulling her into a hug, shocking her and Roesh both. "Congratulations!"

Aylin pulls back, blushing. "Thank you, Majesty. Um, shall we?"

"Yes, I'm sorry."

"Quite all right," Roesh says, laughing. They continue to the meeting room. He glances back at Rafe. "You meant it, when you said she was happy to see us together as a couple."

"I did," Rafe says. "Congratulations, to both of you."

"Thank you," Roesh says. They approach the door. He steps in. "Everything all right in here, Kara?"

She looks up, surprised. "Yes. Is the queen with you?"

"Yes, she is."

"She can come in."

Roesh steps aside, beckoning them to enter. Ana smiles at him as she passes by. "Morning, Kara."

"Ana." She looks at Rafe. "I thought—"

"I'm okay. I asked to come. If you don't mind?"

"Of course not. I'll lead today, if that's okay?"

"Yes, Kara, thank you."

"What are you so happy about?"

"Roesh and Aylin are engaged."

"Oh, that's wonderful news! Now that there are more guardians, I am excited to see them rebuild."

"So are we. Even if I weren't a guardian, I would still want to see that." She looks at Rafe. "What?"

He smiles at her. "I love hearing you say you're a guardian."

"Rafe, do I need to excuse myself?" Kara asks.

He laughs, looking at her. "No, Kara."

They walk to the desk. "How is everything?" Ana asks.

"Very well. No issues or problems. There isn't even a whisper of war between MoonFrost and NightFall."

Ana's eyes close in relief. "Oh, thank God. Peace is all I have wanted for this realm. It is literally the whole reason I came here." She looks over at Rafe, taking his hand. "Okay, maybe not the whole reason…" She smiles at him.

"And now you have both."

"Yes, love."

Kara gags, looking up when Rafe laughs. "What?"

"You! Kara, I swear. What is wrong with you? I get it, you said it yourself you're not about chocolate and flowers, but do you have an ounce of romance in there?"

"I do. I'm just a very private person."

Ana shakes her head. "You always have been. At least, as long as I've known you. I tried to get you to open up more on Earth. I get that you were carrying so many secrets, but even to have a general discussion, on things like dating or relationships, you were so tight-lipped!"

"Ana, all of the things I wanted to say, to tell you, on Earth. I was afraid of letting something slip. That's why I listened and was your friend, but I couldn't open up to you."

"Were you ever going to tell me the truth? If we hadn't been found?"

Rafe looks at Kara, curious. "Well?"

"I don't know. I hadn't thought that far ahead! I was so happy to finally find you and have you in my life." She looks up as people start walking in. "We'll talk more at lunch."

"Yes, sis."

Kara pulls out the chair, getting a look from Ana. "I insist."

Ana sighs, laughing, as she sits down. Kara picks up her paperwork, greeting everyone and starting the briefing. Ana pays attention, listening to the questions and looking interested in what is happening. Kara adjourns the meeting, then turns to Ana.

"I'm going to my chambers to get changed. I'll see about lunch. Evren and I will be there shortly."

"Yes, Kara."

Ana stands up, taking Rafe's hand. He steps out, looking at Roesh. "Our quarters, please."

"Yes, Rafe."

Chapter 11

Rafe goes inside with Roesh while Aylin and Ana stay in the hall. She looks at Aylin. "Can I ask, how did he propose?"

She giggles. "We were in the air."

"Aylin?"

"Do you really want to know?"

She realizes what she's saying and laughs. "Oh, my. Well, that is a great way to get engaged."

"Yes, Majesty. If I may, how are you?"

"I'm doing well. I had a rough day, but I'm much better now."

"Please, feel free to call on me. I want to help, any way I can."

"Thank you, Aylin. I greatly appreciate that."

Roesh and Rafe step out. Taking her hand, Rafe guides her inside. He sets her on the chaise and kneels before her. "You are flushed. Are you okay?"

She laughs, pulling him up to sit next to her. "I am. Aylin was telling me how Roesh proposed."

"Okay?"

"They were… um… they were in the air."

Rafe nearly falls over laughing. "Ana!"

"It's how he asked." She sees the serious expression on his face. "What?"

"I love Kara and Evren, but I really wanted you to make friends with a female guardian. One you can discuss your wings with, and other things if you felt comfortable. This makes me so happy."

"I really like Aylin. She is very kind, and she offered that I could command her to keep my secrets if I needed to. I've had a good feeling about her since we met. You know my instincts are usually right." She looks down. "Usually."

"Ana, we don't need to bring him up. Neither of us saw that coming. Truly."

Kara and Evren arrive, ready to set up lunch. They go to the table. "You said you have files on everyone, does that include the guardians?"

"Yes."

"Good. I'd like to learn more about them. The different ages, who is together, and so on."

"We will. We'll go to my office after we eat. Now, how are you feeling?"

"I told you, Kara. I'm much better. I had a bad morning."

"Ana, you've had a bad couple of days. That's partly my fault, I know. I'm worried about you."

"I know, sis. I mean it. Now, are you going to answer my question?"

"Would I have ever told you the truth? I want to say yes, but I honestly don't know. How would I even tell you?" She faces Rafe. "How did you tell her?"

"Oh, I simply told her the truth."

"And she believed you?"

He laughs. "No. She thought I was high or crazy. Only after she saw my wings would she believe me."

"What were you thinking, Ana, when he told you? Once you knew he was telling the truth?"

"I didn't want to believe him. I tried to tell myself I was dreaming, or that I had finally snapped over him leaving." Seeing the look of guilt on his face, she takes his hand. "I realized, I had healed really fast. Seeing him with wings, I knew he had to be telling me the truth. I thought about it, wondering what would happen if I came here. Knowing lives were on the line, that I could bring peace and save the realm, brought me here." She looks at him, knowing what she's going to say will hurt him. "Also because Rafe told me he would be with me the whole time."

He retreats, his face sullen, and goes to the window. She looks at Kara.

"Ana—"

"No. I knew it would hurt him. It's the truth, though. If he said he was staying on Earth, I would've stayed with him. I love him and wanted nothing more than to be with him. Excuse me." She walks to him and takes his hand. "Please, don't pull away again."

He looks at her with unshed tears in his eyes. "I wish I could go back, change everything. I—" His words die in his throat as she steps up, kissing him hard. She pulls back, gently tracing along his jawline with her fingers.

"Love, we are here now. Please, let go of this guilt! You didn't lie to me. You said you would be with me, and even though we couldn't be together the way we wanted, you were by my side."

"Ana, you took it to mean we would be together. I lied by saying it that way. I hated breaking your heart. It was the worst thing I've ever had to do."

She gasps. "You killed your best friend."

"And that was devastating. Losing you, telling you I didn't love you, breaking your heart, was the hardest thing I've ever done. I… It nearly killed me." He studies her face, his hands on her arms. He sees the pain in her eyes. "Oh, mia estrela. You're right. I do need to let go. I don't want you feeling this!"

"Please. I don't care the reason, but get rid of it. Free yourself from this guilt and heartache." She leans into his chest, wrapping her arms around him. "Please, love. We are getting married. We will rule this kingdom. That pain is in the past, leave it there."

With his eyes closed, he holds her tightly. His mind fills with memories of her, envisioning himself kissing her on the ottoman where he saved her, then taking her to the battlement to propose. "I am, mia estrela. I am leaving it behind."

"Oh, Rafe," she exclaims, looking at him. He wipes the

tear falling down her cheek. "Your love is so strong." She kisses him, holding him with everything she has. He pulls back, chuckling.

"Um, Kara and Evren are staring."

She giggles. "Let's finish lunch."

They walk to the table. "My apologies," Rafe says.

Kara shakes her head. "We were watching because we were concerned. Rafe, are you all right?"

He looks at Ana and smiles. "I am now."

"Okay."

"Sorry. It's still kind of painful for both of us," Ana says to Kara.

"I can't imagine. I didn't mean to—"

"Kara, we brought it up. It's okay," Rafe says.

"Thank you."

"How old would I have lived to on Earth? Would it still be around five hundred years?" She sees the worry on Rafe's face. "I'm curious how aging worked, since I was only gone from here ten years, but I'm twenty-three."

"Honestly, I'm not sure," Kara answers. "I tried to find a planet most similar to ours, but far away."

"What would you have done, once I passed away?"

"Ana," Rafe says, concern in his voice, "why are you asking these things?"

"I'm sorry. I only recently found out I'm immortal, so thinking of death was natural to me. I'm not upset or overwhelmed, I was curious." She looks at Kara.

"I don't know. As I said, I hadn't really thought that far. Finding you and living with you was more than enough at the time. Rafe's right, though. Why are you asking these things?"

"You kidnapped me and took me to Earth. I have a million more questions, but I'm trying to do a little at a time, so as not to overwhelm you or myself."

"Maybe it's best if you and I discuss this tomorrow, when it's just you and me. I don't think Rafe wants to hear this."

"Kara, please don't speak for me. I am concerned for her, is all."

Ana nods at Kara. "We'll talk tomorrow, sis." She gives her attention to Rafe. "I'll be fine. I promise."

He turns to Kara. "If you push her—"

"I promise you, I won't. I've been working on not doing that."

"All right."

They both look over when Ana bursts out laughing, breaking the tension. "What?" Kara asks.

"You two! So protective of me. Thank you."

"I told you, you've suffered enough. From now on, you deserve only love and happiness."

"Thank you, love. That means a lot to me." She looks at Kara. "Are we ready to go to your office?"

"Yes."

She grasps Rafe's hand as she stands up. He takes them out, explaining to Roesh where they're headed.

His eyes meet Kara's. "My apologies, I don't know where that is."

She laughs. "Follow me."

The walk through the corridor is fairly short, and they arrive a few minutes later. They go into her office. Ana spins around, amazed at the sight.

"Kara, this is absolutely beautiful!" She circles the room, taking in how big it truly is. Two couches are placed in the room's center, facing each other with a table between them. The back wall features a fireplace and a smaller sofa. Her desk is in the other corner, by the window. "Oh, I'm envious!"

"Ana, this is your office. I've been using it, while handling my duties."

"Are you… What?" She looks around. "No, Kara. You've earned this office. I'll find a room and make my own. I insist, for everything you have done."

Rafe steps forward. "My old quarters are nearby. They

aren't being used for anything. We could make that into your office, when you want."

"We were going to make it into a rec room," Kara says with a pout.

"I know. I forgot, so much happened since then."

"It's okay," Ana says.

"No. We'll make it into your office. You didn't really get a say in your quarters, so let's create your office together. You can pick everything out and make it your own," Kara offers.

Rafe notices Ana studying him. "Is something wrong?"

"I want to ask a question, but I don't."

He takes a breath. "It's okay."

"What about you? Being Prince or King, will you want an office? Or would you want to share one with me?" She sees him smile as she says it. "Okay. We'll make it our office."

"Sounds great. We'll work on it next week, after we return from NightFall. Who knows, you may find some art or things there for it."

"That sounds wonderful." She looks at Kara. "Where do you want us?"

Kara gestures to the couches. She walks to the filing cabinet by her desk and pulls out files about the guardians. Ana reads through them, asking questions from time to time.

"Dare I ask, how did you get all of this information?"

Kara glances down for a moment. "You probably won't like my answer."

"What do you mean?"

"When Kane was in charge, he hired spies and collected most of this information. I feel bad using it, but since it's here, I see no point letting it go to waste. I went through, recreating the files, with only the most vital information in them. He had blackmail secrets and such. He truly was the vilest man I've ever met!"

"Blackmail? Secrets? No wonder the guards were loyal to him. He was manipulative, desperate to have and keep power,"

Ana says, shaking her head. She looks up when Rafe takes her hand. "I'm okay. I'm over him and everything he did to me, did to us." She looks at Kara. "Rafe and I would like to have a flying lesson, then a private dinner. Will you join us at eight tomorrow morning for breakfast?"

"Of course."

Ana walks to them, hugging her and Evren. "We'll see you then." She turns to Rafe, taking his hand.

They leave the office. He looks at Roesh. "We're going to my old quarters." He laughs when he sees the confusion on his face. "I'll lead the way." They walk down the hall. Rafe gets out his key, opening the door. He stops Roesh from entering. "I'll check."

"Yes, Rafe."

He steps in. Ana looks at Roesh. "Have you two set a date?"

"Probably sometime in the solstice. She wants a winter wedding."

"That will be beautiful! I'm sorry, where do guardians get married?"

"Rafe didn't show you our chapel?" Aylin asks.

"No. We saw so much that day, though. He said he would take me back to show me the rest." She looks up when Rafe steps out. "Let me know if I can do anything to help."

"Yes, Majesty, thank you."

Rafe takes her hand as they step inside. "Oh, wow. You did have very nice quarters." She laughs. "You know, I never saw your apartment on Earth."

"It wasn't nearly as nice as this. I know money wasn't the issue, but I didn't see the point in having a huge place when it was just me." He lights a fire in the fireplace against the wall by the bed.

Her gaze falls upon the dark floors, maroon walls, and ebony bookshelves. She glances at the bed. "Hmm." Taking his hand, she leads him to it. She makes him sit down, and then climbs onto his lap. Their lips meet in a kiss.

"Ana—"

"Hmm. Yes, love?"

"I need to lock the door."

A smile appears on her face as she looks at him. He places her on the bed, hurrying over to lock the door. Returning, he scoops her up and settles on the bed. He holds her, his mouth consuming hers.

"How come I haven't been in here before?"

"Well, when we were forbidden, it would've been way too suspicious for me to bring you in here. Then you passed the treaty and asked me to move in. I didn't think of it." He lowers her down, covering her with his body. "Now, mia estrela. What are we doing?"

"Rafe, if you have a beautiful woman in your bed and have to ask—"

He laughs. "I love that you called yourself beautiful."

She reaches up, tracing his jawline. "I need you to kiss me, please?"

His mouth crashes on hers, his kiss fierce and hungry, as he helps her undress. She stands up, pulling him with her. She undoes his pants and removes them, along with his shorts. He steps out, kicking them to the side. She helps him take off his shirt. His hand comes up, undoing the backing on her gown, which slides down to the floor.

He reaches down, removing her corset. She slips out of her undergarments, kicking them over to his clothes. He picks her up, then gently places her on the bed.

"Love, please," she says, her hands caressing his chest and stomach. "I'm ready. I know we're waiting, but I want you. I want all of you."

He swallows hard. "Ana, we need to wait. You still have walls to bring down. Please, let me tease you. Let me spoil and love you." He leans down, his mouth on her ear. "Let me pleasure you until you cry out and your whole body is spent."

With a gentle tug, she raises him up, her eyes meeting his. "Yes, love. Please me."

He smiles. "As you wish."

Starting from her lips, he kisses his way down to her neck and chest. His lips touch her stomach while his fingers roam. He trembles, as she sends everything into him. He lowers down, letting his mouth explore.

As she pulls him up and kisses him, she begins stroking him. Their hands touch, a shared tremor running through them as he kneels before her. Breathing heavily, she holds back a scream while they both finish at the same time. His touch sends shivers down her spine. With a cry, she grabs his arms. He collapses on her.

"Are you okay?" he asks.

"Oh, yes. That was incredible," she says, rolling over and pulling herself into his arms.

He chuckles. "You truly are. Do you know that?"

"Rafe—"

"You are. I thought we were supposed to have a flying lesson."

She laughs. "You're the one who brought a girl into your bedroom. What did you think was going to happen?"

"Honestly? That we would get ideas for our office." He grins at her. "I enjoyed this much more."

"Me, too," she says, giggling into his chest.

"I love that sound, when you giggle. It's too cute for words."

"Really?"

"Yes, mia estrela. Every sound you make speeds up my heart and makes me love you that much more."

"God, I love you so much. You are so amazing."

"I love you, too, my little warrior." He leans down, kissing her, as his hands caress along her sides.

She shudders, grabbing his arms. "Love, you have done your duty. I am spent," she admits, kissing him. "Now, we need to rinse off and have a flying lesson."

"Hmm. You haven't seen my shower."

"Another first?" she asks, teasing along his waist.

He picks her up and carries her into his washroom. In addition to the shower, there is also a corner tub. "Well?"

"It's nice."

"Not as nice as ours."

"No, but it will work. Do we have clean linens?"

He opens the cabinet. "Yes, we do. Then we'll get dressed and go to the training center, if you aren't too tired."

"I'm not. They need the exercise."

He turns on the water, taking her hand. They step in, rinsing off. She walks up to him, kissing him. "Ana, you need to save your strength for training."

She looks up at him, pouting. "Yes, love."

After cleaning up, they step out and dry. They go into the main chamber and put their clothes back on. She walks to the fireplace, where she opens her wings to let them dry. Rafe stares at her.

"What?"

"Watching you, how natural you are with your wings, the ease of you using them now." He steps over, ruffling through. "You did so well in bed with them."

She smiles up at him, blushing. "You did so well in bed."

"Ana!" He laughs, pulling her to him.

She laughs, pulling back. "Let's fly."

He checks to see the fire is nearly burnt out. "Okay." They step out. "Training center."

"Yes, Rafe."

They follow behind. Aylin sneaks glances at Ana, smiling. "Aylin, do you have a question for me?"

"No, Majesty."

They arrive at the Center. Rafe and Roesh go in. Ana turns to Aylin. "What?"

"I'm so sorry. It's none of my business, Majesty."

She laughs. "We are going to turn his old quarters into our office."

"I see."

She leans in, looking around to be sure it's just the two of them. "But we also enjoyed the time alone."

"Majesty!" Aylin says, laughing. "How did your wings do?"

"Very well. Thank you for the training tip."

"Most welcome, Majesty. Please, don't hesitate to ask me about anything. I truly wish to help you, any way I can."

"Maybe on one of your next days off duty, we could have lunch?"

"That would be nice, Your Majesty. Thank you."

Roesh and Rafe step out. "We'll plan it." She takes Rafe's hand, going inside. She opens her wings.

"Oh, I didn't think to ask if you'd want to change first."

"As I said, since I am normally in gowns, I need to practice in what I usually wear."

"Hmm. Or don't wear?"

"Rafe!" she says, soaring to the ceiling.

He flies after her, laughing when she dodges him. He chases her with all he has, amazed at how fast she is.

"Ana!" He laughs, trying again. She stops evading, hovering instead, and approaches him.

"What?"

"You are incredibly fast! How are you so good at this?"

She flies to him, taking him in her arms. "Because I have an amazing teacher," she says, kissing him. "Now, when were you going to show me the guardian chapel?"

His eyes go wide. "How do you know about that?"

"Aylin told me. Is this some kind of secret?"

He looks down. "No."

"Love, please. Talk to me."

"It's a beautiful chapel. I'm afraid when you'll see it, it's where you'll want to get married. I'm so sorry that we don't really have a say in what should be one of our most important days."

"Rafe, as long as I get to be with you, marrying you, telling you that I will love you and honor you, I don't care where we do it." She kisses him, as they lower back down. "Will you show me the chapel?"

"Yes. Let's get cleaned up and have some dinner, then we'll go down to the barracks. We can meet more guardians."

"Okay."

He takes her hand, leaving the center. "Our quarters, please."

"Yes, Rafe," Roesh responds.

As they walk through the corridor, Ana notices Rafe smiling at her. "What?"

He leans forward, kissing her. "Trying to enjoy a walk with my fiancée."

"Rafe, thank you."

"I'm sorry. What is a fiancée?" Roesh asks.

"It's a word for the person you're going to marry. It's from Earth, where she grew up," Rafe explains.

Roesh looks at Aylin. "I like that word."

She smiles at him. "I do, too."

Ana and Rafe laugh. "I think you started something, love," she says. They arrive at their quarters. Rafe and Roesh step in. She turns to Aylin. "We're going to have dinner, then he's going to show me the chapel you told me about."

"It's beautiful. I'm very excited to get married there. I'm a little jealous, though, Your Majesty."

"How so?"

"You will get married in Penstrella's Cathedral. It's such an incredible place! I'm very envious." She's confused when Ana laughs.

"I'm sorry. I'd give anything to have a small, private ceremony in your chapel, instead. Having already had one wedding in the Cathedral."

"Majesty, when were you married?"

"Oh. Were you one of the guardians rescued from NightFall?"

"Yes, Majesty."

"So you weren't here when I arrived. What have you heard about Archduke Kane? What he did to me?"

Aylin sucks in her breath. "Only a little. I heard he tried to have you killed, because he wanted the throne."

Ana looks up as Rafe and Roesh step out. "Rafe, could I take Aylin inside and speak to her a moment?"

"Yes, Ana."

She nods to the door, and they go in. She and Aylin sit on the chaise. "Kane attacked me, kidnapped my friends, threatened to kill them and me. He forced me to marry him. It was at my wedding that his assassin tried to kill me."

"Why?"

"He was supposed to kill me, once we had said our vows and Kane was crowned. Then Kane would have the throne. Declan and Rafe found out about the assassin, apprehending him in the Cathedral. His bolt shot out, hitting me. It was laced with a fatal poison."

"How are you still alive?"

"Rafe took the poison, saving my life. The wedding was held in the cathedral. It's beautiful, don't get me wrong. I am not thrilled about the idea of getting married there. Can I ask why you are not allowed to?"

"The cathedral is only for royal weddings."

"I wonder if I could change that."

"Oh, Majesty, don't go through any trouble for me."

"It would be for us, both. Let me talk to Kara and Audressa. I'll let you know what I find out."

"Thank you! I appreciate that."

"You're very welcome."

They go to the door, Rafe coming in and Aylin resuming her post. Rafe takes Ana's hand as they go to the closet.

"Everything okay?"

"Yes. Discussing her wedding."

"Oh, okay then."

Ana picks out the silver blue gown she knows Rafe loves. She gathers it up with her undergarments. She places the garments on the ottoman, concealing the gown beneath a robe. Grabbing another robe, she goes into the washroom. She enters and begins rinsing, and he joins her.

"Dinner will be here shortly."

She walks up to him, kissing him. "Are we working up an appetite?"

"After what we did in my old quarters and flying, you should be exhausted."

"Do you forget? I'm a guardian, like you. I'm stronger now."

"Ana, you are still part human. You need to rest. Please, let's get cleaned up, eat, and go see the chapel."

"Yes, Rafe. I'm sorry."

"For what?"

She laughs, kissing him. "It's okay. I am very excited to see this chapel." She meets his gaze when she realizes something. "Where was Audressa? Why wasn't she at the morning briefing?"

"We'll ask Kara tomorrow."

"Okay."

They rinse off and go into the closet. While he's at his dresser, she puts on the undergarments. She effortlessly slides into the gown, then accessorizes with silver shoes, a bracelet, and the diamond teardrop pendant. With a smile, she puts on a circlet adorned with a dangling small diamond star over her forehead. She approaches him.

"Does this look okay for going to the chapel?"

"I'm sure it's—" His breath catches in his throat. He grabs her hand, pulling her to him and kissing her hard. "That's not fair, Ana!"

She laughs. "What?" she innocently asks.

"You know what that dress does to me."

"I have no idea what you mean."

He takes a breath, caressing her face. "Ana, we are going to the chapel." He admires her in the gown. "Oh."

She smiles at him. "Are you sure?" She looks up when the bell is ringing. He runs out, getting the food. He sets it up on their table. She joins him. "Love?"

He puts his hands on her shoulders, gently sitting her down. "Eat."

"Yes, Rafe." He sits beside her, focusing on his food. He looks over when she laughs. "Do I need to change? You can't even look at me in this gown!"

His gaze rakes over her. "Hmm. It's okay."

She finishes eating. She stands up, taking his hand. They go to the middle of the room. She opens her wings, and he ruffles through her feathers, smiling at the moan that escapes her lips. She brings her hand up, caressing along the buttons on his shirt. He grabs her hand, pulling her to him. He kisses her, hard and hungry.

"We're going to the barracks."

"Rafe—"

"Then we're coming back here," he leans down by her ear, "and we will do whatever you want."

Her breath catches in her throat. "Yes, love," she manages. She runs to the washroom, using it and brushing her teeth. Rafe brushes his, then takes her hand.

They go down to the barracks. Melian greets them.

"Is everything all right?" she asks.

"Yes, Melian. Rafe is taking me on another tour. I would like to meet more guardians and see more of where you live."

"Yes, Majesty."

Chapter 12

"Majesty, may I say, that gown is almost too much," Aylin says while Rafe and Roesh inspect the chapel.

"Thank you. It's Rafe's favorite."

They giggle, watching as their men join them. "I think you're going to love it. It's beautiful!"

"Thank you," Ana says to Aylin, taking Rafe's hand.

He leads her inside. They go through an arched set of doors before walking into the chapel. She stops in her tracks at the sight.

"Oh, wow."

She walks forward, admiring the stained-glass windows, depicting guardians in battle. The ceiling is navy blue, adorned with silver stars and gold suns painted on. A royal blue runner adorned with silver stars runs up to the altar.

"Ana, are you okay?"

She looks up at him, only then realizing she had tears running down her cheeks. "I am. It's much more beautiful than I ever could've imagined."

He wipes her tears before kissing her softly. "I wish we could get married here. I truly do. I'm sorry."

"It's okay, Rafe. Bringing me in here means a lot." He takes her hand and escorts her down the aisle. They arrive at the altar. She gives him a smile. "I love you, and I am so excited for the day we get married. I mean it, I don't care where the ceremony is. Being together, being able to marry the love of my life, is what is most important."

"Ana, I know you mean that. I also know what going into the cathedral does to you. I know if you had your way, you would never set foot in there, again. I don't blame you."

"Love, it's okay. Can we go meet some of the other

guardians now?"

"Yes, Ana."

He leads her from the chapel, telling Roesh what they are doing. They walk around the barracks, meeting a few guardians. Most have retired to their quarters for the evening. They decide to do the same. Rafe and Roesh go in.

"What did you think?" Aylin asks.

"You're right. It's stunning. I'd give anything to get married in there."

"I wish you could. I think it's big enough for the dignitaries and ambassadors. I honestly don't see why you couldn't."

"Traditions. I know."

Rafe and Roesh step out. As Ana goes inside, she gives Aylin a shrug of her shoulders. She heads to the closet and pulls out her pajamas.

"Ana, are you okay?"

She looks up to find Rafe leaning in the doorway. "I am. I'd like to turn in."

He makes his way to her. "Oh, mia estrela. I'm so sorry."

"For what?"

"You deny it, but you really want to get married in that chapel, don't you?"

"Yes," she replies. "I'm sorry. I know I shouldn't—"

"What are you going to do about it?" She looks up at him. He smiles. "Oh, I know you better than you think I do. I want to help."

"I was going to talk to Kara and Audressa. I don't know if they can help, but they would know better than anyone else."

Stepping forward, she kisses him, her wings unfurling. She smiles when he does the same. She gently strokes his feathers, savoring the soft texture. He hungrily consumes her mouth, relishing the taste of her lips and tongue.

She presses his lips open, then she explores his mouth. His grip tightens as she undoes his shirt buttons. After dropping it to the floor, she immediately goes for his pants. He steps out of them, walking her to the ottoman. Ana looks up at him, breathless from his kiss.

"I will do anything you ask, anything but what we are saving," he says, stroking along her stomach.

"Yes, love," she whispers.

He lays her on the ottoman, his gaze sweeping over her. "God, that gown is exquisite on you! I long to taste every inch of you!" She blushes, grabbing his hands and pulling him onto her. His hands explore down, pulling the gown up. He removes her undergarments. "Ana, the things I want to do to you while you are in this gown."

"Love, I trust you. I told you, my body is yours. Please, whatever you want, I want, too."

He shifts his position, settling down with her on his lap. Her hand gently strokes him as his head falls back. He brings his fingers trailing up her leg, smiling as she parts for him. One hand gently strokes her while the other plays with her feathers. Her grip tightens on his arm when she is overwhelmed by a rush of emotions.

Ana continues her slow, teasing caress. Smiling, he responds to her affection as she draws near, wanting to be as close to him as possible. She moves faster, smiling at his sudden intake of breath. Her body quivers with pleasure as she pants and trembles. She screams out, falling on him as they finish. He leans back with her head resting on his chest.

"Ana, are you okay?"

She gasps in air and looks at him. "Yes," she croaks out before collapsing on him. "It was wonderful."

She turns over and sits on the edge of the ottoman. Removing the gown and corset, she lies down with him. He draws the blanket over them. Her head rests on his chest as she drifts off to sleep.

Ana wakes up and smiles at Rafe while gently caressing his face and neck. She leans up, kissing him. He opens his eyes, grabbing her to him and kissing her harder.

"I need to use the washroom, love."

"Oh. We both do." He picks her up, carrying her in. He steps into the shower while she relieves herself. She washes her hands then joins him. He takes her into his arms. "How do you feel?"

"Wonderful. Everything you've done for me today has been so incredible. You are the most amazing man to ever live!"

"You are legendary. You are the most rare, unique, beautiful gift the universe has ever given me. There are times I do not feel worthy of your love, because of who you are. You are a goddess, a lover, a warrior, and you belong to me. It doesn't seem possible that I can have you. How is this real?" He looks down when she's trembling in his arms.

"Oh, Rafe. How do you say these things? Your words have just as much impact, overwhelming me and making me feel your love as much as your touch!" She leans up, planting a soft kiss on his lips. "I know we are waiting until August. I am not rushing. I want you to know, I am so excited about marrying you. I cannot wait to be your wife, to say our vows, and finally be together in every way possible!"

"I feel the same for you. To hold your hands, telling everyone how much I love you, how much I treasure you, will care for you, will be there for you, in good times and bad, to be together, always. I long for it more than I have ever wanted anything in over five centuries!"

"Oh, love. Can we wait that long?"

He studies her while thinking about his response. "Ana, please. I truly think it's best. For both of us."

"I know why I need to wait, you're right. What about

you?" His eyes go down. She steps back. "What's the matter?"

"I'm still juggling with the whole prince or king decision."

"Oh, Rafe. It's okay! We'll wait until August, I promise. We won't rush." She steps into his arms, kissing him. "Now, I need sleep. You have worn me out!"

"Bed or ottoman?"

"Bed, please."

"Do we need pajamas?"

"I don't know," she asks, caressing along his waistline. "Do we?"

He grabs her wrists, bringing her hands up and kissing them. "We need sleep."

"Yes, Rafe."

They exit and dry themselves off. As he scoops her up, she lets out a cry of surprise. He carries her to bed, where he joins her and covers them with the blanket. Falling asleep, she snuggles close to his chest. Gazing down at her, he smiles, envisioning her as his bride. He would marry her tomorrow, if he could. Though he knows he must be patient. Love fills his thoughts as he drifts off to sleep.

Chapter 13

As Ana wakes up, she sees it's almost seven. With a flush on her skin, she stares at Rafe, completely consumed by his love. She takes a sharp intake of air, attempting to steady her pounding heart. Rafe sits up.

"Ana, what's wrong?"

She climbs onto him, wrapping her arms around him. "Feel? Your love overwhelmed me, it was so strong! I've never felt this happy or loved in my entire life."

He holds her against his chest. "Oh, mia estrela. You deserve an epic love, love that fills you, top to bottom and never leaves you wanting more."

"Rafe, I swear to you, you give me that every single day." She pulls back, looking up at him. "Kiss me?"

Their lips meet, his touch soft as he traces the length of her back. Her head falls back as he gently trails his fingers between her wings. Her desire for him makes his skin tingle and his breath quicken. She showers his neck, chest, and stomach with kisses as she moves lower. She pushes him down onto the mattress with her hands.

She playfully uses her mouth to tease him while she is on top of him. His hips react with a jerk. He cups her chest and strokes her gently. Lifting her up, he kisses her as his hand travels down.

She kneels beside him, making room for him. He trails his fingers as she trembles. He lays her down, bringing his head down and kissing her until she cries out while her hand is on him. As he runs his hand along her thigh, both bodies tremble. They cry out in ecstasy. He lies down, holding her close.

She sits up, kneeling over him. "Ana?" She smiles at him, kissing him hard. She sits him up, wrapping her arms around him. She opens her wings, pulling them up to the ceiling. "How are you doing this?" He looks down, then meets her gaze.

She smiles at him. "It's actually pretty easy."

Ana wraps her legs around him, holding him tight, as she takes him around the room. He opens his wings, helping her. They hover in the air, as he kisses her with all the love he possesses. He strokes her wings, feeling her tremble under him. They lower back to the bed, landing softly.

"Do you see how incredible you are? You are the Crimson Queen, the winged goddess, and the love of my life."

She smiles at him. "Winged goddess?"

"You know you are."

"Rafe, that's a bit much."

"Ana, look at everything you have done. You have fulfilled the prophecy and attained your status. I assure you, it's not."

"But you still won't believe you are worthy of being crowned King?" She sees the look on his face, feels the heat of his anger. "I'm sorry. I won't bring it up again."

"No, I am. You're right. Here I am calling you a goddess, telling you that you are going to be crowned Empress. At the very least, I should be able to discuss being crowned King. I didn't mean to become angry. Please, forgive me?"

"Rafe, there is nothing to forgive. I've had to change and go through so much, and now that you are facing change, I want to show you the same love and patience you have given me."

"Thank you. At least I have a choice, to become Prince or King. All of this was forced onto you, from growing wings to becoming immortal and finding out you will become Grand Empress of the galaxy. I should not be so upset over a title."

"That's why we talk about it. By discussing it, it makes it seem like it's not such a big thing. When you push it down, trying to forget about it, it will come back to the surface and overwhelm you. I know that better than anyone. Will you let me help you? Will you talk to me about it?"

"Yes, mia estrela. I know you are right. I will discuss it with you, any time you want, and I won't get upset. Now, shall we get clean and get ready for breakfast?"

"Yes, love."

He carries her to the washroom. They rinse and dry off, going into the closet. She runs her fingers through the gowns, letting out a sigh.

"Ana—"

"No, I know." She laughs. "It's okay."

With a flourish, she shows off a purple gown featuring short sleeves, a v-cut bodice, and a flowing skirt. Holding it up, she admires it. Memories from the day before make her blush as she puts on her corset and undergarments. She slips into the gown, donning the silver shoes and circlet. With a graceful stride, she reaches the mirror and spreads her wings. Rafe's low whistle pulls her gaze upward.

"What?" she asks.

"Oh, Ana. That color on you is breathtaking."

"It looks okay with my wings?"

"Yes, mia estrela. It's a little lower cut than I would like."

She brings in her wings, turning to him. "Should I change?"

"No. I want you to be comfortable and to feel as radiant as you are. You look magnificent in that gown."

"Okay. Thank you, love."

Going to the drawers, he gets her rings and puts them on her. He gets dressed, then takes her hand and leads her out. As Rafe welcomes the breakfast service, she stays on the sofa watching the rain. Everything is set up. As the staff departs, Kara and Evren enter. Ana approaches them.

"Oh, Ana," Evren exclaims. "That color is so pretty on you!"

"Thank you, Evren." She smiles at her, sitting at the table. "What are you and Rafe doing after lunch, while Kara and I visit?"

Rafe looks over at Evren. "Any ideas?"

"We could start getting your old quarters empty, to make space for your office."

"That's a great idea."

"Hmm. Could you leave the bed?" Ana asks.

Kara hangs her head, laughing. "Really?"

"What?"

"Can I eat my meal in peace?"

"I mean it. I really like that bed. It's beautiful." She looks at Kara. "What? It's not like I'm hosting ambassadors in there! We have the meeting room and plenty of studies and ballrooms for that."

"Fine. We'll figure something out."

Ana sneaks a glance at Rafe, grinning at him. He winks at her, smiling back.

"What are you and Kara doing today?" Evren asks as she butters her toast.

Ana looks outside. "I don't know now. I had something planned, but not in this rain." She turns to Kara. "Any ideas?"

"I know a few places I would like to show you."

"Okay. As long as we're spending the day together, I don't care what we do."

"Me, too, Ana. You might want to put on a light cloak, as the palace is a bit chilly. We'll start warming up, soon."

"Yes, Kara." She sees the relief on Rafe's face. She laughs. "Really?"

He looks down, blushing. "I'm sorry."

Kara looks at Rafe then Ana. "What?"

Ana shakes her head, turning to Kara. "Rafe thinks my dress is a little too low cut."

Kara bursts out laughing, hitting Rafe in the arm. "Really?"

"What? You don't think so?"

"Rafe, she looks great."

"I know."

"Why now? She's worn gowns like that before."

"Not that low cut."

"Oh, my God!" Kara exclaims. "Do you check everything she wears? Why are you so jealous all of a sudden?"

"This isn't all of a sudden," Ana says. "Remember Bela?" She looks up as Rafe hangs his head. "Oh, love. I'm teasing. Please, don't be embarrassed."

He jumps from his chair, scooping her up and planting kisses all over her face. "Do you submit?"

"Never!" she cries.

Kara and Evren watch as he carries her to the middle of the room, opening his wings and carrying her to the ceiling. He continues to shower her with kisses. "Submit or the kisses will end."

"Oh, no!" she playfully cries out. "I submit!"

He lowers them down to the floor and takes her to the table.

"Rafe, are you trying to make me hate mealtime?" Kara asks. "Because I swear, between the two of you, I am coming really close!"

"I'm sorry, Kara. We are excited about getting married, getting crowned, starting a life together over our kingdom. I didn't mean to embarrass you."

"Rafe, do you mean that? Are you finally excited about getting crowned?" She lowers her head. "Oh. You meant me, didn't you?"

"Ana, I meant both of us. I am trying to be excited."

"Rafe, it's all right. You know I am kidding with you guys. We are in your chambers, not out in public."

"Thank you, Kara." Rafe takes Ana's hand. "Are we going to the briefing?"

"We will. Speaking of which. Where was Audressa yesterday?" Ana asks Kara.

"Oh, her wife had taken ill. She was staying with her and the children. She should be there today."

"Shall we head on? I need to get caught up."

"Kara, you and Ana go ahead. Evren and I will take care of dishes and meet you there shortly."

"Okay."

Kara and Ana go to the door. Kara looks at Roesh. "Meeting room, please."

"Yes, Sage."

"Please, Roesh, call me Kara."

"Yes, Kara."

Roesh inspects the meeting room, then steps out. Ana and Kara go inside. "Kara, is there any way that Rafe and I could get married in the guardian's chapel, instead of the Penstrella one?"

"I don't think so, but we'll look. What does that one look like?"

"Oh, you've never been? It's absolutely breathtaking! I wish desperately that we can get married there." She looks up when Audressa walks in. "How are you? How is your wife?"

"We are both better. I am recovered, and she is feeling better. Thank you."

"You're most welcome. I was wondering, what are the rules and traditions pertaining to a royal wedding? As far as, do they have to get married in the Penstrella Cathedral?"

"Is someone else getting married?"

Ana smiles. "My apologies. I thought you heard. Rafe and I are betrothed."

"Congratulations! Um, let me think." She walks to the desk, getting out a book on customs and traditions. "Give me a moment." She scans through the pages. "Hmm. It says it is traditional for a royal wedding to take place in the cathedral, but it is not law. Every royal wedding in our history has been held there, since it's construction. However, it is not required. Where would you like to get married?"

"In the guardian's chapel. Since we are both guardians, it is where we would like to exchange our vows."

"What do you mean, you are both guardians?"

"When I died and grew my wings, I transformed into a human guardian."

"I was unaware of this. Obviously, I knew you had wings. I mean, how do you know you are technically a guardian? If you don't mind me asking."

"Joph ran tests for me in NightFall. Why? Does it make a difference?"

"No, because of your treaty."

Ana steps closer to her. "What do you mean?"

"It was illegal for a guardian to be on the throne. The law was passed around two thousand years ago."

"What? What would've happened to me had my treaty not passed?"

Audressa sucks in her breath. "Majesty—"

"Please, Audressa. Tell me?"

"You would've been stripped of your title."

"And?"

"You would have been forced to join the other guardians, protecting the new royal. You would serve them, as your guardians have served you. Your Majesty, the treaty was passed and—"

"Kara, I need to return to my quarters."

"You don't look well. What's wrong?"

"I need to lie down."

Kara takes her out into the corridor. "Aylin, please take the queen back to her quarters. I'll be there shortly."

"Yes, Sage."

Rafe looks up, confused when the door opens. Roesh walks in. "Everything all right in here?"

"Yes," Rafe answers. Roesh steps out as Ana walks in. She sits on the chaise, staring at the fire. Rafe looks at Evren. "What is going on?" She is as bewildered as he is. He approaches Ana. "Are you okay?"

"Well, the good news is that we can get married in the guardian chapel," she says, keeping her gaze forward.

"Okay. Is there bad news?" He runs to her when her head goes down. He sits beside her, taking her hand. "Ana?"

"I was right," she says softly, refusing to look at him. "If my treaty had not passed, I would no longer be on the throne. I would be a guardian, forced to serve the next royal."

"What?" Rafe exclaims. "What are you talking about?"

"Audressa said there was a law passed, making it illegal for a guardian to have the throne. It was undone with my treaty."

"I seriously don't think that would've happened. You are not completely a guardian, but a human guardian. And having royal blood—"

"Rafe, please. I really don't want to discuss it. I just wanted you to know why I'm upset. Kara and Audressa are holding the briefing, then Kara will be here with lunch."

Rafe gestures to Evren. "You can go to the briefing, if you want. We're staying here. Kara said she'll bring lunch after."

"Yes, Rafe. Ana, is there anything I can do to help?"

"No, but thank you."

"All right. I'll see you in a little bit." Evren leaves.

Rafe scoots closer to Ana. "What can I do?" She says nothing, watching the flames. "Please?"

She looks at him. "Sorry."

"Overthinking everything?"

"Of course."

"You made that treaty so we could be together. In doing so, you saved your own throne. Everything happens for a reason. You are meant to be Queen. Do you see that?"

"I'm trying to. Really, I'm okay. It was surprising to hear."

"Are you happy about the chapel?"

"Yes. I'm so sorry. Again, here we should be celebrating good news and instead I'm focusing on the negative! Who do we talk to, so we can secure it and make sure it will be available?"

"We'll talk to Sister Ramilda. She oversees it."

"When will we do that?"

"We'll go now, if you feel up to it."

"Yes, Rafe." She takes his hand. "Thank you, for your patience with me."

"Ana, I was as surprised as you were to hear that. It's okay." They step out. "Roesh, we are going to the barracks."

"Oh, Aylin! I'm so sorry."

"For what, Majesty?"

"Rafe, will you and Roesh walk ahead so I can have a moment with her?"

"Of course," Rafe says as Roesh nods. Aylin steps back.

"I'm sorry. I found out Rafe and I can use the guardian's chapel. Then I found out something upsetting. I forgot to ask about you and Roesh with the cathedral. I promise I will find out."

"Majesty, please. It's quite all right. We would be honored to be married in the same chapel as you and Rafe. It truly is not a big deal. Thank you, for your concern."

"I will still ask."

"Only if you get a moment."

"Thank you, Aylin. If I may, I value you and consider you a friend."

"Majesty, thank you. That means a lot to me."

"Of course."

Chapter 14

Navigating the barracks, they descend the stairs and arrive at the chapel. Sister Ramilda is attending to the altar. As Ana and Rafe walk in, she looks up.

"Is there anything I can do for you today?" she inquires.

"Her Majesty and I would like to get married here."

Sister Ramilda's eyes go wide. "My apologies, Majesty." She bows. "I did not recognize you."

"It is quite dim in here. It's all right."

"When would you like to get married?"

"The first of August."

"Let me check." She walks to a podium and flips through the pages of a ledger. "Yes. That is available. I will write you in. What time?"

Rafe looks at Ana. "Mia estrela?"

"Two o'clock?"

"That is fine." She writes in the book. "There you are. Anything else I can assist with today?"

"Thank you so much, Sister Ramilda. We truly appreciate it."

"Yes, Majesty. May Asterin's blessing be upon you."

"You as well," Ana says, taking Rafe's hand. He leads her from the chapel.

"We are returning to our quarters."

"Yes, Rafe."

Aylin looks at Ana. "Were they open for you?" She sees Roesh's jaw tick. "Your Majesty?" she adds.

"Yes. We are slated for the first of August at two o'clock."

"I'm so glad to hear that."

"Thank you, Aylin. Whether because you are on duty that day or because I ask, I truly hope you and Roesh will be there."

"Yes, Majesty. We would not miss it for anything!"

Ana sees Roesh give her a stern look. "Roesh, Aylin is my friend. I am happy she is excited for us."

"Yes, Your Majesty."

They return to their quarters. Roesh and Rafe step inside. "Aylin, has he lightened up any?"

"Yes, Majesty. When we are off duty, he is very sweet. When he is protecting you and teaching me, he can be a bit harsh, but he has been working on it."

"Okay. Don't make me command him to be nice," she says, winking.

Aylin giggles. "Majesty, don't tempt me."

They both laugh as Roesh and Rafe walk out. Rafe takes her hand and guides her into their quarters. "I'm glad to hear you laughing. Everything okay now?"

"Yes, Rafe. I'm sorry. I was overwhelmed when I should not have been."

"It's okay. I am relieved to see you better now." He looks at the clock. "Kara and Evren will be here with lunch shortly. Is that what you want to wear while you are with Kara?" He watches her eyes go down. "Ana, what's wrong?"

"I don't want to leave you, but I know I need to spend the day with her."

"Ana, it's only for an hour or two. We'll have a private dinner tonight. How does that sound?" he asks, pulling her into his arms.

"Wonderful. Thank you. Yes, I'll wear this." She holds him tight, letting his warmth comfort her. "I love how you make me feel. I missed this so much when you were gone."

"Ana—"

"No, I'm sorry. I'm not bringing up the past. I want you to know how much I love being in your arms."

"Always?"

"Rafe, you will forever be my always."

"Oh, mia estrela!" He leans down, kissing her. He looks

up as Kara and Evren walk in.

"Everything okay?" Kara asks, as Evren takes the staff to the table to set up lunch.

"Yes, Kara. I'm okay now. Thank you."

"Audressa was upset with herself for what happened. I told her she did nothing wrong, but her duty as Chancellor."

"I'll speak to her tomorrow."

"Please," Kara says.

"I didn't mean to upset you both."

"It's okay. Can we eat?"

Ana laughs. "Yes, sis."

They sit at the table. Rafe looks at Evren. "Still going to work on emptying my old quarters while they are out?"

"Yes, Rafe. I like spending time with you."

"The feeling is mutual. Evren, you are a good friend."

"Thank you, Rafe. Speaking of which, I want to ask you a favor."

"Go ahead."

"At our dinner the night before the wedding, will you make a speech on my behalf?"

"Evren, I would be honored."

"Thank you."

Ana turns to Kara. "Anything you want to ask me?"

"I've been putting it off, because I know how much you hate speeches."

"Kara, you know I will happily do it for you."

"Thank you."

They finish eating. Rafe takes Ana's hand. "You won't be gone too long, right? I'll miss you."

"We won't, I promise," Kara says, getting to her feet.

Ana kisses Rafe. "I'll miss you, too." She joins Kara by the door. "Lead the way, sis."

Kara steps out into the hall, seeing Roesh and Aylin come to attention. "Follow me," she says.

"Yes, Sage."

"Roesh, we've been over this. Please, call me Kara."

"Yes, Kara."

She turns back to Ana. "You'll miss him?"

"What? I'm sorry, that we have this pull, this need to be together. I don't know if it's because of the prophecies, about our bond, or because I love him so much. Or both."

"No, I'm sorry. You're right. I forgot."

"Majesty, may I ask?" Aylin inquires.

"Yes, Aylin."

"You told me earlier about the one prophecy. Are there others?"

"There are. We'll discuss it more in private."

"Yes, Majesty. Thank you."

"Of course. Kara, Aylin and Roesh are betrothed."

"Congratulations!"

"Thank you," they reply.

Kara stops at the end of the corridor. She opens the door. Roesh steps in, looking around. He gives the all clear. She takes Ana inside.

"What is this?" she asks, walking around. The room is medium-sized and round. There are a few desks against the wall.

"This was one of the original offices for the queen. We keep it like this, because the last queen to use it was rumored to be Celestia herself."

"Really?"

"Yes."

"It's amazing. I don't know if I've ever been in a round room before." She looks at Kara. "What?"

"Sorry. Just thinking of your coronation day. No, the one coming up. It's incredible to think of. Are you worried?"

"I'm a little nervous, of course. Does each of the six realms have a king or queen over them?"

"Yes. This was the only one without once your father died in battle. Although most realms honor the treaty, I'm sure people here were worried they would attack with the throne being vulnerable. I see now why Rafe was sent to find us."

"Kara, I'm sorry."

"For what?"

"Rafe rescued me, but he changed your plans. You never had a chance."

"Honestly, I'm grateful he did. You have him, I have Evren, and we're all happy together. I miss a few things from Earth, but I would give it all up again to be here."

"How much do you want to know?"

"About what?"

Ana looks down. "Everything. What I've been through here, what happened with my foster father and foster brothers. I want you to know you can ask me anything. I know I got upset last time. You are my sister. I want to be able to talk to you, about anything."

"Is there something particular you need to talk about?" she asks as she walks to her. "I want to help, if you'll let me."

"There are some days when I'm with Rafe, that I feel like I am ready to give him all of me. Others, the thought scares me terribly."

"Okay. The days you feel like you want to, what leads up to it? I don't mean the kissing and such, but the emotions behind it?"

"Having a good day. Being happy, loved, feeling safe."

"And when it scares you?"

"Days like this morning. Being overwhelmed, scared, worried. But sometimes, it can be the opposite. No rhyme or reason. I want to be ready by August, and I know it is several months away. I'm so worried I won't be. He has been so sweet, patient, and loving. He deserves more than I can give him."

"Oh, Ana," Kara says, hugging her. "I know how much you love each other. You are everything to him. Don't question how much he loves you, nor your love for him. Everyone sees it. Even when he said he didn't love you, when it was forbidden,

I could see it on his face, hear it in his voice. The first time you were poisoned, and it was just the three of us in the exam room, he was gently stroking your face, so worried about you."

"Really?"

"Yes. Ana, he has been in love with you since the beginning. I know you feel the same, because I never thought you would ever open up to a man. Not like you have with him. I was suspicious of him at first, but he even warmed me over. I tried to hide it, because I was still fighting against trusting him."

"You mean you were starting to trust him on Earth?"

"I did until he left. Now we understand why."

"Kara, what if I'm not ready? He is so excited about getting married. How do I tell him?"

"Ana, you won't have to."

"What? What do you mean?"

"I know you are talking to him, opening up. He can feel what you are feeling. He said you are very powerful about what you send out. Between being open and feeling what you are going through, he will know if you are ready."

"You're right. Thank you."

"What are you most nervous about? Having an episode, or the wedding night itself?"

"I am nervous about being with him. The thought scares me. Not because of him. I know he will be watching over me, making sure I'm okay. He is so good about doing that, but I wish he didn't have to."

"Ana, keep bringing down your walls. Let him in. By your wedding night, maybe he won't have to."

"I want to believe that. I really do. Can we see something else?"

"Is there somewhere particular you want to go?"

"I'd like to see the cathedral."

"Ana, I don't think that's a good idea. Not today."

"All right. Then can we see the throne room? Since that is where I'll be crowned as Empress."

"Yes, Ana." She takes her hand, leading her out. She looks at Roesh. "We are going to the throne room."

"Yes, Kara."

They follow behind. "What does the coronation crown look like for that?" Ana asks. "Is it the same one from before?"

"No. That one is locked up. Once you are crowned, there are additional crowns you can wear. Of course, you can stick with your traditional crowns and circlets, as well."

"Are you nervous about being crowned Empress?" Aylin asks. "Your Majesty," she adds.

"I am, but not like I thought I would be. Rafe said it wouldn't be until after I had been here a year. Why is that?"

"To ensure your reign over this realm. You have to be a king or queen for at least a year before being crowned Empress."

"I see. Can I wear the coronation gown from when I became Queen? Rafe didn't get to see me in that."

Kara laughs. "Of course."

"What? I was crowned Queen, and he wasn't there. You know how worried I was."

"Was that when Kane kidnapped him, Majesty?" Aylin asks.

"Yes."

They arrive at the throne room. Roesh walks in and returns a moment later. "All clear, Your Majesty."

"Could Aylin come in with us?"

"Yes, Majesty."

"Thank you." The three of them step inside. "Aylin, you asked about the prophecies. Please, don't take this against Roesh. I know he is a good and honorable guardian. It's me. I have trust issues, that I am working on. I will answer your question, though. We have fulfilled a few prophecies. Me becoming the Crimson Queen, the soulmates that can heal each other, and the soulmates who die for each other."

"Majesty?"

"At my wedding with Kane, I told you about the fatal poison. Rafe took it from me, healing me and saving my life. He gave his in exchange for mine. Then when I went into battle, I was fatally wounded, defending him. I laid down in the woods and died, then came back as wings of fire erupted from my back, growing into the wings you see now."

"Really?"

"Yes." She looks at Kara. "Can I show her? Only for a second, I promise."

"As long as you'll tell Rafe you did."

"I will."

Aylin looks at her, as she steps back. Ana extends her wings, closing her eyes and focusing. When they turn to fire, Aylin gasps softly, unable to believe the sight. Ana extinguishes the blaze.

"Oh, Majesty, that was incredible!"

"Thank you, Aylin."

"How do you feel?" Kara asks, walking to her.

"I'm okay. It doesn't wear me out like it used to."

"All right. Are we walking up to the throne?"

"Please."

Kara takes her arm, and they approach the throne. Ana sits down.

"How does that feel, now that you are Queen?"

"It's okay. It doesn't scare me like the first time you brought me in here."

"Good." Kara notes the pain in Ana's expression. "I can see how much you are missing him. Let's head back."

"Are you sure? I don't want you to cut our time short on account of me."

"Ana, I see it on your face. We'll have another day together soon. We can work on your office together, too."

"Yes, Kara." She looks at Aylin. "Any questions before we step out?"

"When they are fire, what do they feel like?"

"Warm. They don't burn me or Rafe. They've saved my life, a few times."

"Majesty, am I allowed to tell Roesh about your fire wings?"

"Hmm. I would prefer if you didn't, but I know it's something incredible to see. If you honestly think he will keep it between the two of you, I say go ahead."

"I will keep it to myself."

"Thank you." They walk out to the corridor. "Back to my quarters, please."

"Yes, Majesty."

Roesh enters her quarters, then steps out a moment later. "All clear. If I may, there's no one inside."

"They must still be at his old quarters," Kara says. She looks at Ana. "Do you want to go there?"

"We can go on in and spend more time together until they return."

"All right."

She steps in first, leading Kara. "I'm going to use the washroom. Sit on the sofa in front of the window?"

"Yes, sis."

Kara sits and watches the rain fall. She looks up when Ana sits with her. "I'm sorry."

"For what?" Kara asks.

"We talked about me. What about you and Evren? How are you doing?"

"I'm okay. We're finalizing plans for the wedding."

"Are you nervous?"

"Hmm. Yes and no. I am, because like you, I never thought I would get married. Then I'm not, because I love her so much and am so excited to be with her."

"How is she handling everything?"

"Like you. She pulls inward and tries to carry it herself. She is nervous. I think more because of some of her family coming more than anything."

"Her gown is, wow. Absolutely breathtaking."

"She said you helped her find one. She won't tell me anything! I don't know what to wear, because I want to match."

"All I'll suggest, is you wear a white tux with blue accessories, similar to her hair color."

"Thank you for that! It's been frustrating, trying to get anything out of her. I don't need a detailed description. What you said is perfect."

Ana stands up, taking Kara's hand. "Come here for a sec."

"Okay."

They go to the middle of the room. "I wanted to do this outside, but it's probably going to rain the rest of the month, so we'll do it here."

"What are you—" Ana grabs Kara to her, taking her to the air. "Ana!" she cries out, laughing. She clings to her, as she takes her around the room. She lowers her back down.

"Well?"

"Rafe is right, you are incredible. You're still working them every day?"

"Yes. We stretch and fly around like you and I just did, or we go outside or to the training center."

"Do you want to talk about what else you've done?" She gasps when Ana blushes, looking down. "I'm sorry! You don't have to."

"No, it's okay. We have had fun with our wings. That's all I will say."

"All right." They look up when Rafe and Evren walk in. Rafe looks surprised when Ana runs over and kisses him.

"Missed you," she says, squeezing his hand.

He smiles at her, leaning down and kissing her. "Missed you, too."

"Am I really so bad?" Kara asks with a laugh.

"Sis, shut up!" Ana says, chuckling.

"Yes, Ana."

"Dinner will be here shortly," Rafe says.

He takes Ana to the chaise, holding her to him as they watch the fire. Evren goes to Kara, kissing her.

"We got a lot of his old quarters emptied out and ready. He'll take her there, so she can decide how she wants to set everything up."

"We'll help, if they want us to."

"Yes, Kara. I'm sorry. Are we embarrassing you?"

"No, Ana." The bell rings, and Kara lets staff bring dinner in. They set up and leave. She walks to Ana and Rafe. "Are you ready to eat?"

"We'll be over in a moment," Rafe says. "Is that all right, Kara?"

She laughs. "Of course. We'll go on and sit down."

Ana looks up at him. "Are you all right?"

"Yes. I'm enjoying your warmth. I really did miss you. I didn't just say that back to you."

"Rafe!" She leans up, kissing him. She laughs when her stomach grumbles. "I need to eat."

He helps her up, taking her over to the table. He gives Kara a warm smile. "Where did you girls go today?"

Kara looks at Ana, who nods. "We went to Celestia's office then the throne room. Aylin was with us in there." She looks at Ana. "Are you telling Rafe or do I need to?"

"Kara, it's not a big deal." She turns to Rafe. "I showed Aylin my fire wings. Literally for a second." She takes his hand. "As you see, I am fine. I'm not tired or drained."

"All right. Were you going to tell me if Kara hadn't said anything?"

"Yes, love. I told her I would. She didn't give me a chance." She shoots Kara a playful look, then laughs when Kara sticks her tongue out. "Grow up!"

"Ana, I am over three thousand years old. If I haven't grown up by now, it's not going to happen."

"I'm not giving up," Ana says.

Kara takes her hand. "Please, don't."

Ana's expression grows serious. "Kara—"

"I'm sorry. I didn't mean to ruin your fun." She pulls Ana up, hugging her. "I was thinking about your old scars. I'm so sorry."

"Kara, it's okay. Let's finish dinner."

"Yes, Ana."

She sits back down. "You aren't feeling guilty about all that again?"

"No. Well, maybe a little."

"Kara!" She stands up, taking her hand. "Come with me, sis. Evren, Rafe, give us a moment." She takes Kara to the chaise. "Talk to me."

"Really, Ana. I'm okay. I was thinking back to when you first came here, how worried I was. I was scared to death you were going to hurt yourself. I'm sorry to say that."

"Kara, you have no reason to be sorry. I did hurt myself. You were right to be worried. What's bringing this up now?"

"Seeing you react to Audressa."

"Kara, I am okay now. I still get a little overwhelmed from time to time, but I haven't thought of hurting myself in a long time. I promise you, I'm okay." She hugs her tight. "Now, are you okay?"

"Yes, I'm sorry." Kara pulls back. "I worry about you, and it overwhelms me sometimes. You have been through so much hell, and the thought of losing you scares me more than words can say."

"Kara, I will still have my moments, but with you, Rafe, and Evren, I'm okay. I promised Rafe that I would never put another blade to my body. I make the same promise to you. Really."

"You don't have to do that. I know you won't. This was

on me, not you."

"What can I do? How can I help?"

Kara hugs her again. "I'm okay. Let's finish dinner, then you and Rafe can go check out what he's done to his old quarters."

"You sure?"

"Really. I love you, Ana."

"Love you, too, Kara. Come on."

They return to the table. "Sorry, Rafe, Evren. I was having a moment. It's all good now. Rafe, why don't you take Ana and show her what you guys did today?"

"Good idea," Rafe says, smiling at Ana. They finish eating. "Did you want to go now?"

"Yes, love." She stands up, pulling Kara with her. She hugs her. "I had a good day with you today. We'll do it again soon."

"All right. We'll gather dishes."

"Rafe and I would like breakfast alone tomorrow. We'll meet you for the briefing around nine-thirty."

"See you then."

Rafe takes Ana's hand. They go into the hallway. "Follow me," he tells Roesh. They follow behind as Rafe leads them. They arrive at his old quarters, standing guard as he takes her inside. The bed is moved along the wall to the right. She walks to the window and faces him.

"Are you thinking of having our desks here?"

"I think so." He steps over. "A couch and table by the fireplace, with some privacy panels around the bed. How does that sound?"

"Perfect." She smiles, walking up and kissing him. She wraps her arms around his neck, holding him tight. "I really missed you today."

He smiles at her. "I can tell."

She laughs, blushing. "Sorry."

"For what? Loving me? You never have to apologize for

that. I missed you, too. Now, do you want to stay in here or do you want to get cleaned up after walking around?"

"Let's get cleaned up. We can enjoy some time in here as we go over plans for everything."

"All right." He steps out, holding her hand. "Back to our quarters."

"Yes, Rafe."

They return. Aylin and Ana wait outside as they clear the room. "Majesty, are you better from this morning?"

"Yes, Aylin. Thank you."

"You're welcome."

Rafe and Roesh step out. Rafe leads her inside. They go to the closet and gather up pajamas. He holds her hand as they go to the washroom. He steps in, starting the water while she undresses. She steps in.

"I forgot shorts. Be right back," Rafe says as he leaves.

Ana steps under the water, as the chill is running down her spine. She opens her mouth, gasping for air. She goes to the wall, leaning against it, as the tears are streaming down. Rafe steps in, rushing to her.

"Ana, what's wrong?"

"I'm sorry. It's an episode. I didn't mean—"

He grabs her, pulling her to him. He takes her to the water, holding her tight. "I'm right here. You're safe now. Just stay with me, Ana." He feels her trembling, as the memory overwhelms her. He strokes her hair, reassuring her until the trembling stops.

"Rafe," she says quietly, "please help me get clean and into bed. I'm exhausted now."

"Of course."

He washes her hair, lathering the soap and cleaning her. With her standing by the wall, he washes himself. They dry themselves after he takes her out of the shower. He helps her dress, then places her on the tub while he does the same. He picks her up, stepping out. "Do you want to lay on your ottoman?"

"No, the bed is fine."

"Okay." He gently lays her down. "One moment, mia estrela." He runs to stoke the fire and turn off the overhead light. He climbs into bed, pulling her to him. "There, it's okay now. Do you want to talk about it?"

"In the morning," she mumbles. "For now, I want to go to sleep."

"Yes, that's a good idea." He kisses her forehead. Glancing down, he sees she is already sleeping. "Battle your demons and kick them out, my little warrior," he whispers in her ear, caressing her face. "You know you're strong enough."

Chapter 15

"How do you feel?" Rafe asks as he kisses Ana's forehead.

"Much better. When you get breakfast, could we have cocoa?"

"Of course. Are you ready for me to put in for it?"

"Please."

He pulls away, putting on his robe and going to the door. After requesting breakfast, he crawls onto the bed, sitting up and pulling her onto his lap. "You don't have to, I'm just asking. Are you ready to talk about what happened last night?"

"Yes. Kara mentioned my scars. Even though they're gone, I… sometimes I can still feel them. I was back in the home with my foster brothers. I thought I was stronger. I thought I was over it."

"Stop. You know what I'm going to say. You will take as long as you need, and you will continue to recover, battling your demons. Let me comfort you now. You know how much I love you, and you know how I see you. You have no reason to doubt yourself or me. Tell me you know this."

"I do, love. I know how much you love me. I feel it, even being in your arms. It's overwhelming me, calming me mind and soul. Thank you."

"And how do you see yourself?"

Her eyes squeeze shut. "Rafe, I can't—"

"No, Ana. Please. You are my warrior queen. What will it take for you to see that? For you to see yourself the way I do?"

"A little time. I will, later. Even today, but right now, that's not how I feel. Please, be patient."

"I will be. Whatever you need, mia estrela."

"Thank you, love."

"Are you going to be okay to go to the briefing?"

"Yes. I need to apologize to Audressa. I never meant to make her feel bad."

"If you feel it's necessary."

"I did push a little for her to tell me about the laws. I owe her this, I promise you."

"All right." When the bell rings, he lays her down on the bed. The tray in hand, he walks to their table. He finishes setting things up and returns to her side. "Are you ready to eat?"

Stepping out of bed, she puts on her slippers and robe. With his hand in hers, they walk together. She sees the relief on his face when she eats without being asked. "I'm okay now, really."

"I worry."

She laughs. "It's your duty. Right?"

He leans down, kissing her. "My pleasure to serve, Your Majesty."

"Rafe, behave yourself!"

"Is that an order?"

She smiles at him. "I'm so grateful you are no longer under my command."

"You are the queen, I will always be under your command. I know what you're referring to, though. Ana, the day you freed me was incredible. I didn't want to say too much, because I could see how badly you felt for having such power over me. It felt like chains that were wrapped around my body suddenly broke free."

"Really?"

"Yes, only when you commanded me. It did not feel like that all of the time, or I would've told you."

"So, you want guardians to continue with the indoctrination process?"

"Yes. I agree with it, and I say that, having gone through it myself and been under command for over five hundred years." He looks at her when her head suddenly goes down. "What's wrong?"

"Did… did my father ever command you to do something you didn't want to? Like hurt an innocent person or—"

"It doesn't work like that. We can't be commanded to break a law. We couldn't kill a child, for example."

"Your answer tells me so much about him. I'm sorry I asked."

"Ana, it's okay."

"What does it feel like, when you're commanded to do something?"

"Like I'm a prisoner in my body, watching it react but unable to stop myself. Fighting it is intensely painful."

"Rafe, I—"

"No, we aren't talking about Everard. I was simply answering your question. I don't want you dealing with that until you are ready to."

"Yes, love. Melian said it's impossible to fight."

"Usually, it is. Luckily, I was walking towards you, so I let gravity pull me down. Now, do you want to talk about all of this?"

"No, no, please. I'm sorry."

He gazes at her, noticing the tears welling up in her eyes. "No, I am. It was a bad time for both of us." He stands up, pulling her out of the chair and into his arms. "Forgive me, mia estrela." He takes her to the sofa and wipes away her tears. "Oh, Ana. I'm so sorry."

"No, it's okay. That night, being away from you, was horrible. I—I don't know why I got so angry, why I let it consume me."

Drawing her nearer, he embraces her as she rests her head against his chest. "It was my fault. You told me you saw him, being very adamant about what you saw. I shut you down. I… It was my fault. Running in, seeing you fight him while your wings were fire, then he used his magic on you. I thought for sure I lost you."

"I'm right here, safe and sound."

Rafe looks over when the bell rings. He stands up, laying her on the couch. "Stay right here, mia estrela."

"I will."

He opens the door. "Kara, is everything okay?"

"Yes, I'm sorry to bother you. Can I come in?" He steps back, letting her inside. She looks around. "Where's Ana?"

"I'm over here," Ana says, sitting up.

Kara looks up at Rafe. "Another bad morning?"

"Bad night, leading to a bad morning," he answers softly. "Come on."

They walk to the couch. Kara sits by Ana while Rafe stands by the window. Kara studies her with an expression of concern. "I'm sorry. We have intel there is another assassin in the palace. I wanted to inform you, since you said you were coming to the briefing and having lunch with the countess today."

"Kara, would you do me a favor? Let the countess know what has transpired. If she still wishes to do lunch in the dining hall, I will meet her. If not, tell her we can reschedule once the threat has been taken care of."

"I will see to it and let you know shortly."

"Thank you."

"Are you all right?"

"Yes, Kara. I'll be fine. Do you want me to attend the briefing?"

"I would prefer you stay in here with Rafe until the assassin is caught."

"I will, unless I am having lunch with the countess."

"I understand." Kara hugs her. "I'll be back after the briefing to give you more intel, about everything."

"Thank you, Kara."

"Of course."

As Kara departs, she smiles reassuringly at Rafe. He joins Ana, sitting with her and holding her hands.

"I'm not going to the briefing."

"I heard. Would you like to have a lesson or continue our discussion from this morning?"

"Could we have a lesson?"

"Of course. What do you want to know?" He sees her eyes go down as she blushes. "Ana?"

"Um, what is my last name?" She asks, meeting his gaze. "When I sign my documents, Kara has me sign as 'Queen Maeriana' or 'Queen of the Maristellar Kingdom' but never my full name."

"Your full name is Maeriana Rose Summerhauld."

"Really?"

"Yes."

"I… Not so different from Earth, then?"

"No. Kara said your bracelet had your name on it. I wonder if it was damaged or part of it was unreadable, for them to give you that name."

"Hmm. What is your last name?" She becomes concerned when he pulls away, walking to the window and looking out. She stands up, walking up beside him and taking his hand. "Love?"

"I don't have one. Guardians only have a first name. It's been that way for most of our history."

"How did I not notice that in the files?" She squeezes his hand. "Would you take my name, when we get married?"

He turns to her, surprise on his face. "Really?"

"Yes. It would make me very happy."

"Then yes, Ana. I will take your last name."

She smiles at him, stepping up and kissing him. "Rafe and Ana Summerhauld. I like the sound of that."

He mirrors her smile. "So do I." He carries her back to the sofa and settles her on his lap. His gaze is lowered, observing her as she watches the rain. "You really love your rainy days, don't you?"

"Yes. They are my favorite kind. I know it isn't great, since we need to stretch our wings, but I can't help it. The rain is so beautiful.”

“Speaking of which, how are they today? Do you need to exercise them?”

“We will shortly. Right now, I love being with you.”

“Always.”

“Forever,” she says, sitting up and kissing him. She caresses his chin and jawline, kissing him again. “I love you.”

“I love you, mia estrela.”

“Hmm. I guess we should get dressed and stretch our wings. Who knows what Kara will say when she returns?”

“When you’re ready.”

“Let’s go on. Besides, I’d like to wear my engagement ring.”

Standing up, he smiles at her and carries her into the closet. He places her on the ottoman and lies down next to her. Leaning forward, he softly kisses her.

“We aren’t doing anything this morning while you’re still recovering. I just wanted to kiss you on our ottoman.”

She smiles at him, pulling to him and kissing him harder. “Yes, love.” He sits up, pulling her with him. She wraps her arms and legs around him. “Please, Rafe, hold me like this right now?”

He feels her trembling. “What’s wrong?”

“I’m trying to push down the memories, fighting against the night we fought, and when I nearly died the next day. Losing you, pushing you away, I was so stupid! I don’t know what came over me. I’m so sorry I ever did that to you.”

“Ana, please. It’s said and done. We forgave each other and moved on. Why does it still hurt you so?” He looks down when his arm is wet from her fallen tears.

“I was devastated that you would walk out the door.”

“Ana! Oh, mia estrela. I am so truly sorry. I don’t know what I was thinking. I was so angry at you for commanding me to go, angry at how you were treating me. I’ve worked on my anger. I think I’m doing better. It doesn’t excuse me leaving you then. No matter what, I never should've done that!" He grips her tighter, sending all of his love and comfort into her.

"Rafe, please. I'm sorry. I should be past this. I don't know why it still hurts me so."

"Because it took you back to Earth, to me leaving you for four months. The night we fought, I walked out, and you probably thought I was gone again like that. It's why I should not have left. I had already done it once. It was so wrong of me to do it again."

"I think you're right. About why it affects me, not that it was wrong of you to do. I told you to go, I commanded you. I came in here, and I cried myself to sleep."

"Really?"

"Yes. I made myself get up and go to breakfast the next day, because I knew I would need my strength. I hadn't given up on us. I almost did, but I refused to, after everything we had been through. Then I ran into you on the way to the summit, and I couldn't talk to you. Seeing you made my heart ache and made me feel empty again. I'm sorry I was too afraid to fight for us."

"No, Ana. I doubted you, I left, I broke your heart. Everything that happened was because of me. I don't even remember what I said, only that I turned and walked out. I went to my old quarters and took a shower. I sat on the sofa, watching the fire. I cried, my heart breaking for you. I thought about coming back, trying to talk to you. I thought we were both too upset and needed some time. Waking up without you the next morning, feeling empty as the day went on, was why I decided to come and talk to you."

"And I blew you off."

"You were protecting yourself while also trying to keep the peace."

"Let's get dressed. Kara will be here shortly with news." She pulls back, looking at him. "Thank you for bringing down walls with me this morning. I'm sorry, it wasn't my intention to bring up such a painful time."

He smiles at her. "Ana, we needed to. Thank you for opening up to me."

Standing, he pulls her to her feet. He leads her to the drawers, retrieves her rings, and places them on her fingers. Kissing her hand, he then walks to his dresser.

She looks through her clothes. "When will my new gowns be delivered?"

"Probably tomorrow morning."

"I hope they are. I know of at least two I would like to wear while we are in NightFall."

A lavender gown with long lacy sleeves, embroidered roses on the bodice, and a billowing skirt catches her eye. She sheds her pajamas, replacing them with her corset and dress. She slips on her silver crown and shoes. After approaching the mirror, she admires her reflection.

"You look beautiful."

"Thank you. I'm never sure, lavender with crimson."

He laughs. "I don't really know fashion, but I think it looks great together."

"That makes me think of Earth."

"How so?" he asks, walking to her while buttoning up his shirt.

"I told Kara I was envious of how you and she dressed. You each represented your personalities. She asked if this was because of you, as I had never mentioned fashion in the five years we'd been friends. It's when she bought me new clothes, that I wore when we went to the Italian restaurant for lunch. Fashion was never really my thing. I was more focused on my grades, my reading, my job."

"Having to wear a uniform for so long, it was kind of freeing wearing jeans and leather jackets. I do miss those."

"Me, too."

"You miss your yoga pants."

"Rafe!"

He laughs. "What? I thought you looked really cute in them." He leans down, kissing her, moving his mouth to her ear. "And your butt looked really cute in them." He watches her head go down as her face flushes red.

She looks at him, laughing. "Really?"

"Oh, yes. It was a shame you had to wear sweatshirts over them, hiding it."

She shakes her head. "What am I going to do with you?"

"Marry me?"

"Of course!"

Leaning up, she kisses him before leaving the closet. Knowing Kara will arrive shortly, she approaches the chaise and takes a seat. Her eyes follow Rafe as he enters the room.

"I hope Kara has good news. I am so tired of threats, of dealing with assassins. Kane, Tinsley, and Remus are dead. So, I wonder, who sent this one? Why are they here?"

"Hopefully they will find them and get answers," Rafe says, sitting with her. He takes her hands.

She looks at him when she feels his worry. "What?"

"We didn't finish breakfast. I upset you then Kara showed up. Come on."

"I can't. I'm sorry, I know that makes you mad. I can't eat until we hear something from Kara."

Standing, he approaches and retrieves their plates. He passes one to her. "Will you at least try?"

"Yes," she says, taking the plate.

Despite not wanting to, she eats to avoid upsetting him, knowing it's necessary. She was relieved that she had eaten most of it beforehand. He takes the plates and puts them on the table. The bell rings, and she looks over to see Rafe opening the door.

Kara and Evren step in. Ana stands with her hands clasped together. "What news?"

"Nothing of the assassin, I'm afraid. Countess Anwyn says she will be in the dining hall at eleven, that she is not scared off by threats," Kara says.

"A woman after my own heart. I will join her." She notes the look of concern on Rafe's face. "I will not hide in here all day!"

"No, I know. Stubborn to a fault, like me." He chuckles. He turns to Kara. "Her security?"

Kara looks at Ana, knowing she won't like what she's going to hear. "There are four guardians and four royal guards outside."

"What?"

"It's necessary. After what happened last time—"

"Fine," she says, walking to the window. The thought of stepping out and being surrounded by so many people fills her with dread, but she will not hide. Kara joins her. "I'm sorry. I know you have to. You're trying to protect me. Thank you." She watches Rafe go into the closet, stepping out a moment later with a sword on his belt. She hangs her head.

"What's wrong?" Kara asks.

"Maybe I should stay here."

"Ana, take an hour with the countess then return here. How does that sound?"

"Yes, Kara."

She walks to Rafe and takes his hand. Kara leads them out, telling Roesh they are going to the dining hall. Ana looks around her, seeing Kellan and Erick. "Kellan, how are you?"

"I am recovered, Majesty. Thank you."

"I'm sorry you were forced here—"

"No, Majesty. Kara asked for volunteers. Erick and I gladly serve."

"Thank you, all of you."

Chapter 16

Entering the dining hall, they find the countess is at a small table for two towards the back. Ana steps up to Rafe, kissing him then walks to the countess. Anwyn rises as she approaches.

"Your Majesty," she bows.

"Countess," Ana says as they sit. "I apologize for all of the additional security—"

"Your Sage, Kara, explained the situation. It's understandable."

The first dish is served. Ana looks at Anwyn's plate. "You like the vampyra dishes as well?"

"I do. When I first heard they were being served here, I was skeptical. I must say, this is some of the best food I've had."

"I was the same way. When we were in NightFall, I took small bites so I could hide my dislike, not wishing to offend anyone. Instead, it has become my favorite cuisine."

"Majesty, I'll get straight to the point. I asked you to lunch because the ladies of the court would like to host a high tea in your honor. I apologize for being forward, but I know you aren't the most comfortable in social settings, and I thought it best to ask when it was the two of us, instead of in front of the whole group."

"I appreciate that. Is it that obvious?"

"I apologize if I offend, but yes."

Ana laughs. "Oh, no. You aren't offending me for speaking the truth. Between us? I would be honored to attend a high tea, but I will feel most self-conscious, being the only woman at the table with wings."

"Hmm. I didn't think of that."

"Countess?"

"I'm sorry. I've grown up here, watching and interacting

with the guardians. Some of the other ladies have, as well, while a few are from other realms and have not seen people with wings before.”

“Yes, we will have a high tea. What if we have it in the Lunala Ballroom? It is small enough, that it could be easily guarded.”

“Excellent idea! Of course, you are the queen, so tell us what day and time works best for you.”

“We are leaving tomorrow to go to NightFall. Perhaps next Wednesday at three? Is Kara, my sage, invited as well?”

“She and Evren, both.”

“Thank you.”

“Can I ask about them, about your wings?”

“Countess, ask me anything you want. You will not offend me.”

“What are they like to have?”

Ana laughs. “Um, different. I hated them at first, I was so scared and freaked out. Learning to use them, being able to fly and control them, I’ve learned to accept and even love them.”

“I can’t imagine.” She looks confused when Ana laughs out loud. “Majesty?”

“That is pretty much everyone’s response. My apologies, I hope I did not offend you.”

“No, Majesty, you did not.”

“How many women will be at the tea?”

“Around twenty.”

“Not too bad.”

“May I ask, why do you not like to be a part of social settings?”

“It’s how I am. I am a quiet introvert who would rather be reading a good book and having a cup of tea than being in a room full of people. I am trying to be more social.”

“You remind me of my daughter.”

“Thank you. Will she be at the event?”

“Oh, you don’t know. Um, she died a few years ago,

sickness."

"I'm so sorry. My apologies, Countess."

"Quite all right, thank you. She was very shy, and books were her favorite thing, too. I would get on her relentlessly about being out in court more. I wish I hadn't been so hard on her." She looks up at Ana. "My apologies."

"No, Countess. No apologies are needed. I can't imagine your loss, but I offer my heartfelt sympathy."

"Thank you, Majesty. You truly are a kind and compassionate queen."

"Then I offer you my thanks, for your words. May I ask, what was her name?"

"Aislinn, it means dream."

"Oh, what a beautiful name. May I ask, was it just the two of you?"

"Yes. Her father died in battle when she was a baby. He was on our home realm, MoonSol, fighting for our king."

"Countess, I am so sorry. You have endured such heartbreak, but here you sit, having lunch as though everything in the world is fine. Your strength is beyond measure."

"Majesty, that is high praise. Thank you. If I'm not being too forward, may I ask about your guardian?"

"My fiancé?" She sees the look of confusion on her face. "My apologies. Fiancé is the word for who you are betrothed to on the world I grew up."

"Oh, I see. No, I mean the handsome one with pale blue wings."

"His name is Erick, though I do not know him well. He and Kellan saved me from an assassin. He is an excellent guardian." She takes a bite, then nearly chokes on her food. "Wait, are you—"

The countess laughs. "I would like to meet him," she quietly admits.

Ana looks over, gesturing to Rafe. "Everything all right?" he asks as he approaches them.

"Would you bring Erick over here?"

"Majesty! I didn't mean right this second," the countess says, laughing.

"It's no trouble."

Anwyn looks at Rafe then Ana, then nods. "Please?"

Rafe speaks to Erick, who joins them a moment later. "How can I serve you?" Erick asks, bowing before them.

"Erick, I would like you to meet Countess Anwyn. Countess, this is one of my most esteemed guardians, Erick."

He turns to her, his breath catching in his throat. "Countess," he manages to get out.

"Guardian. If I'm not being too bold, would you join me for dinner when you are off duty next?"

"I am off tomorrow. I could meet you here at five."

Anwyn smiles at him. "I'll see you then."

"Yes, Countess." He turns and quickly returns to his post.

"Anwyn!" Ana exclaims, laughing. "Will you tell me how the date goes?"

"Of course. It wouldn't happen if you hadn't passed your treaty. I saw him once before, but it was forbidden at the time, so I tried to forget him. He is very handsome. Your guardian is easy on the eyes, as well."

Ana nearly spits out her drink, collecting herself. "Countess!"

They both laugh. "My apologies."

"No, it's a compliment. Thank you. Perhaps Tuesday we could meet for lunch, so you can tell me how your dinner went and to discuss the tea party?"

"That would be fine." She looks at the clock. "I must be going. Enjoy your trip to NightFall, and I will see you here Tuesday."

"Thank you, Countess."

She stands and bows, looking over at Erick. "Thank you."

Ana chuckles as she walks away. She finishes eating, looking up when Rafe sits with her. "You two seem to have hit it off. Can I ask, what did she want with Erick?"

"They are having dinner together tomorrow."

"I see. Another couple because of your treaty?"

Ana laughs. "Rafe, it's just dinner. Though, he seems to like her as much as she does him, so who knows? I guess we are returning to our quarters."

"Would you like to go to the training center first?"

"Can we?"

"Of course." He takes her hand, instructing the guards where they are going.

Ana looks at Kara. "We are going to have some training, then return to our quarters."

"We'll go on. If I learn anything new, I'll bring you news. Otherwise, breakfast in the morning?"

"Yes, Kara. We will see you then."

Kara and Evren step away, two royal guards walking with them. Ana shakes her head.

They arrive at the training center, waiting outside as Kellan and Roesh inspect the center, going in once they give the all clear. Ana steps into the middle of the room, opening her wings. Rafe runs to her when she flinches.

"What's wrong?"

"I'm okay. I didn't realize how tight they are."

"You hold them in when you have an episode, don't you?"

Her head goes down. "Yes. I am so sorry."

"Don't apologize. Your whole body literally tenses up, and it's out of your control. It's okay. Let's stretch them out now."

She looks up at him. "Thank you, love." She furls and unfurls them, warming them up. She watches as he's in the air. "Jerk!"

"What?" he asks, laughing.

"I need a moment! I have to warm up. Not all of us have five hundred years of muscle memory."

"Hmm. Sounds like an excuse."

She's angry until she looks at him and sees the grin on his

face. Her wings billow out, and she rushes to him, catching him off guard. She grabs him to her, holding him tight, hovering in the air.

He looks in her eyes, bringing his head down and planting gentle kisses all over her face. "Jerk, huh?"

"No! I'm sorry!" she says with a giggle.

"Submit?"

"Never!"

She pulls away, laughing as she evades him. He goes up, faking before turning and going back down. She catches on and goes backwards.

"Ana, that's incredible. Where did you learn to do that?"

"I saw you do it."

"It is amazing that you can see something I do then do it yourself, without being shown how. Do you realize that? Do you know how amazing you are with your wings?"

She laughs. "Jealous?"

He charges at her again, laughing. She narrowly evades his grasp, falling then flying up over him. He lowers to the ground, watching her. She rushes to him.

"What's wrong? Why did you stop?"

"I was in awe, watching you. I thought for a second your wings had given out. I didn't realize you had such control over them!"

She smiles, kissing him. "Told you, I have a great teacher." She leans her mouth down by his ear, holding him tight. "Now, shall we have some private training in our quarters?"

"Ana!" He laughs, kissing her. "Let's go."

He takes her hand, leading her from the center. He instructs the guards that they are returning to their quarters. They wait as Roesh and Erick inspect inside. Rafe scoops her up, causing Ana to squeal in surprise, and carries her inside. He locks the latch before taking her to the middle of the room.

"Now, what to do with you? Calling me a jerk and teasing me with your wings? What to do?"

"I submit," she whispers, kissing him. "Do with me whatever you want."

He takes her into the air, as she wraps her legs around him, clinging to him. He kisses her, looking into her eyes. Her love for him reflects in her gaze. "Are you sure you're okay?"

"Please, love. I am." His hand comes up, gently slipping off her undergarments. His hand trails along her thigh. "What about you?"

"Oh, trust me. I will enjoy this as much as you."

She realizes they can feel each other, without her having to send it into him. The connection is so strong, she can feel his longing, feel the heat in his veins, the love in his heart.

"Rafe, take me to bed, please?"

He lowers down and lays her on the mattress. "What's wrong?"

She laughs. "No, I need you. I need us to be together." She stands up, unbuttoning his pants and removing his belt.

"Ana, are you—"

Their lips lock in a passionate, fiery kiss. She presses closer, the passion between them growing. Her heart races, and her blood surges with desire. She removes his pants and shorts, allowing them to drop to the floor.

Her fingers work the buttons, letting his shirt fall onto the pile. He removes her gown and lays her on the bed. He leans over her, showering her with kisses. With a flick of her wings, she turns them over, placing herself on top.

"How did you—"

The question dies in his throat as her mouth trails down his stomach. Drawing her up, he kisses her. When he touches her, her legs part for him. She holds him gently, stroking slow and deliberate.

As they soar into the air, she lets out a gasp, her breath catching in her throat. His hand continues its gentle caress as she strokes him. She kisses him hard, her head rolling back as the waves threaten to drown her. They cry out, gripping each other tightly, as he lowers them to the bed.

"Shower, now."

She giggles as a trickle of sweat rolls down her cheek. "Can't even form a sentence, love?"

He carries her in and begins running the water. With his weight, he presses her against the wall, pinning her body. Her eyes, filled with love and trust, gaze up at him. He gently runs his hand along her chest, then moves it down to her stomach.

As she trembles, he lets out a chuckle. She copies him, her hand moving along his waist.

"What to do with you? You said you submit, so you are mine now. Hmm."

She plays along. "Oh, no. What are you going to do to me?"

His smile grows. "I will teach you to call me a jerk!"

With a gentle touch, he strokes her thigh. He moves higher, noting her shudder in response. As she gets closer, he pulls his hand away, kissing her and pressing his body over her.

"Oh, love!" she cries out. "Please, this is torture!"

He smiles at her. "For both of us."

She laughs, forgetting he feels it as well. "Then give me all of you!"

He kneels and lifts his hand again. His tongue glides over her thigh, then playfully teases her apex. Her back hits the wall, as he strokes her desire and explores her most tender spot. She cries out, collapsing on him when they are consumed by the waves. He stands and takes her into his arms. His breathing is ragged, and his heart races. She holds him tight, knowing she will fall to the floor if she lets go.

"Are you all right, mia estrela?"

She laughs. "I am."

"You had me worried for a moment."

"I'm sorry. It slipped out. I didn't mean to call it torture."

"It's okay. For most normal couples, it is. What you've been through, I don't ever want to be the one hurting you."

"Oh, Rafe! No, love. I didn't mean torture like that. Please, it's okay. I want us to be able to use these words without bringing up bad memories."

"We'll continue to work on it."

"Oh, no. More sessions like today?" she asks with a playful wink.

"I have to teach you, don't I?"

"Yes, love. I need to clean up, then get some rest. You have worn me out today."

He laughs. "You, too."

After cleaning up, they step out and head into the closet. She puts on her black pants, shirt, and hoodie. He follows suit, keeping his eye on her as she sits on the ottoman. He approaches and takes a seat next to her.

"Sure you're okay?"

"Oh, yes. Thinking back again, to when we had to hide in here. Even before I had wings. It's weird to think of, that we've been together longer with my wings than without."

"Why is it weird?

She looks down. "It's just, we were both basically human on Earth. No wings on either of us. Now, we both have them. How much things have changed."

"Like my love for you?" He sees the worry on her face when her head jerks up to look at him. "No, Ana. In a good way. My love for you has grown over time, becoming so much deeper and richer. I think you were right, when you said that one night hurt worse than the four months we were apart. We're not going into that, I simply wanted to point it out."

She leans up, planting a gentle kiss. "Could we nap in here?"

"Of course." He walks to the floor lamp and switches it on. He turns off the overhead light, then climbs onto the ottoman with her, pulling her onto his lap. "Bringing you in here, my heart pounding, my fear of discovery being overwhelmed by my need to be with you. It was intense."

"I was equally as scared. If they caught us, you know I would have been executed with you?"

"No, Ana. That's not what the law—"

"I would have ordered it. I would not be able to live with myself if I had been responsible."

"Ana! Oh, mia estrela. I don't know if I would've brought you in here, had I known that."

"I knew, but I took the chance, because being away from you was already killing me. I could handle the fear, I couldn't take the aching of my heart. You were right, our souls were reaching out for each other, even before you and I understood this pull we have."

He kisses her, his hand caressing her face. "God, you're beautiful. Every inch of you, every piece of you, is absolutely breathtaking. What did I ever do to deserve a goddess like you?"

She blushes. "Rafe!"

"I'm sorry. It's the truth."

"Can we get a nap?"

"Yes, mia estrela." He lays down, bringing her with him. She clutches his shirt. "I'm right here. I am not going anywhere."

"Promise?"

"I do."

She laughs. "I can't wait to hear you say that."

"Me, too, Ana. Now get some sleep, then we'll have a nice, private dinner."

"With dessert and cocoa?"

"Yes, mia estrela."

"Hmm! Thank you," she says, snuggling in closer. "I love you, Rafe."

"I love you, too." He watches her fall asleep, closing his eyes as her warmth and love is radiating through him.

Ana wakes up, looking up at Rafe. She nuzzles in closer, holding him tightly. She listens to his heartbeat as his love is flowing through her. Looking at him, she trails her fingers over his chin and cheek. His eyes open, and he smiles when he sees her.

"Hmm, hello, mia estrela. How do you feel?"

"Much better, love."

"What time is it?"

"Almost four. A little early for dinner."

"So, what should we do while waiting?" He looks at her when she giggles. "I love it when you do that."

"I'm spent."

"I was just… teasing."

"Jerk!"

"Ana, what have I said about that?"

He climbs over her, planting soft kisses on her nose, cheek, and chin, as she playfully begs him to stop. "No! Because you were being one!"

"Hmm." She laughs as he does it again. "Am I now?" he asks.

"No, love."

"All right. We'll leave for NightFall tomorrow. Are you excited to fly?"

"What?" she asks, sitting up. "Really?"

"Not the whole way, not while you are still learning and warming them up, but you will fly quite a bit."

"Oh, yes, please!"

"Ana, why are you so excited about this?" He sits up with her.

"Rafe, I've gone from hating my wings, to accepting them, to loving them. I practically begged you last time to let me fly. I can't wait!"

"Oh, shoot. I hope it's not raining."

"What will we do then?"

"Hmm. We could take a carriage, but it will take longer. I'll take a look at the forecast and go from there."

"Oh, I really hope we can fly!" She laughs as his happiness overwhelms her. "Your happiness is radiating into me."

"I can't help it." He holds her tight. "I've waited so long for this!"

She laughs, wrapping around him. "Oh, love. I'm happy to make you happy. It's my lifelong mission, to always make you feel this way."

"You do. Every single day. Just by existing, simply by being here. Did you know that?"

Her breath sucks in. "Really?"

"Yes."

"Oh, love!" she exclaims, trembling in his arms. "You do, too. Waking up every day, seeing you with me, fills me with so much love and happiness. Then you give me your warmth, your patience, and your heart. How do you fill me with so much love and happiness every minute of every day?"

"Ana, I give back to you what you give to me."

"Rafe!"

He laughs. "What? It's the truth. I know you have days where you doubt yourself, doubt what you are capable of, but please, don't ever doubt our love. You feel bad that you aren't ready to be with me, but I can assure you, the love is there. That is never in question."

"Yes, love. Will you put in for dinner?"

"If my queen commands."

She giggles. "Guardian, I need food."

"I shall see to it, mi'lady."

He sits her on the ottoman, bowing, as he turns and runs out. She leaves the closet, going to the sofa. She sits and watches the rain, hoping they can fly to NightFall. Rafe sits beside her, taking her hand.

"I feel worry. What's wrong?"

She nods to the window. "I love the rain, but I really hope it's not doing this tomorrow."

"I asked, and it looks like we will get a break. Let's hope that's the case. Pack extra cloaks and warm clothes, just in case."

"Oh, no. Will we have to find shelter and share a sleeping bag?"

"Ana!"

She laughs. "What?" she innocently asks. "It was quite snug…"

"What am I going to do with you?"

"Feed me?"

"Of course!" He takes the tray and brings it to their small table. Looking up, Ana joins him.

"What is this?" she asks, looking everything over.

"Some of this is your vampyra food, but this plate," he gestures, "has a sampling of dishes from MorningStella."

"Trying to find me something to eat for our honeymoon?"

"I thought it was a way to give you a taste of their dishes."

"Rafe?"

"And to make sure you can find something to eat."

She laughs. "I will. I promise I will. Don't worry, please?"

"Ana, have you met me?" They burst out laughing. "I swear, it's in my DNA to worry about you."

"When I woke up in the hospital, I could hear the concern in your voice, see it on your face. I was so confused as to why a good-looking stranger was so worried about me."

"Good looking, huh?"

"Rafe, focus!"

"Yes, Ana. Oh, seeing you on the ground, blood pouring from your shoulder, I was so scared."

"Really?"

"Yes, I told you. From the moment I saw you, I've felt this pull with us."

"I did, too. I'm sorry I tried to pull away, to build a wall from you."

"Ana, you literally knew nothing about me and were trying to protect yourself. I'm grateful to be here now, bringing down your walls."

"That you are." She looks over the plate, looking at Rafe. "Do you know what they are? The MorningStella dishes?"

"I do."

"Hmm." She picks up a piece, showing him. He nods. She puts it in her mouth, looking up at him as the flavor overwhelms her. "Oh, that is good!"

He laughs. "That is, sarda marinis. A common fish from there."

"Rafe, how long ago did you arrange this? I know Yeona does not keep this in stock, right?"

"She does, so when the ambassadors come and visit, they can have their cuisine. I asked about it when I set up our special dinner. She told me to request it any time."

She looks over the plate, trying not to laugh at the different colored pieces. She picks up a piece, looking it over. "Not sure of the texture on that one."

"Ana—"

"I'll try it." She plops it in, closing her eyes. It has a soft texture with a salty sea flavor. "Hmm. Okay, that was better than I thought. Do I want to know?"

"That is black kingfish. It's a little rarer."

"Rafe, we should've had lessons about the creatures first."

"You wanted to see their faces before you eat?"

"Hmm. Good point. Please tell me this is just fish, right? Nothing like turtles or lobsters or crabs?"

"Just fish."

"All right." She picks up a pale blue piece. She makes a face, looking up when he laughs. "What?"

"Ana, don't play with it. Try it."

"Fine!" she says, laughing as she eats it. "Don't care for

that one."

"That's azure shark."

"What? Rafe, did you make me eat shark?"

"Yes, but—"

She shoots him a look. "I love sharks. Why would you do that?"

"I swear, I didn't know. I've never heard you mention sharks."

"Did you not see the plush one on my bed? The pictures on my desk?"

"No, I'm sorry. I had no idea. That's the only shark on there."

She pushes the plate away. "I've lost my appetite."

"Ana, please. Don't let this ruin our evening."

"You're right. I'm sorry. Let's try something else." While she's trying different pieces, he tells her what they are. "See? I'll be fine there."

"Good. I'll let Yeona know you liked it."

"We can, next time we go to the kitchen." She looks down. "Oh, well, once the assassin is taken care of, I mean."

"Ana, it's okay. You can write a note and send with the dishes."

"That will work, thank you."

At her desk, she composes a thank you note for Yeona. She places it with the dishes. Stepping out, Rafe gives the items to a staff member. She sits on the sofa to watch the rain. Rafe sits beside her, taking her hand. She glances at him.

"Well, I told you I know how to swim, but that was before my wings. I don't know what that will be like."

"We can practice before we go there."

"Practice? How?"

"Your swimming pool."

She sits up, looking at him in surprise. "What? What are you talking about?"

"You have a private swimming pool."

"Why haven't I heard about this before?"

"You can't use it."

"What?"

He laughs. "Too cold. It's inside the palace but has open windows. We'll use it this summer."

"My own pool," she says softly. "I love swimming. Wait, what do I wear? Since we haven't gone to MorningStella yet?"

He raises his eyebrows, laughing when she blushes. "I'm kidding! No, you'll see. Once it warms up, you can buy a bathing suit here. There's a public pool in the village."

"Rafe!"

"What?"

"Making me think I would have to be… without clothes to swim!"

He moves closer to her. "Ana, you can say naked," he teases. Her head immediately goes down. "What's wrong?"

"No, please," she murmurs. "Could you give me a little time?" Pulling her hand away, she hugs her knees to her chest.

He lifts her into his lap and holds her close. "I won't ask. Just stay with me."

"I will," she replies, burying her face into his chest. "Hold me right now, please." His grip tightens when she trembles in his arms. "I'm okay," she says.

"Ana, you're not. Stay with me, feel my warmth. What can I do to help? What do you need?"

When she doesn't say anything, he looks down to see she fell asleep. As he sits, he watches the rain and holds her tightly. While stroking her face, he becomes aware of the shame and anger emanating from her. Focusing on her, he closes his eyes to send love and comfort. Lying on the couch, he holds her on his chest, dozing off to the rain outside.

Chapter 17

Ana's eyes open, gazing downwards. It hits her that she nodded off while on the couch with him. Aware that he will ask again, she wants to distance herself from him. Discussing it is off the table for her right now. His chest moves softly with each breath, and she finds comfort in it, unable to pull away just yet.

"Ana, how are you? You don't have to tell me what happened, but are you okay?" Sitting up together, she keeps her eyes averted.

"Please," she begs.

"What?"

"I don't… I can't…"

"Ana, talk to me. What can I do?" He looks down when she trembles again. "You are scaring me to death! Mia estrela, what do you need?"

She takes a deep breath. "I'm sorry. I'll be okay in a moment."

"I never meant to cause an episode."

"No, you didn't."

"It wasn't what I said?"

"Well, yes, but—"

"I'm so sorry."

"No, Rafe. Please, don't. This wasn't your fault. I was trying to push down memories, already hiding from you at the mention of the pool, when you said that. This was completely my fault."

"Ana, why were you hiding?"

"It's too much. I'm not ready."

"You are. You are so strong and brave, and I am right here with you. Please, mia estrela. Let me help you? Let me in?"

She takes a deep breath, looking up at him. "If I do, I'll need a shower, then I'm sure I'll need more sleep."

"Okay. I'll see to it, whatever you need."

She braces herself, knowing this may be the very thing that pushes Rafe away. Unshed tears glisten in her eyes as she concentrates.

"My foster father decided he wanted us to have a pool. Of course, it never happened, but he tried. He would drink a few beers then go out back, digging in the ground. He had a pretty deep hole dug, when I was around seven, I think. I went outside to let him know his friend was calling him, because he asked me to keep his phone. He took it from me, turning away to answer it.

"When he did, the shovel hit me, knocking me into the hole. He laughed, putting his phone in his pocket and throwing dirt on me. I cried and begged to be let out, for him to please help me. He did it a few more times, then yelled at me for crying, saying it was a joke, all in good fun. He grabbed my arm and yanked me out, throwing me to the ground. He realized how muddy I was and started screaming at me for ruining my clothes."

She looks down, swallowing hard. "He yanked them all off me, throwing them into the trash. He… He took me inside and made me take a bath. He washed me himself, to be sure he got all of the mud. Then he took me to my room." She looks at him. "I can't. Please, Rafe. I can't!"

"You don't have to. You've told me enough. I know what he would do in your room. It's okay. You're safe now. I have you. Go get a shower. I'll be right here when you're done."

"I'm sorry I need to by myself."

"Ana, no. Go ahead. I trust you."

"Thank you."

She goes to the washroom and turns on the water while stripping down. Her sobs grow as she steps under the water. Rafe walks in a moment later.

"I want to make sure you're okay. I could hear you out there."

"Will you come in here with me?" she asks, trying to keep her tone steady.

"If you want me to."

"Yes, please."

She looks up as he steps in. Shame and pain are written on her face as she makes her way to him. He takes her hand, then embraces her.

"You're safe now. He will never hurt you again. Feel my warmth, let the water cleanse you, body and soul. You're okay now." He moves her under the shower head, holding her tight. He helps her clean up and dry off.

After putting on his robe, he carries her to the closet. He gets her dressed in her pajamas. While he changes, she reclines on the ottoman. Glancing over, he realizes she fell asleep. He picks her up and takes her to bed.

Opening her eyes, Ana notices it's a quarter past four. Rafe is peacefully sleeping as she looks up at him. Her smile widens as she buries her face into his chest, enjoying the warmth of his embrace. She drifts off to sleep again.

She wakes up once more, noticing that it's seven. Leaning forward, she gently touches Rafe's cheek. "Love?"

"Hmm. What time is it?"

"Seven."

"Do you want breakfast or more sleep?"

"Breakfast, please."

"I'll see to it." He slips away, going to the door.

She sits up and moves to the edge of the bed. She takes the blanket Evren made and wraps it around herself. As Rafe approaches her, she glances his way.

She shivers slightly and admits, "I'm a little cold."

He sits beside her. "Ana, I'm not angry or upset. I want you to know that. I have to ask, why did you hide last night? Why didn't you tell me?"

She looks down, wrapping the blanket tighter. "I'm sorry."

"Ana, please. I don't want an apology."

"You want an explanation," she says in a reserved tone. "You deserve one, but I can't give you what I don't have."

"What do you mean?"

"I don't know why I hid. I mean, I do, but I don't know if it was my shame, or my fear of losing you, or—"

"What do you mean, fear of losing me?"

"I told you, it's not you. It's how I am. I worry I'm going to tell you something about myself, then watch you walk out the door."

"Then it is because of me. I left you twice. I told you I didn't love you, I hurt you. The last thing I ever wanted to do, and I did it. I'm sorry. Please, believe me when I tell you that I am never leaving again. I know I've said that, and I still left. I'm telling you now, I promise on everything I am, that I am never going to leave you again. No matter what."

She looks up at him. "Really?" she asks as tears start to fall.

"Oh, mia estrela," he says, pulling her to him. "Really. What can I do, how can I convince you that I'm not going anywhere?"

"I know you're not. I know this. I told you, it's me, not you. I'm sorry."

"No, Ana. No apologies, remember?"

"Yes, love."

He gets breakfast and brings it to their table. As he returns, his gaze lingers on her face. "Are you able to eat?

"I will." She stands up, dropping the blanket onto the bed. She walks to the table, smiling when she sees the pancakes and cocoa. "Really? Thank you. You know that's my favorite."

He smiles. "Of course." He watches her eat, grateful to see she is. "Are you up for going to the briefing?"

"No, but I can't miss another one."

"Ana, there is an assassin about, too. Kara will understand."

"You won't tell her what happened?"

"Why don't you want her to know?"

"She's worried enough. I'll tell her when she and I have another day together."

"Okay."

"Are we still going to NightFall?"

"Yes. The rain has stopped and very few people know we are leaving. I think it should be safe."

"Who is accompanying us?"

"Who would you like?"

"Roesh and Aylin."

He sees her smile. "You really like Aylin, don't you?"

"I do. She's very kind and sweet. I trust her."

"That's good. I'm glad to hear that. Now, since we aren't going to the briefing, what do you want to do until we leave?"

"We'll get cleaned up and change into clothes. I'd like a lesson, if that's okay?"

"Of course."

He looks up when the bell rings. He walks to the door and opens it. Kara and Evren wait in the corridor. "Don't tell Ana I told you this, but she's having another bad morning. I told her we're staying in because of the assassin, you know how she is. We already ate."

"Yes, I do. Good thinking. We'll have breakfast then go to the briefing. We'll bring lunch and any intel or news after."

"Thanks. We'll leave after lunch."

"I won't tell her, you have my confidence."

"Thank you, Kara. See you in a while." He shuts the door and returns to Ana. She's finished her breakfast and cocoa. "Ready to get cleaned up?"

"Yes, Rafe."

They go to the washroom, cleaning and drying off. She takes his hand, going into the closet. She slips on black pants, a corset, and a navy-blue shirt. Seeing the look on his face makes her laugh.

"I need a break from gowns."

"You won't hear me complain. As long as you're comfortable."

"I am."

He walks up behind her and gently ruffles her feathers. "How are they this morning?"

"They need to stretch. We'll do that, then have your lesson."

"Okay." He gets dressed, matching her.

She leaves the closet and goes to the middle of the room, extending out her wings. "Just a warm-up, since you said I will be flying today."

"All right. Yes, it's best if we stay in and rest until our travels."

Her wings furl and unfurl. "What?" she asks when she notices him watching her intently.

"You're blushing. Are you feeling self-conscious?"

"I am. I shouldn't be, I know."

He joins her, opening and closing his wings. "Better?"

She laughs. "Yes, love. Thank you. When are we leaving?"

"After lunch."

"Wait, I thought it took a day to travel there?"

"That's because we walked. It's much faster when we fly. Especially since we aren't injured or recovering."

"I see."

"Bela knows we'll get there a little late, so it's no big deal. Then we'll sleep, so tomorrow we can go into their village, see the shops, meet the people."

"That sounds wonderful. I'm excited to go. This will be a fun trip for us. Not going to find out results, or save someone, or keep the peace."

"Yes, we need a trip like this." He looks up as she's suddenly in the air. "Ana! We're supposed to be taking it easy."

She laughs. "I know. They needed a little more than stretching. I'll be down in a minute."

He flies up to her, pulling her into his arms. "Are you okay?"

"Yes, Rafe. I am now. I'm sorry about last night."

"You don't have to—"

"No. I know you said no apologies, but I should know better. We are getting married in August. I worry about not being ready, and what I did last night was the last thing I should've done."

"I want you to open up to me because you want to, not because of the wedding night."

She lowers down and stalks to the chaise. He joins her, taking her hand, and surprised at her feelings.

"Ana, why are you angry?"

"Why do you do that? You always think everything is about the wedding night! Yes, I brought it up, but only to make the point that I should not hide. While I am worried about the wedding night, it is the least of my concerns right now."

"Ana, stop."

"What?"

"You're getting angry at me, so I won't be angry at you. Like you did in NightFall. I'm not angry because you hid. I mean it."

She looks down. "But you have every right to be."

"Ana, no, I don't. You react, having episodes and moments, and dealing with how you need to. Yes, I wish you wouldn't hide. I know sometimes you have to, in order to cope because you can't face it yet. That's why I'm not upset. Now, would you like to have a lesson?"

"Yes, please."

"What do you want to learn about?"

"The Crimson Queen."

"Um, what?"

She laughs. "I mean, what did you grow up hearing? What versions or variations did you know? You said you had heard it as both a legend and a prophecy, but most everyone else said they only heard it as a legend."

"I assume because the legend was about a queen with wings, it is an extremely popular legend amongst the guardians. We grow up learning it. I'll tell you the story the way we hear it. There was a great battle raging, one to take the throne. The queen and her great love rode out together, ready to defend the kingdom.

"She fights with all she has, determined to protect her people. As the battle rages on, she looks over, seeing her love on the field, about to be killed. She runs with all she has, no strength left within her to fight, and she sacrifices herself on him. She is pulled away, left alone to die, when great wings of fire erupt from her back, wrapping around and saving her life."

"So, it's word for word what happened to me."

"Do you want me to tell the story or not?" he asks, winking at her.

"Please continue," she responds while stifling a laugh.

"Hmm. Let's see. She woke up, alone and scared. She walked out onto the battlefield, her wings opening. At the sight of her, every soldier dropped their weapon and knelt before her. She was joined by her great love, and together they brought peace across the realm."

"I hadn't heard that part."

"Which part?"

"That together we would bring peace. Think about it, you went to save Bela, which started peace with NightFall. The prophecy was about you, too. Not only being my great love, but what you've done to help keep the peace. You messaged Bela from MoonFrost, you saved him and me at NightFall. The prophecy is truly about both of us."

Rafe shakes his head. "Wow. I never thought about it like that. I knew the healing soulmate prophecy was."

"Fate wouldn't be so cruel." His jaw drops, and she squeezes his hand. "What? I swear you said that every time you healed me in the beginning."

"You heard that?"

"A couple of times. I didn't know what you meant at first, because I didn't know about the legend. So, wait. You knew about it. Is that why you said you loved me, because you knew you were healing me?"

"Ana, no. First, I didn't know if we were healing each other, because I had healed you, but you hadn't healed me. Secondly, you know how unplanned that was. You said it yourself; I yelled it at you. I was in the moment, listening to you doubt yourself. I had to convince you why you are so important. So, no, it had nothing to do with the legend."

"I'm sorry."

He laughs. "I'm not mad. I probably would've wondered the same thing."

"Any other prophecies I should be aware of?"

"I honestly don't know. I know quite a few of them, but there are literally dozens if not hundreds of books of myths, prophecies, and legends in your libraries."

"Maybe one day next week we can look through them."

"What has you so curious all of a sudden?"

"Please, don't take this the wrong way."

"Okay," he says with confusion written across his expression.

"After what happened in battle, me dying and sprouting wings, I'd like to avoid any more surprises if I can. Like I told you, even if I knew it was going to happen, I would still do it."

"I understand. Yes, we'll look next week." He looks at the clock on the fireplace mantel. "Kara and Evren will be here shortly with lunch. Let's pack while we're waiting on them." He takes her hand, leading her to the closet.

"What should I pack?"

"A little variety. One winter gown, one or two evening gowns, and everyday clothes for going into the market. Of course, any jewelry or accessories, extra shoes and underwear."

"Rafe!" she exclaims as her cheeks turn crimson.

"What? Do you really need that? I don't think you do."

"Jerk!" she says, laughing. He rushes to her, kissing her on her face and neck. "Okay, okay! I submit!" she cries out, laughing and falling into his arms.

"What? You started it," he says, kissing her softly on her lips.

"Oh, love. Thank you."

"For what?"

"Being you," she says as she retrieves her bag. She lays it on the ottoman and packs for the weekend. "When will we leave NightFall to come back? Sunday night or Monday morning?"

"Monday Morning."

"Okay." She looks up when the bell rings.

Rafe steps out to answer the door while she finishes packing. She walks out as the staff leave. Kara and Evren enter. She joins them at their table.

"Are you doing better?" Kara asks.

Rafe nearly drops his fork. "Kara!"

"Crap. I'm sorry. Ana, please don't be mad at Rafe."

Ana smiles at him, then she kisses him. "I'm not mad. It's okay. He was right to tell you, as I shouldn't keep anything from any of you. I was going to talk to you about it next time we had a day together. I'm sorry."

"It's all right. He didn't tell me anything, except it was a bad morning. Anything I can do to help?"

"No, thanks. I'm okay now. Any news on the assassin?"

"Conflicting reports. It's frustrating. Honestly, I'm glad you're getting out of the palace for the weekend, until I can get some actual intel."

"I am, too. I'll miss you, though."

"Oh, sis. I'll miss you, too. At least this should be a fun trip, right?"

"That's what we were talking about. Yes." She laughs. "Oh, Rafe made me eat shark last night."

"Rafe! What is wrong with you?" Kara asks.

"I swear, I didn't know she loves sharks that much! I was only trying to get her to try some of the cuisine from MorningStella."

"I see his point, Ana. Still, the fact that you didn't murder him…"

"Kara! Be nice. He didn't know. It's not his fault."

"Yes, sis."

"Ana, when Kara and I get married, will I also be your sister?" Evren asks. She looks at Kara when she tilts her head and furrows her brows. "What?"

"Yes, Evren," Ana says. "I already consider you my sister. You have been nothing but loyal and wonderful from the moment we met."

"Thank you. I appreciate your praise."

"Evren, can I be honest without offending you?"

"You know you won't offend me."

"Thanks. I tried so hard not to stare at you the first time we met. I was in a new place, and you were the first elf I had ever seen."

"You did stare," Evren says, laughing. "It's okay, though. I knew you had been raised on Earth and that everything here was new to you. I was taken back by how polite and kind you were. Can I ask?"

"Evren, ask anything."

"What happened to you on Earth? I mean, I know you and Kara were separated after she took you. I don't mean the bad stuff, but where did you grow up? Did you have a family?"

"It's all kind of tied in together, good and bad. All I'll say is, I grew up in a small town, which is where Kara found me. I never had a family of my own, until she became my sister. Now, the three of you are my family."

"Thank you, Ana. I consider you as my sister as well." She looks at Rafe. "And you as a big brother."

Rafe smiles at her. "Wow. Thank you, Evren." He looks at Ana. "Are we ready to go? Look, even the sun is out."

"I'll take that as a good omen," Ana says. "Yes, I'm ready. Let me use the washroom." She runs inside.

Kara looks at Rafe. "I am sorry. I swear, I didn't mean to break your confidence. So much going on, with the threat of an assassin, you two leaving the palace, and trying to disband the last of Remus' men, I honestly wasn't thinking."

"Kara, that's twice this week you've slipped. Are you okay? Do you need help? I know Ana worries you are overwhelmed."

"No, I'm fine. Really. Evren is helping, too. It was just my mistake."

"All right. If I can do anything, though, please don't hesitate to ask."

"I appreciate the offer, Rafe. Trust me, helping her is enough."

He looks over when Ana steps out of the washroom. They get their bags together. She hugs Kara and Evren. "We'll see you guys Monday."

Rafe takes her hand, stepping out. Roesh and Aylin pick up their bags, leading them out of the palace. Rafe looks at Ana, smiling. "Ready to fly?"

"Yes!"

"You need to stretch first. Come, I'll stretch with you." He extends his out. She does the same, and they stretch together. They go into the air, heading for NightFall. Rafe holds her hand. "Ana, tell me if you start to get tired or need to rest a bit."

"I promise, I will. Right now? I'm loving every moment of this!"

He smiles as her happiness overwhelms him. He watches

her as they fly. She looks at him, confused. "Ana, I'm loving this as much as you are." She squeezes his hand, smiling at him. They stop long enough to eat a snack and relieve themselves, then head back into the skies. Rafe studies her for a moment. "You don't feel tired, but I want to ask."

"I'm okay, really. We've warmed them up and been working with them. If I start to get tired or hurt, I promise I will let you know."

Chapter 18

Arriving at NightFall, Rafe lowers down with Ana. They approach the gate. "Queen Maeriana is here to visit Count Bela," Rafe says. The doors open, and they are lead inside the city walls.

Guards lead them to the capitol. Ana pushes down memories from before. Once they are inside, Bela and Joph come over to greet them. Bela becomes concerned when Ana practically collapses against Rafe.

"I'm okay," she assures him. "Exhausted from our trip."

"We need to message Kara to let her know we made it safely," he says, glancing a look down at Ana. "Bela, I hate to impose—"

"It's no trouble. I'll see to it."

"Thank you. Please explain to her that Ana overdid it, as usual," Rafe says with anger in his voice, "and had to rest."

"I'll send word while Joph takes you to your quarters. Everything should be as you requested."

"Thank you, Count." He turns to Roesh and Aylin. "Will one of you be standing guard while the other sleeps?"

"I am," Roesh says.

"Rafe, please. Let them both rest. I'm sure Bela could post a guard outside of our quarters. Please?"

He looks at Bela, who nods. "Yes, that is fine. Roesh and Aylin, go to your quarters for the night. We'll see you in the morning."

Aylin smiles at Ana, nodding. "Thank you," she mouths, as they are led down the corridor. Ana smiles back.

"Now to our quarters, please," Rafe says. He holds Ana close, following Joph.

Nothing is said as they walk down the corridor. Once they

arrive, Joph opens the door and gestures them inside, while he hangs back.

"Breakfast will be here at eight. We thought you might like a quiet breakfast in before starting everything. We will be here at nine to escort you through the quadrant. Is that all right?"

"That is wonderful. Thank you, Joph," Ana says. "Have a good night."

"Until the morrow."

Ana takes her bag to the dresser and sets it down. She stands there, wrapping her arms around herself and fighting down the tears. Rafe gently grips her shoulder, causing her to jump.

"What's wrong?"

"You were so angry at me, and—"

"No. I was angry at myself. I am your trainer. Even if you weren't tired yet, I should've made you rest. I swear, I am not angry at you."

"Your voice was so thick with it when you were talking to Bela."

"I'm sorry. I never meant to scare or upset you! Please, mia estrela. What can I do? What do you need?"

She shakes her head. "I love this room, it's beautiful. But right now, I really need a shower, and I know we can't do that."

"Come here," Rafe says, taking her hand and leading her into the washroom. She gasps at the sight of the shower built into the corner. "You like it?"

"This is what you and Bela talked about?"

"Yes. I explained to him that you have moments, but that a hot shower is a coping tool for you. He was very happy to oblige."

"Thank you, love!" She leans up, kissing him. "Oh, what did I do to deserve someone as thoughtful as you?"

His eyes go down. "I wasn't just now."

"Rafe, no. It's okay. There are times I honestly forget we can feel each other, too. It happens. Help me clean up and into bed?”

“Yes, Majesty.”

Laughing, she enters with him. He starts the water while they undress. He goes to the linen closet to find fresh cloths and towels for them. They clean up, then step into the bedroom. She retrieves her pajamas from her bag. He carries her to bed, holding her close.

“Thank you,” she says, planting a soft kiss on his mouth.
“For what?”

She smiles at him. “Being wonderful.”

“Ana, I told you. It’s what you deserve. You deserve all of the love, warmth, comfort, and kindness. I don’t ever want you to doubt our love, but instead to be so overwhelmed you never need to.”

“Thank you.” She yawns while snuggling into his chest. “For everything.”

“I love you, my warrior queen.”

She giggles. “I love you, too, guardian of my heart.”

“Ana, I don’t know what to say to that.”

“Do you like it?”

“Of course!” He kisses her softly. “Now, sleep.”

“Yes, love.”

***

Ana wakes up to the first rays of sunlight. Her gaze falls on Rafe as he opens his eyes. She kisses him softly, murmuring a sleepy “Morning, Guardian.”

He laughs, returning her kiss. “Morning, Majesty. What do you need? It is my pleasure to serve.”

“Rafe!” she says, crawling up and kissing him. “Hmm.” She closes her eyes, kissing him and thinking of being in the air in their quarters. “How’s that?”

“Shower, now.”

"Really? We're on our romantic getaway. That doesn't sound very romantic to me," she says, teasing his waistline with her fingers.

"My apologies, Majesty. I can't help that you got me… excited."

"Oh, my… Rafe!"

He sits up, pulling her with him and kissing her softly, at first. His kiss grows in intensity as he holds her tighter.

"What do you want?"

She smiles at him. "All of you."

Wrapping her arms and legs around him, she kisses his face and jawline. He lowers his head to the crook of her neck, trailing soft kisses to her mouth.

"Ana, how do you feel? I'm sorry. I should've asked that first thing. After flying so much yesterday."

"Love, I know you can feel me. I'm okay. I needed rest and a chance to recover." She brings her mouth to his ear. "And I am fully recovered and ready for you."

Picking her up, he carries her into the washroom. With his eyes fixed on her, he starts the shower. She walks up to him, nodding, and kisses him. As she undresses him, he helps her out of her pajamas with a smile. He leads her into the shower. Gazing up at him, she runs her hand across his chest and stomach.

"God, you're perfect," she says, looking at his chest then meeting his gaze. "What? You are!"

He laughs, pulling her to him. "So are you. In every way, inside and out. Every piece of you, every heartbeat, every breath, is perfect." He feels her trembling in his arms. "Ana, happy tears?"

"Yes, love, but I'm sorry."

"For what?"

"I am still tired. I didn't feel like this in bed."

"Let's get cleaned up and dressed. We'll have breakfast then tour the quadrant. I wasn't thinking this morning, we have a lot of walking to do. Best to save our strength."

"Yes, love."

They wash and step out. She braids her hair, pulling it up and pinning it. She looks at Rafe.

"Is it okay?"

"It's perfect, like you." His response elicits a quiet giggle from her. "What? You know you are."

"Rafe, please—"

"What?"

With a shake of her head, she steps out. She retrieves a pale pink gown from her bag and puts it on. She adds silver shoes with a matching crown, which she pins into her braids.

Rafe steps out, getting dressed in black slacks and a button up shirt with a charcoal vest. He strides towards her, checking her out.

"What's wrong?"

"You are too beautiful. What am I going to do?"

She smiles as he leans down and kisses her. "Thank you."

"Now, let's stretch our wings, then breakfast should be here shortly."

"Yes, love." She opens her wings, crying out and flinching. Rafe runs to her.

"What's wrong? Are you hurt?"

"Give me a moment, please. I'm not sure." She furls and unfurls them, flinching again, as the tightness begins to ease. "I'm okay. I think they were tight from being used so much yesterday." She puts her hand on his arm, as she stretches them again. "See? No pain now."

He gently turns her, massaging her neck and back along her wings. "Yes, they are. Here," he says, continuing to work through the taut muscles. "Better?"

"Yes. Thank you. I'm sorry. I swear, they didn't hurt until I opened them!"

"Ana, it's okay. I know." He watches her head go down. "What?"

"Are we… Can we still fly home?"

"Of course. We may stop to rest a little longer."

She turns to him and her eyes meet his. "Oh, no. Not the sleeping bag?" she teases. She laughs when he blushes. She caresses his face. "I guess that will be okay."

He kisses her while gently stroking through her wings. She grabs him, kissing him hard.

"Ana, right now, you need—"

"I need you," she says, breathless from his kiss. "Please?"

Carrying her, he goes to the bed and lays her across the duvet. After climbing on beside her, he lifts her gown. His hand teases her thigh and hip. She shudders as he caresses the fabric of her undergarment.

He kisses her as he continues, trembling as she reacts to him. Teasing again, he slows down, while she writhes under his hand. With wide eyes, she glances at him, panting for air while he builds up speed. He cries out as she is overcome. He lies beside her while they catch their breath.

"How was that, Majesty?"

"It really is your pleasure to serve, isn't it?"

He laughs as he sits up. "Yes, it is."

She sits up with him. "How bad is my hair?"

"Here." He fixes a loose strand, then he readjusts her crown. "Perfect."

She crawls up to him, kissing him. "Thank you, love. So were you."

"I need to use the washroom. Be right out."

He runs inside and shuts the door. A knock makes her look up. Opening the door, she finds a vampyra woman she doesn't know, carrying a breakfast tray. She gestures for her to come inside, and Aylin walks in with her. Breakfast is set up on the small table, then they leave. Ana sits down, waiting for Rafe, who steps out a moment later.

"Oh, good. Breakfast." He joins her.

"I'm not sure what some of this is, but it looks good."

They eat every bite, impressed at how good it all is. She takes a sip of her steaming drink and smiles at Rafe.

"Bela remembered my cocoa."

"He is a good friend. I'm glad we have him and Joph."

"So do I. I'm excited to tour the quadrant and meet more of his people."

"I wonder what else he has planned while we're here?"

Ana realizes it's almost nine o'clock. "They'll be here soon. We can ask." She stands so she can stretch her wings. She notices the worry on Rafe's face. "See? All good now. They were a little tight." Looking up, she sees how low the ceilings in their quarters are. "I'll need to fly a bit and warm up over the weekend before the return trip. I wonder where we can do that? Or will we have to go outside?"

"We'll ask Bela. I'm sure he knows of somewhere. It would be a good idea for both of us to stretch."

She walks to the door, opening it and seeing Roesh and Aylin outside. "Aylin, could I see you for a moment?"

"Yes, Majesty." She walks inside as Rafe steps out to give them privacy. "Is something the matter?"

"No, not with me. I'd forgotten you had been brought here. I did not think of that when I requested you and Roesh. Are you okay to be here?"

"Yes, Majesty. I was unconscious for most of it. There are no bad memories for me here. If I may, these were our days off—"

"Aylin, I'm so sorry."

"No, please, Majesty. As I was saying, even though these were our days off, we wanted to come here, hoping for a little time to ourselves as well. I had a feeling you would do that," she laughs, "like last night. So, thank you."

"Of course." She looks up as Rafe walks in.

"Bela and Joph are here."

"Thank you, love. We're finished talking."

She steps out with Aylin, who resumes her post with

Roesh, following behind. Ana takes Rafe's hand as they follow Bela and Joph.

In the market, they go to different vendors, with Ana trying to buy a little something from each one. Rafe laughs, as Bela instructs each vendor where to bring the purchases later. Around eleven, Ana gets hungry.

"Bela, is there somewhere to eat nearby? I'm ready for lunch."

"Of course. We have a nice eatery nearby. We'll go in for a rest."

"Thank you."

They follow him in. Ana looks at Rafe in amazement. "They have a restaurant?"

Bela shakes his head as his brow furrows. "I don't know this word, restaurant."

"My apologies, Bela. On Earth, it's a place similar this."

A hostess walks up to them and nearly drops the menus at the sight of Ana. "Majesty," she manages while bowing. "Welcome."

"Thank you."

"This way, please." She leads them to a round table in the back.

"Could Aylin and Roesh sit over there?" she asks Rafe, pointing at a table for two next to where they will be sitting.

"Yes, if they want to."

"Thank you, Majesty," Aylin says.

Ana smiles at Rafe. "I know they are on duty, but I want them to have time to celebrate their engagement."

"Of course. It's fine."

They sit at their table. Ana scans through the menu, finally looking at Bela. "I apologize, as I haven't learned all of your cuisine names yet."

"It's no trouble. With your permission, shall I order for you?"

"Thank you, Bela."

"You're most welcome. Oh, do you and Rafe have fancy attire for this evening? I'm so sorry, I know it's last moment."

"Bela, what do you have planned?"

"It's a surprise. An engagement gift for you both. If you don't have clothing for it, we can go to the merchant next."

"Can Aylin and Roesh dress up as well?"

Rafe sighs. "Ana, I know they are celebrating, but they are still on duty."

Ana laughs while pinching his arm. "Are you telling me she can't protect me while wearing a gown?"

He hangs his head, laughing as he relents. "You're right. Yes, Bela, we'll go there next."

The server approaches to take everyone's order. She bows before walking away. Ana turns to Bela. "I think she's nervous I'm here. Is it because of my wings or that I am Queen? Or both?"

Bela chuckles. "Probably both, if I'm being honest."

"That is all you have ever been to me, Bela. I can always count on you for that. It means a lot to me." She sees a look of regret flash across his face. "Count, what's wrong?"

"Hmm. I have carried this for a while, but I didn't want to tell you."

"What do you mean?"

"Rafe rescued me from NightFall, from execution. I showed him the guardians, helped free them. Then they marched on you to reclaim me, for revenge for helping you."

"I don't understand?"

"You died in that battle and grew your wings."

"Bela, do you blame yourself for what I became?"

"They were coming because of me."

"It's not your fault. It was fate. It was prophecy. It

happened for a reason, and believe me, nothing was going to stop it. What happened wasn't anyone's fault. Why have you carried this so long?"

"I know it was prophecy, still I blame myself."

"Bela, don't. Whether it was that battle or another, it was going to happen to me either way. Is that why you asked about my wings? You usually aren't so forward with me."

"It is. I was afraid of how they made you feel, afraid they were hurting you. I didn't want that."

Rafe looks at Joph, seeing he's just as surprised. "Bela, as Ana said, this was prophecy. We had scouts out, gathering intel. Nothing could change it from happening."

"Yes, Rafe. Thank you."

"Bela, I'm sorry you carried this. Why didn't you tell me this sooner?"

"Watching you struggle with what you've become, hearing you talk of the pain from your wings, my shame was too great."

"Bela! Oh, I'm so sorry. You never should've felt that in the first place. None of us knew what would happen. If it is because of you, I should be thanking you. I love who I am and how I am. It made me and Rafe more alike, bringing us closer, and gave me immortality to be with him. So, if you still think it was because of you, then accept my thanks for it."

"You are always most gracious with us. Thank you for your patience and kindness. We do not deserve it."

"I told you, I do not give my friendship or trust easily. You and Joph have earned your place among us. I assure you." They look up as their meals are brought out. Ana looks at her plate, smiling at everything she sees. She gasps when cocoa is put in front of her. "Bela, thank you."

"You are most welcome." He looks at Rafe. "Did she like the new shower?"

Rafe nearly chokes on his drink. He swallows hard. "Yes, thank you."

"Bela, that was too much."

"Ana, I didn't mean to offend—"

"Oh, no! No, sorry. I meant, having that put in the washroom for me. I greatly appreciate it. I hope it didn't put you out."

"Not at all."

Ana eats every bite, enjoying her meal and cocoa. "This is really nice. It takes me back to Earth. Kara would like this."

"We'll have to bring her and Evren sometime." He faces Bela. "Would that be all right?"

"Of course. Evren may feel a little self-conscious though, as we don't see many elves here."

"Understandable."

Ana looks up when Aylin steps up beside her. "Is everything all right?"

"Yes, Majesty. The server asked if we wanted a cocoa trifle? I don't know what that is. I didn't wish to look ignorant in front of her."

"It's a dessert, with layers of chocolate cake and fruit. You and Roesh get whatever you want, I insist."

"Thank you, Majesty." She returns to Roesh.

"Personally, I don't have room for dessert," Ana says, looking at Rafe. "You?"

"Oh, no."

Bela gestures for the server to come to them. "We are finished."

"Yes, Count." She hands him a slip of paper and walks away. Rafe gets out Ana's purse, when Bela stops him.

"Rafe, you all are our guests. This is on us."

"Count—"

"Ana, I insist. Your guardians, as well."

"In that case, thank you, Bela. Everything was delicious."

"I'm glad you liked it."

"You never thought you would see me eat like this, did you?" Ana asks Rafe.

"Not after watching you push your food around so

much." He leans down, kissing her. He pulls back, then he looks at Bela. "My apologies, Count."

"Quite all right. Now, shall we head to the clothing merchant?"

"Yes."

She stands as Roesh and Aylin join them. Rafe takes her hand, walking out and following Bela to the shop. Ana turns to Roesh and Aylin.

"The count has invited us to a formal event this evening. You and Roesh need to get appropriate clothing for it. Aylin, will you accompany me while Roesh and Rafe look?"

"Yes, Majesty."

They go inside. Aylin and Ana go to the gown side, looking through various dresses while Roesh and Rafe look at tuxes. Ana pulls out a gown, then examines the back.

"Oh."

"Majesty, is something the matter?"

"Our wings. I don't know if they can work with that." She looks up as a beautiful vampyra woman walks in. Her black hair is wrapped in braids while she's dressed in a long black gown with silver accents.

"Hello, Majesty," she says, bowing. "I am Sadira. How may I serve?"

"We need formal gowns for this evening."

"Ah, yes. The count mentioned you might be stopping by. Please, peruse at your leisure, and let me know how I can assist."

"I apologize, as I do not intend to offend you. Our wings—"

"Majesty, it is no trouble."

"Thank you, Sadira."

Aylin and Ana continue looking. Ana picks out a crimson gown, off shoulder with a tight bodice, billowing skirt, and draped with rose lace from the shoulders down. She holds it up to show Aylin.

"Oh, Majesty. That is exquisite! If I may, that will look beautiful with your wings."

"Thank you, Aylin."

Aylin lifts up a long-sleeve silver gown, V-neck and tight bodice, with billowing skirt. She shows Ana. "What do you think?"

"That is perfect for you! The contrast of silver with black will look fantastic."

"Thank you." They hand the gowns to Sadira.

"I will have these mended momentarily." She steps into a small room.

"Do you know why we are dressing up, Majesty?"

"I don't. Bela said it's a surprise."

"Okay. I'm sure Rafe is over there interrogating him." Ana's expression darkens, and she notices. "What's wrong?" Aylin asks as everyone walks in.

"Apologies, Aylin. Memories from before. You sure you're okay here?"

She glances at Roesh, then back to Ana. "I'm fine."

Roesh takes her hand. "Aylin, what is she talking about?"

"She's worried about me, from when I was brought here. I told you, I was unconscious for most of it and don't remember much."

"Some crazy scientist experimented on you. I see why she's worried."

Joph steps forward. "I never did a single experiment. I took some blood samples, that was all."

Roesh turns to Joph. "It was you?" His hand flies to his hilt.

"Roesh, I command you to stand down!" Ana cries out. "Listen to him."

Reluctantly, he faces Joph. "Go ahead."

"I lied to the council, fudging numbers and pretending to do what they asked. I respect the guardians far too much to ever hurt you. I give you my word, I never experimented."

Roesh looks at Rafe, who nods. "I believe you, Joph. Both Ana and I do. You are a good man. You've never done wrong by us. Roesh, he saved you when we came after Remus."

Roesh removes his hand from his hilt, his posture easing. "My apologies, everyone."

Bela steps up to him. "Quite all right. If I was in the same room with someone I thought hurt the person I love, I would react the same way."

"Roesh, are you okay to be here? You and Aylin could return to the palace if you need to. Rafe and I would be fine with Bela's guards."

"I am ready to serve and perform my duties. Though I must confess, I am a bit embarrassed now."

"No, Roesh. It's all right. Why don't you and Rafe step out for some fresh air? We have to try our gowns on, once they are mended for us."

Rafe puts his hand on Roesh's shoulder. "Come on." They exit the shop.

Aylin looks at Ana. "Your Majesty, I am so sorry."

"Not necessary. It's okay. I had a similar reaction not too long ago, myself. Almost cost an innocent man his life." They look up as Sadira returns with their gowns. Aylin helps Ana into hers, then gets her own gown on. They step out, walking up to the mirrors. "I was right, Aylin. That gown is perfect on you."

"Thank you, Majesty. Yours is beautiful."

They extend their wings, feeling the openings and making sure everything fits just right. "Mine fits perfectly."

"As does mine."

They change back, handing the gowns to Sadira. Ana steps outside. "Love, I need my purse."

"Of course."

Bela stops him. "No, Ana. This is on us. Sadira knows to send me the bill, for everything."

"Bela—"

"We put you on the spot last minute, and we are

celebrating your betrothal. I insist."

"Thank you, Count. We are excited about tonight." She steps back in. Sadira hands them their gowns, now in garment bags.

"Thank you, ladies, for coming here. You are most welcome any time."

They give their thanks and step out. Rafe takes the garment bag, draping it over his. "Are we heading back, Bela?"

"Yes." He looks at Ana. "After you drop off your purchases, I would like to take you on a tour of the Citadel."

"That would be fine." Ana lowers her gaze while she clasps her hands. "But not the sublevel, though. Right?"

"No, Ana."

"Thank you."

They drop off their bags and freshen up. Ana uses the washroom, then steps out. Rafe is drinking some water while watching the fire. She walks up beside him.

"Are you having a good time?"

"I am," he says, "other than what happened at the store."

"I thought Roesh knew all of this. Otherwise, I wouldn't have said anything."

"You are concerned with how she is, but how are you? You mentioned the sublevel to Bela. Are memories trying to push up?"

"No," she says. "They already are."

"Ana, we can tell Bela you need a break."

"I'm all right. Walking around and learning about everything will help take my mind off things."

"Okay." He takes her hand. They step into the hall, where everyone is waiting. "All right, Count. Where to?"

"Follow me."

Aylin steps back, next to Ana. "Majesty, did the count pay for our meal and clothes?"

"Yes, Aylin."

"Thank you." She walks up, moving next to Bela. "Count, thank you for everything for today. Roesh and I truly appreciate it."

"It's my pleasure."

He takes them around and shows them meeting rooms, studies, and the library. Looking at the books, Ana is most curious about what their literature is like.

"Count, may I?"

"Yes, Ana. You can look at any book you want."

"Thank you."

She notices Aylin looking as well. Ana studies history books. A book titled *Maristellar Prophecies* catches her eye. She comes upon the prophecies she knows, with the healing soulmates and the Crimson Queen. A prophecy foretells the Crimson Queen's battle to save her throne and the fate of the galaxy. Sitting down, she slowly reads it. Rafe joins her.

"What did you find?"

She shows him the cover, crying out when he takes the book from her. "What are you doing?"

"Ana, I thought you learned your lesson after what happened with Kara. You do not need to be reading this right now. We have this book in our library. We will go through these next week."

"I know, but I want to—"

"What do you want?" he snaps.

Her skin grows warm as the anger rises in her. "Count, I need fresh air."

Bela helps her to her feet. "Come with me."

"We'll be back. Stay here!" she commands Rafe.

"Ana—" He stops when he sees the pained look on her face. "Yes, Majesty."

Bela takes Ana out into the corridor, then to a balcony.

She steps out, letting the air cool her warm skin.

"My apologies, Bela."

"Is everything all right?"

"There are so many stories, legends, and prophecies about the Crimson Queen. I get overwhelmed sometimes. Rafe didn't want me to read about them here. I know he was trying to protect me, but it made me angry."

"I can understand."

She turns to him. "I need to stretch my wings today and have some warm-up before we fly home Monday. Where would you recommend Rafe and I do that?"

"We have a training room. The ceiling is over forty feet high, and the room itself is quite large."

"That would work. If it's not imposing?"

"Ana, it's not. Let me or a guard know, and we'll escort you there."

"Thank you. I feel better now. Let's go back inside."

He takes her to the library. She takes Rafe's hand and walks with him to the back wall for privacy. "I'm sorry. I know you were worried. I didn't mean to get so upset." She lowers her gaze.

"It's okay," Rafe says, gently raising her head. He leans forward and kisses her. "I should've talked to you, instead of taking the book away. I'm sorry, too."

"Thank you. Bela said they have a training room we should be able to fly in. Do we want to before dinner?"

"Yes, that would be fine." They walk back over. "Bela, was there anywhere else you wanted to show us?"

"Not at the moment."

"Could we go to the training room?"

"Of course. Come on." They follow through the corridor, going towards the back of the building. He opens the doors. They step inside, looking at the massive training room. "Well?"

"Count, this is perfect! Thank you," Ana says, walking around.

"Aylin, Roesh, if you will stand guard outside. Ana and I are having flying lessons." Rafe watches them go out. He turns to Bela. "Thank you."

"Please, help yourselves. Dinner will be at five. Is our banquet room okay?"

"Yes, Bela," Ana answers.

"Then your event is at eight. There will be a guard outside your quarters shortly before then to escort you there."

"Yes, Bela. We will see you at five for dinner."

Bela takes Joph's hand, "Come along, Joph. Let them have privacy."

Ana turns to Rafe, laughing. "I think Joph was sure he was going to watch."

"He is fascinated by you." He gently strokes through her feathers. "Are you ready to work them?"

"Yes, love."

She extends her wings to their full span. With excitement for the workout, she gazes at the high ceiling. She takes flight, and her laughter echoes the room as he gives chase.

"Ana, we need to not overdo it."

She lowers down and waits for him. "You're right," she says. "I'm not upset. I know we do." She takes him in her arms, kissing him. "But I do need to get cleaned up now."

He smiles at her. "Does Her Majesty need a shower?"

"Yes, please."

They step out. Rafe instructs Roesh they are returning to their quarters. "While Ana and I take it easy, why don't you two get some rest as well? You can meet us here at five to escort us to the banquet room."

"Thank you, Rafe," Aylin says.

They arrive at the quarters. Roesh checks inside, then gestures them in.

"We'll see you at five," she says, taking Roesh's hand as they walk off.

Rafe escorts Ana in. From her bag, she takes out clean

clothes to wear to dinner. Placing them on the bed, she approaches Rafe. Smiling, she opens her wings. He returns the smile, as his hand ruffles through them. He traces the space between as she bites her lip. Pulling her close, he kisses her while he continues.

She looks at him. "I know you want me to take it easy."

"Ana, we will do whatever you want."

She grabs the back of his head as her mouth crashes on his, devouring him. She unbuttons his shirt, tossing it to the side. "Rafe, I need to get my crown off," she says, as he's undoing her gown.

She moves back, entering the bathroom. Taking off the crown, she places it inside her bag. She unties the braids and allows her hair to fall freely. She gathers her hair and forms a casual bun. Stepping out, she walks up to him. With a smile, he removes her corset and allows it to drop to the ground. His hand caresses along her stomach.

Her lips are pressed against his while her hands are on his belt. Removing it, she unbuttons his pants. He slides down his shorts, then steps out, leaving them behind. He brings down her undergarments, then removes them. Scooping her into his arms, he takes her to the bed. His hand caresses along her thigh as her hand is slowly working around him.

As she teases him, he inhales sharply. She bends down over him, spreading her legs for him. With each move, he matches her speed and passion, caressing and stroking her. She eases up, mirroring his pace, and then playfully taunts him. His touch sends shivers down her spine, causing her to writhe and tremble.

"Rafe!" she cries out, shuddering. "Oh!"

He looks up at her, smiling. "Yes?"

"Oh, you're mean!" She leans down, kissing him, as he submits to her demands. She cries out again, collapsing on him as they both give in to the waves overtaking them. "Thank you, love."

"Mia estrela, you are absolutely incredible. I love every inch of your body. The way you move, the way you make me feel. Every inch of you."

She smiles at him, caressing his face. "Only you can make me feel this way. I have never wanted anyone the way I want you. I have never trusted anyone, the way I trust you. You own every inch of me, inside and out. You own my body, my heart, and my soul. I am completely yours."

"Ready for a shower?"

"Just a shower, right?"

He chuckles. "Yes, mia estrela. Then we can get a short nap before dinner."

"I need that, thanks to you!"

They clean up and slip into pajamas. He carries her to bed and snuggles with her. "Are you enjoying your time here?"

"I am. It's nice being here, visiting with friends."

"You're thinking of MorningStella, aren't you?"

She laughs. "How did you know?"

"I could feel how excited you are. It wasn't hard to guess." He kisses her forehead. "Now, get some rest."

"Yes, love." They fall asleep in each other's arms.

Chapter 19

"Rafe, love. We have to get up."

Hearing the urgency in her voice, he sits up. "What's wrong?"

She laughs. "No. It's almost five! We'll be late to meet with Bela and Joph. I hate being late for them, since they are always punctual."

He picks her up, helps her to her feet, and kisses her. "Then let's get ready."

Reaching into his bag, he pulls out his clothes. She slips on a pale blue gown. Adorned with a silver circlet and shoes, she approaches the full-length mirror behind the washroom door. Checking her appearance, she unfurls her wings.

"Oh, mia estrela. You know what that color does to me, especially with your wings!"

She blushes. "Do I need to change?"

"No. It's okay."

When he hears knocking, he opens the door. Aylin walks in.

"Are you ready to go to dinner?"

"Yes, Aylin. Thank you. Are you and Roesh rested?"

"Yes, Majesty."

They go to the banquet room to find Bela and Joph already there. They make their way to their table.

"Ana, that gown is spectacular."

"Thank you, Bela." Their meals are served. "Our weekend has been so nice already. We are enjoying our time here."

"I'm glad to hear that. I know the past couple times you were here it was… unpleasant. I really hoped this would be better."

"Thank you for letting us use your training room, too. It

was perfect."

"You are most welcome, Rafe."

Ana turns to Joph. "Can I ask you something?" She waits until he nods. "What did the council ask you to do, when you had the guardians? I know they tried to learn the secret of their immortality, but how? What exactly did they want you to do?"

"They wanted me to put them through pain, torture, and whatever else to see how long they would last. Was it something in their skin? Was it in their DNA? What gives them immortality? I tried to outright refuse, but the council took Bela and threatened to kill him, after they found out about us. They used him as a pawn while making me do their dirty work. I wrote up reports, ran blood samples, pretended to do what they asked."

"How did they not know?"

"Simple. They never bothered to come down to the sublevel and see for themselves. My reports were quite detailed and lengthy, trying to hide the fact there was no relevant information. I ran their blood, but I did not know what was behind their immortality." He looks down. "Until I ran yours."

Ana's blood runs cold. "Joph, do I want to know? Because you do not have to tell me. We can go on, pretending this conversation never happened."

"I compared your DNA with the guardians. That is how I knew what was similar and what was different, in trying to identify you. It is hardwired into your DNA, the immortality. I could not find it in the guardians, as though it was hidden away. With you, it was almost a beacon, as though it wanted to be found."

"What does that mean?"

"Ana, you were not just brought here to save your kingdom and end the war. You were brought here to save your people as well. We would have gone extinct within the next few centuries if you had not become the Crimson Queen. Our life span was continuously decreasing. You did not only battle for your kingdom, but you also battled for us, even without knowing you did so."

Rafe studies her face, but he is unable to read her emotion. He takes her hand. "Ana, are you all right?"

"I am. There was time I kept thinking Rafe made a mistake in bringing me here, that I was not meant to be queen. Then I hear of couples being together, peace between the quadrants, and now this. No matter what I tried to tell myself, no matter how hard I fought it, I know now beyond a doubt. This is where I was destined to be. I don't see how I could ever question it again."

Rafe lets out a sigh of relief. "You had me worried."

"I mean it, I'm okay. Joph, you saved your people. You are the one who developed and dispersed the serum."

"I could not have done it without you, Ana. You were key to its creation."

"I'm not saying I wasn't, but give yourself credit, too." She looks at Bela. "Now do you see what I was saying earlier? You have no reason to feel guilty about what happened to me in battle. Rafe is always telling me, everything that has happened, happened for a reason."

"Yes, Ana. You're right." He pulls out the book she was reading in the library. "I looked through this while you and Rafe were resting. I think you and he should look it over, after dinner."

She faces Rafe. "It's your decision. I won't get angry if you don't want to read it with me."

"I'm assuming there's a reason you want us to?" Rafe asks. Bela nods, and Rafe takes the book. "Then we'll look through it."

They finish their meal. Bela smiles at Ana. "A guard will be outside your door a little before eight to bring you and Rafe to tonight's event."

"Yes, Bela. We will see you then," Rafe says, getting to his feet. He gently pulls Ana up.

They walk to Roesh and Aylin, who escort them back to their quarters.

"Around seven, you and Aylin may go to your quarters to get ready for tonight."

"Thank you, Rafe." Roesh walks in, checking their quarters. "All clear."

"Roesh, thanks," Ana says, as Rafe takes her inside. They walk to the small sofa in front of the fireplace. He pulls out the book. She gnaws on her lower lip. "Rafe, we don't have to."

"Bela didn't insist, but I could tell there is something he wants us to see in here. It's okay." He opens it to a bookmarked page. He moves the small satin ribbon and reads a few paragraphs. "Now I see."

She takes the book and reads as well. "Do you believe this?"

"I mean, it's sort of already happened. We can feel each other, feel what we're sending out. So, what's the big deal if we gain the ability to read each other's minds?"

"It doesn't matter. It's simply a book, full of whatever else nonsense," she says, getting to her feet. When she looks at him, her eyes glisten with unshed tears. "You said it yourself, there are so many variations and prophecies and legends. It's all bullshit!"

Rafe stands and walks up to her. He gently runs his hand through her wings. "Not all of it."

She collapses against his chest as tears stream down her face. "I don't want it to be true! I never want you to see or feel what I've endured."

He wipes her tears before planting a soft kiss on her lips. "Ana, it's okay. It may or may not be true. This is why I didn't want you reading this book yet. I didn't want to upset you. Please, mia estrela." She sobs into his chest. He carries her to the bed. He sits down, holding her in his lap. "Ana, it's going to be okay. Do you want to reach out to me and see if you can read me like that?"

"No, please," she begs. "I can't!"

"What if it proves you right?"

"What if it proves me wrong?" she asks, looking up at him. "No."

"All right. Just stay in my arms. Let me hold you. I promise, we won't do anything but sit here."

His love and warmth flow into her. Taking deep breaths, she attempts to calm her racing mind and her pounding heart.

If it comes where he can read my mind, I will end my life. I never want him to feel anything I went through!

She closes her eyes and falls asleep against his chest.

"Oh, mia estrela. Please, don't think like that. I won't lose you," he says, lying down with her.

He wakes up, looks at the clock, and sees it's after seven. "Ana, we need to get up and get ready for Bela."

"Hmm. Okay."

"How do you feel?"

"Better."

Standing up, she grabs her gown and heads to the washroom. As she examines herself in the mirror, she notices her tired expression. At the sink, she splashes cold water onto her face. She changes into the gown. She brushes her hair, putting on a gold crown. While gazing at her engagement ring, she slides on her other ring.

This is my promise, that I am right here. I'm not going anywhere.

Her eyes close as she thinks on Rafe's words.

He means that. He really does. I have to know this, I know it's the truth. I can't question him, question what we have. Not after everything we have been through.

"Ana, are you all right?"

"Yes, love. Almost ready. I'll be right out." Unexpectedly,

she is surprised by how calm her voice sounds.

Looking at her ring once more, she takes a deep breath. Stepping outside, she recalls that night and the sight of the battlement. She was surprised at the Eiffel Tower he had made for her.

The thought makes her smile. The image of him putting the ring box on the table and asking her to be his wife occupies her mind. Filled with happiness and love, she exits the washroom.

"Oh, mia estrela. What a gorgeous gown!"

"Thank you. You always look fantastic in all black."

He walks up, taking her hands and kissing them. "You're okay?"

She nods, smiling up at him. "I am. Because of you. Thank you, for all of your love and patience with me. I'm sorry. I don't know why it upset me so. I'll leave it up to you, whether we continue looking into prophecies or not."

"We don't have to decide anything right now."

"Yes, love." She steps up, kissing him. "Thank you."

"You're welcome. Now, we have a few minutes before we leave. Will you open your wings for me? I would love to see them with your dress."

With a smile, she takes a step back. Her wings unfurl, and her cheeks flush. She gazes into his loving eyes.

"You really like this color on me, don't you?"

"Not as much as Bela," he says, chuckling.

"Rafe! Jealous?" she asks playfully.

"Never," he cries, running up to her and showering her with gentle kisses, laughing as she begs him to stop. "Hmm. I guess you really are okay."

"Oh, love, everything is perfect."

"Especially you." He laughs when she blushes again.

"Thank you. Are you ready to see what Bela has planned?"

"Yes."

He takes her hand, leading her out of their quarters. Roesh

and Aylin greet them. Ana smiles at the sight of them. "You two make such a lovely couple."

"Thank you, Your Majesty," Aylin replies.

They follow Bela's guards. Rafe feels Ana growing nervous. His warm breath brushes over the shell of her ear. "Mia estrela, it's okay. No need for that."

"Yes, Rafe." She takes a deep, calming breath.

They're lead into a ballroom, where tables are set up with fancy linens, two buffets, a drink and dessert table, and hanging lanterns.

"This is beautiful!" Ana looks over as Bela and Joph approach.

"Well, Majesty, what do you think?"

"It's incredible. What is this?"

Bela laughs. "It's my first attempt at hosting a ball. It's in honor of you and Rafe. We will announce it once everyone is here."

"Oh, Bela! Thank you." She runs up and hugs him tight. She pulls back. "I'm sorry. I know affection is not something you prefer."

He lets out a chuckle. "It's quite all right. I will always take a hug from the woman who saved our people. Oh, did you read the book I gave you?" He sees the pained look on her face. "My apologies. Should I not have done that?"

"It's okay. As I said, I seem to get upset reading them." She grins at Joph. "You would probably faint if I came to you and said we could read each other's minds."

Joph laughs. "Yes, Majesty. It would be—"

Bela interrupts. "Please, Joph. Don't say fascinating."

Joph shifts uncomfortably, chuckling. "No, but it is interesting. The fact you can feel what the other feels is worthy of study itself."

"Joph!"

Ana and Rafe laugh. "Bela, he's right. It is a rare gift," she says. She glances around once more. "This is absolutely perfect!

Thank you."

"You and Rafe are most welcome. I'm glad it worked out. Now, follow me, please," he says, leading them to their table. "Do I have your permission to announce your engagement tonight?"

"Yes, Bela."

They sit and watch as the room starts to fill. Ana sees worry on Aylin's face. She leans over to her. "Are you all right?"

"Majesty? Yes, sorry. Feeling a little like the odd one out."

"I understand. How do you think I feel?"

"Right. Of course, everyone wants to stare at the queen. I didn't realize how nerve-wracking it could be for you."

"It's all right. I've learned to live with it."

They look over as Bela stands up. He pulls out a small sound amplifier, welcoming everyone to the ball. "It is with great honor and pleasure, that I get to announce tonight, Queen Maeriana is betrothed to the Guardian Rafe." He pauses as they applaud the news. "Enjoy the evening!" He pockets the amplifier and sits back down. "Well?"

"Very good, Count. Thank you." Rafe takes Ana's hand, leading her over to get food. He smiles when she fills her plate. They sit and eat. She leans up to Rafe. "Their music is so… different from ours."

"Yes, it is. We don't have to dance, if you don't want to."

She looks out, seeing the floor full of vampyra. "No, I don't. Sorry."

He laughs. "It's quite all right." He watches her eat. "I'm thankful you're better, after earlier."

"Embarrassed," she admits, "but better."

"You have no reason to feel that way. After becoming a legend yourself, I can understand your reluctance."

Bela stands up, taking Joph's hand. "We are going to dance. Are you joining us, Ana?"

Before meeting his gaze. Ana forces a smile. "Yes, Bela." She takes Rafe's hand, standing up. He takes her to the dance floor, seeing all eyes are on them. She holds him tight.

"Mia estrela, it's okay. No need to feel nervous. Everyone stopped staring and is focused on dancing." He feels her ease up. "There you are."

"Thank you, love." She sighs in relief when the song ends. They walk over and get some dessert, before returning to their table. She looks at Aylin. "What do you think of their food?"

"Everything is delicious. We've had some of it back at the palace, but I have yet to try anything I didn't like."

"Oh, just so you know. You and Roesh will retire to your quarters tonight. We will have two of Bela's guards posted."

"Majesty, thank you. Even though we are on duty, this has been a nice little trip. It means a lot to me, so thank you."

"Aylin, you are very welcome. In case we don't get to speak again until tomorrow, we will see you at your post at eight tomorrow morning."

"Yes, Majesty."

Ana turns to Rafe. "So how early can we leave without being rude?"

He bursts into laughter. "Ana!"

"I'm sorry. I am still tired from earlier."

"I see that. Hmm. We'll stay a little longer."

"I know. He put a lot of work into this." Bela and Joph join them. "Bela, everything is perfect. I would've thought this was something you had done many times before!"

"Thank you, Majesty. Kara was a lot of help."

"Really?"

"Oh, yes."

She looks at Rafe. "On top of everything else, she was doing this and keeping it a secret? I know she's getting married soon, but when we get back, I think she needs a little vacation."

"I could not agree more." Rafe looks at Bela. "We will head back shortly. She needs her rest."

"Oh, of course! I understand. Are we doing breakfast, or shall we have it sent to your room?"

"Could we have it in our quarters, then we'll join you for lunch? Is that all right?"

"Of course, Ana." He chuckles when she tries to stifle a yawn. "Please, Majesty. You can go on. You won't hurt my feelings, I promise."

"I'm sorry."

"Quite all right."

"Thank you for such a wonderful day."

Two of his guards walk up to escort them. Ana takes Rafe's hand, and she sees the confusion on his face.

"Aylin and Roesh need some time, too."

"Right," he says. "I forget they are celebrating, as well."

They go into their chambers. He looks everything over and checks the washroom. He looks confused when she laughs.

"What?"

"You will always be my guardian, won't you?"

"Yes, Your Majesty," he says, bowing.

"Rafe!" She laughs, falling into his arms. She kisses him. "I need cleaned up and to go to sleep."

"Then that's what we'll do, mi'lady," he says, taking her hand and kissing it.

She smiles as she walks to her bag and pulls out clean clothes. They step into the washroom. She removes her crown, brushes her hair, then undresses.

She steps into the shower, washing her hair when Rafe joins her. He lathers up the soap and cleans her off. She steps out and dries as he finishes cleaning up. She relieves herself and brushes her teeth before returning to the main chamber.

He leaves the washroom, walking to her on the sofa in front of the fireplace. "Are you all right?"

She smiles up at him. "Waiting for my guardian to escort me."

He returns her smile before picking her up and carrying her to the bed. "Get some sleep, my little warrior."

"Yes, love. Goodnight."

"Goodnight, mia estrela."

She clutches his shirt, falling asleep as his love is overwhelming her. He caresses her hair and face, planting a gentle kiss. He prays she sleeps through the whole night.

Rafe is in the washroom when Ana wakes up. As she turns on the lamp, a shadow descends over her, causing her to cry out. Before she can move, a dagger plunges into her abdomen. Her efforts to turn are in vain as she is stabbed in the chest. Her movement causes her to roll off the bed and land on the floor.

Her skin runs hot and cold, as shock weaves its way through her. She watches the assassin go and wait by the door, hiding out of sight. While she tries to call out for Rafe, her mouth becomes filled with blood. The coppery taste causes her to choke.

Opening the door, he is stabbed twice by the assassin. While falling, he grabs her arm, takes the dagger, and slits her throat.

Ana tries making her way to him, but everything is going dark and numb. She closes her eyes, focusing on turning her wings to fire. As the warmth erupts from her back, her wounds heal. She crawls towards Rafe, praying she makes it in time.

Chapter 20

Ana comes to, seeing it's been almost an hour since the attack. She examines Rafe, opening his shirt and relieved to see his wounds healed.

"Rafe?" She caresses his face. "Love?" Still no response.

Despite falling once, she eventually gets to her feet and walks to the door. As she opens it, her gaze falls on the two murdered guards. She is aware Roesh and Aylin are in the adjacent quarters. Despite exhaustion, she makes her way there. Holding on to the frame for dear life, she knocks on the door.

"Ana!" Aylin cries out at the sight of her.

"I'm okay," she assures her. "We're okay, but we need help. The assassin is dead, so you have time to get dressed before coming to my quarters."

"I'll get Bela," Roesh says as he runs from the room.

Aylin puts her arm around Ana and returns with her to her quarters. "We will attend to you first." She gasps at the sight of Rafe on the floor.

"He'll be all right. We are both healed but exhausted beyond words."

"What can I do?"

"I need cleaned up and dressed, then Rafe will, too. We'll sleep as we recover." She goes to her bag, getting out pants and a shirt. "Will you help me clean up?"

"Yes, Your Majesty."

"Aylin, please. For tonight, call me Ana?"

"Let's get you cleaned up, Ana." She takes her into the washroom. Ana strips out of her bloody clothes. "I'll handle these," Aylin states as she walks out. She tosses them into the fireplace. Kneeling beside Rafe, she carefully inspects him. She returns inside. "Rafe hasn't woken up yet."

"Aylin, are you okay to help me here? I don't want to embarrass you or make you feel uneasy."

"Ana, you won't."

"Thank you," she says, stepping out. She nearly falls into Aylin's arms. "Sorry. The exhaustion is taking over."

"Quite all right." Aylin helps her dry and dress. "What now?"

"Let's step out and see what's going on."

"All right."

Aylin takes her out to see Bela and Roesh are checking Rafe as everything else is getting cleaned up. Bela looks up, seeing Ana. He rushes to her.

"Are you all right?"

"Yes, Bela. We both are. Roesh, can you help get him cleaned up and into bed? We're healed, but we need to rest."

"Your Majesty, I will see to it," Roesh says, helping Rafe to his feet.

Ana grabs his bag and gets him out fresh pajamas. Bela takes them from her and into the washroom. He steps out to give Rafe privacy.

"You need sleep," Aylin says.

"I want to wait for Rafe, please," she pleads in a softened tone.

"He'll be out in a moment."

Ana collapses against her. Lifting her, she carries her to bed and lays her down. Roesh escorts Rafe to bed.

"Do you want to see something?" Bela asks her guardians. Roesh looks at him. "What?"

"Put Rafe in bed, but on the other side, away from her."

"Okay," Roesh says, confused. He does as Bela instructs. They watch in wonder as Rafe and Ana reach for each other, pulling into each other's arms. "What is that?"

"It's because they are soulmates," Bela answers.

Roesh looks at Aylin. "You knew that, didn't you?"

"A little. The queen has kept me in her confidence. I'm

sorry I didn't tell you."

"Aylin, no. You are performing your duty by keeping her secrets. I never want you to feel like you have to tell me anything."

"Yes, Roesh." She turns to Bela. "Will you stay with them while he and I get into uniform?"

"Of course."

"Thank you, Count," Roesh says, taking Aylin's hand and leading her out.

Bela stands by the bed, watching until Joph walks in.

"My apologies."

"I know you have a sick patient. They are healing each other, it's okay."

"What happened?" Joph inquires.

"I don't know the details. An Asarian assassin for sure. I've doubled the guards and am looking into how she got in. Her guardians stepped out to change. They will be back any moment."

Joph walks to the bed, checking Rafe's pulse and lifting his shirt, feeling around. He goes to Ana, checking hers as well and feeling around. "You are correct. They have healed."

"They will need rest today. This always takes it out of them." He looks over as Aylin walks back in.

"Roesh will stand guard outside. I will stay in here, in case they need anything. Is that all right?"

"Yes, Aylin. Call on us if they do."

"Thank you, Count." She gets a chair from the table and brings it to the bed, then she sits down.

Bela and Joph step out. She studies Rafe and Ana, who are peacefully asleep. She watches over them all night.

⁓

"Morning, love."

Rafe nuzzles into the crook of her neck, planting soft kisses. "Morning."

"How do you feel?"

"Oddly enough, recovered and not as tired. Do you know why that is?"

"I had to use my wings of fire."

"Ana!"

"What? I was too hurt to get to you." She glances over when Aylin clears her throat. "Aylin, you stayed here?"

"My apologies, Majesty. Yes, I stayed in here in case you woke up and needed anything. I didn't mean—"

"It's all right, Aylin. Thank you for everything." She pulls tighter to Rafe. "I used my wings to heal, then made my way to you."

"Majesty, what happened?"

"The assassin got me in bed, then waited for Rafe since he was in the washroom. He managed to fight her off and kill her. I was too wounded. She stabbed me twice, once in the abdomen then again in the chest. I tried to warn him, but…" She closes her eyes, still tasting the copper in her mouth.

"But?" Rafe asks.

"My mouth was filling with blood."

"Oh, mia estrela!" He clutches her tightly. "Thank you for saving my life."

"I told you, love. I will always save you."

"Ana, you healed yourself and me. How are you feeling?"

"Like you, not as exhausted as I thought I would be." She looks at Aylin. "I hate to bother you, but would you see about breakfast?"

Aylin stands. "Majesty, it is never a bother. I'll see to it."

"Thank you." She watches Aylin step out. "Rafe, you aren't mad at me, are you? Like before?"

"Ana, no. I wasn't mad that time, either. I gave in to my fear. I swear right now, I'm not mad at you about anything." He leans down, planting a gentle kiss on her lips. "I feel love and gratitude."

She smiles as it flows into her. "I feel it, too."

Aylin steps in. "Breakfast will be here shortly. Roesh and I will eat with you, if you don't mind."

"You know you are always welcome. We'll discuss what we're doing today and go from there."

"Yes, Majesty."

"Aylin, will you help me to the washroom?"

"Ana, I can take you."

She looks up at him. "Yes, love." He helps her up and escorts her in. Blushing, she looks at him.

"Ana, please. It's not a big deal. We're getting married before end of the year, and I assure you, this is something married people do."

"It's not just that," she says quietly.

"Okay. I'll step out."

He leaves and shuts the door behind him. "Thank you," he says to Aylin.

"It was our duty," she says as she approaches him.

"Even, so—"

"Rafe, can you come here please?"

"Excuse me," he says as he walks in. Ana's leaning over the vanity, trying to keep conscious. "What's wrong?"

"I'm dizzy. I feel like I'm going to pass out."

He picks her up, carrying her to bed. "You need food. It will be here any moment. You'll feel better once we eat."

"Yes, love."

Roesh walks in, escorting the staff with breakfast. Everything is set up. Rafe helps Ana to the table. She eats quickly, mumbling an apology when she finishes.

"Ana, you needed that. No need to be embarrassed."

"Do you think Bela has canceled our plans for today? I need to see him, to let him know you and I are recovered."

"No, Ana. You are still recovering. I know this isn't like before, where it would take us all day, but you still need to rest."

"Aylin, would you let Bela know we will join them for lunch?"

"Yes, Majesty," she says, standing and walking out.

Ana looks at Rafe. "It's lunch in the banquet room. I promise, I'll be okay for that." She takes his hand. "See?"

"Hmm. You do feel tired, but not exhausted. You definitely feel better since you've eaten." He looks over, seeing the look on Roesh's face. "Are you okay?"

"Yes, my apologies. Another prophecy? Can you feel what she is feeling?"

"Yes to both."

"We saw a little last night, when you were unconscious and reaching for each other. It was incredible to see."

"We have this pull, this need, to be together always. We can't explain it." He squeezes her hand. "Don't need to, either."

She smiles at him. "Let's not embarrass Roesh."

He chuckles. "Quite all right, Majesty. Aylin and I don't quite have that, but we do like to spend every minute together we can. If I'm being honest, I was a little upset at first that you had requested us, because we were looking forward to our weekend together. Then, coming here, staying in beautiful quarters, and you giving us time to ourselves, I really appreciate what you've done for us."

"I'm glad. I'm sorry we ruined it," she says.

"Majesty, you did not ruin anything. I feel as though I have failed you, as it is our duty to be watching over you."

"Roesh, I am telling you right now. You did not fail me. Rafe will tell you the same." She looks at Rafe, who nods in agreement. "We are alive and safe now. Do not blame yourself."

"Thank you."

Aylin returns. "Bela said he will see you at eleven in the banquet room."

"Thank you for doing that for me."

"Most welcome, Majesty. Roesh and I will resume our

post, unless you need anything else."

"Thank you, both. I am blessed to have you as my guardians."

Aylin blushes. "Thank you. We are honored to serve." She and Roesh step out.

Rafe turns to Ana, caressing her face. "How are your wings?"

"They need to stretch," she says, standing up.

He takes her hand, walking her to the middle of the room. She expands them out, looking up at him. She smiles as she wraps her arms around his neck.

"Ana, you need to rest. We will have lunch, fly a bit, then we will do whatever you want. As long as you take it easy this morning."

She folds into him, touching ever possible inch of him she can. "Love, please."

"Ana, I know. I feel it, too. You need to rest, mia estrela." He pulls her back, looking into her eyes. He scoops her up and takes her to the bed. "This is just about you, while you recover."

"Rafe—"

"No, please. We will have time together later today." His hand trails her waistline. He gently pulls on her pants. She nods, as he slides them off. He continues trailing her undergarment, teasing at first. He smiles as she trembles under him. "Like this?" he asks, kissing her.

"Yes, please," she begs, as her body writhes. He caresses while he kisses her, smiling when she gasps in air. His touch sends shivers through her as she cries, "Love!" Taking his hands, she pulls him down beside her. She holds him close.

"Was that what you needed, mia estrela?"

"Yes," she whispers, panting for air. She catches her breath and calms her heart.

He sits up, pulling her onto his lap. "Now, we need to stretch your wings."

She giggles into his chest. "Yes, love."

"Be right back," he says, laying her on the bed.

He runs to the washroom. She stands up, slipping her pants back up, then waits for him. He steps out and joins her. Her wings extend out.

"How do they feel?"

"Okay. I want to fly back tomorrow, but I think we should stop and rest, or you can carry me for part of it."

"I wanted to ask, but I didn't want to upset you. I was afraid you would think I was doubting you, when you know that's not the case."

"Yes, Rafe. I know."

"You're ready to be outside and really flying, aren't you?"

"Yes. Spring will be here soon. Oh, to go outside and fly in the sun? I'm very excited! It was wonderful to do on the way here." Rafe chuckles, and she tilts her head at him. "What?"

"You, my little warrior. I never expected this. I knew one day you would accept your wings, but I was doubtful you would ever love them like I do."

"Rafe, I don't know if anyone loves their wings as much as you do."

"How dare you?" he asks, grabbing her face and planting kisses. "Do you take it back?"

"No!" she says with defiance, laughing as he kisses her again.

"Submit, or it'll only grow!"

"I'll never submit!" she says, laughing harder as he kisses her face and neck. She grabs him to her, kissing him hard. She jumps up, wrapping her legs around his waist, her arms around his neck. "Rafe, please, love."

"Ana, you need to rest! You feel like you're going to pass out in my arms. Please, lay down?"

"Yes, love."

He places her on the bed. They lay together, and he laces his fingers with hers. "Sleep. I'll be right here when you wake up."

"I'm not tired!" she argues while stifling a yawn.

"Where do you get this stubborn streak?" he asks, a chuckle escaping his lips. "Go to sleep."

"Yes, love."

⸺⸺⸺ ❧ ⸺⸺⸺

He wakes her at ten-thirty to get ready for lunch. "How do you feel?"

"Much better. Are we going to lunch?"

"Yes."

Getting up, she heads towards her bag. No gown catches her eye as something she would wear. She goes to the dresser, pulling out a short sleeve navy-blue gown. As she holds it up, she notices that it ends right below the knees. It features a corset and lace sleeves, with lace draping down the back, nearly reaching the feet. She looks at Rafe.

"Um, am I allowed to wear a dress this short?"

He turns to her, swallowing hard at the sight. "Well, but I mean—"

"Rafe, not your permission," she clarifies while laughing.

"I don't know all of the customs for your gowns."

"You know what? It's fine. We're on vacation." She removes her pajamas and slips the gown on. She laughs when his eyes go wide. "Do I need to change?"

"No, Ana. I'm not used to seeing you in something like that." He slips on his black pants and charcoal shirt.

She puts on silver shoes and a crown, as he slips into his black dress shoes. "I hope Bela still wants to do something today."

"We'll discuss it with him. He's probably not used to you recovering this quickly."

"Of course."

She takes his hand as they step out. "Banquet room," Rafe

instructs.

They follow Aylin and Roesh. Aylin looks back at Ana's gown.

"Aylin?"

"Majesty, I apologize. I'm not used to seeing a gown that short."

"The vampyra fashion is a little different from ours. I don't know that I would ever wear this at the palace, but I figured since we are on vacation…"

Aylin laughs. "It looks fantastic on you."

"Thank you."

Chapter 21

They go into the banquet room. Bela and Joph stand at the sight of them. Bela admires her gown. "Ana, you look wonderful."

"Thank you, Count. It's a beautiful dress. What are we doing after lunch?"

"Do you need to rest?"

"No, I used my wings of fire this time. Rafe and I are already recovered."

"Fascinating!" Joph exclaims, hanging his head when Bela shoots him a sharp look. "My apologies, Majesty."

"Bela, Joph, please, stop this. Neither of you are going to embarrass me or Rafe. Bela, please let Joph express himself with us. I truly mean that."

"Yes, Ana. Would you like to go back into the village? See more shops?"

"Your shops are open on Sundays?"

"Oh, yes."

She looks at Rafe. "Could we?"

"Yes, mia estrela." He looks at Bela. "Do you have a jewelry vendor?"

"We do."

"We'd like to go there." He sees the smile on Ana's face.

They eat their meal, then head for the village. Bela leads them to the jewelry vendor. Rafe takes Ana inside, followed by Bela and Joph. Roesh and Aylin stay outside at their post. Ana walks up to the counter, trying not to be overwhelmed from the last jewelry store encounter. She pushes it down, admiring the rings instead.

"Wow. These stones are like nothing I have ever seen!"

He walks up beside her and looks at the various rings. "I

see that. We're looking at bands, right?"

"Yes, love."

"Ana, we can look at whatever you want." He leans down, kissing her. He pulls away when someone clears their throat. A female vampyra steps up behind the counter. "Our apologies."

She smiles at him. "Quite all right. Welcome." She realizes who Ana is. She steps back and bows. "Majesty. I am Eirian. How may I help you today?"

"We would like to look at wedding bands." She sees the confusion on her face. "I apologize. I was raised on Earth, where they are a tradition. We are getting married this year and would like matching bands."

"We can do that. It would be our honor. Follow me." They walk over to another counter. "Here are some various bands."

She pulls out the display case, laying it on the counter. Ana looks them over, seeing a white gold band with star and moon etchings. She looks up at Eirian, who nods. She takes the band out, showing it to Rafe.

"What about this?"

"It's beautiful, but do you want a simple band or something with stones in it? I'm fine with either."

"Oh, I'm not sure."

"That's why we're looking, mia estrela."

"Yes, love." She puts the band back in. She sees Eirian staring at her engagement ring.

"Majesty, is that—"

"It is," Rafe says.

"Where in the world did you find one?" she asks.

He laughs. "I know the right people." He faces Ana. "If we have matching bands, what will become of your engagement ring?"

She smiles at him as she slips it off, moving it to her right hand. "Like this?" she asks with a smile.

"I see."

Once more, she examines the rings and notices a white gold band with petite star-shaped diamonds set flush. She lifts it up and tries it on.

"Wow, this is absolutely stunning!"

Rafe looks at the band, seeing a similar one with moons. He picks it up, showing it to her. "We could match with these."

"Oh, Rafe. I love that!"

They go over sizes with the vendor. "I can have these made and delivered to you by Friday. Is that all right?"

"Yes," Ana answers.

Rafe pays for them. He walks back, taking her hand and leaving the shop.

"Where next?" Bela asks.

"Shall we walk the market again? Meet more of your people?"

"That is fine."

They walk into the market, seeing the looks of surprise on people's faces when they realize the queen is walking amongst them. A sweets vendor catches Ana's eye.

"Could we see this booth?" she asks Bela.

"Yes, Ana."

At the booth, Bela points at each piece and explains their flavors. Rafe purchases various sweets for Ana. They walk around some more. Holding Ana's hand, Rafe feels her exhaustion.

"We need to head back. I feel how tired you are getting."

"Rafe, I want to stay."

"Please, don't argue. Bela says we are welcome any time. We'll come again in the spring, when the weather is nice."

"Yes, love." She looks at Bela. "My apologies."

"After what you survived, no apologies are needed. We'll head back. Do you feel up to dining with us this evening?"

"Yes, Bela. We'll get some rest then join you."

⁘

Ana looks at Rafe as he locks the door inside their quarters. "What?" he asks when he see her gnawing on her lower lip.

"Do I want to know how much the rings cost?"

"No," he responds, a little quicker than he meant to.

"Rafe!"

He laughs. "I paid for them, not you."

"Love, we're going to get married. Everything we have belongs to the other."

"I know, but until then, I didn't want you to worry about the cost. They are absolutely beautiful bands."

"So, all currency is coin? There is no paper currency here?"

"Right."

"I told you I wouldn't remember."

He laughs, pulling her to him. "That's why we'll study them again. Now, do you want to get cleaned up and get a nap?"

"Yes, please." He looks her up and down. "What?" she asks.

"Admiring you in that dress."

"Well, look all you want, because it's staying here. No way would I wear this at home."

"Could you imagine the look on Kara's face?"

Ana doubles over with laughter. "Oh, what would she think?"

She walks to her bag to retrieve fresh clothes to sleep in. They clean up and change. He carries her to bed, holding her tight.

"Please, let's sleep and not have any more attempts!"

She looks up at him, kissing him. "I can't make promises."

"Ana!"

"What? Roesh and Aylin are outside. It's daytime. We

should be safe."

"All right. Get some sleep."

"Yes, love." She snuggles into his chest, clutching his shirt. "I'm having a wonderful weekend with you."

"Me, too."

He looks down as she falls asleep. Trying to suppress the memory of walking out and finding her bleeding on the floor, his heart pounds in his ears. His gentle touch on her face reassures him they're both fine. He drifts off into a restless sleep.

Ana wakes up, seeing it's after four. She sits up and looks at Rafe. She caresses his face, when he suddenly brings his arm up and hits her, knocking her off the bed.

"Stop!" he cries out. "Don't touch her!"

Getting to her feet, she realizes he's having a nightmare. She rushes to him, shaking him.

"Rafe! Rafe, love! Wake up!" She looks up when Roesh and Aylin rush in. "We're all right. Nightmare," she explains. They look around the room then step back out.

Rafe looks at her as he sits up. "I'm sorry," he says.

"For what? Last night was scary. I don't blame you for having a nightmare. Are you okay to join our friends or should we have food brought in?"

"No, I'm okay now. Thank you." He watches her strip out of her pajamas, getting to his feet when he sees the red marks on her stomach and leg. "Ana, what is that?"

She examines them, then she runs towards the washroom. He grabs her hand, pulling her to him.

"Rafe—"

"Did I cause that?"

She calms down and meets his gaze. "It's okay."

He gently grips her chin when he sees another red mark. "Oh, Ana! What did I do?"

"You were having a nightmare! It's okay. I'm not hurt."

He pulls her to him, focusing with all his love as he heals her. "I'm so sorry," he says, tears streaming down.

"We've survived so much already. Please, don't let this ruin our weekend! It was an accident, and you've already healed me! Please, love?" She clings tighter to him. "Please? I can't… I can't take your anger right now." She closes her eyes, concentrating on their love, on his comfort and happiness.

"I'm okay. Don't get me wrong, I still feel awful for what happened, but I won't get angry again." He buries his head in the crook of her neck, breathing in her love and warmth.

She gently caresses his neck and back while holding him tight. "We're okay now. We're safe and okay. That's what matters."

"Yes, mia estrela. I'm so sorry."

"It's all right. It was an accident."

He caresses her face. "Are you all right mentally? I didn't trigger anything?"

"No, love. I'm all right. Are you ready to eat?"

"If you are."

She smiles up at him, kissing him. "I am."

He lets her go, sitting back down on the bed. She gets her bag, getting out a gown when she looks up at him. When he hangs his head, she approaches him.

"I'm going to send word to Bela that we're staying in."

"No, it's okay. We're leaving in the morning. I'm okay. Really."

"Rafe, look at me." She patiently waits. "Love?"

He meets her gaze. "I'm okay."

She leans down, kissing him. "I love you. You know that, right? You know how much I love you, how much you mean to me?"

"I know, mia estrela. I love you, too. More than there are

stars in the sky, more than my words could ever say."

"Now let's get dressed and visit with our good friends."

"Yes, Ana." He goes to his bag and gets out dress clothes. He changes, watching her slip into her gown. "Whatever you wear or don't, you are always so sexy. You know that, right?"

"Rafe!" she exclaims, laughing. She steps up to him, wrapping her arms around his neck. "What has gotten into you?"

He devours her lips while stroking teasingly through her wings. "You have, my love."

"Oh! We're supposed to be going to dinner."

"I know. This is for when we get back."

She gasps, as his hand slowly brings up her gown, teasing along her thigh. "Love," she moans, her head rolling back. "Now you're being mean!"

She brings her hand up to his chest, working her way down. She slowly caresses along the zipper of his pants, folding into him.

"Ana!" he says, grabbing her arms. He kisses her hard. "Mia estrela, what are you doing?"

She looks up at him, smiling. "Whatever do you mean, love?" she innocently asks, biting her lip.

"They are waiting on us."

"They're not the only ones waiting."

"Ana, I swear!" he cries out, kissing her hard. "We're going to dinner," he leans down by her ear, "then you and I are going to have a very intense training session."

She smiles up at him, kissing him. "Promise?"

"Yes, mia estrela."

She takes his hand, laughing at the look on his face. They step out, Roesh and Aylin ready to escort them. It's a quiet walk down the corridor. They arrive at the banquet room. Bela and Joph are waiting for them.

"How are you feeling?" Joph asks.

"We're okay," Ana answers before turning to Bela. "I'm

so sorry about your two guards. I feel awful."

"Ana, they know the risks when they join. Even so, thank you for your sympathy."

"Other than that, we've had a perfect weekend here. Thank you for hosting us and for everything you've done."

"You are most welcome! Will you be joining us for breakfast in the morning?"

"Yes," Rafe answers, "then leaving after. We have had a good time this weekend. As Ana said, thank you for everything."

"You are welcome, and you know you can come here any time you want? We truly enjoy spending time with you both."

"Thank you," Ana says, yawning. "My apologies."

"No, it's quite all right. I know you and Rafe need to get to bed soon."

Ana stifles a laugh, turning it into a cough. She takes a sip of her drink. "Yes, Bela. Thank you." She looks up at Rafe, who winks at her. She shakes her head. "Oh, we've decided on March fifteenth for our Rose Ball. I will send you an invite once I've had them made up." A pain tugs at Ana's stomach, but she ignores it.

"We will be there," Bela says.

They finish eating. "Good night," Ana says.

"Until the morrow," Bela replies.

Rafe takes Ana's hand, leading her back to their quarters. Roesh steps inside, checking the room. He gestures them in once he's sure it's all clear. Rafe picks up Ana and carries her inside.

"Rafe!" she says, as he puts her on her feet. He locks the door.

"Yes, mia estrela?"

"Hmm. I need a shower."

"Not yet you don't."

"What?" she asks, squealing in surprise when he scoops her up and carries her to the bed. He lays her down, laying over her. "Love, I want to try something."

"Ana?"

"No, not that. Something like that." She sees the confusion on his face. "We undress, but leave our undergarments on. Like… like a practice run? So I can get used to having your body over me, to feel you…" She takes a breath. "You know?"

"Are you sure?"

"Yes. If we start now, then it won't seem so overwhelming on our wedding night. Please?"

"We'll start, but if you—"

"Rafe, I swear."

He studies her face, leaning down and kissing her. "Let's try this."

They stand up and undress, doing as she said. She lays down on the bed, smiling as his body covers hers. He leans down, kissing her as her hands caress along his neck and chest. He lowers down on her, his weight on top of her, when she tenses up.

"Ana—"

"I'm okay," she quietly replies. "Really. Let's keep going."

He studies her for a moment. "Yes, mia estrela." He kisses her again, moving his hips, his body rubbing against hers. "Like this, Ana?"

"Yes, love."

Her legs wrap around him. Tenderly, he kisses her neck and face. He lowers down more. With his touch, she becomes tense. She takes a deep breath and forces the memories away, directing her attention towards him. Sitting upright, he pulls her onto his lap.

"Rafe, what's wrong?"

"You are too tense. I'm worried."

"That's the point, though. I have to work past everything."

"We will, one step, one wall, at a time."

She wraps her arms around his neck, tears streaming

down. "I've ruined this. I'm sorry."

"No. You haven't ruined anything. This is why we're doing this. Were you back in his camp just now?"

"Yes," she quietly replies. She pulls away, sitting on the edge of the bed. "I didn't tell you everything."

"What do you mean?"

Her head goes down. "I lied to you."

Rafe crawls over, sitting beside her. "About what?"

She glances at him before hanging her head in shame. "When you asked me if he was inside me, in the camp," she says, her voice small and breaking.

"Ana, did he—"

"Not the way you're thinking."

"I don't understand."

With her fingertips, she follows the contours of his hand as they intertwine. When she looks at him, she sees understanding in his eyes.

"Oh, Ana. Why didn't you tell me this sooner? Why have you been carrying this on your own?"

"I was too humiliated and ashamed." She pulls away, getting to her feet, wrapping her arms around herself. She looks at him. "I'm so sorry I kept this from you. Please, just go. I know you want to," she says, wiping her tears. "I wouldn't blame you if you do."

He stands up, walking to her and picking her up. He takes her to the sofa in front of the fireplace. "Ana, in what universe would I ever leave you? I told you, and I meant it, that there is nothing you could ever tell me that would stop the love I have for you. I will never see you differently because of anything you tell me. I'm so sorry for everything you've endured."

"How can you still love me?" she asks, pushing down the tears.

"I will always love you. When we say always and forever, it's not only a saying between us. It means eternity for us. Our love, our life, our souls. We are together forever. Can you see that? Will you see that?"

"I want to," she answers. "I really do. I told you, it's not fair to you though. We keep breaking down walls just as more get built."

"If I have to break down a wall every single day until you are free of them, that is what I will do. You were so angry in sword training, saying it was typical that I wouldn't fight for you. I have spent every day since proving how wrong you were. I will fight for you with every breath, every beat of my heart." She looks up at him, disbelief on her face. He lowers down, planting a soft kiss on her mouth. "I mean that. Every single day."

She climbs up, kissing him and wrapping her arms around him. "How can I prove my love to you? How can I prove myself worthy of you? Everything you have done for me, every wound healed, every episode you've held me through."

"Ana, you battled Kane, jumping on me to save me life. You died for me. You laid down in the woods, saying goodbye to me, after you gave yourself. Remember we talked about the little things you do? You show me every single day how much you love me, from gentle kisses to holding my shirt. I have never doubted or questioned your love for me, even when you did mine. I am the one who is not worthy of a woman like you."

"Rafe—"

"You are the queen of my heart, the goddess of my soul, and empress of my very being. I worship every piece of you, broken or whole. I'm sorry if I haven't made that obvious by now."

She loses the battle, as the tears stream down. "You have! You truly have. I know how much you love me, I really do. It's me! You know it's me."

"We fought about Everard, and I walked out the door when you needed me to believe you the most. Then you nearly died. Do you see? I'm the one who isn't worthy of you." He places her on the sofa, then goes to get his pants on.

"You're leaving me, aren't you?" she asks, trying to look at him.

Turning back, she hangs her head. Her eyes meet his as he stands before her. He drops to his knees, taking her hands.

"How can I convince you that I am here to stay? What will it take to prove to you that I will never leave again? Because this is killing me, knowing how much pain I have caused you. You should be recovering from his camp, and instead you are so scared of losing me! What can I do?" He kisses her hands, sitting next to her. "Please, mia estrela? What do you need?"

"I need you."

"What do you need?"

"You want to prove yourself to me? Give yourself to me."

Chapter 22

He lifts her up while kissing her and takes her to the bed. He lays her down, covering her with himself. She grinds against him, until his full weight rests on her.

Rolling away, he positions himself next to her. Rising on his elbow, he peers down at her.

"Ana, that's as far as we're going tonight."

"But—"

"No. I feel how tense you are, and your fear is pouring out of you. I won't risk you for myself. If you're going to hurt no matter what I do, believing I don't love you or sending you into an episode, this is what I choose. I can tell you how much I love you, I can tell you how much you mean to me. What you're asking for? I can't undo if it hurts you. I'm not ready for that, either."

"Rafe, that is exactly what I was hoping you would say."

"What? Was that a test?"

"No, love. Please, no. Not a test, not for you. If you had been willing to give yourself to me, I would've felt guilty because I'm not there yet. I would've stopped you. This proves to me that we both need to wait." She sits up, pulling herself to him. "It proves to me how much you love me, that you would put me before yourself." She kisses him, wrapping her arms and legs around him. "I'm sorry if that hurts you or upsets you, as it was never my intention." She kisses him again. "You have more than proven yourself to me. I'm sorry I asked you to. That wasn't fair to you."

"I asked you to show me what you needed. You did."

"I need a shower now. Will you join me?"

"Yes, Ana," he says, helping her out of her corset. He takes her into the shower. He holds her tight as she cries, gently caressing her back. "Are you okay now?" he asks, stroking through her wet hair.

"Yes, love. I am. We brought down walls and showed each other our love. I can think of nothing better. Can you?"

"Being with you, holding you in my arms, is the best thing in my life. You truly are my everything."

"I'm sorry I ever doubted."

"I'm sorry I gave you reason to. Know this, I will always love you. I will always be here for you. Nothing you say or do will ever turn me away from you."

"I believe you. With every ounce of my being, I believe you." She kisses him hard, running her hands through his hair and clutching him tight.

"Now, let's get cleaned up and sleep. Will you do that for me? Will you sleep tonight with no nightmares?

"I would ask the same of you."

"Yes, mia estrela. We both will," he says. "Hmm, maybe tomorrow we can really enjoy this shower."

She looks up, hearing him laugh. She turns to him, punching his shoulder. "Jerk!"

"What did I say about that?"

Her eyes go wide as he is reaching for her. "No!" she playfully cries out as he plants kisses on her face and neck. He pulls back, holding the back of her head, looking into her eyes. She reaches up and kisses him, wrapping her arms around him. "I love when you do that to me."

"I'm a little uneasy, hearing you say no."

"You can tell in this instance, that I don't mean it. Any other time with me, even if it's my body saying it and not me, you hesitate, checking on me. You hit the brakes and make sure I'm okay. That's why it doesn't bother me for you to ignore this one no from me. Because I'm playing along with you."

"All right. Now, will you submit?"

"Never!" she cries out, as his mouth is on hers, kissing her neck and down to her chest. "Rafe," she says, as his mouth is around her, playfully teasing. "Love, please," she says, as he stands back up. She looks up at him, longing in her eyes.

"We need to get clean. We're traveling tomorrow."

"Yes, love," she says, facing the shower head.

She washes and rinses her hair. Battling her embarrassment, she glances at him. He steps up behind her, pulling her against his chest.

"Please?" she begs.

He kneels down, bringing his hand up, gently caressing along her legs. She grabs his shoulders, holding onto him with everything she has as he moves faster.

Ana cries out, grabbing him and kissing him as she's overwhelmed. She pulls back, panting for air. He holds her to his chest, gripping her tight. She feels his racing heart, smiling as he's trying to catch his breath as well.

"We both enjoyed that," he says.

"Thank you, love," she says, kissing him gently.

"Now, will you finish getting clean so we can turn in?"

"Yes, Rafe. Sorry I'm so needy," she says, grinning at him.

"Ana!" He kisses her hard, his mouth over hers, his tongue probing inside. He holds her tightly, wanting to be on every possible inch of her he can. "We needed each other."

She pulls back, looking at him. "You like to hear me beg, don't you?"

He looks down but quickly meets her gaze. "I do. I'm sorry."

"Rafe!" she says, stepping up to him. "How dare you?" she asks, laughing. "You'll pay for that!"

"Oh, really?" he asks. "How do you plan to do that?"

"I'm not telling you anything. You'll see."

"All right, mia estrela. If you say so."

After cleaning up, she goes to get her bag. She retrieves the lacy lingerie he adores. She puts them on, then walks to the bed and lies down. Stepping out, he changes into his shorts and pajama bottoms. The sight of her amuses him.

"What?" she asks.

"Is that the best you can do?"

"I have no idea what you mean. I'm a little warm, and this feels comfy to sleep in."

"Right," he says while walking towards her. He climbs into bed with her. "Oh, no. This payback is horrible!" he says with a wink.

"Oh, this isn't it."

"What?" he asks when she lays him down.

As she climbs over him, her hand glides down his pants. With a slow movement, she brings her hand under the fabric, gently wrapping around him. His head rolls back, as she teases along his length. While leaning over him, she kisses him and continues stroking. She feels him trembling, his breathing ragged. She pulls back.

"I need to use the washroom," she says as she climbs out of bed.

She steps inside, brushing her teeth and relieving herself. Then she joins him in bed.

"Good night, love," she says, turning away.

"Ana, please."

"Yes, Rafe?" she asks, fighting her grin while trying to sound serious. "Do you… need something?"

"No," he says, though his face turns red. "I'm okay."

"All right then." She covers herself with the blanket.

"Ana, please! I need you. Don't leave me like this!" he cries out.

She rolls over, laughing hysterically. "Yes, love." She climbs on him, kissing him. "What do you need?"

"This is too mean!" he says, kissing her hard. "I've learned my lesson. I'm sorry I made you beg. Please, mia estrela, will you take care of me?"

She runs to the washroom, getting a towel and bringing over. "Lift your hips, love," she says.

She lowers his pajamas and shorts while he lifts himself

up. As she climbs over him, her hand on him, she kisses him. Her smile widens as he responds to her touch, his head rolling back and a moan escaping his lips as he collapses onto the bed. She cleans him up, taking the towel into the washroom and tossing it into the hamper.

She washes her hands then returns to him, as he's pulling his pajama bottoms back up. He looks up at her as she climbs into bed. He pulls her to his chest, holding her against him.

"Better?" she asks.

"Yes, mia estrela." He looks down at her, caressing her face. "Thank you."

"It's my pleasure to serve my king," she responds.

"Ana!" He plants kisses all over her face. "Really?"

"I'm sorry. Too much?"

"No. It's okay. I still haven't decided, though."

"Love, whatever you decide, I am happy with. Whether you are Prince Rafe or King Rafe, as long as I can call you my husband, that's the only title I care about. Now, let's get some sleep. We travel tomorrow."

"Yes, mia estrela."

She snuggles into his chest, holding his shirt. "I love you, Rafe."

"Ana, I love you, too." He kisses her forehead. "God, you're amazing!"

She giggles into his shirt. "I learned from the best." She looks up at him, kissing him. "Good night, my love."

"Good night, mia estrela."

She falls asleep listening to his heartbeat. Rafe studies her for a moment, admiring her beauty in the firelight.

She continues to surprise me. I can't believe the hell she has survived, but she still trusts me with every inch of her. She is so amazing, so incredible, so beautiful that I don't understand how she could ever doubt herself. If she can go through everything she has, then I can handle a simple title. I can see how badly she wants me to be her king, so that is what I will become.

***

Near midnight, Ana stirs. She wraps the robe around herself and opens the door. Roesh is standing at his post. "Where is Aylin?" she asks.

He turns to her. "She is resting, Majesty."

"You both should be."

"Majesty—"

"Roesh, I insist."

"After last night, I really don't want to leave you unguarded."

"Bela's guards—"

"I wish to remain at my post."

"You can sleep in here, if need be. There is a sofa. I know you need to sleep, too. Please?"

"Yes, Majesty." He walks inside and goes to the sofa. He pulls it over to the door before lying down. "Thank you."

"Sleep," she says.

Walking to the washroom, she splashes cold water on her face. Inhaling deeply, she reflects on what they had done earlier. Her focus is on his love for her, as he has wrapped his heart around hers. With a smile on her face, she steps back out. Snuggling into bed, she clings to his shirt, allowing his warmth to seep into her. She drifts off to sleep again.

***

Rafe plants a soft kiss on her mouth. She smiles at him, wrapping her arms around his neck.

"We have an hour until breakfast. What should we do?" he asks, kissing her again. He looks at her when she giggles.

"Roesh is in here."

He looks over and sees the sofa by the door. "You?"

"I insisted. He needed his sleep."

"I'm awake, Majesty."

"Roesh, you can go be with Aylin," Rafe says. "I will protect the queen."

"Yes, Rafe. We'll be back in an hour to escort you to breakfast."

"Thank you."

"Majesty, thank you." He pushes the sofa back before slipping his uniform jacket on and leaving the room.

Rafe looks at Ana. "What time did that happen?"

"I had to use the washroom around midnight. I was going to ask Aylin a question, but he told me she was sleeping. I told him he needed to do the same." She sees the look on his face. "What?"

"You were going to ask Aylin a question?"

She laughs. "Girl stuff, Rafe!"

"Hmm. All right, I won't ask." He nuzzles into the crook of her neck. "Now, where were we?"

"Taking it easy since we're traveling today."

He pulls back, looking at her. He studies her face, leaning down and kissing her. "Good answer."

"What?" she asks.

"I want to ask you something."

"Rafe, go ahead."

"Does Kara know about what happened in the camp?"

"No. I have been keeping that to myself, unable to even think of dealing with it until I couldn't hold it anymore." Her eyes close. "I'm sorry, for everything. I never should've hid from you. Not about that."

"Ana, I can't begin to imagine how scared you were, how violated you felt. I am not upset or angry that you hid from me, only that it happened to you in the first place. I'd give anything to reach over and heal your mental pains the way I can your physical ones."

She sits up, moving to the edge of the bed. "There are no

words for what I went through. I was hurt, humiliated, and ashamed." She looks at him as he's pulling her back into his arms. "Rafe, it's too strong."

"So am I. I won't feel anything you don't want me to. Let me comfort you. Can you do that? Can you feel my love and comfort flowing to you?"

She closes her eyes, laying her head against his chest. "Yes, love."

"I am right here. That man is dead and will never lay another hand on you again. I'm sorry I didn't get to you sooner."

"Rafe, don't. You saved my life. Please, let's not go there. I can't… I can't deal with that right now," she says, burying her face into his shirt. "I can't."

"Okay. We don't have to." He gently caresses through her hair. "I'm sorry."

"I'd like to get cleaned up before breakfast. Will you help me with that?"

"Of course, mia estrela." He stands up, bringing her with him. He takes her to the washroom, turning the water on. "Can I undress you?"

She looks up at him, seeing love in his eyes. "Yes, please."

He removes her undergarments, putting them in her bag. She steps up to him, pulling his shirt off then his pants. They step into the water. He takes her hand, pulling her to the shower head. He washes her hair, her body, then her wings. "Dry off, Ana. Sit in front of the fire to warm up. I'll be with you in a few minutes."

"Thank you, love," she says, stepping out.

After drying off, she steps out and dresses in a pale blue gown, complete with silver shoes and a circlet. Making her way to the sofa, she relishes the cozy fire. When Rafe steps out, she glances over. She stands and walks to him.

He smiles at the sight of her. "You and your blue gowns. Can I see your wings with that dress?"

She expands them out, then she faces him. "Well?"

"You know how beautiful they look with that color."

Thoughts of returning home race through her mind. "Oh, I'm so nervous about Wednesday."

"What's Wednesday?"

"I didn't even tell you. That's why Anwyn wanted to have lunch with me. The ladies of the court are hosting a high tea, in my honor. It's Wednesday at three." She looks down. "I don't want to be away from you, but we agreed I need to interact more."

"Ana, I'm not upset. I'm glad you agreed to it, but why are you so nervous?" He sees the look on her face when their eyes meet. "Because you'll be the only one there with wings?"

"Yes. You know I love my wings, I'm not ashamed of them anymore. Still, being at a table with so many women and being the only one—"

"What if Aylin could join you?"

"Hmm. I'll find out when we get back. Kara and Evren can be there, as well. That helps some."

Rafe takes her hand. "Let's go see our friends."

"Yes, love."

They step out, seeing Roesh and Aylin waiting for them. They escort them to the banquet room, where Bela is already seated.

"My apologies," he says, getting to his feet and bowing. "Joph is doing rounds and will be here shortly."

"No apology needed, Count. We understand," Ana says as they sit and the first course is brought out. "We are leaving after breakfast. I wanted to thank you again, for your hospitality, for the ball, for everything this weekend."

Bela smiles at her, taking her hand. "Ana, it is the least I can do for you and Rafe, after all you have done for our people." He resumes eating, looking up when Joph joins them.

"Good morning, Joph," Ana says as he sits.

"Good morrow, to you and Rafe. The skies are clear, so

you should be good for flying home."

"Thank you. Bela, if you have any more issues with MoonFrost, or any of Remus' men, please don't hesitate to reach out to me. I want so desperately to maintain the peace we finally have."

"You and me both. I will, thank you."

Ana looks at Joph, who quickly averts her gaze. "Joph?"

He continues eating. "Yes, Majesty?"

"Is something wrong?"

He looks at her, realizing they're all looking at him. "Can Bela and I watch you leave?"

Ana laughs. "Of course. Joph, I'm not nearly as self-conscious with my wings as I used to be. Really. We'll have to get our bags first."

"Yes, Ana. Thank you."

"You love to watch her fly, don't you?" Rafe asks.

Joph shifts uncomfortably in his seat. "I… erm…"

"Joph, it's okay," Ana reassures him. "Can I ask why?"

He looks at her. "You are a new, unique species. Everything about you is fascinating to me."

Rafe laughs. "Should I be jealous?"

Bela chuckles. "Really, Joph?"

"Of course not!" he stammers out, looking down. "My apologies. Studying and researching is my life, so you can imagine why I would be intrigued by you. I apologize if I ever made you feel embarrassed or uncomfortable, Your Majesty, as that has never been my intention." He looks up when Ana's hand is on his.

"Joph, you have been nothing but a good friend to me. I will always be in your debt, for everything you have done to help me through my transition. I truly wish you would feel more comfortable with me, instead of being embarrassed to ask your questions."

"I will work on that, Ana."

"Please, do. We need to do a few things before we leave.

We will meet you outside our quarters in half an hour."

"Yes, Ana."

She gets to her feet, taking Rafe's hand. "Come along, love."

"Yes, mia estrela." They follow behind Roesh and Aylin back to their quarters. Roesh checks inside then gives the all clear. "Go pack and be here in half an hour."

"Yes, Rafe," Roesh says, taking Aylin's hand as they go next door.

Rafe leads Ana in. "What are we doing before we leave?"

She laughs, pulling into his arms. "Warming up my wings," she answers. "They're a little tight for travel."

She expands them out. Their eyes meet as he opens his as well.

"Why do you think Joph and Kara are so fascinated by my wings? As you said, I could understand if this was Earth and I was the only one who had them. They've seen guardians, been around people with wings. Why me specifically?"

"Well, as Joph said, you are unique. As a researcher, I'm sure he would give anything to be able to study you extensively. Kara? Who knows with her? I never expected her to be so jealous, though!"

"How do you think I felt? She humiliated me! I had told her how sensitive they are. I know she said it was an accident, but I really had to wonder after she admitted how jealous she was!"

"Ana, it was an accident. She was really excited to see them again. I could see the look on her face, she was so upset about it."

"That makes me feel a little better."

He steps up to her, gently ruffling through. "Are they ready for travel?"

"Yes, love. I've enjoyed our time here, but I'm ready for us to get home."

"Me, too."

She changes into travel clothing, packing everything up. She uses the washroom and steps out. "Ready?"

"Ready," he says, slinging his bag over his shoulder. She does the same, taking his hand as they step out, seeing everyone is waiting for them. Bela and Joph lead them out. Rafe shakes Bela's hand. "Thank you, for everything."

He turns as Ana pulls him into a hug. "Yes, thank you."

Bela chuckles. "You are most welcome! All of your purchases will be delivered by Friday at the latest."

"Thank you, Count. We will see you again soon, I hope?"

"Yes, Ana."

She hugs Joph, pulling back and looking at him. "Thank you for hosting us."

Joph steps back, bowing. "Always a pleasure, Majesty."

Rafe takes Ana's hand and flies into the air. She looks down, seeing the amazement on Joph's face. She laughs, turning back to Rafe. They travel a few hours before landing. "How are you feeling, Ana?"

"I'm okay. I think we can fly through to get home."

Rafe squeezes her hand, concentrating. "We'll rest for a little while, then keep going." He looks over, seeing clouds in the distance. "Hmm, or not. We need to get in front of those if we want to fly home all right."

"Love, I swear. I'm okay. I have lunch with the countess tomorrow but nothing else planned. I can take it easy. Really."

"Roesh, Aylin, are you okay to keep going?"

"Yes, Rafe. You're right. We don't want to get caught in that," Roesh replies. He looks at Aylin. "Ever flown in a storm?" She shakes her head. "Then you're lucky."

"Let's go," Rafe says, taking Ana's hand and flying back into the air.

They fly fast and hard, trying to get around the clouds moving their way. It grows dark and windy, as the storm picks up speed. Rafe looks over at Ana, seeing the worry on her face.

"We have to land!" he says, looking down. "We'll have to

find shelter until it passes." She nods in agreement. He looks over, unable to see Roesh or Aylin. She looks around.

"Where are they?"

"I don't know."

They lower down, looking up. She pulls to Rafe. "Oh, I hope they're okay!"

He takes her to a small cave, pulling her in just as it starts to rain. He wraps his arms around her as she's shivering from the sudden cold. He looks further in, finding wood. He makes a fire, as she gets out a cloak and wraps it around.

"Ana, they'll be all right. They know if we get separated to continue to the palace. It's protocol."

She looks up at him, trying to fight down her worry and anxiety. "Yes, love." The wind blows the rain in, and she wraps her arms around herself.

Rafe pulls her flush against his chest. "Get by the fire and warm up. I don't need you getting sick."

They sit by the fire. She holds his hand, shivering from the cold. "I can't help it. I'm so worried about them."

"It'll pass in a moment, then we'll see if we can find them. It'll be a short storm. You can tell from the wind and chill it brings."

She looks out to watch as it starts to dissipate. "I see." She gets to her feet, stepping towards the opening of the cave and watching the sun shine through. "Can we go yet?"

"Let's give it a minute to warm back up." He takes her hand, pulling her to the fire. "Please, stay warm for now." She lays back in his arms, her worry growing more with each minute that passes. He gets to his feet, bringing her with him. "All right. I can't take it anymore."

She takes her cloak off and puts it back in the bag. He puts the fire out, taking her hand. They leave the cave, going back into the air. He looks around, happy to see the skies have completely cleared. They speed towards the palace, hoping to see Roesh or Aylin. She squeezes his hand.

"There!" she says, pointing with her other hand. He looks over, seeing Roesh carrying Aylin. Ana speeds up, pulling Rafe to him. Roesh looks up, surprised to see them. They land.

"What happened?" Rafe asks.

"We got separated. Her wings were overcome from the water. She fell, and I caught her before she could hit. I don't know what's wrong with her."

Chapter 23

"Lay her down," Ana orders. Her hands trace the contours of Aylin's head, neck, back, and wings. "She hurt her wing. We need to get her to the Medical Center as quickly as possible, and I'm the fastest one."

"Ana—" Rafe starts.

"No, please. We have to help her!" she says, picking her up. She sees the concern on his face as she takes to the air, flying as fast and hard as she ever has.

As she approaches the kingdom, exhaustion washes over her. Fighting with everything she has, she makes it to the palace. Melian and Kara are near the entrance, shocked when Ana rushes in.

"She needs Winslow, now!" Ana cries out, collapsing to her knees.

Melian takes Aylin as Kara gets Ana to her feet. She helps her to her quarters. "What do you need?" Kara asks.

Ana closes her eyes. "I need a bath. I need to soak my wings, after flying like that."

Kara gets her into the washroom, running a bath as Ana undresses. Kara helps her in. "What else can I do?"

"Wait for Rafe. I know he's going to be angry with me, for overdoing it."

"I'll take care of him," Kara says. "You soak and relax."

"Thank you," she says, sinking down into the water.

"Evren will be in shortly to help you. I'll see to Rafe."

Kara leaves, and Ana worries about how Rafe is going to react to her leaving. She closes her eyes, focusing on easing her wings. Evren steps in. She brings her a glass of water and some bread with cheese.

"Kara said you need this."

"Thanks, Evren." She eats and drinks slowly, though she wants to devour everything. "Would you start the shower for me?"

"Of course," Evren says as she turns on the tap. She adjusts the temperature. Ana goes from the tub to the shower, letting the water wash over her wings and back. "I'll get you clean clothes," Evren says, stepping out.

"Where is she?"

Ana's eyes close at the anger in Rafe's voice. "I'm in here," she answers. Her body trembles at the thought of seeing him.

"How do you feel?" he asks as he enters the room.

"Rafe, do you need pajamas?" Evren inquires.

"Yes, please. You can set them on the vanity with her clothes. Thanks." He turns back to Ana. "How are you?"

"I'm okay," she says. "A little tired." She jumps when his hand is on her arm. "Please—"

"Ana, what's wrong?"

Reluctantly, she meets his gaze. "You're angry I left."

"No, no! I'm not. I'm worried, but you did what any of us would do for a hurt guardian. I swear, I'm not mad," he says, pulling her to him. He massages her back and around her wings. "Kara said you were worried I'd be angry. I was at first, but Aylin's going to be okay. Winslow said you got her here in time. I can't be angry at you for saving her."

"She's going to be okay?"

"Her accelerated healing has finally kicked in. She'll be fine."

"Does he know what happened?"

"He thinks she overextended it, trying to fly in the storm. Then as she was falling, she probably panicked and tried to use it, making it worse. The circulation was completely cut off. She almost lost her wing. He was able to set it, so the blood could flow through, letting her healing work. Thanks to you, she'll be recovered by tomorrow."

"Oh, I'm glad to hear that!" She falls into his chest,

holding him tight. "I'm so sorry."

"You did what you had to do. I'm not angry. I'm sorry that you had to be worried about me when you're recovering yourself."

"I'm okay, too. I'll probably be a little sore." She looks up at him. "I swear, I won't hide from you. Any pain or soreness or anything, I will tell you."

"That's all I can ask," he says, massaging the space around her wings. "Are you ready to get out, or do you need a little longer?"

"I'm ready to step out. I am beyond exhausted. No pain, only tired."

"I can feel that."

He assists her by drying her and helping her get dressed. In a rush, he dries and dresses her while sitting her on the tub. With care, he escorts her to the chaise and settles down, keeping her on his lap.

"Did you eat?"

"Yes. Evren brought me food."

Evren walks in, having heard her name. "Did you need something, Ana?"

"No, I'm sorry. I was telling Rafe you took care of me."

"Oh, yes. Rafe, do you need food as well?"

"Please, Evren."

She steps out, returning with Kara. "Dinner will be here shortly." Kara walks up to Ana, kneeling in front of her. "How do you feel?"

"Like I can hardly keep my eyes open."

Rafe stands up, carrying her to the bed. "Sleep. You can eat more in a little while."

"Yes, love."

He lays her down, covering her with the blanket. He kisses her forehead, watching her fall asleep. He walks to Kara. "I hope she's okay from this. She's never flown so hard before."

"She seems to be okay. I'm more worried about her walls."

Kara notices the confused look on Rafe's face. "She took a bath before she got into the shower, to soak her body and wings."

Rafe looks at Ana. "Oh. You're right. That was her first time by herself since she was a child." He turns to Kara. "I'm going to lay with her for a little bit."

"Of course."

He takes off his shoes and climbs into bed with her. Embracing her, he reflects on his love, the joy she brings, and her immense significance to him. Holding her tightly, he prays for her to remain free from episodes or nightmares. As exhaustion consumes him, he falls into a deep slumber.

Kara moves towards Evren. "I hope they're okay."

"What do you mean?"

"Flying so much, so quickly. He worries over her when she's staying in her quarters, so I can't imagine what he's feeling now. After what she did."

"He told her he wasn't mad."

"Really?"

"Yes. He told her she did what any of them would do for a hurt guardian."

"I hope they stay that way. She is already dealing with so much, still recovering from his camp and everything else. She doesn't need to deal with Rafe's anger right now."

"I think they're okay. He's been working on that, hasn't he?"

"He says he has. I guess we'll see." The bell rings. She and Evren take the food and drinks to set up. She walks to the bed and sees they are both asleep. She gently shakes him. "Rafe? Food is here. Do you want to eat, or do you need more sleep?"

"Could you bring me a plate?"

"Of course," she says. She gets a plate and cup, then brings them to him. He sits up to eat. "We'll get her up in a little bit, since she ate some already for Evren."

"Okay." He finishes and hands her the plate. "Thanks, Kara."

"You're welcome. By the way, we're staying in here tonight."

"That's fine. Thank you." He settles back down, holding Ana, and falling asleep.

Kara takes his plate and cup to the table. "At least he ate," she tells Evren. "They're sleeping now." She takes Evren's hand. "Let's get cleaned up and changed for bed."

"All right."

They go next door, getting cleaned up. They hurry back over, checking on Ana and Rafe, grateful they are still asleep. Kara walks up to Ana, feeling her face and forehead to make sure she's not sick. She sighs in relief when she feels fine. Ana looks up at her.

"What you do?" she mumbles, falling back to sleep.

Kara joins Evren. "She's out for the night. We'll keep her food covered. If she wakes up hungry, it'll be here for her. Are you ready to turn in?"

"Yes, Kara."

With Evren by her side, she takes a blanket from the linen closet and heads to the sofa. She lays her down, tucks her in, and gives her a goodnight kiss. Pushing the chaise closer to the bed, she settles on the soft cushions and covers herself with the blanket. With closed eyes, she prays for a night free from any disturbances.

***

Waking up, Ana's gaze falls on Rafe. With a gentle touch, she runs her hand over his face. She climbs up and gently kisses him on the lips. "Love?"

He looks up at her. "Are you okay?"

"I am. I'm hungry."

Kara approaches them. "We have food. I'll bring it to you."

"What time is it?"

"It's a little after four."

"Kara, I'm so sorry."

"No, Ana. It's okay. Here," she says, getting her the plate of food. "Eat what you can, then we'll get more rest."

"Yes, sis."

Rafe sits up with her, helping her eat. "How do your wings feel?"

She kneels beside him, extending them out. She opens and retracts them. "Okay. A little tight, but not as bad as I was expecting." She looks at him. "That's because of you, isn't it?" He grins at her. "Rafe!"

"What? We fell asleep together. Of course, I'm going to heal you."

"Love, how are you? Are you okay?"

"Ana, I'm fine. You weren't shot or stabbed; it was just your wings. I'm fine, I promise."

She sighs in relief. "Don't do that to me!" She leans over, kissing him all over his face and neck. "I swear!" she cries out as he's laughing. She looks at Kara. "What am I going to do with him?"

Kara laughs, taking the plate and setting it on the table. "For now? Get more sleep with him. It's what you both need."

"Yes, sis." She lays down, clutching his shirt. She looks up at him. "Jerk!"

"Ana," he says, laughing. He kisses her. "Get more sleep, mia estrela."

"Oh, yes. I need to be well rested for my revenge!"

"Ana, Rafe, go to sleep," Kara orders in a playful tone.

"Yes, Kara," Ana responds with a grin.

As he kisses her once more, she smiles. She cuddles against him and drifts back to sleep. Gently touching her face, he holds her hand, searching for signs of pain or fear. His smile reflects her inner peace. He kisses her forehead and falls to sleep with her.

Looking at the clock, Ana sees it's almost seven. She climbs on top of Rafe, kissing him gently.

"Ana?" he asks, as she's kissing his neck and chest. "Kara and Evren are in here," he murmurs. He gasps when her hand is on him, gently teasing. "Ana!" he tries again, his breath catching in his throat.

She looks at him as she gets out of bed, lust reflecting in her eyes. "I'm getting a shower."

His head falls back on the pillow, as his body arches. He takes deep breaths, concentrating, until he can get to his feet. Rushing into the washroom, he slams and locks the door. Her gaze lifts to his in surprise.

"Ana!"

"What?" she asks, stripping out of her pajamas and turning on the water. "Did you need something?"

After undressing, he casually tosses his clothes into the hamper. He steps forward and gives her a passionate, fiery kiss, then stares longingly at her lips.

"I need you," he says.

"Rafe!" she cries out, clinging to him. "Whatever you need, I am yours."

He leads her to the wall, his body pressing against hers. As he kisses her, his hand gently caresses her neck and chest. She embraces him, matching the intensity of his kiss. With a firm grasp on her head, he senses her touch on him. Slowly and teasingly, she moves along. When his breath gets caught and his head rolls back, she smiles. Leaning forward, he kisses her passionately while she quickens her pace. His body leans onto her, his hand reaching out to the wall for support.

"How was that, my love?" she asks, smiling at him.

"Amazing," he says, still catching his breath.

He lowers himself, placing a gentle kiss on her. Continuing downward, he showers her neck and chest with kisses. Her moans intensify as his mouth envelops her, causing him to break into a smile. He teases and gently nibbles, sensing her wriggling beneath him.

Moving down, he positions himself on his knees in front of her. Leaning on the wall, she spreads her legs for him. He explores her hips, her thighs, and in between. Her body quivers with his touch, her cries echoing as she collapses into his embrace. As they sit on the shower floor, he places her on his lap. He raises his hand and gently strokes her thigh. With a tight grip on his wrist, she lifts his hand.

"I can't," she says with a gentle laugh. "Please, love. I'm spent."

He wraps his arms around her, holding her to his chest. "As you should be."

They rest for a moment, catching their breath and calming their hearts. He stands up, getting her under the shower head. He washes her off, then himself. They slip on robes and run to the closet. She puts on one of her new gowns. She walks to the mirror and opens her wings.

He smiles as he walks to her. "That's one of your new ones?"

"Yes. What do you think?"

He looks at the silver blue fabric. The dress is floor length, with silver beads hanging off the shoulders. Silver tulle fabric hangs over the dress, coming down her back and along the front of the gown.

"You did very good picking this out."

"Really?"

He leans by her ear. "You know how much I love that color on you."

"Rafe!" She smiles, bringing her wings in. She turns around and kisses him. "You need to finish getting dressed."

"Yes, Your Majesty."

A silver crown and shoes complete her ensemble. She retrieves her jewelry from the bowl in the washroom. As she walks out, she slides on her rings. Kara switches on the overhead light.

"Ana, that gown is gorgeous."

"Thanks, sis. It's one of my new ones."

"Oh, right! I can't wait to see the rest. Are you and Rafe recovered from yesterday?"

"We are."

"All right. Breakfast will be here shortly. We're going to step over and get dressed. We'll be back in a minute."

"Thanks, Kara."

"Of course!" She gently wakes Evren up. They leave as Rafe steps out of the closet.

"Kara and Evren went to get dressed. Food should be here shortly," Ana explains.

"Okay," he says, walking up to her. "So, your revenge this morning?"

"Oh, that wasn't my revenge."

"What?"

She laughs. "That's still coming."

"Ana, please. Like NightFall?"

"That was merciful compared to what I have in store!"

He grabs her quickly, pulling her into his arms and has her in the air. He showers her with kisses. "Tell me you won't."

"Never!" she cries out, laughing. His kisses grow in hunger, holding her tightly to him. She pulls back, caressing his face. "Oh, love. You know you deserve it."

He gasps, kissing her again. "What do you have planned?"

She smiles at him, biting her lip. "You'll have to wait and see."

They lower back to the ground. "Hmm."

The bell rings. He opens the door, letting breakfast be set up and watching them leave. He walks to her, kissing her again.

"I don't think you have anything planned," he challenges.

She caresses his face, then her hand moves lower, stroking his chest and stomach. While kissing him, her hand continues down and wraps around him. He trembles as she moves quickly, stopping and pulling her hand out. He looks at her, hunger in his eyes. His mouth crashes on hers, devouring her. She brings her hand back down, gently at first then moving faster.

"I'm hungry," she says, pulling away.

She goes to the washroom, relieving herself and washing her hands. She goes to the table and sits, laughing when she sees him standing there.

"Aren't you going to eat?" She laughs when he falls over onto the bed. She walks to him and leans over. "What's wrong?"

She takes his hand, leading him to the table. She sits with him, as Kara and Evren walk in. He takes deep breaths, trying to calm his body. They sit down to eat. "Kara, I'm having lunch with the countess today."

"Oh, right. The tea party tomorrow. We got our invitation while you were in NightFall." She looks at Rafe. "Are you all right?"

"Fine," he answers, eating.

Ana laughs. "You and Evren will be there, right?"

"Of course. I wouldn't make you go to that by yourself."

"Thank you. I'm a little nervous."

"It'll be fine. I know most of the women who will be there. They are kind and compassionate women."

"That makes me feel a little better." Her hand gently rubs along his stomach, trailing down. "How do you feel, love?"

"Fine," he answers.

Kara and Evren gather dishes. "We'll be back."

"Thanks, sis." She watches her and Evren leave. She looks back at Rafe. "So, you still think it's funny to make me worry myself to death over you?"

"It was a joke."

"Oh, love," she says, getting to her feet.

Helping him to his feet, she brings him inside the closet. Locking the door, she guides him to the ottoman. She undresses him, laying him down after removing his pants and shorts. Kneeling beside him, she raises her hand and starts working slowly. Her legs open as his hand moves up, gently caressing her. As they cry out with pleasure, she falls over him while kissing him. She goes to the drawer and takes out a towel. Bringing it over, she cleans him up.

"Better?" she asks, throwing it into the small hamper she'd had brought in.

"Ana, I swear, what am I going to do with you?"

"Hmm. Marry me?"

"Yes, mia estrela. We will, in the chapel."

"Oh, right! I need to speak to Audressa."

"We can go see her, then check on Aylin."

"Please?" she asks, getting to her feet. She helps him get dressed, laughing when he pulls her onto his lap. She kisses him. "Thank you."

"For what?"

"Not being angry about yesterday."

"I wanted to be. How are you so much faster than me?"

She gasps. "Are you jealous?"

"No," he says, looking down.

She laughs, getting to her feet. "Really?"

He looks at her. She takes his hand, helping him up. "I've been flying over five hundred years, and you took to it like a fish to water! It's incredible to watch you."

They leave the closet, seeing Kara and Evren on the sofa. Kara looks over, shaking her head at them. "I don't want to know, but promise me you will both rest today? After everything you went through yesterday!"

"We will," Ana answers. She takes him to the washroom, washing their hands and brushing their teeth. Ana steps out and walks to Kara. "We're going to see Audressa then check on

Aylin."

"Audressa should be in the briefing room."

"All right. I don't know how much time I'll spend with Aylin. If we don't make it back for the briefing, I'll be in the dining hall at eleven to meet with the countess."

"We'll see you there."

Rafe takes her hand, leading her out. Kellan and Erick are at their post. "Meeting room," Rafe instructs. They follow behind, as he sees Ana looking at Erick's wings. "Really?"

"What? I can't get over how pretty they are!"

He laughs, pulling her closer to him. "All right."

They arrive at the meeting room. Kellan walks in. "Everything all right in here, Chancellor?"

She looks up, surprised. "Yes, of course. The queen may enter."

She steps out, gesturing her in. Ana walks up to Audressa. "I am so sorry about last week. You had no reason to feel bad about anything. All you did was your duty, explaining the laws and telling me the truth. My apologies."

"Thank you, Majesty. It was never my intention to upset you so. I can't imagine what you were feeling, as I told you that. I am sorry."

"No, Audressa. You owe no apology. You did your duty. Thank you."

"I did a little research, and I was wrong."

"What do you mean?"

"Since you were born a royal, that would take precedence over whether you are a guardian or not. You would not have lost your title or your throne, especially since you gave everything to protect your kingdom. You died to become a guardian, you were not born one. I'm sorry that I was wrong."

"It's all right. Either way, the treaty passed, and all is good. I do have two questions for you, if you don't mind."

"I don't. Please, Majesty."

"Since I will be crowned as Grand Empress, that means

Rafe can be crowned as King, right?"

"Yes, Majesty. He does not have to, though."

"Of course. Also, I was wondering, is the Penstrella Cathedral only for royal weddings?"

"What do you mean?"

"I have two guardians who are getting married this solstice, and she would love to get married in the cathedral. I would be happy to oblige."

"Hmm. One moment," she asks, getting out the book on customs. "There is nothing in here stating it is only for a Royal Wedding. I think most people believe that since that is the only type that has occurred in there. Tell your guardian she may get married there."

"Oh, thank you so much! I have to go check on her, as she was wounded on our return trip. Thank you, for your time and your research."

"Yes, Majesty."

Ana walks out, smiling at Rafe. "Let's go see Aylin, please."

He takes her hand, looking at Kellan. "Medical Center."

"Yes, Rafe."

Chapter 24

Winslow approaches Ana when they enter, studying her face for a moment. "Majesty, is everything all right?"

"Yes. I would like to see Aylin, if she is up for company."

"She is. Right this way."

She and Rafe follow behind him. They reach her room, and he knocks.

"Come in," Aylin says.

Winslow steps in. "The queen and her guardian would like to see you."

"Please, let them in."

Ana and Rafe step inside. Winslow offers a small bow before walking away. Ana hugs Aylin.

"How do you feel?"

"Much better. They'll be discharging me soon. Winslow says I have you to thank, for getting me here so quickly. I appreciate you saving me."

"Aylin, you are my friend and trusted guardian. It was the least I could do."

"Still, thank you."

"Where's Roesh?" She steps up to the bed when Aylin begins to cry.

"He's angry I tried to fly in the storm. I told him I didn't know what to do! I couldn't see him, or either of you, and I did try to land."

Ana turns to Rafe. He nods in understanding and steps out. Ana takes Aylin's hand. "I'm sorry. He can be the same way, you know. Rafe accidentally hurt me a couple of times in training, and he would get so angry at himself. He's doing better, but I know how you feel. Roesh will come to his senses. You'll be all right."

"Thank you, Majesty."

"Aylin, please. While we're in here, you don't have to use my title. I insist. Now, in case you and Roesh work things out, I do have some good news for you. The cathedral is yours if you still want to get married there."

"Really?"

"Yes. I spoke to the chancellor, and she said it is fine."

"Thank you!" She looks down. "I hope he still wants me."

"I do," Roesh says, stepping in with Rafe following behind. "If you'll forgive me for my temper."

"Look who I found in the hallway," Rafe says.

"We'll give you two some privacy." Ana takes Rafe's hand. "Aylin, you and Roesh take the rest of the week. Recover. I insist."

"Thank you," she says. She looks up at Roesh. "I'm sorry."

"No, angel. This was my doing. I'm the one who is sorry." He walks up, taking her into his arms. "Will you forgive me?"

"Yes," she says, kissing him.

Rafe and Ana step out. "Well, I'm glad they're okay. Déjà vu, huh?"

He chuckles. "Yes. Oh, your tea party?"

Ana shakes her head. "She has more important things to focus on."

"I see. Are we going to the briefing?"

"I'd like to rest before lunch. Could we go back to our quarters?"

"Yes, we'll go back." He nods to Kellan.

She and Erick escort them back, with Erick checking inside.

"Thank you," Rafe says to him as he gestures for them to go in. Ana walks to the chaise and sits, watching the fire. "You sure you're okay?"

"A little tired from this morning. I'll have lunch with the countess, then we can stretch our wings a bit and have a nap before dinner."

"Sounds good." He sits next to her, turning her so he can massage her back and wings. "Not as tight as I thought they would be. Would you open them up?"

She looks at him, smiling. "Yes, love," she says as they expand out. They furl and unfurl. "See? No pain. You healed me, so thank you."

"I have never seen anyone who is so selfless, so compassionate and kind, as you are. It is incredible to witness."

"Thank you, Rafe. I know what it's like, to feel unloved, unwanted. I mean it, when I say I never want anyone to ever feel that way."

"If you were anyone else, I would want you to do everything as you have. Ana, you are queen. There will be times you may have to put yourself above someone else, because the kingdom and the galaxy need you. If you were killed, the chaos, the battles, the death would be too much."

"How did I not think of that?"

"What?"

"That everyone was battling for the throne, so they could be Emperor or Empress of the galaxy." She looks at him. "I'm not upset, but maybe you should have told me that from the beginning."

"Why? What difference would it make?"

"I wouldn't have been so reckless, for starters. I see what you mean about how important I am. Having no heirs or anyone to take the throne, it would be chaos! It also helps me understand why Kane was desperate for the throne." She looks down, tracing her finger along his hand. "You're right. It's better I didn't know. I probably wouldn't have gone into battle if I had known the fate of an entire galaxy was resting on my shoulders." She sits up. "The prophecy!"

"What are you talking about?"

"When we were in Bela's library, I was reading through the book of prophecies. There was a prophecy that said the Crimson Queen would battle, not just for her throne, but for the galaxy. I was worried it meant another battle. I see now, it's referring to the one I fought in. If I had not saved our kingdom, who knows what would have happened? War between the realms?"

"I'm grateful you saved Aylin, that you risked your life for me jumping at an armed assassin, but this is why I would get so angry. It wasn't only your life or mine, or even the kingdom. So much hinges on you. Do you see that now?"

"I do. I won't promise that I'll never do any of that again, but I see now how important it is for me to stay alive, for our people and our realm." She looks up at him. "We're still going to MorningStella for our honeymoon, right?"

"Yes, mia estrela. I promise you, we will." He looks at the clock. "Almost time for lunch."

"I need to freshen up," she says, getting up and going into the washroom.

Rafe walks to the window to watch the falling rain. He thinks of Ana, how much she loves the rain, the peace it brings her. He looks down when she's taking his hand.

"What's made you so happy?" she asks.

"You," he replies, kissing her. He leads her out, looking at Kellan. "Dining hall, please."

"Yes, Rafe."

He looks at Ana when he feels worry. "What's wrong?"

"Nothing. Sorry. I'm a little worried about lunch." She looks at Erick. "Oh, right! You had dinner with her Friday, didn't you?"

"Yes, Majesty."

"How was that, if you don't mind me asking?"

"It went very nice. I think she had a good time, but I'm not sure."

"I see." She glances at Rafe, noticing his equally confused expression. "Do you like her?"

"Oh, very much."

"So, what's the problem?"

"I was too shy to ask her."

"Erick, that's okay."

"You won't say anything, will you?"

"Not unless you tell me to," she says as they approach the dining hall. "I mean it. I won't get in your business."

"Thank you, Majesty."

They walk inside. She looks over, seeing the countess. She steps up to Rafe, kissing him. "I'll see you shortly?"

"Yes, mia estrela. I'll be right over here."

She walks to the countess, who stands and bows. "Majesty."

"Countess. How are you?"

"I'm quite well." She glances at Erick. "Mi'lady, I hate to be forward, but did he say anything?"

"He did, but I told him I won't get in your business."

"I understand. It's just, I would like to have another dinner with him, but I was surprised he didn't ask me."

"All I'll say is, you asked first. Maybe that is what he prefers?" she offers.

"I see. I will take that into consideration. Thank you. How was your trip to NightFall?"

"It was very nice. The people and food, everything was fantastic. The assassin came after us, but she has been dispatched."

"Never a dull moment for you, is there?"

Ana laughs. "No. Now, about the tea party tomorrow. Would it be possible if Kellan joined us? She is the guardian over there with Erick. She saved my life. I would like to repay her by having her join us."

"Majesty, are you that worried about your wings?"

Ana looks at her, shaking her head. "Countess, I will say, at least you aren't afraid to speak what's on your mind. I find it refreshing."

"I'm sorry. I can't help it sometimes."

"It's quite all right. Yes, it's also because I don't want to be the only one at the table with wings.”

"Of course, she can join us. We'll take care of it.”

"Thank you." She looks up, startled when Anwyn gestures Erick to come over. He bows before them.

"How can I serve?" he asks.

"Erick, when are you available again? I would like to have dinner with you, if you wish to as well." He looks at Ana. "She didn't say a word, I promise. I realized I asked you the first time. Perhaps I should ask again."

"Yes, I would like to have another dinner with you. I am off Friday."

"I look forward to seeing you Friday, in my chambers for dinner."

"Yes, Countess," he says, blushing. "Until then, I will return to my post."

Anwyn laughs when he walks away. "I don't think he expected me to be quite that forward."

"I didn't, either," Ana confesses. "Have you ever dated someone who was shy?"

"What do you mean, dated? I don't know that word."

"Sorry. I believe the word you use here is courting."

"Ah, yes. I see. No, I have not."

"A little advice from someone who used to be afraid of their own shadow?" Ana asks, as Anwyn nods. "It's okay to take the lead, like you just did. However, take it easy and slow. Please, don't push."

"I see. I will try and remember that. Thank you."

"You're most welcome."

They finish eating. "I have somewhere I have to be. I will see you tomorrow at three for the tea party."

"Thank you, Countess. I am excited."

"And nervous?"

Ana laughs. "Yes."

"You'll be fine, I promise."

"Thank you. I'll see you tomorrow," Ana says, getting to

her feet. She walks to Rafe, who is eating. She sits with him, taking his hand.

"Still nervous?" he asks.

"Yes," she answers. "At least Kellan can join me for the tea party."

"That is good. Now, are you ready for training?"

"Then a nap, right?"

He looks at her. "Maybe we should rest first."

"No, I don't want to keep changing clothes. We'll train then sleep."

"Hmm. All right."

They go to the training center. As she spreads her wings, she observes him soaring towards the ceiling. Before joining him, she warms up by stretching. She flies to him.

"I'm sorry."

He looks at her. "For what?"

"That we didn't get to fly home together. I was really looking forward to that."

"Ana, you were saving someone's life. It's all right. How do your wings feel? Are they hurting today?"

"No. They feel perfectly fine. I expected a little pain or tightness, but it seems you took care of that." She flies up to him, taking him in her arms and kissing him. "Thank you."

"Of course! Are you up for real practice, or do you want to take it easy?"

"What do you have in mind?"

"I'll make you a wager. I catch you, I'll do anything you want with you tonight. You catch me, I get to choose."

"Rafe, that's not fair. You know how fast I am."

"Oh, cocky now, are you?"

She laughs. "No, of course not! Fine. I'll take your wager. How do you want to start?"

He takes her to the middle of the room, pulling away. "Ready?"

"Ready," she says, flying backwards.

"Go!"

Amazed by her speed, he chases after her. Evading his grasp, she falls beneath him, only to fly over instead. She knows she could end it any time by catching him. The thrill of the chase excites her. She loves watching him pursue her. A smile touches her lips as he draws near.

"Are you even trying?" he asks.

Her smile grows as she increases her speed. His inability to keep up with her amuses her. She flies under him, surprising him when her arms wrap around him.

"I win!" she declares, kissing him.

"Yes, mia estrela. You win." He kisses her back. "Ready to clean up and rest?"

"I am," she says, as they lower back down. She takes his hand as they leave the center. "Our quarters," she tells Kellan. "By the way, are you assigned to us tomorrow?"

"I am," she answers.

"Would you join me for a tea party with ladies of the court? My way of saying thank you for saving me."

"I would be honored. How should I dress?"

"I'm not really sure myself. We can ask Evren."

"Yes, Majesty. Thank you." She goes inside to inspect their quarters. Once finished, she steps out and announces, "All clear."

"Thanks," Rafe says as he takes Ana in. They clean up and change into pajamas. He carries her to bed, laying down with her. "Sleep now. We both need it. Especially for whatever you have planned for tonight."

She smiles at him, winking. "Hmm… Who knows?"

"Ana, what?"

She kisses him. "You'll see."

"Yes, mia estrela."

"Rafe, I love you. I love you so much, I feel I could burst with it."

"I love you, too, my warrior queen. Believe me when I tell

you I feel exactly the same way."

He smiles when she grabs the bottom of his shirt, holding it tightly as she falls asleep. He gently touches her face while running his fingers through her hair. The exhaustion is overwhelming, but his only desire is to be with her. Ultimately, he surrenders and dozes off.

Chapter 25

Rafe wakes up and realizes Ana's shivering and whimpering beside him. "Ana?" He gently shakes her shoulder. "Wake up!"

Sitting up, she looks around the room. Tears stream down her face. "I'm sorry."

"For what? What happened?"

She swallows hard while averting her gaze. "I had a nightmare."

"Do you want to tell me about it?" he asks, pulling her onto his lap. She wraps around him, clinging to him.

"Please, don't make me. Not yet," she begs.

"Okay. You know you don't have to. Whenever you're ready. Was this because you took a bath?" Her body tenses against him. "You're with me and safe." He feels her easing up while he quietly reassures her.

"I'd like to get ready for dinner."

"Do you want to eat in here?"

"Yes, please."

"Of course. Put on something comfortable. I'll get Kara and Evren, if you want them with us."

"I do."

Getting up, he helps her stand. As he puts on his shoes and exits, she enters the closet. Taking a moment to survey her surroundings, she considers what to wear.

We're staying in, so I can be comfortable. Then again, Kellan may come in to look at gowns so we know how to dress tomorrow.

She sits on the ottoman, wrapping the blanket around herself. As Rafe enters, she lifts her head and wipes away her tears.

"They'll be right over." He sits with her and clasps her

hand. "What's wrong?"

She shakes her head. "I'm okay. I needed a moment before I get dressed."

"Ana, you can put on whatever you want, since we're staying in."

She walks to the dresser and picks out a black pair of pants with a silver top. "Is this okay?"

"It's fine."

He takes off his pajamas and gets dressed. With concern, he gazes at her as she settles on the ottoman. He joins her.

"Are you sure you're all right?"

"I'm okay. After Kara and Evren leave, we'll talk."

"You won the wager, so you decide what we do tonight."

"Why do I have the feeling, even if you had won, you'd still let me choose, after what's happened?"

He smiles at her. "Because you know me so well." He kisses her forehead. "Come along. Food will be here soon."

He stands up, pulling her with him, and takes her to the table. As she's sitting down, the bell rings. He walks to the door, opens it, and lets food service in. Kara and Evren enter behind the staff. They sit together to eat. Kara studies Ana.

"Are you all right?"

"Still tired from everything," she explains.

"Of course."

"Will you help Kellan and me figure out what to wear for the tea party tomorrow?" Ana asks Evren while buttering her bread.

"I would be happy to."

She looks at Kara. "Will you be in a gown?"

"Yes, unfortunately." Kara sighs.

Evren takes her hand. "You look so lovely in them."

Ana laughs when Kara blushes. "She's right, Kara. You are very pretty."

"Okay, enough about me! How was your trip, besides the assassin, of course?"

"It was wonderful. We had a great time. We'll have some things delivered from there this week. We bought a few things for our office and bought our wedding bands."

"Already?" Kara asks.

"I didn't plan on it," Ana says. "I thought we were looking for ideas. When you see them, you'll understand why we didn't wait."

"All right. You're waiting until August to get married, right?"

"We are."

"Do you still have nightmares?" Evren asks. Her eyes go down when Kara gives her a sharp look. "My apologies."

"Evren, it's all right. Kara, she is my friend as well and can ask me anything. Yes, I still have nightmares. We're dealing with them, though."

"Like the one you just had?" Rafe asks.

She drops her fork, looking at him. "Really?"

"Ana, you are in a room full of people who love you. Let them help, too."

She looks at Kara and Evren, seeing the concern on their faces. "You're right, Rafe. Yes, like the one I had earlier. The bath triggered it."

"I'm sorry. Are you sure you'll be up for tomorrow?" Kara asks.

"I'm fine now. I had my episode, and I—"

"Episode or nightmare?" Rafe asks. Her eyes go down. "Which is it?"

"Both," she admits.

"Why didn't you tell me?" he demands.

"Please! I told you I wasn't ready to discuss it. Why are you pushing me so hard?" She looks up when Kara pulls her into her arms while she shoots Rafe an accusatory look.

Kara takes Ana to the chaise. "Just us. You don't have to tell me anything, but I want to comfort you," Kara explains, sitting down with her. She's surprised when Ana grabs her tighter and cries in her arms. "Shh. You're all right now. It's okay."

"Why does he do that? Why does he push me so hard?"

"In his defense, sometimes it's the only way to get you to open up. I'm not saying he should've this time, but I understand why he does it." She pulls back, looking at her. "Are you okay to come eat?"

"Can I tell you about it?"

"You know you can."

Evren looks at Rafe. "Will she be okay?" They watch Kara and Ana talk.

"She will. I'm sorry. She's right, I don't mean to push her so hard."

"What did she mean, a bath triggered her? I don't understand that."

"She endured horrible things as a child. For you or me, taking a bath is soothing and relaxing. It's scary for her, what she's been through. It brings back memories of the horrors she suffered through."

"I see. Kara told me a little, but I didn't know it was so bad."

"I don't see how she is still alive, with everything she has been through. Then to come here." He hangs his head, taking a deep breath. "It's been too much for her from the beginning."

"She is brave and strong. She killed a man to save me, carried Aylin here, and came back after dying in battle. Right now, she is scared, but you've seen how strong she is."

"I know that. Believe me, I know. She's the one who refuses to see it." He looks up when they make their way back to the table. "Ana, I'm so sorry. Can we eat? Are you okay?"

"Yes, love," she says, taking his hand as she sits down. "I'll eat. Everything's okay. Thank you, Kara."

"Of course. We'll look at gowns when we're done."

After Ana finishes her meal, she turns to Rafe. "Why do you push me so?"

"Because I worry about you. Not that you'll hurt yourself, I swear. You promised me, and I believe you. However, I worry you're carrying too much. I want to help you. I'm sorry that I do. I'll work on it, like I have my anger."

"Please do. I love you, and I'm sorry I still hide sometimes, but you can't begin to imagine what it feels like to me, what I have to deal with. Sometimes I have to deal on my own before I can let you in. Like with the camp."

Kara's head snaps up. "What about the camp?"

Ana looks at her. "Not now, please? Look, you and Rafe can talk about it while Evren and I look at gowns. I can't go through it again."

Rafe looks at Kara and nods. "Yes," she says. "You go ahead."

Ana walks to the door, opens it, and gestures for Kellan to come inside. "Evren is going to show us what to wear for the tea party."

They all go into the closet. Kellan smiles at all the gowns. "Oh, you have so many beautiful dresses!"

Ana laughs. "Thanks." She consults Evren. "What would you suggest?"

They search through the racks. Ana pulls out a pink gown, with darker pink roses embroidered down the bodice and lace trailing down the skirt.

"Would this be okay?"

"Yes," Evren says.

Kellan looks at Ana. "My apologies, as I don't have any gowns like that. Mine are mostly long and form fitting, for evening wear."

"Do you see one here you would wear?"

Kellan continues to look, finding a royal blue gown with silver roses embroidered. "Would this work?"

Evren steps up beside her. "Yes."

"I'll need to try it on."

Evren opens the door to the other closet. Kellan enters,

then shuts the door. Evren turns to Ana. "Accessories?"

"Right." She opens the drawer. "Are these Royal Jewels too formal for a tea party?"

"No, Ana. Any of those will be fine. Along with a crown or circlet."

"Okay. You and Kara have gowns for tomorrow?"

"Yes. She is not happy about wearing one."

Ana laughs. "She has never cared for dresses. Honestly, neither did I." She shakes her head. "Didn't know I'd be wearing one every single day."

Kellan steps out. "How does this look?" she asks. Ana opens the doors to the mirror. "Oh. It looks nice, doesn't it?"

"It does. Thank you for joining us. I'm going to be honest with you, and I truly hope I do not offend."

"Majesty?"

"I was nervous about being the only woman at the table with wings." She looks over when Kellan laughs.

"It's quite all right! I'm not offended."

"Thank you."

Kellan steps back into the closet to change. She walks out and hangs the gown up. "Is it okay to leave it here? We'll change before the tea party?"

"Yes, Kellan."

"Thank you. I will return to my post, unless you have further need of me?"

"We're good. Thank you."

Kellan bows and steps out. Ana turns to Evren.

"I guess we'll check on Kara and Rafe." She walks out of the closet, surprised to see the tears on Kara's face.

"What's wrong?" Evren asks, running to her.

"I'm okay, but Ana, are you?" Kara asks, getting to her feet. She walks up to her looking her in the eyes. "Please, tell me if you are."

"I'm okay. I've dealt with what happened at his camp. Really."

"Why didn't you tell us? I had you in my arms, so scared and worried over you! Why did you lie to me?"

Her eyes go down. "Kara, my shame was too great. I pushed it down, unable to even face it myself. I'm sorry."

Kara pulls her into her arms, crying on her shoulder. "Ana, I can't imagine what that was like. I'm so sorry you've been dealing with it."

"Kara, really. I'm okay now."

"What he did with his hand, you may never be okay from this."

She gasps softly. "Kara!"

Ana falls to her knees, sobbing into her hands. Kara helps her to her feet and taking her to the sofa. Rafe and Evren join them. Kara looks up, seeing Rafe next to her. She stands up, taking his hand so he sits with Ana.

"I'm sorry, Ana. I never meant to make you feel like this."

"You were speaking the truth. You are right, that I may never be okay." She meets Rafe's gaze. "I won't question us, or question you, I swear. Please, will you hold me?"

He pulls her to him, looking at Kara. "I guess we both push, don't we?"

"Yes. I am so sorry."

"Kara, it's all right. Like you said, you wouldn't have to if I would open up. I do hide, and I'm sorry."

"What do you mean, with his hand?" Evren asks. Kara takes her aside and tells her what happened in the camp.

Rafe looks down as Ana is trembling, with tears falling fast. "Ana, what can I do? What do you need?"

She clutches his shirt. "What you're doing," she replies in a hushed tone, wiping her tears. She looks up when Kara stands before them.

"We're going to let you have privacy. Ana, I am so sorry. For everything."

"Thank you, Kara." She watches them leave, turning back to Rafe. "I'm sorry, too. I thought I was over this."

"The way you were hurt, it's going to take you a long time to recover. I'm right here with you, through all of it. Kara is wrong. You will move past this, in your own time. I wish I could do more for you."

"Do you not know how warm and comforting you are? Laying here, in your arms, feeling your strength and love is more than I could ever hope for. Believe me, you are doing so much to help. I hate that you have to keep seeing me like this."

Her shame flows into him. He closes his eyes, seeing her strength, her beauty, warming up as he feels her love for him, his heart with hers. "Is that better?"

"Yes, thank you. Can we get a shower and turn in? I know it's early, but I'm exhausted now."

"Stay here while I get us fresh clothes. You've soaked through both of ours."

She smiles at him. "Thank you."

Going into the closet, he gets their clothes and takes them to the washroom. He sets them on the vanity, then goes to her, lifting her up to carry her inside.

First, he turns on the water, and then he assists her in undressing. As he undresses, she steps in. He enters, embracing her tightly against his chest. Turning towards him, she gives him a kiss.

"Ana—"

"I needed a kiss. I know I'm not in any shape for anything more. Please, love, kiss me?"

He leans down, kissing her gently. He pulls her into his chest, wrapping his arms tightly around her. "I'm right here, mia estrela."

"Will you help me get clean?"

He takes her under the shower head, washing her hair. He lathers the soap, cleaning her over. His hands run along her leg, washing, when her body goes tense. "Ana?"

"I'm okay," she says, softly.

He continues to wash her. When he moves the cloth down

her stomach, she falls into his arms, sobbing. He pulls her into his embrace. "What happened?"

"MoonFrost," she answers, trembling against him. "You can put me down. I'm okay. Do you want me to clean you?"

"Ana, I am going to rinse you off, then you will dry off and dress while I get cleaned. I will slip into my robe, carrying you to bed. Then I will finish drying and changing."

"Yes, love."

He does just that, laying her in bed and covering her with the blanket. "I will be right out." He runs back in, drying off and changing into pajamas. He rushes to her side, seeing her asleep. He climbs into bed, pulling her to him. Her hand reaches up, grabbing his shirt.

"Please," she begs, half asleep, "don't let him hurt me again."

"He never will, I promise." He closes his eyes, feeling her fall into a deeper sleep, feeling love and peace. "Please, mia estrela, sleep all night. You need your rest, as you recover from so much." He falls asleep listening to her soft breathing.

***

"Are you ready for breakfast?" Rafe asks before placing a gentle kiss on her forehead,

"Could it just be us, until I have to leave for the tea party?"

"Of course. I'll take care of it." He slips on his shoes and robe, stepping out. He flags down a staff member, putting in for their breakfast. He goes next door. Kara opens the door.

"Everything okay?" she asks.

"Yes. Ana would like it to be her and me, until the tea party. She's not upset with you. She wants some time while she's recovering."

"I understand. We'll come over around two so we can help her get ready."

"Thank you."

He goes back in and finds Ana resting on the chaise. He sits next to her. She looks up at him. "Just us?"

"Yes, mia estrela. Breakfast will be here soon."

"Can we still do what I wanted to do last night? Since I won the wager?"

He looks her over, studying her face. "What do you want to do?"

"Ever heard of Truth or Dare?"

"It's a game, right? The person says truth, and the other person has to answer the question honestly, or if they choose dare, they have to do what the person says?"

"Yes."

"Are you sure?"

"I am."

The bell rings, and Rafe answers the door. The staff set up and leave. He takes her to their small table. "Now or after breakfast?"

"After."

"And what does the winner get?" He smiles when she blushes. "Ana?"

"You'll see."

"All right. Are you still nervous about the tea party?"

"Not as much, since Kellan, Evren, and Kara will be there with me. Of course, I wish you could be there."

"Do you see me drinking fancy tea and eating scones?"

She nearly chokes on her drink. "Rafe! Yes, actually, I can." She finishes eating, taking his hand and leading him to the sofa. "Since I won the wager, I'll ask you first. Truth or dare?"

He thinks for a moment, worried about how this could go. "Truth."

"What is one thing you wish you could change about me, that you don't like?"

"Ana—"

"No, it's okay. I won't get angry or offended. I've thought

a lot about this. Please, answer the question."

"I wish you could have more self-confidence. To see yourself as I do, as strong, courageous, beautiful. When you see yourself as small or weak, it hurts me, knowing you have never been either of those."

"I'll work on it. Your turn."

He brings his hand up, caressing her face. "All right. Truth or dare?"

"Truth."

"What's something about me you don't like?"

"Rafe, that's against the rules. You can't ask the same question."

"I don't see a ref here. It's okay. Will you answer it?"

She looks down. "Yes. You know the answer, after last night. I wish you wouldn't push me so hard. There are times you feel you have to, I understand. Last night was not one of them."

"You're right. I am sorry for that. I will work on it."

"Truth or dare?"

"Truth."

"If you had gone back to your apartment, reading about the soulmate legend in the journal and realized it was about us, without being pulled back here, what would you have done?" She sees the confusion on his face. "Would you have come back to me and told me everything? What were you thinking about before they brought you back?"

"I hadn't given that much thought. I read the passage, then packed the journal in a box when the portal opened and swallowed me up. If I had read that, I probably would have come back to you. I would've taken you into your room, and I would've told you everything. Then I would let you decide whether to stay there with me or come here. I couldn't have told you about us being forbidden, because I did believe there was a curse. All right. Truth or dare?"

"Dare."

"I dare you to stare into my eyes, without looking down or away. Can you do that?"

She swallows hard, looking up at him. She keeps her gaze. "I love your silver-emerald eyes. They are the most beautiful eyes I have ever seen." Her eyes begin to water, as she desperately wants to look away. "For how long?" she asks, as her voice is breaking.

"Ana!" He pulls her to him, reassuring her. "It's okay. Why did that upset you so? What's wrong?"

"I was never allowed to look at my foster father. My head had to stay down any time I was with him. The only time he made me look at him was when we were… when—"

"Shh. It's okay. I'm so sorry. I never would've asked you to, if I had known. Please, mia estrela. Forgive me?"

"No, because this was my fault. I didn't tell you about it. If I had, it wouldn't have happened." She leans up, kissing him, then pulls back. "I'm okay now. It's your turn."

"Ana—"

"Really. Truth or dare?"

"Dare."

She smiles at him. "I dare you to kiss me, only with your lips on mine, your hands to yourself."

He looks at her, thinking this is an easy dare. "Okay."

His lips are on hers, devouring her. He starts to bring his hands up but instead lets them lay in his lap. She kisses harder, grabbing the back of his head. His hands start to come up again, but he holds them together. Her hand caresses down his neck as her lips part for him. Unable to help himself, his hands are up, grabbing her hair and kissing her, hard and hungry.

She pulls back. "I win!"

He laughs, shaking his head. "That was harder than I thought it would be."

"Really?"

"Yes! From the moment my lips were on yours, my hands were reaching for you. Oh, wait, you've never done that either, have you?"

"No. Is that my dare?" she asks, winking at him.

"Yes," he responds, as her lips are back on his.

She laces her fingers together, keeping her hands down to her lap. He wraps his hand around the back of her neck, gently holding her as his mouth continues to explore hers. He brings his other hand up, caressing along her back and ruffling through her wings.

A small groan of frustration escapes, as she struggles to keep her hands to herself. He gently runs his fingers through her wing, spreading his fingers and laughing as she grabs him with both hands and kisses him with everything she has.

"See what I mean?"

She pulls back, laughing. "That was hard! Now, are we still playing?"

"If you want."

"Truth or dare?"

"Dare," he says.

She leans up, her mouth on his ear. "I dare you to strip out of your pajamas."

Chapter 26

"Ana!" he says, getting to his feet. He strips to his shorts, sitting back with her. "All right. Your turn."

"Truth," she playfully says, seeing the look on his face. She laughs. "What?"

"Okay. Did you ask me to strip down because you have something in mind?"

She gasps, smiling at him. "Yes, I did."

He returns the smile, fire in his eyes. "Dare," he says. He watches her bite her lip, looking at him with love and want.

"I dare you to take me to bed."

"And do what?" he asks, picking her up and carrying her over. He lays her in the bed. "Ana, truth or dare?"

"Dare," she replies, looking up at him.

"I dare you to open up to me."

She sits up, looking at him. "What do you mean?"

He sits on the edge of the bed, looking at her. "I want you to talk to me, about what we're doing, without getting embarrassed."

"Rafe—"

"Can you do that?"

"I want to try." She looks up at his body is over hers, covering her and kissing her. "Oh, love." He sits her up, removing her pajamas. He smiles at the sight of her. "I'm going to pull down my undergarments for you," she says, as she slowly lowers them down. She kneels in front of him. "I'm going to take you in my hand, holding you as I touch you."

"You're doing very well. As your hand is caressing me, mine will be exploring every inch of you I can touch." He stops, as her face turns red. "Ana, we can stop if this is too much."

"I've already lost, getting embarrassed." She looks up at

him. "Could we just be together, how we usually are? Please?"

"Of course, mia estrela," he says, laying her back down.

He smiles when she tugs at his shorts. He pulls them off, letting them fall to the floor. She turns him over, kissing his chest and stomach. She starts with her hand, then her mouth wraps around, teasing and tantalizing. His breath sucks in as his heart is pounding in his chest. He grabs her up, pulling her to him as he's overwhelmed.

She kisses him hard, parting her legs as his hand caresses along. He smiles at her, feeling her ready for him. He pulls her up, laying her on her back, as he lowers down. His mouth leaves wet kisses along her stomach and hip. He brings his face down, kissing her thigh.

She trembles and writhes under him as his mouth continues to explore. A shudder wracks through his body as he responds to his own touches. He smiles up at her, moving faster. She cries out, falling back against the pillow, when he goes again.

Her body trembles and shakes, giving in to the waves crashing down on her. She screams out, grabbing his head and kissing him with everything she has left to give. He collapses on top of her, as they try to catch their breath.

"Ana, how long have you been wanting to do that, to play that?"

She laughs. "A while now."

"I see. Why didn't you ask?"

"I was waiting for the right time. This morning was it." She looks up at him, kissing him. "Thank you."

"For what?"

"Everything. I need a shower."

"Can we try something first?" he asks. He laughs at the look on her face. "No, I know we are both spent."

"I trust you. You know that, right?"

"I do."

"Okay. Then, yes. What do you have in mind?"

He sits up, pulling her with him. He takes her in his arms, her legs wrapping around his waist. She gasps when they are in the air. He takes her around the room, holding her against him. She looks up at him, kissing him as they slowly lower back to the bed. He sits on the edge, holding her wrapped around him.

"How was that?"

She smiles up at him. "Wonderful." He starts to stand. "Can we sit like this? Just being together with nothing between us?"

He sits back down, holding her to him. "As long as you need. Or if you start to get cold." He smiles when she extends her wings, wrapping them around both of them. He laughs as he gently ruffles through, her body trembling in response.

"Rafe! Don't be mean," she says, kissing him again.

"I'm sorry."

She looks at him, smiling. "No, you aren't."

He laughs. "You're right. It's too much fun seeing your whole body react to your wings like that. I am sorry, though."

She brings her hand up, caressing his jawline and chin. "Love, I am ready for you. Are you ready?"

He takes her hand, kissing it. "Ana, we will both be prepared by August."

"Yes, love."

"I'm happy that you're getting excited, for the wedding, for being with me. Please, don't be upset or embarrassed that I want to wait."

"I'm not, because I know you're right. Thank you."

"Now, let's get cleaned up and ready to have lunch brought in. You certainly worked up my appetite!"

"Of course."

He carries her into the washroom and turns on the shower. She looks over at the tub. "Thinking of a romantic bath with me?" he asks.

She puts a smile on her face then looks at him. "That would be nice. Maybe not for a little while, though."

"Ana, whenever you're ready."

"I see now, what you mean. I get these moments, when I truly feel like I am ready. So how will I know when I really am? Ready to be with you?"

"We both will."

"I hate that," she says.

"What?" he asks, walking up to her. "Hate what? Feeling what I feel?"

"No! No, not that. The fact that you have to watch over me, looking and feeling for unease, for an episode or trigger." She hangs her head. "I hate that you can't let go and enjoy being with me."

"Ana, I do. Did we not enjoy what we did?"

She looks up at him, blushing. "Very much, but—"

"See? You have nothing to be ashamed of or embarrassed about. We can be together, doing everything but that, and truly enjoy it. You know how much I do."

"I do, Rafe. Thank you, for your patience with me."

"Shower, now!" he orders with a wink.

She laughs, falling into his arms. "Yes, Guardian."

They clean up and step out. He picks her up, carrying her to the closet. "Now, what are you wearing until your tea party?"

She surveys her new gowns. At his dresser, she watches him change his clothes. She slips into the gown, putting on gold shoes and crown. She makes her way towards him. "Like this?"

He looks at her, stopping in his tracks, his breath in his throat. "Ana!"

She blushes. "You like it?"

He looks her over, shaking his head. "This is different. Yes, I like it."

She walks to the mirror, admiring the gown. It's deep purple, with long lace sleeves and a split skirt. Satin purple riding under lace, with a low back. "I thought you would."

"This is one you picked out?"

"It is."

"You do have good taste!" He watches her blush. "Ana, I am talking about the gown. Now, take a breath before you pass out."

"Yes, love."

"Are we flying after lunch?"

"Yes."

"Promise me you'll wear that gown."

She turns to him, returning his smile. "What?"

"Oh, mia estrela. I want to see you in the air with that gown. I am sure it will be a beautiful sight!" He leans down, kissing her. "I'll see about lunch."

She watches him step out. As she approaches the mirror, her wings expand. Her mind drifts back to the forest, as she sat up with an intense burning pain in her shoulders.

"Lunch will be here any time."

Ana startles at Rafe's voice. "Thank you."

"Then we'll go to the training center."

"Yes, love."

They step out of the closet as the bell is ringing. Rafe steps over, taking the tray. He sets up their lunch on their private table.

She joins him. "My favorites from NightFall. Thank you," she says, picking up her mug of cocoa.

"You're welcome, Your Majesty."

"Guardian!"

They laugh as they continue eating. "Ana, are you upset you have wings?"

"No! Nothing like that. I was thinking back to the day it happened, wondering why it was me. What's special about me?"

"Everything," he says. He watches her eyes go down. "Ana, you know it's the truth. You went into battle for your throne, were tortured to defend the vampyra, tortured to defend the guardians. Yet you are still here, having won every battle you've been in. Do you see now why I could never see you as small or weak? Do you understand why you should have more confidence?"

"Rafe, I want to. I've always admired Kara for being so sure of herself. I don't know if I could ever be like that."

"Why not?"

Setting her fork down, she averts her eyes. Rising from her seat, she makes her way to the sofa. Sitting down, she watches as the rain falls. She pulls her knees up to her chest, knowing he's going to come over. While she closes her eyes, he takes a seat next to her.

She's surprised when he says nothing. He takes her hand, looking out the window. She looks at him before quickly turning back to watch the rain. They sit in silence for a few minutes, before she can't take it anymore.

"This is almost worse than you pushing."

"What?" he asks, confused. "How so?"

"Because when you ask, I can hear in your voice if you're upset with me. Sitting in silence like this, not knowing—"

"Ana, do you not feel the love coming from me?"

"You're better at controlling it."

"Maeriana Rose!" She swallows hard, looking at him. "I would never use this to lie or be deceptive to you. I am not angry that you came over here. I was trying to give you some space by not asking, while taking your hand to let you know I am here for you."

"I'm sorry. I'm so sorry!"

He scoots over, wrapping his arm around her. "Stop. It's okay. I was trying to do as you asked, trying not to push you."

"I know."

"Will you finish your lunch?"

"Would you bring me my plate?"

He jumps to his feet, getting it off the table and bringing it over. "Eat, mia estrela."

"I will," she says, taking the plate. She finishes eating and sets it on the table beside her. She looks up at him, taking his hand. "Thank you."

"Will you tell me about it?"

"There's really nothing to tell. I… I had to be small, be quiet, any time my foster father was home. If he saw me or heard me," she swallows hard, closing her eyes. She can hear the belt buckle hitting the shelf as he pulled it off. "He would use his belt. I learned very quickly not to make waves, not to talk back or speak up, to only speak when spoken to. I guess after almost four years of that, then dealing with the matron, who treated me like I was a burden, it stuck with me, made me into who I am." She looks back down, tracing her finger along his hand.

"You suffered so much on Earth. How you sit here, so calm, so full of love and compassion and warmth, is beyond me. I can't imagine how I would feel if I lived through that, but I think I would be angry and bitter."

"I have that sometimes, too. When I screamed at you to go because you didn't believe me about Everard or when I would get angry talking about marriage. You weren't the only one who had to work on their anger. I tried to hide mine better."

"We both hide from each other, don't we?"

She looks up at him. "Yes, we do." She looks at the clock. "Did you want a flying session before I go to the tea party?"

"Yes, if you're up for it."

"I am. I need to stretch them."

"Let's go." He takes her hand, leading her out. Kellan and Erick come to attention. "Training center."

Kellan leads the way. Rafe sees Ana trying not to stare at Erick's wings. She looks up at him, blushing. "What?"

"Really?"

"Is this going to be like Bela all over again, because I swear—"

"No!" he says, laughing. "It's not."

"Okay."

Kellan gives the all clear, and they go inside. She expands her wings and works them. Rafe takes to the air, growing concerned when she shakes her head.

"What?" he asks, lowering back down.

"I have to stretch and warm up."

"I know."

"Jerk!" she yells as she flies after him, easily catching him. "Told you I was faster!"

"Yeah, I know."

She backs away, giving him a hurt look. "Wow. You are jealous, aren't you?" She flies up to him. "Really?"

"No, I'm not. I'm just play—"

Hearing the anger in his voice, she backs away again. "Do you think I wanted this? Do you think I wanted any of this? It was forced on me, and I have tried my best to accept it. Now that I finally have, you're going to make me feel bad for it?"

"Ana, no. I'm sorry. Please—" he tries, as she lowers back down.

"I want to go back to our quarters."

"Ana—"

"Stop!" she cries out, looking up at him. "I'll attend this tea party, since I am expected, then I want to be alone tonight."

He rushes to her and grasps her hands. He kneels before her, kissing them. "I'm so sorry. I never meant to make you feel that way. Don't send me away again. Please, forgive me?"

She kneels down with him, looking up into his eyes. "Why do you do that? Why do you make me feel so bad about myself, because I'm better at something than you? You always seem so happy with my accomplishments, unless it's something I'm better at. Like using a sword. I could tell you were jealous of that, too. Why?"

"I've been flying and training for over five hundred years. You walk in, and you're a natural at everything you do. I am impressed at how great you are at everything you do. I am jealous, and I swear, I don't mean to be! I thought I was doing better with it, not letting you see or feel it. I am truly sorry. Please, mia estrela. Please, can you forgive me?"

She stands up, pulling him to his feet. "I already have such issues, such self-doubt, that for you to add to it." She looks up him, seeing the shame on his face. She caresses his jawline. "If you mean it, that you'll work on it, then yes, I forgive you."

"I am, I am working on it. I swear it. Now, please, will you fly some more? I know they need to stretch, after yesterday."

"I will, if you'll step out into the hall."

"What?"

"I want to do this alone."

"Yes, Ana."

She watches him step out. In a rush, she makes her way to the washroom, where she collapses onto the vanity, sobbing. She begins to run the water as she calms down. Cupping her hands, she cleans her face and takes a small drink.

Stepping back outside, she ascends into the air and completes a few laps of flight. As she descends, her wings give out, and she lets out a cry. Colliding forcefully with the mat, she struggles to catch her breath. She remains motionless, overwhelmed with shock.

Chapter 27

Ana tries to calm her pounding heart. In an effort to regain her breath, she rolls onto her side. Slowly, she rises to her feet and begins exploring her leg and stomach with her hands. Upon the realization that nothing is injured, she heaves a sigh. She walks out and spots Rafe conversing with Kellan and Erick.

"I'm ready to go to our quarters," she says. She keeps her arms crossed, trying to get warm. Rafe looks at her but says nothing as they go back.

Once inside, she looks at him.

"I need to rinse off, then Kara and Evren will be here to get Kellan and me ready for the tea party."

"You want to shower by yourself?"

"Just a quick rinse."

"All right."

She enters the closet. Shedding her gown and undergarments, she slips on a robe and goes for the washroom. Observing Rafe, she notices the worry etched onto his face.

"What?"

He rushes to her and rips the robe off. "What happened?"

Glancing down, she notices bruises developing on her leg and stomach. She runs to the washroom and slams the door behind her.

"I'm not mad. Please, what happened?" he asks, pounding on the door. She closes her eyes, focusing on her wings. They turn to fire and heal her body. As they return to her crimson feathers, she falls against the door. "What was that? Are you okay?"

Ignoring him, she starts the water and steps under it. She sighs in relief at the feel of it. Stepping out, she dries off and wraps herself in a towel.

She opens the door to find him staring at her. "I'd like to get dressed."

He studies her, seeing her injuries have mended. "You used your wings!"

"I'm fine."

"Tell me what happened."

She swallows hard. "My wings gave out and… I fell. It wasn't very far, as I was already lowering down. I landed on a mat. I'm fine." She cries out in surprise when he pulls her to him.

"I never should leave you alone. Why do you do that? I leave, and you get hurt. I can't take that."

"But I'm fine now."

"I left to get snacks, and you were nearly killed by an assassin. I left when we fought about Everard, and he nearly took your life. Do you see, I can't leave you alone!"

"Rafe, this was nothing compared to what you just said. I'm perfectly fine. It's not a big deal."

"This time it wasn't. What if you had been up at the ceiling? Or what if you had been up in the battlement?"

"Rafe—"

"No! This is why I worry, and why I push. I knew I should've stayed in there, but after how I acted, I was trying to give you some space."

She lets out a small gasp. "You're blaming yourself again. I would've fallen whether you were in there or not. This wasn't your fault." She grips his chin and makes him look at her. "Tell me this wasn't your fault!"

He stares into her eyes. "All right. It wasn't. It wasn't my fault, what happened just now."

"We're okay. I'm going to this tea party to make new friends, then we'll have dinner with Kara and Evren. You and I can spend all evening together. Please?" She steps up, kissing him. "Please, love?"

"Yes, Ana."

"You're still upset. I can feel it."

"I'm upset with myself and upset because you had to use your wings. Why didn't you let me heal you?"

"I was afraid if I told you what happened while you were looking at the bruises, it would be too much for you. I love you, but I cannot take your anger. Not right now, not while I'm still dealing with his camp!"

His eyes close in shame. "I am sorry. You're right. I put so much more on you right now. You are already trying to heal and recover, and I only made it worse."

"No, love. It's okay. You had every right to be worried about me, once you saw I was hurt. I don't blame you for that."

"Come on. You're shivering." He scoops her into his arms and takes her into the closet. He sits with her on the ottoman, holding her with all the love he has for her.

"Hmm. This brings back memories," she says, looking at him.

He leans down and kisses her. "Yes, it does. I doubted you. I doubted every day that this was enough for you. Looking back, I know how much you love me, how lost you were when I broke your heart. I can see why you doubted me, why you were so worried I would leave you again. I never want you to feel that way as long as we live."

"Rafe, you're angry I wanted to be alone tonight, aren't you?"

"Yes and no. Yes, because I never want to be without you. No, because you were only trying to protect yourself from my anger, so I can understand."

"It wouldn't have happened."

He cocks his head. "What do you mean?"

"I could feel my own heart breaking as soon as I said the words, so I knew I would not be able to be without you tonight. Even if I had to beg you to stay."

"I promise you, it would not come to that. You saw how devastated I was."

"I'm so sorry!"

"No, no. I'm not trying to make you feel guilty. I wanted to point out how badly I didn't want to be away from you."

"Rafe, I'm getting cold."

He stands her up, taking her towel. "Yes, mia estrela."

She gets dressed, slipping on the pink gown she had picked out. She puts on silver shoes and crown, looking at him. "What do you think?"

He smiles, looking at her. "I think you're perfect." His smile grows when she blushes. "Ana?"

She looks up at him. "Yes, love?"

"You are truly beautiful. Are you ready to be in a room full of women who are jealous of you?"

She takes a breath before lowering her gaze. "Rafe—"

"Ana, ask Kellan or Kara. They will tell you the same thing."

The bell rings. "Speaking of which," she says on her way to open the door.

She steps back as the three of them enter. Kara helps Ana with her hair while Evren gets Kellan dressed and ready. Kellan and Ana step out, sitting on the chaise.

"We'll get ready and be right back," Kara says, taking Evren out the door.

Ana looks at Kellan. "Are you as nervous as I am?"

She lets out a laugh. "I don't know. I'm pretty nervous."

"You're both going to be fine. I swear, you can stare down an assassin but get scared at the thought of drinking tea with other women?"

"He's right," Ana admits.

"That's the sad part, Majesty!"

They both laugh. She looks up when Kara and Evren return. Evren is dressed in a white gown with lace sleeves. Kara is in a navy-blue gown with a cinched bodice and billowing skirt. Ana jumps to her feet.

"Kara, you and Evren look great. You should dress like

that more often."

"No, thank you," Kara says, laughing. "This is not something I prefer to wear. I'd much rather be in my pants and shirts."

"Honestly, I feel the same," Kellan says.

"Are we ready?" Rafe asks, taking Ana's arm.

"Let's get this over with," Kara says.

"Sis!" Ana exclaims.

"What? I'm thinking what we all want to say."

"Kara, Anwyn went to a lot of trouble to set this up. Be nice, please?"

"I will. I promise."

Rafe leads them to the Lunala ballroom. The doors are standing open, with a few ladies already inside. Ana swallows hard. "What are you doing while we're in here?"

"I'll be out here with Erick, as your second guardian."

"Rafe!"

"What? I want to. It's okay. He and I get along fine."

"All right." She kisses him again before going inside. She looks at Kara, who appears completely at ease.

I do wish I could be more like her. My heart is pounding, my hands are sweating, I would give anything to get out of here.

She takes a deep breath, calming her mind and heart. She walks with Kara to meet ladies of the court. Anwyn walks in, greeting everyone and gesturing for them to sit at the long banquet table set up. Three-tier stands are spread every few feet. Each stand has sandwiches on the bottom, scones and biscuits in the middle, and sweets on top.

"Sweets are for last," Kara whispers to her. Ana shoots her a look. "What?"

"I would like each lady to stand up, introduce yourself, and tell us what realm you are from."

Ana looks at Kara, panic in her eyes. Kara leans over. "Ana, it's fine. You are Queen Maeriana of the Sea-Stellar Realm."

Even taking deep breaths, her heart races by the time it comes to her. She stands up, introducing herself. "I am Queen Maeriana of the Sea-Stellar Realm." She sits down.

"Thank you, ladies. Now, shall we?" Anwyn asks, taking a tea pot and pouring into her cup. Ana accepts and steeps her tea, watching Kara. She looks up when she realizes everyone is watching her.

Her face grows crimson as she faces Kara. "My wings opened up, didn't they?" Kara slowly nods. Ana takes a breath, focusing on retracting them in. She stares down at her plate but her head snaps up when Kara stands.

"Our apologies. The queen is still tired from her travels, and she is still adjusting to her wings. They can be a little harder to manage while she is recovering."

"We understand. Thank you," Anwyn says. "Majesty, if you need to rest—"

"I'm all right, Countess. Thank you, though." Relief washes over her when she realizes the ladies have resumed talking to each other. She looks at Kara. "Thank you, sis," she whispers to her. "That could've been so much worse."

"Ana, it's okay." Kara grins at Kellan. "So, I've heard that you are courting someone. Want to spill any details?"

Kellan smiles at Kara. "What have you heard?"

"Hmm. That he is a squire."

"Incorrect."

"What?" Kara asks. "Who is it?"

"Ramin."

"Ramin as in Captain of the Royal Guard?"

She laughs. "Yes. We just started, so I don't know how serious it's going to get." She looks at Ana. "We couldn't be together, if you had not passed your treaty."

Anwyn stands up. "If you aren't too embarrassed, I would like any lady here who is able to be in their current relationship because of the treaty to raise their hand."

Ana looks around as most of them go up. "Really?" she

asks, looking at Anwyn.

"Majesty, that is the main reason we wanted to have this today, in your honor. To thank you."

"You are all very welcome."

"The ladies who did not raise their hands are grateful because you ended the war, returning their spouses or children home to them."

Ana gets to her feet. "I am not very comfortable speaking in front of a group of people, but I want to thank you for having me today. I have questioned myself at times. Questioned if I was right for the throne, right to be queen. I laid my life down in battle, defending the ones I love. I passed the treaty, freeing slaves, and making love legal. I feel as though I am queen, not because of the blood flowing through my veins, but through my actions for my kingdom and my realm." She sits back down, seeing Kara with the biggest smile. "What?"

"Ana, that was brilliant! You have to tell Rafe about that."

"I'll let you tell him over dinner." She looks up as Anwyn approaches. "Is everything all right?"

"Yes, Majesty. I want to tell you, your speech was spectacular! You absolutely have earned your throne, proving your worth, even if you never needed to. We are so grateful to have you as our queen."

"I appreciate your words, Countess. Thank you."

"Now, will you please eat?" She looks at Ana as she blushes. "Majesty?"

"My apologies. I did not realize everyone was waiting on me."

"Oh, no. That's my fault. I forget you are new here. I'm sorry."

"Quite all right. Would you mind helping me?"

"I'll be glad to help." She shows Ana the various foods and helps her fix her plate. Ana watches as the other ladies do the same.

She sits back down, looking at Kara. "I had no idea they

were waiting on me to eat."

"I didn't, either. It's okay. They are now. So, are you enjoying yourself?"

"I'm still nervous, but I feel better than I did when we first arrived." She looks over to see a young baroness staring at her. "Kara, who is she again?"

"That is Baroness Amaris. I do not know why she is looking at you so intently, though."

"Should I walk over and say hi?"

Kara laughs. "Ana!"

"What?"

"No. When everyone starts to leave, we'll approach her."

"All right."

"Now, please, eat."

"I will."

With uncertainty, she gazes at the sandwich on her plate. Picking it up, she takes a small bite. She nearly gags when she realizes it is some sort of fish salad. She looks at Kara, who takes the sandwich and eats it. She devours her biscuit and sweets.

"I should've known."

"Kara!" They both laugh. She finishes her tea. "Kara, I could use some water." She looks up as a pitcher and glass are brought over. "Thank you," she says to the young woman who poured her drink. She bows and backs away.

Kara sees the confusion on Ana's face. "She's here to help serve. She is not a slave, I promise you."

"Thank you."

"Are you okay? You look as though you could pass out."

"I had an incident in the training center, but I'm okay."

"What happened now? Who hurt who?"

"Kara, it wasn't like that. He wasn't even in the room. I fell."

"You fell!"

"Quiet! I don't want everyone staring at us. I'm okay,

Kara."

"What happened?"

"I'll tell you about it at dinner. I really don't want to discuss it here."

"All right. You swear you're okay?"

"Do you really think he would've let me come if I wasn't?"

"Hmm. Fine. We'll talk in a little bit."

"Thank you."

The baroness approaches her. "Majesty," she says, bowing. "I am Amaris, Baroness of MoonSol."

"Baroness, how can I help?"

"I wanted to meet you, and I wanted to thank you. Without your treaty, my sister would not be able to be with the person she loves. At least, not openly. So, thank you."

"Is your sister here?"

"She is not. She is on bedrest."

"I'm sorry to hear that." Ana sees the concern on her face. "Will she be all right?"

"She is pregnant by a guardian. He would have been killed and she would've been punished if not for the protection in your treaty."

"I am grateful they will be okay now. Even if I were not in love with a guardian myself, I still would have put that in there, because love should never be illegal!" She notices the women are all looking at her. "I would not rule over a kingdom where it was."

"Thank you," Anwyn says. "Every one of us here appreciates that."

Ana looks up when Rafe and Erick run in. Rafe rushes to her. "Apologies, Majesty. There has been an incident. Please, come with me now."

"Rafe, what is happening?"

Without another word, he lifts her from her seat and carries her out of the ballroom.

Chapter 28

They rush inside their quarters. Kara stays with Ana and Evren by the fireplace as Rafe and Erick inspect all the rooms. "All clear," Rafe says. Erick steps out and joins Kellan in the corridor.

"What is going on?" Ana demands.

"We caught one assassin. During interrogation, he claims there were two more assassins with him."

"Who sent them?"

"He won't say. They are still interrogating him. As soon as I heard, I came and got you. I apologize if I scared you, as that was never my intention. I needed to get you to safety as quickly as possible."

"No, it's okay. I understand." She looks at Kara and Evren. "Can't ever have a normal day, can I?"

"I guess not," Kara responds. "Do you want to get changed for staying in?"

"Yes."

Rafe takes her hand, going with her to the closet. He helps her out of her gown. She slips on her black pants, shirt, and hoodie. Then she sits on the ottoman.

"What's wrong?"

"I wanted a nice day with the ladies of the court. What must they be thinking? I'm embarrassed now."

"Ana, I can assure you, they are going to their quarters, as well. Everything is essentially locked down until we find the assassins. Four more guardians and ten royal guards are on their way up, to guard outside your door."

"Rafe, that is way too many! Use some of them to search the palace."

"It's protocol, nothing I can do. I agree with you, though."

He joins her and takes her hand. "Now, your friends are out here. Let's visit with them."

"Yes, Rafe." She stands up, leaning against him. He takes her hand.

"You are exhausted! Why didn't you say anything?"

"I didn't want to ruin her tea party. She put a lot of time and effort into it. I know it's from earlier, but I'm okay."

He takes her to the chaise and helps her recline. Kara and Evren walk to her. "Sis, are you okay?"

"I am."

"Will you tell me what happened?"

Ana yawns. "I'm too tired. Rafe will tell you."

Kara faces him. "What happened to her in the training center?"

"Apparently her wings gave out, causing her to fall. She was not too high and landed on one of the mats. She's okay, but she had some bruises that she healed."

"*She* healed? Meaning she used her wings?"

"Yes."

Kara wants to ask but sees she's asleep. She pulls the blanket over her. Rafe sits on the chaise, looking down at her.

He turns to Kara. "Are you both staying in here tonight?"

"Yes. I know she will want us to. We'll get cleaned up and come right back."

"Kara, take Kellan with you. Have her inspect your quarters and watch over you, please? You know Ana would want that."

"Yes, Rafe. Then we'll bring her with us so she can change back into her uniform. I know she's not crazy about being in a gown."

"Like you?" Rafe asks, chuckling.

"Shut up."

"What? You look very nice."

"Whatever." She sticks her tongue out at him. She takes Evren's hand to go next door.

He feels her forehead and face. "At least you aren't sick. I'm worried enough as it is."

"Hmm, love?"

"Yes, Ana?"

"I hardly ate at the tea party. Will we have dinner soon?"

"I'm sorry. Everything is closed down right now, including food service. We will have food brought in, but I'm not sure how long it will be."

"Oh, okay."

He takes her hand, closing his eyes. "Why didn't you eat there?"

"I tried," she explains, yawning, "but the sandwich was some horrible fish thing I couldn't stomach. I did have a biscuit and some cookies."

Kara and Evren walk in. Kara runs to Ana, unable to hide the concern etched on her face. "What's wrong?"

"After healing herself, she needs to eat. Stay with her. I'll go get some."

"Rafe, no. It's too dangerous. Let them conduct their sweep, then we'll have food brought in."

"Kara, I can feel how hungry she is. She needs to eat."

"Then I'll get it," Evren says. "We have some bread and cheese from a snack earlier. I'll bring it over."

"Kara—"

"I'm going with her. We'll be right back." They step out, as Kellan walks in.

"Apologies, Majesty. I am changing back into my uniform."

"It's all right," Ana says softly. She looks when Evren and Kara return. They bring the tray to her.

"Ana, please eat."

Rafe helps her sit up, feeding her pieces of bread and cheese. "Thank you, both. She needs this."

Kara gets her a glass of water. "Drink, sis. Then get some sleep."

"Why are you all so worried about me?" she asks, laughing. "I'm okay, just tired. Really."

"We know. I'll take you to the washroom then Rafe will put you to bed."

"We'll sleep on the ottoman so you guys can have the bed."

"No, Ana. I'm moving the chaise over by the bed."

"Kara—"

"Please, don't argue. It's for your protection."

"All right." She finishes eating and drinking. Kara takes her to the washroom. Evren sits with Rafe.

"I didn't think she got so tired using her wings to heal? Not anymore?"

"I think between rushing here Monday, then what happened today, her body is a little overwhelmed. She needs rest, then she'll be fine. At least she's not sick. I checked."

Kara walks back out with Ana. Rafe carries her to bed. Laying her down, he covers her with the blanket. He takes her hand, feeling her in a deep sleep. He returns to Kara and Evren.

"How is she?" Evren asks.

"Sleeping good."

"Oh, Rafe, I meant to tell you. You should've seen her at the tea party. She made a speech about earning her place on the throne. She was fantastic! I wish you could've heard her."

"We talked a little this morning, about how I wish she could be more confident. She really admires how you are and wishes she could be more like you."

"I was a lot like her when I was her age."

"What changed?"

"Everything. Where we were, it became illegal to use magic. My mother, two sisters, and myself fled to another galaxy. There was… an accident, and I refused to practice magic. I came to the MoonSol Realm, where I befriended a beautiful countess, who was pregnant. I stayed along, helping as her aid. When Rosalina was born, I felt a bond with her.

When she became engaged to Caelum, we came here."

"Does Ana know any of this?" Rafe asks.

"A little."

"But you still won't tell us why you stopped using magic?"

"No. I swore I would never speak of it again. My apologies."

"It's all right. We all have our secrets, don't we?" He looks at the bed. "Believe me, I was shocked when she showed me her tattoo!" He turns back to Kara. "So, what happened at the club?"

Kara laughs. "Oh, no. She begged me never to speak of that again."

"Please?"

"No. Not unless she gives me her permission."

"All right then."

"Rafe?"

He looks over when Ana calls his name. "On my way." He looks at Kara, getting to his feet. He goes to Ana. "What's wrong?"

"Will you take me to the washroom?"

He scoops her up and carries her in, growing concerned when she vomits. He feels her forehead. "You have a fever."

"I don't feel well," she says, walking to the vanity and rinsing her mouth. She brushes her teeth. He picks her up, taking her back to bed. He goes to Kara and Evren.

"I have to get Winslow in here. She's sick."

"We'll stay with her."

Rafe steps out, seeing all her guards and guardians. He decides to get Winslow himself, knowing it's dangerous. He goes to the Medical Center. Winslow is in his office. He gets to his feet at the sight of Rafe.

"Ana is ill."

He grabs his bag and follows him back to their quarters. Winslow walks up to her and pulls out his machine. He takes a blood sample and runs it as he's taking her temperature. "She has a fever." He looks at the screen when it beeps. "Hmm. This isn't good."

"What's wrong?"

"She has andelaise and pneumonia."

"How serious is that?"

"It could be fatal." He gets out his syringes, giving her two injections. "She'll sleep through this. The most important thing is keeping her temperature down. Keep a cold, wet cloth on her head as much as you can. I have to get back to the center, but I'll come by to check on her."

"Winslow, let me escort you back. It's dangerous right now."

"I'll have one of the guards outside take me. It's all right."

"Thank you."

Kara and Evren walk to Rafe and Ana as soon as he leaves. She sees the worried look on Rafe's face. "What's wrong?"

"It's serious."

"What? What do you mean?"

"She has andelaise and pneumonia."

"Shit," Kara responds. "Evren, come into the washroom with me." They go inside.

Rafe goes with them. "I need a cloth soaked with cold water."

Kara fixes it up and hands it to him. "We'll be out in a moment."

He takes the cloth and lays it gently on Ana's forehead. He kisses her cheek, knowing she doesn't like to be kissed on the mouth when she's sick.

"I'm right here, mia estrela. Please, get better." He sits by her, holding her hand. He looks up when Kara and Evren join them.

"We're going to try something. I don't know if it will help, but I can't just sit here and do nothing while she is so sick."

"What do you need?"

"For her to drink this." Kara has a bowl in her hands, with

a bright pink liquid inside. Rafe grimaces. "I swear, this is made to help her. If it doesn't work, it will not hurt her."

He looks at Evren, who nods. "Okay. I don't see that we have any choice. She needs to be in the Medical Center, but we can't chance that until the assassins are caught. Go ahead." He caresses Ana's face. "Mia estrela? Ana, can you wake up for me?"

"Hmm, no," she says, turning away. "I need sleep."

"You need to drink this medicine, then we'll let you sleep."

She rolls back over. "Promise?"

"I do."

"Okay." He helps her sit up, holding her head as Kara slowly pours the liquid down her throat. She gags. "That tastes awful!"

"It will help," Kara says. "Now get more sleep."

"Okay." Rafe helps her lay back down. "You're laying with me, aren't you?"

"I will soon. Now get some sleep." He looks down, realizing she's already out. He looks at Kara. "How soon will we know if it helps?"

"Could be an hour or two. It's not a cure all, but it should help her fever and help with the pneumonia, at least. I'm hoping it will work on the andelaise, but I can't say for sure."

"Kara, how long have you planned this? The medicine?"

"We picked up the herbs and supplies when we were in the market. I had a feeling she would get sick again. I had to do something."

"I understand. Let's pray this works. I'm going to change into pajamas. I'll get into bed with her, but I can't hold her to me. We have to get her temperature down." He takes the cloth with him, running it under cold water.

Placing it back on her forehead, then Rafe goes into the closet and changes. He walks out and climbs into bed. He instinctively wants to reach for her. When he turns away, he sees the look of understanding on Kara's face.

"You have to fight it, don't you?"

"Yes. I didn't realize our pull was that strong."

"Rafe, even unconscious you reach for each other."

"I didn't think of that. Maybe I shouldn't sleep in the bed with her."

"It'll be okay. I'll keep an eye on both of you."

"Thanks, Kara."

"I'll let you know if we hear any news on the assassins." She looks at Evren, then back to him. "What happens if we don't find them?"

"We'll stay locked down for another twenty-four hours, then the palace will resume normal business. Additional guards and guardians will be posted, but otherwise it will go back to how it was."

She walks to the chaise and sits with Evren. When Ana trembles against him, his gaze falls upon her. He touches her cheek, noting its warmth. With his eyes closed, he longs to hold her desperately. He rolls over again, attempting to go to sleep.

⁂

Kara checks on Ana. She removes the cloth before feeling her face and neck. Rafe turns to her and watches.

"How is she?"

"She doesn't feel as warm. I'm not sure if that's us or the medicine Winslow gave her, or both. I really hope she is getting better."

Kara goes to the washroom, wetting the cloth and putting it back on her forehead. The bell rings.

"I'll get it. Stay with her," Kara says, then she walks to the door. Kellan is outside. They speak for a few moments, then Kara returns.

"They caught another of the assassins, who confirmed what the first one said, that there are three of them. They're still questioning him."

"I know she is curious to find out who has hired them. Why now? All of her enemies are dead. Who could be behind this?"

"I don't know. Like you, I hope we find out soon enough."

"No!" Ana cries out, rolling over. "Please, don't hurt me!"

Rafe crawls over to her, gently shaking her. "Ana! Wake up. You're having a nightmare. You're okay now."

She opens her eyes, looking at him. She reaches up, caressing his face. "My love," she says, passing out. He feels around her face and neck.

"You are right, her fever is going down. That's good. I wonder what her nightmare was about?"

"Honestly, as sick as she is, she may not even remember," Kara says. "We'll let you both get rest. Let me know if you need anything."

"Thanks, Kara."

Chapter 29

Kara feels Ana's face, shocked that her fever is gone. She walks to Rafe and gently wakes him.

"Hey."

"What's wrong?" he asks, sitting up.

"No, it's good. Her fever is gone."

He rolls over, feeling Ana's cheek. "Oh, thank goodness." He smiles at Kara. "Thank you, you and Evren both."

"Of course."

He takes Ana in his arms. "Kara, she's going to need a shower. Her whole body is drenched in sweat. I'll get her in, if you'll get her clean clothes."

"Yes, Rafe. Evren will change the bedding."

Rising to his feet, he carries her to the washroom. He undresses them both while turning on the water. He takes her in, washing her all over. He lowers her to the shower floor, leaning against the wall. After cleaning and drying himself, he changes into his pajamas. Kara knocks.

"Come in."

She steps in. He gets Ana up, as Kara helps him dry her off and get dressed. "Evren almost has the bed made up."

"Thank you both."

Kara fills a glass with water and gets Ana to drink it. "Hmm. Kara, I need to go."

"Where?"

Ana laughs. "No, you know."

"I'll step out while you help her," Rafe says. He walks into the main chamber and helps Evren finish making the bed. "Thanks, Evren."

"She did sweat a lot. She'll feel better on fresh sheets."

Rafe glances over when Kara steps out, holding Ana up.

He runs to them and carries her to bed. "Maybe now we can all sleep tonight."

"Here's hoping." Kara walks to the chaise with Evren.

"Rafe?"

He jerks awake and sits up. "What's wrong?"

"Nothing, but I'm hungry. Did we ever get food?"

"I'll check." He walks to the table, relieved to see plates of food. Kara sees him and steps up beside him.

"Is she awake?"

"She is, and she's hungry."

"It was just delivered."

Rafe takes the lid off. He tries a bite of everything, then notices Kara staring at him. "I'm not taking any chances."

"I don't blame you," she says. He takes the plate to bed, helping Ana eat. Kara approaches. "How do you feel?"

"Better," Ana says. "Tired and hungry."

"To be expected. Eat then get more rest. We are two assassins down, waiting for news on the third."

"Okay." She finishes eating. "I need more sleep."

Kara takes the plate, watching Rafe lay down with Ana. "Rafe, you need to eat as well. I'll bring you a plate."

"Thanks."

He takes the plate and devours his meal before handing it back to her. She takes it to the table, then eats with Evren. When she hears the bell, she opens the door to find Winslow. She gestures for him to come in.

"Dare I ask, how is she?"

"Much better. She ate, and now she's resting." She sees the surprise on his face. "Evren and I cooked something up. Once things have calmed down, we'll stop by and go over it with you."

"You cured andelaise?"

"Well, I won't know that until you examine her."

He approaches Ana, who wakes up. "Winslow?"

"I'm taking a small sample to run. My apologies."

"No, it's okay. Thank you."

He pulls out his machine and scans her blood. There's a beep, and he checks the screen. "Her temperature is normal, and this shows no sickness or infection." He looks at Kara. "I will be most curious to hear about your treatment."

"We'll come by tomorrow."

"Please, do." He turns back to Ana. "Rest, Majesty. I will check on you again in the morning."

"Thank you, Winslow."

He leaves. Kara walks up to her and feels her forehead. "How do you feel?"

"Much better, thanks to you and Evren. I am exhausted, though. Can I go back to sleep?"

Kara chuckles, pulling the blanket up. "Of course. Sleep, sis."

She looks at Rafe as Ana falls back to sleep. Rafe takes her into his arms. Kara returns to the chaise and moves it a little closer to the bed. She kisses Evren good night.

Ana opens her eyes and turns to Rafe. She smiles at him while tracing his jawline with her fingers.

"Morning, mia estrela. Are you recovered?"

"I am. Any news on the third assassin?"

Kara stretches and joins them. "Nothing yet. I'll see if we can get breakfast." She steps out into the hallway.

"Do you remember having a nightmare last night?"

"No. Did I?"

"You cried out but fell back to sleep."

She shakes her head. "I don't remember. I do remember waking up, drenched in sweat when my fever broke. You and Kara helped clean me up. I remember eating a little. Was Winslow here?"

"Yes, a couple of times."

"That's really all I remember."

"Okay." He looks over as Kara walks back in.

"No news on the third assassin, but food is on the way."

She gestures for Rafe to follow her. He looks down at Ana, seeing she fell back to sleep. He gently lays her down, then walks to Kara. They go to the fireplace and push the chaise back to its original location.

"We found out who is behind this."

"Who?"

"You're not going to believe it."

"Kara, just tell me."

"It's Emory."

He steps back in shock. "What? I thought—"

"We all did. The assassins have been kept separated, but during interrogation they both admitted to being hired by him."

"There must be some greater plot. This doesn't make sense, at all."

"I know. That's why I pulled you over here to talk. I'm not telling Ana, not until we can confirm this."

"I think that's best. I know she hates it when we do this, but we aren't keeping it from her. We are waiting on more information."

"Exactly."

"I'm going to check on her." He walks back over to the bed, seeing her still asleep. He lays with her, taking her hand. He nearly gasps as he's overwhelmed with feelings of shame. He looks at her, seeing and feeling her trembling. "Ana? Ana, wake up," he tries, gently shaking her. "Please, Ana."

Kara runs over. "What's wrong?"

Ana opens her eyes, looking up at him. Tears start

streaming down as she clings to him. "Rafe! Please," she begs.

"What is it? What happened?" he asks.

"I was… I was back in his camp. I'm sorry."

"No, Ana. No apology. I'm right here. You're safe now. It's all right." He holds her to him, wiping her tears. He looks at Kara, seeing the worry on her face. He looks back down at Ana. "You're safe, mia estrela. We're here with you."

She clings to him tighter. "Please don't leave."

"I won't. I swear to you I won't. I'm right here." He caresses her face, gently stroking her hair. "Right here, mia estrela." He looks down, seeing that she fell back to sleep.

The bell rings, and Kara opens the door. She has food set up then approaches the bed. "Rafe, breakfast has been brought in."

"I'd like to eat at the table," Ana says.

"Ana, you need to—"

"Please?"

"All right."

He stands and carries her over. Kara gets her a plate while he settles Ana in her seat. He samples it, ensuring it's all right. He places the meal before her.

"It should be okay."

They sit down. "What am I doing today?" Ana asks. "I know we're staying in, but what, a pajama party?"

Kara laughs. "Of course not. We can have a lesson and talk about anything you want. Right?"

"Yes," Rafe answers. "While you continue to rest. It's your choice, bed, sofa or chaise."

"Rafe—"

"No, Ana. You were hurt yesterday and sick last night. Please, don't argue with me about this."

"Yes, love. Would you bring me my hoodie? I'm cold."

He goes to her nightstand, getting the hoodie and helping her slip it on. His hand traces the contours of her face and neck. "You don't feel sick, so that's good."

"I feel okay, just a little tired."

"A little?"

"Fine. Yes, I am still exhausted. I will take it easy today, I promise."

"Now, what do you want to learn about?"

"Yesterday at the tea party, you only said your first name and said our realm. Where are you really from?"

"Why are you asking me this?" Kara asks, turning away.

"I don't need to get into your family history. What's the name of your realm? Where is it? I'm curious, is all. You don't have to answer, if you don't want to."

Kara sighs. "I am from the Lunox Realm, which is pretty far from here. I was traveling through portals and accidentally ended up on MoonSol, where I met your grandmother while she was pregnant with your mother. I acted as an aid and midwife to her, helping raise your mother."

"Wow. You meant it when you said you knew my mother her whole life."

"I did."

"Was my mother born into a noble family, or did she earn her title?"

"A bit of both. Her mother was a countess, but later married a baron after her first husband passed. That's when your mother grew up to be a baroness."

"I see." She looks at Rafe. "Things are so different here."

"I know. How do you think I felt on Earth?"

"And you were by yourself. I have all of you, at least." She leans against him. "I think you're right. I need more sleep."

He picks her up and carries her to bed. She strips off the hoodie, which he sets on her nightstand.

"Sleep, mia estrela. We'll be here when you wake up."

"Will you lay with me?"

"Yes," he says, climbing into bed. "Of course, I will." He holds her until she falls asleep. He walks back over to Kara and Evren. "We'll let her rest, then maybe we'll have more news."

"How does she feel to you?"

"Better. No pain or sickness, just tired."

"It's a shame, because she was starting to really enjoy the tea party. She was doing well on her own and meeting the court. I'll get with Anwyn and perhaps we can try again."

"If Ana wants to. Don't push her, Kara."

"We both do."

"I know. We talked about that. I'm working on it."

"Kara, why are you so hard on Ana?" Evren asks.

"How do you mean?"

"Like you said, you push her. Why?"

Kara is distracted when the bell rings. She opens the door and speaks with Kellan, then she returns to them. "All three assassins are accounted for. They are still being questioned, but the palace is going back to normal."

"I'm very happy to hear that," Evren says.

Rafe walks to Ana and places his palm on her forehead. He watches her sleep, planting a soft kiss on her lips. He returns to Kara and Evren. "We'll let her get more sleep before we tell her the news."

"Maybe she can have a normal day tomorrow then recover over the weekend. She hates when she misses days like this."

"I know," Rafe says. "She gets so angry at herself. I have a feeling she wasn't allowed to have sick days when she was growing up."

Kara's head snaps up. "I didn't even think of that! No wonder she feels like she's useless when she's recovering. That explains so much."

"I hadn't thought of it, either." He looks over, watching her sleep. "She has suffered through so much. I only want her to be happy and loved now."

"Rafe, she is. She and I talked when we toured the other day. She knows how much you love her. She questions herself."

"Sometimes I wonder if August is too soon. We talk about how we push her, but she tries to push herself harder than we do. I think maybe we're closer to her walls coming down, then I learn something new."

Kara walks up to him, putting her hand on his arm. "Rafe, she will be ready by August. I can see it in her eyes, hear it in her voice, how much she wants that. Even if you think it's best for her, she won't want to wait."

"I know you're right. She is doing well, but then she has those days where she is so overwhelmed from what has happened. I hold and comfort her, but I don't know what else to do! I feel so helpless when she's like that."

"Evren and I are going to get cleaned up and changed. We'll see about lunch and be back shortly."

"Okay. Thanks."

He watches them leave, then sits on the chaise. He looks at Ana, unaware she heard everything they said. He looks up when he hears her sniffling. He walks up to her, caressing her face as tears are falling down.

"Are you having a nightmare?"

She turns away. "I'm fine, but I need more sleep."

He takes off his shoes and climbs into bed with her, pulling her to him and kissing her forehead. "You heard us talking, didn't you?"

"Yes," she admits. "If you think we should wait, I won't be upset. I would rather wait than risk ruining—"

"Please, please, stop this! What will it take to show you, you have never ruined anything? Why do you think it's ruined? Why are you so afraid?"

Turning over, she looks at him. "I'm sorry."

"Ana, what have we talked about?"

Her eyes go down. "No apologies, just an explanation."

"Can you do that for me?"

"Rafe, please. I don't want to talk about it. I'm not hiding, I'm too tired and already dealing with so much. Please, let it go?"

"I will when you do."

His words cut deep. The hurt and anger is undeniable in her eyes. "Easy for you to say!"

Jumping up, she races towards the washroom and slams the door shut behind her. Tears stream down her face as she sits on the edge of the tub. A moment later, Rafe knocks on the door.

"Ana, please. Let me in. I'm sorry."

She walks to the door and leans against it. "Rafe, no. I need to clean up by myself. If I feel like it, we'll talk after."

She strips down before getting into the shower. Leaning against the wall, she hugs herself.

*How could he say that? Either he wants me to open up and tell him everything, or it's too much and he acts like he doesn't want to know! What do I do? Do I pretend everything is fine now and never mention it again? I need to be past what happened at the camp. How do I—*She glances up to find Rafe watching her.

She turns away. "Please," she tries.

He steps in but stays back. "I'm letting you know I'm here. I won't say or do anything until you tell me to."

Her head goes down as the tears continue to flow. "Why did you say that?"

"I didn't mean to. I'm so sorry. I don't know what came over me."

"It's because I'm right," she replies in a hushed tone.

"About what?"

"That you will get tired of dealing with me, tired of all my nightmares and episodes." She turns to him. "That you'll see I'm not worth the effort you've been putting into me."

Stripping down, he rushes to her, wrapping her in his arms. "That will never happen! I will cut my wings off again before I would ever hurt you like that." He pulls back, looking her in the eyes. "How can I convince you of that?"

"By not hurting me like you did." She watches as his shoulders slump. "Rafe, I love you. I know we love each other. Maybe… maybe we do need a break from each other. I don't want you to see me like this all the time."

His head jerks up when she says they need a break. "How could you even think that? Being away from you while you were having tea was almost more than my heart could bear. Could you be away from me?"

"Yes," she replies, knowing she doesn't mean it, but she wants to give him space from her and her episodes.

Exiting the shower, he dries himself and puts on clothes. She collapses against the wall, crying with her hands covering her face. Sliding downward, she lets the water envelop her on the floor.

Getting up, she cleans her hair and shuts off the water. She dries off and steps out, not seeing him. In the closet, she drops the towel, collapses onto the ottoman, and cries herself to sleep. Rafe walks to her and takes her hand.

"Oh, mia estrela. Why do you feel like this? Why do you think I would ever get tired of you, of what you're going through?"

He takes out a nightgown and wraps it around her, fastening the buttons. He brings her onto his lap. Cradling her as she sleeps he strokes her hair. He softly caresses her back and neck. As she awakens, her eyes land on him.

"Rafe?"

"I'm right here. I was by the bed when you stepped out of the washroom. I waited, thinking you were coming in here to get dressed. When you didn't come out, I walked in to check on you, finding you asleep."

"I thought you left," she admits. "I didn't mean it, when I said I could be away from you."

"I know. It's not okay that you said that, but I know why you did. I'm not leaving. I'm not going away. I would give anything to prove that to you."

"The fact that you're in here with me, and not back in your old quarters or out the door proves that to me. I've told you, it isn't you. I thought I was working on it, doing better, but—"

"You were, until you heard me and Kara talking. Then what I said to you. This was both of us. I am truly sorry."

"I want to open up, I want to tell you. Then you said you didn't realize how much I was still dealing with. It… You made it sound like it was more than you want to handle."

He lies down, bringing her with him and caressing her cheek. "I'm sorry you thought that. I thought we brought down most of your walls. Then you tell me about food, or punishment, and I realize we still have work to do. It makes me angry because I hate how much you have gone through, how much you have survived. It makes me sad, because I love you so much and would give anything to take your pain. I never meant to take it out on you. That is the last thing I would ever want to do, as much as you have already had to deal with."

"We are both learning as we go through this. For everything you've helped me through, from my nightmares and episodes, you have done a wonderful job. Given you didn't know all of this when you fell in love with me. Seeing that you choose to stay by me, choose to love me every day, should show me that you are here to stay, that you aren't leaving me." She blushes when her stomach growls. "Um, can we get lunch?"

He kisses her. "Then we'll continue to talk about this? If you want to, I mean."

"Yes. I'll get dressed while you do that."

He steps out. She goes to her gowns, knowing they probably won't leave their quarters. She opens up the garment bag with one of her new gowns. She looks it over. White satin with silver lace, and short, billow sleeves with a small V-neck. The gown fits snug, down to her ankles. She slips it on, wearing matching shoes and crown. She gets her rings on and steps out.

"Lunch will be here any moment," Rafe says, walking up to her. "Is that another new gown?"

"Yes."

"It is fantastic. Oh, mia estrela! You sparkle like moonlight on the ocean in that gown!"

She looks up at him, leaning up and kissing him. "Thank you. I wanted to wear this in NightFall, but they hadn't arrived before we left."

"Dressing up for Bela?"

She laughs, as he wraps his arms around her. "No! Jealous much?"

He kisses her forehead. "Not anymore. I am so glad you have Bela and Joph as your friends. Not just as allies, but actual friends. I see how much they mean to you and to know that you don't even care if they are vampyra or human or elf but accept them as they are."

"I'm guessing my father didn't," she says, pulling back and looking up at him. "I'm sorry. You don't have to answer."

"It's all right. No, he didn't care for them. He didn't go to war with them because they are different, but because of his greed. Same reason he went after all of the quadrants. Still, they weren't welcome to the palace under his rule."

"That's why we didn't have their cuisine."

"Exactly," he says, leading her to the chaise. He sits with her, holding her hands. "There is something we need to discuss. I want you to listen to me. Listen to every word I'm about to say, without interrupting. Can you do that?"

"Yes, love."

Chapter 30

Rafe kisses Ana's hands while looking into her eyes. "Maeriana Rose, you and I are getting married in August. You will be crowned as Grand Empress, and I will be crowned as King." He sees the surprise on her face as her mouth opens slightly and her eyes go wide. "We will rule our kingdom, we will bring down walls, we will keep the peace. That is the future we have ahead of us. Is that the future you want?"

She swallows hard, fighting back tears threatening to escape. "More than anything," she replies.

"Then that is the future we will have."

"Rafe, what changed your mind? About becoming the king?"

"Thinking of everything you have gone through. You were crowned queen, died in battle and grew wings, survived torture to protect your people, thought to get critical intel while being hurt in his camp. And I'm what, upset about you wanting me to be King? I see how badly you want this for me because you feel I have earned it, the way you have earned your place as Queen. It's a lot to take in, something I'm still dealing with, but it is the least I can do, for the woman who has given me everything."

"Not everything," she says as her eyes go down.

"Ana, you have given me your heart and soul. That is everything to me."

He looks up when the bell rings. He kisses her hands, then lets Kara and Evren come in with lunch. Everything is set up. He takes Ana's hand and escorts her to the table.

"How do you feel?" Kara asks.

"Much better. Thank you. Do I want to ask what was in the medicine you gave me? I'm glad it made me better, but it was so gross!"

"Probably better if you don't," Kara says, laughing. "We need to go see Winslow. He's very curious, himself."

"I would imagine," Ana says, her eyes going down.

"Did you have something you want to ask me?"

"I—" She looks at her. "Did you use magic?"

"Evren and I did. It was worth it, to make you better."

"Kara, I'm sorry."

"No, it's okay. We've actually practiced a little. Everything that has happened, we figured it would probably be useful. We were right."

"Will you ever tell me why you stopped?"

"No, Ana. I'm sorry."

"It's okay. You saved my life, thank you."

Kara examines her. "Is that a new gown?"

"I picked it out from the fabrics and patterns."

"It's beautiful."

"Thanks. I needed something besides pink or blue."

"You do have a lot of those."

"So, a week and a half until the wedding. Are you ready?"

"We are. We're excited. She's done writing her vows, but I'm still working on mine."

"Shall I compare thee to a summer's day?"

"Ana, I swear, if you even think about it—" She looks up when Ana is doubled over with laughter. "It's not funny!"

"What? I thought it was."

Kara looks at Evren, confusion written across her face. "It's from our college days. The captain of the swim team had a crush on me and tried to slip that into my book."

"What's wrong with that?" Rafe asks.

"He tried to pass it off as if he'd written it."

"Um, I'm not from Earth, even I know who Shakespeare is."

"See? That's why it was so ridiculous!"

"I thought it was sweet," Ana says. "You didn't have to be

so mean to him."

"What did you do?" Evren asks.

"I was friends with the yearbook staff. They published it under 'worst idea' for that year. With his name and picture."

Rafe laughs, wiping his eyes. "Kara! I think that was perfect. Did he leave you alone after that?"

"You bet he did!"

"She always had guys trying to get her attention. A few girls, too. I didn't ask, as I wasn't interested in dating, myself. I figured you had your reasons but didn't want to talk about them."

"Now you know. I didn't want to love someone knowing I would lose them. Honestly, I never felt any attraction to anyone, until I saw Evren." She takes her hand and smiles. "I thought you were the most beautiful thing I had ever seen."

"Kara!" Rafe exclaims. "Whoa. Where is this coming from?"

She looks at him, blushing. "I think you two have been a bad influence on me!" She turns when Evren laughs. "What?"

"I thought the same thing," she admits. "I wasn't sure if I should say anything, since it was forbidden because of my status. When Ana was hurt, and you were so scared of losing her, I couldn't help it."

"You admitted your feelings while we were in the Medical Center?"

"Yes, Ana. You were stabbed by an assassin, and I was comforting Kara. I confessed my feelings then she kissed me."

"You two!" Ana says. "That's sweet." She looks at Evren, concerned when her smile fades. "What's wrong?"

"Royse said he may or may not come. He is worried how it will look to the court, for him to come to my wedding."

"Evren, I'm so sorry. You don't deserve to be treated this way! Especially since he was the one who did this to you."

"Thank you, Ana. Kara, do we want to go see Winslow? I'm sure he is very curious about our medicine for andelaise."

"Yes, Evren, we'll go on. Ana, you and Rafe have the rest of the day together. We'll do breakfast tomorrow, the briefing, lunch, then go over more information on the people in your kingdom."

"That sounds great. Thanks."

Kara stands up, taking Evren's hand. "We'll see you in the morning."

Ana turns back to Rafe. "I'm sorry."

"For what?"

"Everything. How I reacted in the training center, hiding from you, doubting you. I mean it. I'm truly sorry."

"I am, too. I'm sorry for what I said, for being jealous, for leaving the shower when I should've stayed. I thought we would get dressed and talk. I never meant for you to think I was leaving. I can't do right by you. Whether I push or try to give you space, I upset you. What can I do?"

"What can we do?" she asks, smiling at him. "It's both of us. I need to stop hiding, you need to stop pushing. We can work on that together, if that's what you want?"

"Of course, it is. I want to help you. I want to work with you, to help you battle your demons and bring down your walls."

"You already are." She stands up, walking to the middle of the room. She expands her wings, furling and unfurling them.

"We can go to the training center. I promise, I'll do better."

She nods to the window. "How about outside?" She sees the look on his face. "You're worried because I fell. If we go out, I'll hold your hand the entire time, no matter how well I'm doing. I promise."

He leans down, kissing her. "Will you wear that gown?"

She smiles up at him. "Hmm. Maybe. Do you want me to change into something more appropriate?"

"No," he answers, cupping her face. He kisses her again.

"Everyone should see how beautiful you are." He takes her hand. "Ready to go?"

"Yes, love."

They step out and find Asuin and Rayan at their post.

"We're going to our battlement."

"Yes, Guardian. Sorry. Yes, Rafe."

"It's all right."

She smiles at Rafe. "What?" he asks.

She looks at Rayan's wings. "Well?"

"It's fine."

She smiles at him, squeezing his hand. "They are pretty," she says.

"Ana!"

She laughs, looking back at him. "I'm teasing."

They arrive at their battlement. Asuin and Rayan stand guard. Rafe takes her up the steps. She breathes in the fresh air, smiling at the sun.

"Rainy days are my favorite, but knowing we get to be out in this is making me very happy."

"I can feel it! Maybe the sun isn't so bad?" He looks concerned when she releases his hand. "Ana?"

"I'm not flying yet. I need to stretch first. Remember? Not all of us have been doing it over five hundred years?"

"Of course."

She walks to the middle and looks down. "This is where our fire pit was." She smiles at him. "That was one of the best nights of my life."

"One of?" he asks as he joins her.

"Rafe, you have given me so many. The night you danced with me at the masquerade, the night before our first battle together—" She gasps when his lips are on hers. Her arms wrap around his neck. "Rafe, I'm sorry. I need to stretch my wings, then rest."

"It's okay. We'll fly a bit then rest before dinner. You're recovering from being sick. Relax tonight, do your duties tomorrow, then we'll have the weekend together. Just the two of us. Sound good?"

"Yes, love."

"Now, stretch your wings for me."

She smiles at him. "You want to see them with this gown."

"Ana! I am your instructor. You need to stretch before we fly."

"Admit it, and I will."

"Yes, I want to see your wings with that gown. The crimson and silver will be spectacular together." He sucks in his breath when her wings open. "I was right."

She giggles, stretching her wings. "Thank you. You truly know how to make me feel beautiful."

"Ana, because you are beautiful."

"Thank you, Rafe. Now, are we ready to fly?" she asks, taking his hand. He takes her into the air, flying over the palace. "What do you think of our kingdom?"

He smiles at her. "I love hearing you say that. Our kingdom is beautiful."

"Rafe, are you sure you'll be okay to be crowned King? I don't want you to do it because it's something I want. I want you to want it, too."

"I do, Ana. I thought a lot about it."

She smiles at him and squeezes his hand as they go around. He takes her over the village and market, above the farmhouses then back to the palace. He hovers with her above the battlement.

"What's wrong?"

"Do you want to fly a little on your own?"

"Not right now. I am still tired. We'll continue to train and build up my endurance. Then I'll really put you through your paces."

"Ana, I will be so happy to fly around with you. I love the chase," he says, lowering them to the ground. "I won't be jealous, I promise. Envious, maybe." He smiles at her. "You are amazing with your wings.'

"Thank you, love. I have a great instructor." She hovers up, kissing him. She laughs at the look on his face. "You really like this, don't you?"

"It's incredible."

She lowers to the ground. "Are we ready to return?"

"Rest and dinner?"

"With cocoa and dessert?" she sheepishly asks.

"I knew you would drink cocoa after winter!"

She laughs. "I can't help it."

They walk down the steps, going out into the hallway. "Back to our quarters, please."

"Yes, Rafe."

They follow behind. Asuin goes in and checks the rooms. "All clear."

Ana takes Rafe inside and proceeds to the washroom. While he starts the water, she begins to undress. Once she puts her clothes in the hamper, she steps into the water while he begins undressing. Struggling to stay awake, she leans against the wall. When he enters, she raises her gaze.

"I'm okay, just really tired."

He approaches her and lends a hand in cleaning up. Sitting her on the tub's edge, he proceeds to dry her off. Wrapping the robe around her, she enters the closet. Slipping into undergarments and pajamas, she settles on the ottoman and drifts off to sleep. He walks in, shaking his head. After changing into his pajamas, he turns off the overhead light and joins her on the ottoman, pulling her towards him. Before falling asleep, he kisses the back of her head.

***

Ana wakes up, looking up and seeing Rafe. She smiles at him, as she nuzzles into his chest. His warmth spreads throughout her. She leans up, propping up on her elbow, and planting a soft kiss. "Rafe?"

"Hmm. Yes, Ana?"

"Are you awake?"

"No."

She laughs. "All right. I'll see about dinner."

"I'm getting up." He stands up, pulling her with him. "Get dressed however you want. We'll stay in tonight."

"Thank you."

She walks to the dresser, getting out black satin pants with a pale blue satin blouse. She changes and steps out as he walks back in.

"Dinner will be here shortly."

She sits on the chaise while he goes to the closet, getting dressed. He dresses to match before joining her.

"Comfy?" she asks.

"Yes," he replies, kissing her. He gently ruffles through her wings. "How are they feeling?"

"Much better since we worked them. I wish I had been doing it sooner. You were right to push for flying lessons. They don't hurt anymore."

"Really?"

"Yes. I'm sorry it took me so long."

"Ana, it's okay. You had to adapt and adjust, and now, we're here. Everything happens for a reason, in its time and place. Do you still question why it happened to you?"

"No. I see now it was meant to be. I had to die and change, to bring freedom to the realm. I became the Crimson Queen to protect the throne and free the people. It paved the way to everything that has happened and to everything that will happen."

"What do you mean?"

"To us getting married, being crowned, creating an heir. None of that would've been possible without the treaty, which came about because of what happened to me."

"Ana, have you finally accepted yourself? Your wings, your immortality, everything you are?"

She looks at him, smiling. "I have." She gasps when his lips are on hers, kissing her with so much happiness and love. "Rafe! I'm sorry, I'm tired."

"I was showing you how happy I am. I promise you, we won't do anything tonight but eat dinner and talk."

"Thank you."

"Speaking of which," he says when the bell is ringing.

He stands up, letting the staff in. Ana watches them go to the table and set food up. She looks up when a woman she doesn't know approaches her.

"Can I help you?" Ana asks, getting to her feet.

The woman says nothing as she pulls out her dagger. Ana steps back. She cries out for Rafe while grabbing the woman's wrist and struggling against her.

The assassin manages to get Ana to the ground, bringing the blade down when Rafe tackles her away. Ana jumps to her feet, seeing Rafe stand up, covered in blood.

"Rafe!"

"It's not mine." They look down to find the assassin with the dagger in her abdomen. "Are you all right?"

"I'm okay. She didn't hurt me." She runs into his arms, holding him tight. He strokes through her hair. The staff run to them.

"Our sincerest of apologies! She had only been with us a few weeks. We had no idea she was an assassin!"

"We need to get everything cleaned up," Rafe says. "We need fresh food, delivered by Yeona herself. The queen and I will get cleaned up as you get this taken care of."

"Yes, Guardian. Thank you."

He takes Ana to the washroom. "Stay right here. I'll get us clean clothes." He runs to the closet then quickly returns. He gets her into the shower, washing her off when she's trembling.

"Ana?" He turns her around when she doesn't respond.

He wipes the tears from her eyes. "You're safe now," he says, wrapping her in his arms. "We're safe."

"Oh, love. Please, just hold me."

"I will. I'm right here."

She wraps in tighter, letting his warmth and comfort penetrate her to the core, easing her worries. She takes slow, deep breaths, listening to his heartbeat. "I'm okay now. Let's get clean and see if we have food."

"You'll eat?"

"I promise."

They dry off and dress, stepping out. Yeona is standing over by their small table. Rafe takes Ana's hand and walks her over.

"Majesty, Guardian. I am so sorry." She bows.

"No," Ana says. "It was not your fault. Rafe and I are okay."

"I saw to this food myself. I will personally see to your meals from here on out and bring them to you."

"Yeona, we appreciate that, but you have a full kitchen to run. It isn't necessary," Ana tries.

"Majesty, please—"

"You may see to our meals being prepared but are not responsible for their delivery. I insist."

"Yes, Majesty. Thank you. I will return to the kitchen. Please, let me know if I can give any other assistance."

"Thank you, Yeona," Rafe says. She turns and leaves. Rafe sits at the table with Ana, watching her eat. He jumps up when the bell is ringing. "Stay here, Ana. Please?"

"I will."

He opens the door, surprised to see Kara. She rushes in. "Is Ana all right?" Her eyes scan the room, spotting her at the table. She sprints to her, lifts her up, and hugs her tightly. Rafe watches as Evren walks in. They make their way to Kara and Ana.

"What is going on?" Rafe asks.

"We found evidence that the three assassins were decoys, to hide the real assassin. We're still looking into it."

"Rafe killed her."

"What?" Kara asks.

"She came in with the staff to set up dinner. She pulled a dagger on Ana. I was able to tackle her, plunging the dagger into her. Everything was cleaned up then Yeona saw to our dinner herself."

"Ana, I am so sorry."

"For what?"

"I was too late. I—"

"Kara, stop. Rafe and I are fine. The assassin is dead. I know you are getting married and going on your honeymoon, but I swear you need a break. What can we do? How can we help?"

"Audressa has been preparing to take over while we are gone. I'm okay, Ana. I promise you."

"Kara, no. You have taken on too much! Why didn't you ask me to help? I know I've had a few bad days, but I would've pushed that down to take care of my kingdom!"

"Ana, that's why I didn't ask. You need to heal and recover, from everything you have suffered through to protect your people. Evren and I are handling things. I've given Audressa's wife clearance, so they can work together to run things while Evren and I are gone."

"If you're sure. Kara, I'm doing much better."

"We will continue to learn about the people in your kingdom until Evren and I leave. When we get back, you and I can go over everything as you continue your duties. Is that okay?"

"Yes, Kara. Thank you for everything you are doing. For me and for the kingdom. I don't know how I can repay you for all the responsibility you are carrying in my stead!"

"Ana, you gave me everything I ever wanted the day you passed your treaty. I am still in your debt. I do what I can for this kingdom, to repay you and your mother. I assure you, I am fine. I am not overwhelmed."

"She really isn't," Evren adds. "We have several advisors who assist, and Ramin and Melian are really great about keeping us up to date."

"All right, sis. If you start to get overwhelmed—"

"I will let you know, I promise. I'm grateful you are both okay. Please, finish your dinner. We will see you in the morning for breakfast."

"Yes, Kara. We will see you then," Ana says, hugging her again. Kara steps away, taking Evren's hand and leaving. She sits back down, finishing her meal. She looks at Rafe when he joins her. "I hope she's telling the truth. I do worry over her and how much she is doing."

"I understand, but as I said, your advisors and captains take on most of the responsibility. Plus, she has Evren and Audressa to help."

"What are her duties? What does she do all day?"

"Well, you know about her preparing for then having the morning briefing. She receives intelligence reports and information throughout the day, acting accordingly. She was a little overwhelmed when she was helping Bela plan his ball, planning her wedding, dealing with Remus and threats of assassins. That's not the case now."

"I see what you mean." She gets up and walks to the window. Her eyes scan the kingdom spread out below her. Rafe approaches and gently holds her hand. Her gaze lifts towards him. "I still can't believe this is real, that this is ours. I… growing up and being told how worthless I was, that I would never amount to anything. I look out and see a kingdom that needs me, a kingdom that we have saved."

He caresses along her back, his hand gently going through her wings. "You gave everything you have, everything you are, for your people." He cocks his head when she laughs. "What?"

"I realized something. You got angry at me in NightFall

for diving at the assassin because I thought you were coming into the room, telling me I am too important and never should've done that. What if I hadn't done it in battle? Did you ever stop to think about that? About how different things would be?"

"I see your point. You're absolutely right. No, I had not thought about that. You broke your promise to me, and in doing so saved your kingdom. I say your kingdom because that's what it was at the time."

"Rafe, this has been your kingdom from the time you picked up a sword and fought for it."

"Ana—"

"I mean it. Your family, your life, your duty has been to protect this kingdom. Even having your wings removed to find me. Believe me when I tell you that you have earned this kingdom just as much as I have."

"I lost my wings to save the kingdom, you grew yours to do the same."

"Yes, we did." She yawns.

"Ana, why didn't you tell me you were tired? We can get ready to turn in."

"It's still early. I don't want to turn in yet."

"You need to rest."

She takes his hand, sitting on the sofa. "Please, after what happened earlier, I want to spend time with you."

"I do with you, too. I also know you are recovering."

"I'll go to bed soon, really." She scoots over, laying against his chest. He brings their legs up, laying on the sofa. "Thank you for saving me."

"I will always be there for you. I told you I would, and I mean that. I'm grateful you called out instead of trying to take her on yourself."

"I didn't want to, because I hate the thought of you getting hurt for me. I knew I had to, though. I know you're right about being too important to the realm and galaxy. I had no idea what she wanted when she walked over. I saw the dagger and reacted."

"Lucky you were watching us set up. She probably would've… No, it's too close to bed. We won't go there."

"She would've slit my throat."

"Ana!"

"It was already on my mind. I'm okay now. No nightmares or episodes tonight, I promise. Not from this."

"If you do, please wake me. I'll try to be better about not pushing, but I at least want to help and comfort you. Will you let me do that?"

"Yes, love. Thank you. I'll try not to hide."

"That's all I can ask. Now, are you ready to go to bed?"

"No, but I can tell you're worried about me. That's okay. Let me use the washroom, and we'll go to sleep."

"All right."

He stands up, helping her up. She goes into the washroom while he waits outside. She sits on the chaise while he does the same. He scoops her up, kissing her and carrying her to bed. He lays her down, covering her with the blanket. She grabs his hands as he climbs into bed. She pulls up to him, kissing him with all the love she feels for him.

"My brave guardian, coming in to save me. Thank you, Rafe."

"Anything for my warrior queen, ruler of my heart and domain over my soul."

She smiles up at him, kissing him again. "I love you."

"I love you, too, mia estrela. Now, get some sleep. We will have a normal day tomorrow then spend the weekend together."

"That sounds wonderful. I truly hope we can, with no sickness or assassins or anything like that!"

"We will. I promise."

Chapter 31

Ana is startled awake and gazes down at a sleeping Rafe. Before lying back down, she checks the time. She crawls to him, letting him take her in his arms. With his warmth surrounding her, her heart and mind begin to relax.

"Ana, do you want to tell me about it?"

"I thought you were asleep. I didn't mean to wake you."

"It's all right. Do you want me to hold you?"

"I… it was a nightmare. I'm okay now, really. You pulled me into your arms and calmed my entire being. I love how you do that to me."

"I told you, you do the same for me."

"Yes, Rafe. I was back in his camp. I keep thinking I'm going to move past it, but then I get overwhelmed again. I don't know what to do!"

"How can I help?"

"Let's get more sleep. In the morning, I want us to get a bath, like we did in NightFall. Please?"

"If that's what you want. I'll gladly fix that up for you. Are you sure you'll go back to sleep?"

"I will."

"You'll wake me if you need me?"

"Yes, love. I'm sorry."

"It's all right. Get more sleep." He kisses her forehead. "I'm right here, watching over you. Nothing is going to hurt you while I'm here."

"My personal Guardian."

"Yes, Your Majesty."

She giggles into his chest, clutching his shirt. She falls back to sleep, overwhelmed with his love. He pulls her in tighter, praying for her to sleep all night. He watches her sleep, feeling her love.

"Rafe, can we get a bath?"

"What time is it?"

"Four."

He sits up, turning on the lamp, then he studies her. "What happened?"

Her body trembles from crying as he pulls her onto his lap. He scoops her up, carrying her into the washroom. While they undress, he begins filling up the tub. Adding soap, he keeps his shorts on and lends a hand to help her inside.

He pulls her up against his chest, and they lie down together. Her shame and anger flow through him, stopped by his thoughts of comfort and strength for her. He sends them into her with everything he has.

"Thank you. I'm sorry I woke you so early."

"Ana—"

"I know. No apologies."

"You don't have to, but will you tell me about it? Was it the camp again?"

"No. It was MoonFrost, when he told me he killed you and showed me the bloody feather. I didn't want to believe him when he said that, but seeing the feather was too much. I thought I had lost you."

"I'm right here, mia estrela. Right with you, not going anywhere. Everything you suffered through to protect the guardians, to protect me, I can never thank you enough for. I'm so sorry for what you've been through."

"I'm trying to get better, to move past it. I keep thinking I am, then I have a nightmare or episode. I don't understand what's causing it."

"What do you think it could be?" He watches her head go

down. "Ana?"

"My wings," she admits with reluctance. "Remus came after me because I have them. I don't hate them or anything like that. I won't revert to that, I promise. Not after everything we've done with them."

"Is that why you've been pushing yourself so hard with them?"

"Partly." She traces her fingers along his arm and hand. "I wanted to work with them, knowing I needed to. The more we worked them, the more I was thinking about Remus and what he wanted to do, killing all of us. I didn't mean for that to happen."

"How can I help you move past this? What do you need from me?"

"Time and patience. I am moving past it; I can feel it. I'm not there yet." She looks up at him. "I'm ready to rinse off and go back to bed. Will you get more sleep? I'll stay up with you if you can't."

"We'll both get more sleep."

"Yes, love."

He helps her to her feet, sitting her on the edge while he goes over to start the shower. She stands up and joins him. He washes her off. They dry and change back into pajamas. With her in his arms, he carries her to bed, never letting go. He realizes she fell back to sleep. Observing her, he smiles down at her. He stays awake, wanting to ensure her comfort. Glancing at the clock, he realizes it's after seven. He lets her sleep a little more before waking her up.

"Kara and Evren will be here shortly with breakfast. Do you want to get dressed before they do?"

"Please."

"Are you staying in or going to the morning briefing?"

"I'd like to attend the briefing."

"Then we will." He gets her to her feet, going to the closet. She fingers through various gowns, smiling at the thought that it's finally spring. She slips on a pale-yellow gown with off shoulder sleeves and billow skirt. She puts on gold shoes and crown. She looks in the mirror, opening her wings.

"Hmm. I don't think I like the yellow."

"Ana, it looks great on you. Why don't you like it?"

She looks back at the mirror, looking up and down. "Maybe because I'm not used to it. It really looks okay?"

"Yes, mia estrela. I mean that." Rafe finishes getting dressed and walks to her. "It almost looks gold."

"Hmm. Okay. I really don't want to change," she says, laughing. "It's just for breakfast and the briefing."

"Are we flying after?"

"I'd like to."

"Then we will." He takes her hand, stepping out with her as the bell rings. He lets staff in to set up. Kara and Evren walk in.

"I like the yellow!" Kara exclaims, walking up to Ana. "You haven't really worn much of that, have you?"

"I don't know if I like it."

"Why not? It's a great color on you."

Ana gives her a small smile. "Thanks." They sit at the table. "What did Winslow think of your medicine?"

"He processed it and ran some tests, thinking it might actually help andelaise. Maybe not a cure, but certainly reducing the time and symptoms. He's working on a synthetic version."

"Thank you. I hate when I'm sick with that. It's awful!" She looks at Rafe. "You're jealous of how fast I can fly, while I'm jealous that you never get sick. I wish I had gotten that, too!"

"I know, mia estrela. Believe me, I feel so helpless when you're sick."

"Wait, Rafe is jealous?"

"Yes," Ana says. "I'm faster than him."

"Rafe!"

"I didn't mean to be. Watching her take to the skies as if

she had done it her whole life was incredible. I always want you to feel good about yourself, about what you can do. I never meant to make you feel bad," he says, kissing her forehead.

"Is that why you fell in the training center?" Kara asks.

Ana realizes they're all looking at her. She hangs her head. "No," she quietly replies.

"Ana?"

"Rafe, I—"

"No, I'm sorry. What happened?"

"I was lowering down and grew angrier, thinking about what happened. I lost my focus and fell. It was my fault, not yours." She looks up at him. "Please, don't get upset. I'm okay now."

"I'm not upset." He takes her hand. "I'm not. I was worried, but I'm glad you're okay." He turns to Kara. "We're coming to the briefing this morning."

"Yes," Ana agrees. "I'd like to go to that, have lunch, then go to your office to learn more about the kingdom."

"We can do all of that."

"Great! I'll use the washroom then we'll head to the meeting room." Ana goes to the washroom.

Kara looks at Rafe. "How is she? Really?"

Rafe shakes his head. "She is recovering and getting better, but she needs time. She's repressed and pushed so much down, it's a wonder she can still walk and talk."

"I meant from her fall. Did she have an episode last night?"

"And a nightmare. She swears she wants to have a normal day, so I'm not arguing with her. I'll make sure she rests this weekend."

"We'll let you have the weekend together, since last weekend was a working weekend. Plus battling an assassin."

"Thanks. She'll appreciate that." He looks up as she steps out. He goes to her, taking her hand. "Ready?"

"Yes, love."

They go to the meeting room. Audressa rises to her feet, bowing. "Your Majesty."

"Chancellor. How are things looking?"

"Everything is going well. We have questioned the assassins extensively. They claim to have been hired by Emory of MoonFrost, but each gave a different description. Someone is trying to set him up. We have agents looking into it."

"I knew it wasn't Emory," Kara says. She sees the look Ana gives her. "Sorry. We didn't want to say anything until we knew for sure."

"I understand."

"Majesty, please have a seat. I insist."

"Thank you," Ana says, walking around the desk and sitting. "Audressa, while Kara and Evren are on their honeymoon, please don't hesitate to come to me with any issues or concerns. I'm learning more about the kingdom and resuming my duties."

"Yes, Majesty. Thank you."

The room starts to fill. Audressa gets the reports together and with Kara, has the briefing. There are no questions or concerns, so she adjourns the meeting. Ana gets to her feet, taking Rafe's hand. They return to their quarters for lunch.

"Evren and I are going to see about lunch then get changed. We'll be back shortly."

"No rush. The meeting didn't last as long as I thought it would." Ana sits on the chaise, joined by Rafe. She looks up at him. "I'm okay. I'm a little tired, but that's to be expected. I really want a normal day, then we'll recover over the weekend. Please?"

"We will. I told you we will. As long as you are honest with me about how you're feeling."

"Thank you. I will be."

"All right."

He looks up when the bell rings. He goes to the door, opening it. Before he can say anything, a shot rings out, and he's hit in the chest. Ana jumps to her feet, seeing him fall to the floor. She flies to the other fireplace, getting her sword as the assassin is reloading their pistol while running towards her.

While Ana is flying towards her, she shoots and hits her in the stomach. Bringing the assassin down, she falls to the ground with her sword in hand. Her eyes shut as her wings ignite into flames. On her knees, she slowly makes her way towards Rafe. The world fades into darkness as she inches closer to him.

Chapter 32

Reaching him, Ana collapses onto him, her focus solely on healing him. "Rafe—" she whispers as she is losing consciousness. With her last bit of strength, she forces her wings to remain on fire. Once she passes out, the flames extinguish as well.

Kara and Evren run in. Kara turns away, fearing they are dead. She makes herself go to them, relieved to find they're still alive. She turns to Evren.

"They're okay. You know the routine." She pulls away Ana, who mumbles in protest. "You have to get clean, then you can stay with Rafe."

"I'm still healing him," she manages to get out.

Kara lowers Ana down beside him. "All right."

Kara and Evren move them aside so staff can come in to clean up and get rid of the assassin's body. Kara takes Ana into the washroom, getting her clean while Evren grabs her and Rafe fresh clothes. Kara gets her dried off and dressed, laying her on the chaise.

She and Evren get Rafe cleaned and dressed, carrying him to the bed. Kara goes to Ana, helping her to her feet and with Rafe. She watches as they reach for each other, Rafe pulling her into his arms.

"They'll be okay now?" Evren asks.

"Yes. So much for a normal day. How did this happen? Who is behind this?"

"Who do you think?"

"I have some theories. Is Remus still alive? Is it someone avenging him or Kane or Tinsley? I need more information. What I have is only speculation." She looks up when staff walk in with lunch. Kara helps set it up, then watches them leave, walking back over to Ana and Rafe. "They need to eat, but I don't even know if we can wake them while they're healing."

Evren walks up to Ana, gently shaking her. "Ana? We have lunch. You need to eat, then you can sleep some more."

"Give us a little while, then we'll eat. Please?"

Kara cocks her head. "Ana, did you use your wings?"

"Yes."

"Then you need to eat."

"All right." Kara brings the plate over and helps her eat. "Thank you. Will you help Rafe? I'm about to pass out."

"I'll make sure he eats. Get more rest," Kara says, taking her plate over and grabbing Rafe a plate. She comes back, getting him to eat. She and Evren sit at the small table to eat their lunch. "I see why they had this brought in. It's a nice place to eat."

"Yes, it is."

"We'll let them sleep and recover. We'll eat then get some paperwork done. I don't want to leave them while they're like this."

"All right." Evren looks over at them. "I wonder what happened. I heard the shots, but don't know where they were hit."

"Kara?"

She jumps to her feet, running over. "What's wrong, Ana?"

"I need the washroom."

Kara helps her up, taking her. Evren walks up beside the bed and examines Rafe. "Are you awake? Rafe?"

She laughs when he mumbles something. She goes to the table to let him sleep. Kara gets Ana into bed. She crawls to Rafe as he wraps her in his arms. Kara shakes her head as she returns to Evren.

"Her paperwork is on her desk. Let's get it knocked out. I know she wanted to do this herself, but she'll have to understand."

Kara and Evren work for a while, occasionally checking on Rafe and Ana. Evren takes the paperwork and to see about dinner.

"Ana, are you awake?" Kara asks as she walks up to her.

"Yes."

"Dinner will be here soon. How do you feel?"

"Okay."

"Can you tell me what happened?"

"There was an assassin."

Kara chuckles. "I know that. What exactly happened?"

"Oh, sorry. The bell was ringing, so Rafe went to open the door and was shot. I flew to my sword above the fireplace then charged at the assassin. She was reloading her pistol and managed to hit me in the stomach as I was bringing my sword down. I used my wings to heal before getting to Rafe."

"Where was he shot?"

"In the chest."

"Oh, my! I'm so glad you're both alive."

"Kara, please. Don't cry. I don't have the strength for that."

She wipes the unshed tears. "I won't. Get more rest. I'll wake you when food has arrived."

"Thanks." She falls back to sleep.

Kara goes to the sofa, looking out at the kingdom. She looks up when Evren joins her, taking her hand. "You're missing Earth, aren't you?" Evren asks.

"A little. Like her, I'm grateful to be here, especially since I found you. I miss the time she and I had together, ordering a pizza and watching movies. We would talk and have snacks. We try to spend some time here, but it's not the same."

"Anything I can do?"

"No, sweetheart. Thank you, though. Things have changed, and I have to accept that."

"Kara, at least you didn't have to change as much as she did."

"That is very true. I was a little cold about it when it happened, saying she would have to deal with it. I was so scared and worried, but I hid by being callous. I don't know what I was thinking."

"She knows how much she means to you. I know you don't like to cook, but I think that was the most fun she's had with you since arriving here."

"You're right. I'll see if she wants to do that again, once she's recovered, that is." She shakes her head. "She's going to be so mad! All she wanted was a normal day, with a nice, quiet weekend with Rafe."

"She can still have that. They'll recover together over the weekend."

"I know you're right. Still, I wish they didn't have to."

"Kara, we're going to get to the bottom of this. You know we will. Then maybe we can finally have peace and quiet in the palace."

"That's all I want for her, for them. She's suffered enough, without having to be in fear of assassins!"

"Shh. It's all right, dear. You know we'll find out. As many scouts and agents as you have out, gathering intel."

"Thank you, Evren. Ana says she couldn't do what she does without Rafe. I feel the same about you." She leans forward, kissing her. "How was I so lucky to meet the love of my life here?"

Evren looks down, blushing. "We both were."

"Sweetie!" Kara exclaims, kissing her again. "Our wedding is coming up. Are you still nervous?"

"I know we both are. I'm not as nervous as I was. Whatever happens with Royse will happen, so I can't worry myself over it. I know our ceremony will be wonderful. I'm looking forward to finally having some time with you, just the two of us. That's what I'm most excited about!"

"I am, too. We both need a vacation, a break from the day to day of palace affairs and reports." She hears the bell ringing.

She lets staff bring dinner in. They set up and leave. She walks to Ana. "Food is here. Can you eat?"

"We'll come to the table."

"Ana—"

"I'm okay, really."

Rafe sits up, pulling her to him. He feels her head and face. "Okay." He helps her to her feet, walking with her to the table. Kara and Evren join them. Kara gets up when the bell rings again. She opens the door, stepping back as their packages from NightFall are delivered. They leave, and Kara joins them.

"Did some shopping, I see."

"Shut up, sis," Ana says, laughing. "Most of that will be for our office." She looks at Kara. "Wait! What happened to Kellan and Erick?"

"The assassin used some sort of powder on them, knocking them unconscious. They are recovering in the Medical Center. Roesh and Aylin are outside."

"She's supposed to be recovering, too!" Ana says, getting to her feet. She goes to the door, looking Aylin. "How are you feeling?"

"Much better, Majesty," Aylin replies.

"I know but—"

"We volunteered," Roesh explains. "Melian told us what happened. We wanted to be here, watching over you. It's our duty, Majesty."

"Thank you, both." She goes inside and returns to the table. "They said they volunteered. I hope she really is recovered."

"Ana, she is. Between you getting her here so quickly and her accelerated healing, she truly is. Speaking of recovering, how do you feel?"

"Rafe, really? I told you, I'm okay. I'm tired, but that's to be expected. How do you feel?"

"I feel fine, since you did all the work this time."

"Ana, when I pulled you away you said he was still healing.

How do you know that? What do you feel when you heal each other?" Kara asks.

"I feel his wound, feel the pain."

"What?" Rafe asks. "I don't feel yours when I heal you."

"It's only when I use my wings. It's different, somehow."

"What do you mean? You used your wings to help heal me, too?"

"Yes. It accelerates what we already have. It's only for a moment, I swear. Then I feel you healing, but not the pain."

"Why didn't you tell me about that sooner?"

"Tell you what, Rafe? There's nothing to tell."

"Ana, you know that I never want you to hurt."

"I would much rather have a few seconds of pain than live the rest of my life without you. Which sounds more painful to you?"

"I know you're right, still. I wish it didn't hurt at all." He watches her get to her feet. He stands up and joins her. She goes through the packages from NightFall, finding a small box. She takes it to the table, sitting back down. "Our rings?"

"I think so." She opens the box, nearly gasping at the sight. "They are even more beautiful than I remembered!" She hands him his band as she slips hers on. She rolls it around a bit, pulling it on and off. "Mine fits perfect."

"As does mine."

She puts them back in the box, handing it to Kara. She and Evren look them over. "Okay. I see why you went ahead and bought bands. These are very nice."

Ana takes the box into the closet, locking it with the Royal Jewels. She walks back over to Rafe, kissing him. "I can't wait until we're saying our vows and putting those on each other!"

"We'll have to remind Audressa, since that's not a normal part of the wedding ceremony here."

"Oh, right." She looks at Kara. "Do they have a rehearsal here?"

"Yes. You didn't get to because—" She sees the angry

look on Rafe's face. "I'm sorry. I won't bring that up."

Ana looks at Rafe. "It's okay. I have moved past Kane, and what he's done. I really have." She turns back to Kara. "You're right, we didn't have time."

"Ana, we will clean up dishes and leave for the evening. You and Rafe have a weekend together, I insist. We'll see you Sunday for dinner, unless anything happens that you need to know."

"Thank you, Kara. You and Evren, both. You know how much you mean to me? That I don't just say that, but I love you both."

"We do. We love you, too," Kara says, hugging her. "Now, enjoy your weekend. Relax." They get the dishes and leave.

"I know we're supposed to be relaxing, but can we go to the training center? My wings need to stretch a bit. They… they're actually hurting a little today."

"Yes, we'll go. Let's get dressed." He helps her up. "What?"

"My yellow dress. How many gowns have to be ruined?"

"Ana, they are dresses. As you see, it's no trouble to go have more made up. You are what matters, not a piece of fabric."

"Rafe, some of these are my mother's."

"It doesn't matter. You are what's important. She would say the same thing."

She follows him into the closet, trying to decide how to dress for a quick flying session. She sighs in frustration, looking up at him. "Sorry."

"What's wrong?"

"Nothing."

She walks to the drawers, getting out black slacks and a pale blue shirt. She sits on the ottoman to get her boots on, looking up when Rafe kneels before her. He helps her into her boots, then sits beside her.

"Ana, I know I'm not supposed to push, but we're about

to fly. You can understand why I would be worried."

"Yes, I know. I'm okay now. I was trying to figure out what to wear."

"You don't have to wear a gown this weekend."

"Really?"

"Really. Even if we go out, you can dress like this."

"Oh, that'll be a nice break. Thank you." She leans up, kissing him.

"Of course, if I had my way, you wouldn't have to wear anything at all."

"Rafe!" she says, laughing. She kneels on the ottoman, wrapping her arms around his neck and kissing him again. "Now, my wings need to stretch."

"Yes, Majesty."

"Jerk!" she says, hitting his shoulder. He scoops her up, taking to the air. He plants kisses all over her face and neck, lowering back down.

"Let's go." They go to the training center. He watches her step over, expanding her wings and stretching them out. He steps up to her, taking her hand and kissing it. "I promise, this won't be like last time."

"I really hope not." She smirks at him.

"Ana!" He kisses her, startled when she flies up and away. He opens his wings and chases after her. "You're supposed to be taking it easy!"

She laughs as she evades him. "I need this. Believe me, they need the exercise. I'm okay, really!" She takes off again, watching him try and catch up to her. She slows down, flying to him and into his arms. "Feel?"

"You are getting tired, but I think you're okay for a little more."

"Hold my hand?"

"Always."

She smiles at him. "Forever."

They fly a few laps before lowering back down. "Are we

returning to our quarters or is there somewhere you would like to see?"

"Our quarters. Tomorrow, I would like to see our chapel again, if that's okay?"

"You're really excited about getting married there, aren't you?"

"Rafe, that is the most beautiful chapel I've ever seen!"

He chuckles. "All right. We'll go there tomorrow after breakfast."

"Thank you," she replies, kissing him. They step out of the center. Rafe turns to Roesh.

"Our quarters, please."

They follow them back. Rafe is back to watching every movement. Ana sighs but understands with the assassins they've just dealt with. At their quarters, he and Roesh go inside. They step back out.

"Could Aylin and I have a moment?"

"Yes, Majesty," Roesh says while Rafe nods.

She and Aylin go inside, sitting on the chaise.

"Are you and Roesh all right now?"

"We are. We talked. He apologized and made it up to me."

"I don't need to know." They both laugh. "I wanted to talk a little more, if you're sure you're comfortable talking to me?"

"Majesty, I meant what I said. I do not embarrass easily."

"Thank you. How do I begin?" she asks, a nervous chuckle escaping. "Um, we have sort of been practicing for our wedding night. Him on top while we're still dressed."

"Why?" Aylin looks down. "I am so sorry, Majesty. That was—"

"No, it's okay. I was hurt when I was on Earth, a trusted figure did things. It's why I'm uncomfortable talking about it, much less thinking of doing it. He never—" She takes a breath.

"Majesty, I want you to know that you can trust me. I meant it, when I said you can command me to keep your confidence.”

"Trusting you isn't the issue. Just being able to talk about it is. It's me, not you, Aylin. This is why I need to, though. If I want to be ready by our wedding night.”

"How can I help?”

"I wonder what it's like, if I'm—” She looks down.

"If you're on top?” She watches Ana's face flush. "Majesty, I worry you are going to pass out.”

"I'm okay, really. Um, yes. If I'm on top. I have no experience, and I don't want to ruin our wedding night!”

"You aren't going to ruin anything. Like you said, talking about it and working through it now will help. If you are on top, you have control. If that's what you need, to help you not feel overwhelmed. Also, if your wings were to open, it would be easier that way.”

"I didn't think of that.”

"May I ask? How they have been doing when you and he are engaging in personal activities?”

"They've done really well. Better than I expected, actually. Your training tip definitely helped.”

"I'm glad to hear that. I want to help you with this.”

"I'm grateful for your help. I don't mean to embarrass so easily. I'm sorry.”

"For what? You have no need to apologize, Majesty.”

"Aylin, while we are in here discussing these things, you can call me Ana. It would actually make it a little easier. If you're okay to do so.”

"Yes, Ana. That's fine.”

"Thank you. I wonder about the wedding night, if I'm too tired or not up for it.”

"You aren't going to ruin in. I'm sure you've been talking with him about this, correct?”

"Yes. He says the same thing. I still worry.”

"What time is your wedding?”

"Two.”

"Sleep in late if you can, or try to have an early lunch then get a nap. That's the best advice I could give."

"Thank you. That is a good idea. I appreciate you helping me through this. It truly means the world to me."

"Ana, you freed your people, brought about peace, and saved my life. I am happy to serve and happy to help you, I insist."

"Thank you, Aylin."

"I'll return to my post, sending Rafe back in."

"Thanks, for everything."

"You are most welcome."

Aylin steps out, nodding to Rafe. "Everything okay?" he asks.

"Yes, Rafe."

He walks in, joining Ana on the chaise. He looks at her, taking her hand. "Why are you so embarrassed?"

"I'm sorry. I… We were talking about the wedding night. She wants to help me with any questions I have."

"I am grateful you have her."

"Me, too. I'm okay now. Can we get cleaned up?"

"Just a shower, right?"

"Yes, love. I am exhausted."

He goes into the closet, getting them fresh clothes. He takes them into the washroom, setting them on the vanity. He starts the water as she steps in. She strips out of her clothes, tossing everything she was wearing into the hamper. She steps into the water, letting it run over her back and wings. She sees the concern on his face when he joins her.

"Are you all right?"

"I am. Still a little tight. We need to work them more, after Monday."

"We will." He steps up, massaging her neck and shoulders. He works around her wings. "Let's recover and get you rested, then we'll work them tomorrow."

"Thank you." She turns to him, stepping up and kissing

him. "You opened the door, and I thought I lost you when you went down. I heard the shot, and my heart was in my throat!"

He pulls her to him, holding her to his chest. "I'm right here."

"I know. I know we're okay. Still, I was so scared."

He strokes her hair, gently caressing around her wings. "I didn't have a chance to be."

She looks up at him. "You're not upset with me, are you? I didn't have a choice! It was just me, and she was reloading, and—"

"Ana, shh." He pulls her to him. "No, I'm not upset. Please, mia estrela. Please calm down." He looks down as she's trembling in his arms. "Oh, Ana. It's all right. I'm not upset. I know you had to defend yourself."

"I'm sorry."

"For what?"

"Getting so worked up."

"We were both nearly killed. It's understandable. Being as tired as you are, that doesn't help either. Let's finish getting cleaned up. We'll sit on the sofa and talk a bit before turning in. Okay?"

"Yes, love."

She rinses off and exits. After drying off, she puts on her pajamas and wraps the robe around her. She moves towards the chaise and nudges it closer to the fireplace. She sits, hoping to get cozy and warm. Stepping out, Rafe walks up and kneels before her.

"Are you sick?"

"No, but I'm a little cold."

"There is still a bit of a chill in the air." He sits beside her, pulling her to him. "I'll help you get warm."

"Rafe, are you nervous about the wedding night?"

"Yes, I am."

"Because of me?"

"Ana, it will be a first for both of us, so of course I'm

worried. You are worried about so many things, please. Let that go for a while. We have several months and are working together to make that a wonderful night."

"I can't help but worry. I'm excited to marry you, but I'm afraid of what will happen on our wedding night. I know we're bringing down walls, but this is—" She pulls away from him and looks down. "I'm tired. I'd like to turn in."

"Ana, are you okay?"

"Yes."

"Look at me."

She swallows hard, meeting his gaze. "Yes?"

"Will you talk to me?"

Getting up, she makes her way to the washroom. On the chaise, he patiently waits for her to come out. When he can no longer bear it, he steps forward and knocks on the door. Her crying causes him to become concerned. He opens the door, where he discovers her sitting on the tub's edge. When he comes in, she lifts her eyes.

"I'm sorry."

"It's okay." He picks her up, carrying her to bed. "I need to brush my teeth. I'll be right back, then we can talk if you want to."

"Okay."

With her head on the pillow, she fights to quiet her fears and worries. She thinks of him proposing to her, focusing on his love for her. She dozes off before he returns.

Rafe leaves, locking the door behind him and turning off the overhead light. Walking to the bed, he discovers Ana is asleep. Crawling in, he pulls her to him., then he kisses her forehead.

"Please, don't hide from me. I swear, whatever you need to say, I'm right here. I love you, mia estrela."

Chapter 33

Rafe wakes up and rolls onto his back. Glancing at the clock, he notes it's a quarter past midnight. On the verge of falling sleep, he is awakened by Ana's sniffling. He turns on the lamp, then crawls to her.

"What's wrong? Did you have a nightmare?"

"I'm okay."

"Ana, please. I know I'm not supposed to push, but I can't leave you like this. What can I do?"

"I need more sleep."

He turns off the lamp, pulling her back against him. "You don't have to say a word. Just lay here with me until you fall back to sleep."

She rolls onto her side, now facing him. "I'm not only worried about the wedding night."

"I don't understand."

"What if our wedding night is wonderful, goes off without any issues? That's great. I want that more than anything. What if one night we're being a married couple, and I have an episode? What will we do—"

"It's okay. You will never be one hundred percent over everything that has happened to you. We'll deal with episodes and nightmares as they come. We'll work through them, together." He takes a breath, focusing on his love for her. "Were you laying here, thinking I would be better off without you?" He looks down when she's crying again. "Oh, mia estrela. Please, stop doubting us. Stop doubting yourself. Look at what we've overcome together." He wipes her tears, kissing her softly. "Why are you getting worked up over it now? The wedding is so far away."

"Because I think about it every day, as I'm trying to bring

down walls and prepare myself for the wedding night. I tell myself it's really not a big deal, that people do this every single day. I should be okay. Then I'm back in his camp or in my childhood room, and I feel as though I am drowning. I don't doubt you or your love, I really don't. Even talking to Aylin, I got so embarrassed, so flushed with it. I should be able to talk about marrying the man I love without feeling like this!"

"It's why we talk. We will continue to slowly discuss it, making it easier for you. That's why I dared you to talk about what we were doing. I thought if you talked about it as you were enjoying it, maybe it would be easier. Let Kara help, too. She may not be able to give advice about the act itself, but she can listen to you and help you with your confidence." He takes a deep breath. "I want to say something, but I'm afraid of upsetting you."

"Please, Rafe. Just say it. I'll listen with an open mind."

"Do you want to wait until next year to get married?"

She sits up, looking at him in shock. "What? Why would you possibly think that? I'm already worrying myself to death over it. Do you want me to be like this even longer?"

"I didn't think of it like that," he says, sitting up with her. "I only meant, to give you more time to deal with everything. I would marry you tomorrow if I could." He sees the hurt expression on her face. She pulls away, running into the washroom and slamming the door. He gets to his feet, turning on the lights. "Ana?" He knocks on the door. "Please, what did I do wrong?"

"It's not you!"

He shakes his head. "I don't understand. Please, talk to me." He leans against the door, listening as she cries and blows her nose. "Please?" he tries again. He leans against the door, growing concerned when he hears the shower running. "Ana? Ana!" He opens the door, not seeing her.

Entering the shower, he finds her sitting on the floor, her back to the wall. Her knees are drawn up to her chest. He strips out of his clothes and runs in. He sits on the floor, scooping her up and pulling her to him.

"Please, what's wrong?"

"You're so ready to get married while I can't even think of it."

He lets out a small gasp. "Ana, that's not what I meant."

"Don't. Please, don't. I know exactly what you mean."

"You're overwhelmed right now because you are exhausted! You need a good night sleep. We'll talk about everything tomorrow. Please, come back to bed with me."

She lays her head against his chest. "I'm so tired of feeling like this. I know you must be tired of seeing me like this! It's not fair to you."

He assists her to her feet, getting her out of the water and drying her off. While she's getting dressed, he turns off the water. After drying, he puts his pajamas on. As she reaches for the door, he scoops her up and carries her out. Her confusion is evident as he pulls her into the closet. He sits on the ottoman, wrapping the blanket around both of them.

"Ana, I brought you in here every day after telling you I loved you. I risked my life, my reputation, everything I am, to be with you. I took the poison, saving your life. You know how much I love you. Then what did you do? You threw yourself on me, not knowing if I was even alive! You laid in the woods, dying.

"What were your final thoughts? You were saying you were sorry to me, telling me how much you love me. How can you even think of questioning us, when we have lived and died for each other? How can you think I would ever want anything other than what I have, right now, with you?"

"Made for each other?"

"Yes, Ana. That's exactly what we are. Just because I'm excited about marrying you, doesn't mean I'm pushing you. I never meant for you to feel that way. I'm sorry."

She looks up at him, caressing his face. She traces along

his jawline with her fingers. "I know now what you were trying to say. I'm the one who is sorry, as I took it the wrong way. We are both excited about getting married. I mentioned the chapel, and of course that would make you think that."

"Ana, I love you more than I could ever show you. I could kiss you for every star in the sky, touch your heart with every piece of mine, and still not show you how much love I have for you." He brings his hand up and gently wipes her tears. "Happy tears?"

"Yes, love. Thank you. Your patience, your calm, your words, are everything I need right now. I love you, so much." She leans up, kissing him. He lays down with her on the ottoman, his body over hers, as he kisses her harder. He pulls back.

"You need rest."

"I need you," she says, pulling him back on her and devouring his lips.

"Give me a moment." He gets up and secures the door. He heads to the floor lamp, illuminating it before extinguishing the overhead light. Rushing back to her, he smiles when he sees her asleep. "Oh, mia estrela. Sleep through the night. Please?"

***

Waking up, Ana is momentarily confused as she realizes they are in the closet. She thinks of him bringing her in there and smiles. As she looks at him, she realizes he is still asleep. She gently kisses his mouth and face.

"Hmm. Morning, mia estrela."

"Morning, love."

"How do you feel this morning?"

"Much better. I'm sorry about last night. I let my fears take over, turning inward instead of talking to you. Thank you for your patience with me. It helps me more than you could possibly know."

"Did we bring down any walls?"

"We did." She leans up, kissing him. She sits up, pulling him with him. She wraps her arms and legs around him. "Please, love? I need you," she says, kissing him again. He puts her on her feet as they strip out of their clothes, letting them fall to the floor. He pulls her back to the ottoman with him, smiling as she kneels over him. His hand traces up her leg as she kisses him harder. She wraps her hand around, gently moving as his hand teases.

"Ana!" he moans, as she moves faster.

She smiles at him as his mouth is crashing on hers. Her body trembles as the waves are threatening to consume her. She collapses on him as they both cry out. He lays down, pulling her onto his chest. She lays with him, matching his breaths.

"Thank you. I have needed you for a while, but so much happened."

"I would say the same." He looks down at her, caressing her face. "You sure you're okay?"

"Rafe, I didn't even tense up when your hand was on my leg. I am making progress. I am moving past what happened, with your help. Thank you, love."

"I told you I want to help you, and I meant it. I will always do what I can to help you bring down your walls. I love you, so much, Ana."

"Oh, Rafe! I love you, too."

"Let's get dressed and see about breakfast."

"Yes, love."

They stand up. She walks to her dresser, getting out her black pants and shirt, slipping her hoodie on over them.

"Hoodie?"

"That's okay, isn't it?"

He laughs, slipping his on, too. "Of course! I told you, we'll relax and be comfortable this weekend." He steps out to put in for breakfast. She walks to the sofa, looking outside. She sees the sun is out, wishing more than anything it was raining. She looks up when Rafe sits beside her. "You don't have to. Any time I ask, you know you don't. Will you tell me what happened last night?"

"What do you mean?"

"That you thought I would be better off without you. Were you thinking of leaving me?"

"I could never!" she says, standing up. "How could you think that? Yes, I was thinking that you deserve better than me, but I would not leave you. My heart can't even bear the thought of it!" she says, crying into her hands.

He rushes to her, picking her up and sitting on the sofa with her. "I'm so sorry. I worry over you, over everything you carry on yourself. This is why I ask to be let in, why I ask to help you. Please don't carry this on your own."

She looks up at him. "How did you know?" She sees the confusion on his face. "I mean, that I was carrying so much," she adds.

"It wasn't hard to see."

"After breakfast, could we do some work on our office?"

"You'll have to change."

"I know."

"You don't have to wear a gown."

"We'll see," she says. The bell rings, and Rafe lets breakfast in. He helps set up, then the staff leave. Ana smiles when she sees her favorites. She squeezes his hand as she eats. "Thank you."

"Anything for you. You know that, right?"

"Yes, love."

They finish eating. She walks to the sofa and notes the concern on his face when he sits with her. "Sure you're okay?"

"A little tired."

"That's to be expected." He takes her hand between his. He closes his eyes, focusing. "Hmm. You don't feel angry or worried like last night."

"You don't believe me?"

"I do. I also know sometimes it lingers beneath the surface, where even you are unaware it's about to burst."

"I didn't know you could read me so well. I'm not sure how I feel about that," she admits.

"I need to, so I can help you. I won't use it for evil," he says, grinning at her.

"Rafe." She laughs. "I don't know if I believe you."

"What?" he says, showering her face with kisses. "Submit!"

"No," she cries out, laughing.

"Then pay the price," he says, as he kisses her harder.

He pulls back, then plants a soft kiss on her lips. He smiles as he pulls back, seeing the love and happiness in her eyes.

"What?"

"You."

"I don't understand?"

"Your love for me is overwhelming me. It's so powerful." He takes her hand again, sending it back to her. "Do you see now? How could you ever think I doubt your love, when it's so strong?" He wipes the tear as it falls down her cheek.

"You're right. I didn't realize. I'm sorry. I never should've doubted. You have shown me so much love and patience during my trials. How can I ever repay that?"

"Ana, you already have." His hand gently ruffles through her feathers. "The day you died and grew these."

She moves over by him, taking his hand. She leans up, kissing him. "I'm grateful I did. It brought peace, brought us together in so many ways, and made me into who I am. I am the Crimson Queen who will rule with her great love, bringing peace to the galaxy."

"Do you know how happy that makes me? Hearing you say that, it means more to me than you know."

"King Rafe and Queen Maeriana Summerhauld of the Sea-Stellar Realm."

"That will be us, by the end of autumn. Married and crowned."

"I am excited!"

"Now, did you want to go see the chapel then work on our office? Or do you want to stay in and rest?"

"The chapel and our office, if that's okay?"

"Of course."

"Rafe, it's your weekend, too."

"I want to do whatever you do."

"All right."

She gets up and goes into the closet, where she looks through the gowns she purchased. As she slips her clothes off, she smiles and lays them on the ottoman. After getting dressed, she puts her rings on, then slips on gold shoes and a small gold crown. Rafe is sitting on the ottoman to put his boots on, and he looks up when she approaches him.

"What do you think?"

His eyes trace over her, taking in the sight, as he stands. "You look fantastic. Another one of yours?"

"Yes," she says, blushing.

He takes her to the mirror. "Ana?"

"Yes, love?" she asks, struggling to keep a serious expression on her face.

"Don't make me beg."

She laughs and opens her wings. She looks at her reflection, admiring the navy-blue gown. Thin straps with a tight fit. A golden lace shawl extends from the shoulders down the front and back of the gown.

"I really like this one." She takes his hand. "Are we ready?"

"Yes, mia estrela."

He takes her out, seeing Roesh and Aylin. "Aylin! I thought this was supposed to be your weekend off?" Ana asks.

"Erick and Kellan are still recovering from whatever the assassin used on them. We volunteered, Majesty."

"Thank you. We're going to the guardian's chapel." She

sees the confusion on Aylin's face. "I'd like to see it again."

"You owe me no explanation, Majesty."

They lead the way. Rafe looks at Ana, realizing her gown is the same colors as the chapel. He chuckles, keeping it to himself. They go down through the barracks.

Melian greets them. "Everything okay, Majesty?"

"Yes. We are taking a small tour."

"Of course. Let me know if I can be of any assistance."

"Thank you, Captain."

They continue walking. "Would you like to see the guardian children?" Rafe asks Ana.

She looks at Roesh and Aylin, then back to him. "Okay."

They go through an arch and down steps. "This is similar to what you would call a daycare or preschool."

"How young are they?" Ana asks.

"Most of them are under ten."

Ana sucks in her breath. "Okay."

They step inside. The children are sitting around a guardian who is reading to them. Ana and Rafe stay back, listening to the story of the Crimson Queen. Ana gives Rafe a knowing smile, which he returns. She shakes her head.

"Is she really real?" a young child asks.

Ana looks at their tiny wings, still unable to believe the sight. "Yes, I am," she says, stepping forward.

The children all gasp at the sight of her. The guardian stands to greet her. "Majesty," she says, bowing. "I am Luxana. It is an honor to meet you."

"So, you are learning about the Crimson Queen?"

Luxana shifts uncomfortably. "Yes, Majesty. It's one of their favorite stories. They ask for it almost daily."

Rafe laughs. "I told you it was popular with us."

A young girl gets to her feet and bows. "Are you really the Crimson Queen? The one from the stories?"

"I am," Ana says, expanding her wings. All the children get to their feet, watching in awe.

"Children, this is your Queen. What do you do when you see your Queen?"

They all bow before her. She gives a nod. "Children, as you were." They sit back down. "Thank you." She furls her wings back in. "We appreciate your time. I hope this wasn't disruptive."

"Not at all, Majesty. You are most welcome any time. Children?"

"Thank you, Your Majesty."

"You are most welcome, little ones." She smiles at Luxana as she takes Rafe's hand. They leave, going to the chapel. He takes her inside. She's happy it is brighter this time. She walks around, admiring the stained glass.

"You really love this chapel, don't you?"

"Rafe, it's the most beautiful room I've ever seen."

"Why do you love it so much?"

"Is it not obvious?" She smiles at him. "The colors, the guardians in the stain glass, the size. It's absolutely breathtaking!"

"You will be, too. When you walk down the aisle to become my wife." He kisses her, pulling back when someone clears their throat. He turns, smiling. "Our apologies, Sister Ramilda. We are most excited about getting married here."

She chuckles. "We are honored to have you. Is there anything I can assist you with, Your Majesty?"

Ana looks from Rafe to her. "How many guardians are getting married this year? If you don't mind."

"Quite a few. Not just guardians, but guardians with members of Court. I never thought I would see the day. I am most pleased to see this. Thank you, Majesty, for making it possible."

"Really? I thought you were against guardians intermingling?" Rafe asks.

"On paper, we are. I for one always thought it was unnecessary. Now, seeing how few of us are left, do we really have a choice?"

"Sister, are you allowed to marry or do you have to take vows when you became a Sister?"

"We are allowed to marry, if we choose. I have yet to meet anyone I would want to spend that much time with." She looks down a moment, before looking at Ana. "My apologies, Majesty."

"It's all right. You were answering my question. May I ask, how old are you?"

"I am eight hundred and sixty-seven years old."

Ana sucks in her breath, taking in her answer. "Oh, my." She looks at Rafe. "I'm ready to continue on." She looks at Ramilda. "Thank you for your time."

"Majesty."

Rafe leads her from the chapel. "We're going to our office now, what used to be my old quarters."

"Right," Roesh says. They go upstairs and down the corridor she knows so well. They stop outside his quarters. He gets out his key, unlocking the door. Roesh steps in, checking the rooms. "All clear."

Rafe takes her inside. "Ana, we need to go to the Housing Office and request what we need for this."

"I know." She smiles at him.

"You are still recovering."

"Rafe, relax. I was… teasing."

He leads her to the bed. "That's my job."

"Rafe!"

He laughs, pulling her into his arms. "I was kidding, mia estrela! Now, let's see. What all do we need? Two desks with chairs, a couch, and a small table. What do you think?"

She looks around. "A rug would be nice."

"Okay."

"And an additional bookshelf."

"For?"

"Books on prophecies and legends. We will look through

them together, slowly over time. I won't get overwhelmed."

"Hmm. All right. Let's go put in the request."

They step out, telling Roesh. He leads the way. They arrive at the office. Rafe puts in the requests, happy to hear they can have everything in there by the evening.

"We'll come tomorrow after breakfast?"

"If that's what you want."

"Thank you. It will be nice to have somewhere for us to work and study. Now, I'm ready for lunch."

"Dining hall or quarters?"

She thinks for a moment. "Quarters, please."

"Right. Quarters it is."

Rafe catches a staff member while Roesh checks inside. Ana turns to Aylin. "I'm sorry you gave up your weekend. How can I make that up to you?"

"Majesty, it's all right. We are off next weekend together."

"Are you sure? I feel bad."

"Please, Majesty, don't. We volunteered. It's all right."

Rafe takes Ana's hand, leading her in once Roesh has cleared the rooms. "Everything okay?"

"Yes."

"Lunch will be here shortly."

"Then maybe we could go outside? Fly a little?"

"That would be a good idea. How do they feel?"

"Okay." She stretches them out. "They definitely need some exercise, though."

Rafe approaches her, then he examines her wings. "What aren't you telling me?"

She looks at him while bringing them in. "I don't know what you mean."

"Why are they so tight?"

"I told you, they just need the exercise."

"No. Did you have an episode last night?"

She takes a breath. "I thought you were going to work on not pushing me?"

"Like you will open up with me?"

Her head goes down. "You're right. Yes, I had an episode last night. I was back in his camp. I didn't want to tell you, because this is our weekend to relax, to be together. I wanted one weekend where you weren't worried over me!" The heat from his anger penetrates her. "Please, I'm so sorry!"

Stepping away, he breathes deeply. He calms his heart and thinks of their love. Returning to her, he embraces her.

"I understand why you feel that way, but if you want to keep moving forward, to bringing down walls, we need to work together."

She lays her head on his chest, listening to his heartbeat. "You're right. How can I stop hiding? It's so hard for me to be open."

"Why is that?"

"Because I should be over it by now."

His eyes close at her words. "Ana, no. You were kidnapped, watched a man die, and were scared! I am so sorry I said that. Please, believe me when I say I would give anything to take that back. You will take as long as you need to recover!" He pulls back, placing his hand under her chin and gently tilting her face to him. "I am sorry."

"Me, too."

The bell rings. He opens the door and lets lunch service in. It's set up on their table. He takes her hand, walking with her.

"Will you eat for me?"

"Yes, love," she says as she sits down. She makes herself eat, worrying that he is going to get upset with her if she doesn't.

"Why are you worried?" he asks after taking her hand. "What's wrong?"

"I don't want you to get angry with me."

"Because you hid?"

"Yes."

"Ana, I'm not. I'm worried about you because I want to help you. I swear to you right here and now, I'm not angry. We are both working on our issues, together. It's a day-to-day process. Right?"

"Yes."

"We both deserve time and patience."

"Thank you." She looks at the window and sees it's raining. "I guess we'll go to the training center." She smiles at him. "Where you won't be jealous, right?"

He returns her smile while leaning down. "Only of how sexy you are in that gown."

"Rafe! Really?" she asks, laughing. "What am I to do with you?"

"Hmm, after flying, anything you want."

"After flying I'll probably need to rest."

"Don't worry. I'll do all the work."

She leans up, kissing him. "What's gotten into you?"

"Seeing you, in that gown, in the chapel. You are more beautiful than I could describe. You are such a goddess." He sees her eyes go down. "What's wrong?"

"I love you. I have given you my heart and soul, everything I am, because I am so deeply, madly, in love with you. It makes me angry with myself that I keep hiding, when I know how much you love me, too."

"Ana, I have loved you from the moment I saw you, and I will love you every day for all time. What you've survived, what you've endured, I don't blame you for hiding. I used to get angry, taking it as a slight against me.

"Now, that I can feel what you feel, I understand that sometimes it's too much for even you to deal with, much less to talk about. Believe me when I say, I wish you would tell me everything, but I know that's not always the case. Tell me when you need me, whether it's to talk about what you're dealing with or so I can take you in my arms. Waking up, hearing you crying, my heart ached so badly for you."

"I never meant—"

"Ana, no. I'm not scolding you or calling you out. I want you to understand why I want to help you."

"What about you? What about your walls? I want to help you, too."

"Ask me anything."

She takes his hand, leading him to the sofa. She sits down, while he lays with his head in her lap. "Are you really over everything from your mother?"

"No."

"I could tell, as much anger as you still carried for her."

"Growing up, she wasn't big on being affectionate. Honestly, most guardians aren't. We don't really show emotion. Our duty is our life, training and protecting. Rowenne was affectionate, giving me hugs and telling me how proud of me he was. When she left, I thought it would be okay. I knew I could still go and see her, so I tried not to worry too much."

"What happened?"

"A few nights after she had left, I went to see her. She asked me why I was there. I told her she was my mom, that I love her, and wanted to see her. She explained to me that she was starting a new family, and that I was not allowed to come there again."

"Rafe, I'm so sorry! You were just a child. That's awful."

"She never should've went into battle."

"What do you mean?"

"She was pregnant."

"Oh, God. Why have you carried this? Why haven't you told me about this sooner? Love, it's not fair that you take my pain while keeping yours bottled up!"

"Ana, it was a long, long time ago. Over five hundred years."

"Then why do you still feel it in your heart as though it were yesterday?" She looks down at him, running her fingers through his hair.

"You can feel that?"

"Like you said, I am stronger with it."

"I was asleep when Rowenne came to me, telling me she had been killed. He sat on the edge of my bed, watching for a reaction. I don't know if he thought I would cry or get angry. I thanked him for telling me and went back to sleep."

"Rafe!"

"What's that word you've used? Disassociating? I'm pretty sure that's what I did when he told me that. I didn't want to think about it. I pushed it down and moved on."

"You pushed it down, and you went on with life. You haven't moved on."

"What do you mean?"

"It's why you didn't want children, isn't it?"

He sits up, looking at her. "I never really thought of that. I won't say it's the main reason, but probably a factor, yes."

"We both have much to deal with."

"Ana, I don't."

"I feel so much anger and regret, when it comes to her. We will deal with this together. What is it you always say to me? Let me in. Let me help." She moves over to him, snuggling into his chest. "Please?"

"You're right. Yes, Ana. I won't hide. Like you do."

She looks up at him, angry until she sees the grin on his face. "Jerk!"

"Ana!"

She pulls away, flying to the ceiling. "What?"

He shakes his head. "Let's go to the training center."

She lowers back down, kissing him. "Yes, love. Do I need to change?"

"Only if you want to."

"I'll be all right."

Chapter 34

Ana takes Rafe's hand as they leave their quarters. "The training center," she instructs Roesh.

"Yes, Majesty."

Aylin looks back at her. Ana flashes her a smile. "Yes, Aylin?"

"After the training center, could we see the cathedral, Majesty?"

"Of course!" She faces Rafe. "They are getting married there."

"Are you sure you'll be all right to go in there? You haven't been there since you nearly died."

Roesh looks at Aylin. "Did you know that?"

"Yes, but—"

"Aylin! No, Majesty. She and I can go to the cathedral when we are off duty."

"Roesh, I insist we go there after the training center. I want to see it myself. I asked Kara to take me there not too long ago. I want to."

"Yes, Majesty."

"I'm so sorry."

"No, Aylin. It's okay. We are going to see where two of my best guardians are getting married. I want to."

"Thank you, Majesty."

They arrive at the center. Roesh and Rafe go in to check it's empty. Ana looks at Aylin. "Please, don't feel bad. I want to go there."

"I do, though. I wasn't thinking."

"Aylin, it's all right. It was a bad day, because I nearly died. It's also the day Rafe took me in his arms and confessed his love for me, even though it was still forbidden. Believe me, it wasn't all bad memories."

"How long did you have to hide, before your treaty was passed?"

"Long enough. I was so nervous about trying to pass the treaty."

"Freeing slaves and freeing love, while trying to bring peace? I can't imagine!"

"I mean it, when I said I refused to rule over a kingdom where love was illegal. Such archaic customs and laws!"

"Majesty, I couldn't agree more. When I was returned here and heard what had happened, that the war was over and a treaty in place, I couldn't believe it!" She looks up as Rafe and Roesh walk out.

"We'll talk more."

"Yes, Majesty."

Rafe takes her inside. "Everything okay?"

"I was reassuring her that I want to see the cathedral, too. She felt bad for asking. It is their weekend off, but they volunteered to watch over us. The least we could do is let them see where they are getting married."

She steps over, opening her wings. She looks at the mat where she fell. Rafe walks up, taking her hand. "What's wrong?"

"Looking at where I landed."

He looks over at the mat, turning back to her. "I'm so sorry."

"Rafe, it's okay. We've moved past that." She pulls away, flying up to the ceiling. "Now, what are you going to do?"

He races up to her, laughing when she evades him. "Ana! You are supposed—"

"I swear, if you tell me to take it easy, I will fly laps around you!"

He laughs, trying again to catch her. She turns back, flying up to him and into his arms, kissing him. "Ana, are you okay?"

"I am. Are we ready to see the cathedral?"

"We are." They lower down.

"I need to use the washroom before we go." She lets go of his hand, running in. He walks around the center, admiring the equipment. He looks up when he hears a noise from the washroom.

"Ana?" he asks, walking in. She's leaning over the sink, washing her hands. She looks up at him.

"What's wrong?"

"I thought I heard something. I wanted to make sure you're okay."

She dries her hands. "Good to go." She kisses him, taking his hand. They leave the center. "Roesh, to the cathedral, please."

"Yes, Majesty."

"Ana, what am I feeling from you? Fear, love, worry?"

Roesh spins on his heel. "Majesty—"

"Roesh, cathedral. Now."

"Yes, Majesty," he says, turning back around. Aylin takes his hand.

Ana smiles at them, looking back at Rafe. "I'm okay. So much happened that day, but I mean it when I say it was one of the best days of my life. Everything I went through was worth it, for you to pull me into your arms and tell me you love me."

"Wait," Roesh says. "Wasn't that forbidden then?"

"It was. We had to hide, until I grew my wings and passed the treaty."

Roesh stops, looking at her. "I was in the field that day, Majesty. I was there when you emerged from the woods, your wings expanding."

"Really?"

"Yes. I was in such shock."

"Roesh, you didn't tell me that," Aylin says. "Did you fall to your knees? Like the prophecy?"

"Yes. We all did." He turns back, continuing to the cathedral. "I can't imagine."

Ana laughs. "Believe me, literally everyone has said they can't imagine what I went through. It's okay."

They arrive. They go inside, happy to find it empty. Ana and Rafe walk around the pews, admiring the huge marble pillars. She looks up at the ceiling, seeing it's painted navy blue with constellations painted on. She looks at Rafe.

"Do you know the different constellations?"

"I do. I'll teach you."

"Please, do."

"Are you okay to go up to the altar?"

"I'm fine. I swear, I'm not hiding."

"All right." He leads her up the aisle, walking to the altar. He puts his hands on her shoulders, gently positioning her.

"What are you doing?"

"This is where you were, when I saw the bolt go through you. I was so sure I had lost you. I was in the rafters, apprehending the assassin. I flew down to you, once he was in custody."

"You flew to me? I didn't even get to see it! I was unconscious."

"I had to make sure you were alive. I was so scared."

"I'm right here, love," she says, kissing him. She steps back, looking up and around. "It is a beautiful cathedral, but I am most excited to get married in the chapel."

"I am, too. You were right. This is a little much for us."

"Aylin, is this what you want? For your wedding?"

"Yes, Majesty. It is. Thank you, so much."

"You're most welcome." She sees worry on Roesh's face. "Are you all right?"

"Yes, Majesty. I'm thinking of the wedding day. I have a good size family, but Aylin does not."

"I'm sure she has more than enough friends to help fill her side."

"Her side?"

Ana looks at Rafe. "They don't have that here?"

"What are you talking about?"

"On Earth, the bride's family and friends sit on the side she stands on, the groom's on his."

"No, here everyone sits wherever."

"I see."

Rafe looks at her. "I feel how tired you are. We need to have dinner then rest tonight."

She wants to argue, but she knows he's right. "Yes, love."

He grabs her to him, taking her to the air. He kisses her. "Happier memories here? Yes?"

She kisses him back as they lower down. "Yes, thank you." She looks over, seeing Aylin and Roesh watching them. "Our apologies."

Roesh laughs. "No problem, Majesty. I'm glad you're okay in here."

"Thank you, for your concern. I am sorry, but I need rest. You are both welcome to come back here when you are off duty."

"We appreciate that."

Roesh takes Aylin's hand, leading them back to their quarters. He and Rafe step in to inspect them. "Majesty, are you sure you're okay?"

"Yes, Aylin. Really. It's been long enough, the memories don't bother me anymore. I've moved past it."

"Still, I'm sorry."

"For what?"

"What happened to you, what you went through."

"I'm okay now. Thank you, though. It was terrifying at the time, but I overcame that. Kane is dead, while I'm still here. He nearly took me with him."

"Really?"

"I stabbed him with my sword, going through his chest. He fell on me. As I was trying to get away from him, he stabbed me with a poisoned dagger."

"It's a wonder you're still here!" She blushes. "I'm sorry,

Majesty."

"Quite all right. Rafe and I healed each other." She looks up as they step out. "We're going to have dinner then rest."

"Yes, Majesty. We will have dinner brought in for you. Thank you for letting us see the cathedral this afternoon."

"Aylin, you are most welcome."

Rafe takes her inside. She goes to the closet, getting out pajamas. She looks up at him, seeing a look on his face. She walks up, taking his hand.

"Ana, what are you doing?"

"Why are you so angry?"

"I was thinking of my mother again. What we talked about."

"Let's get cleaned up. We'll talk over dinner, if that's all right?"

"It is." He leans down, kissing her. "Thank you."

"For what?"

"Being amazing." He smiles when she blushes. "You are!"

"Rafe! Let's get cleaned up." They go to the washroom. He starts the water as she removes the gown. She strips down, looking up at him. He kisses her, softly at first, but it grows in hunger. "Love, please—"

"Just wanted a kiss."

"Thank you."

They clean up and put on their pajamas, stepping out as the bell is ringing. He seats her on the chaise, and then guides the staff to their table. Food is set up, and they leave. He walks back to her, taking her hand.

"How do your wings feel?"

"So much better. They needed the exercise. Thank you for showing me the guardian children."

"They love their Crimson Queen."

She laughs, taking a drink. "That they do."

"But you still don't want any?"

She nearly drops her cup. "I... what? Do you?"

"No, of course not."

She finishes eating and walks to the sofa, where she sits down. A moment later, Rafe joins her. "Then why did you ask?"

"I'm sorry. If a time ever did come, that you might want children, I want you to know we can at least discuss it. I won't shut you down, like I have with other things."

She scoots over, laying her head on his chest. He brings her legs up, laying her on the sofa. "Thank you. I... Honestly, I think that's another wall of mine. I don't want children, but it's difficult to talk about. I don't know why."

"Ana, even though I grew up here with wings and training, I still had a more normal childhood than you. Of course it would be difficult to talk about having one of your own. It's understandable."

"My childhood was spent going foster home to foster home, until I spent four years with him. Then I was taking care of the house while he worked and drank."

"Did you have any friends?"

"Not allowed."

"What?"

"I went to school, came home, and took care of him. If we had food in the house, I would fix what I could. Usually the pantry was empty and the only thing in the fridge was beer. I had to clean house and do laundry. I didn't go to other kid's birthday parties or have anyone to play with. Once he would pass out for the night, I would go to my room and read. I could easily hide books."

"Nothing about your childhood was normal, was it?"

"I guess not. It was what it was. I'm moving past it, bringing down these walls with you. I don't feel as much hate or anger as I used to."

"What do you feel?"

"Sad. I grieve for the life I should've had. The one you told me about, growing up here in the palace. It's not Kara's fault. My mother died, and Kara did what she had to in order to protect me from my father. I try to think of growing up here, but all it does is make me sick to my stomach."

"Are you okay to talk about this now, so close to going to bed?"

"I am. Trust me, as tired as I am, I will sleep good tonight." She looks up at him. "What about you? Losing your mother the way you did, I'm sure life was different for you after that."

"I focused on training. I used my anger as my strength. Letting it build up over the centuries, no wonder it took me so long to work on it, not wanting to hurt you anymore."

"If you could say anything to your mother, what would it be?"

Rafe thinks for a moment, thinking of the look on his mother's face when she told him to leave and not come back. "I would tell her I forgive her. I don't know why she left Rowenne, or why she left me. All I know is, I'm done carrying this anger. You and I both deserve better."

"You've been doing so much better, about not getting angry. You… It scared me sometimes, how angry you would get."

"That's why I've worked on it. Even if you deserved it, like lying to me to go rescue Bela, I never should've let it consume me. You had just suffered hell, and I couldn't even see it because of my anger. You needed me, but I was more concerned with how I felt. Then finding out what you really went through, I knew I had to do something. I never want you to feel that kind of anger from me again. No matter what, you don't deserve that. Not from someone you love."

"Thank you. That means so much to me, that you would do that for me. Growing up in an angry house, hearing him scream and yell." She looks down. "I never wanted to be around that again. I know we've had our fights, but I promise you, you were never like him!"

"We need to do something, before turning in."

"What do you mean?"

"I don't want this on your mind as we're going to sleep." He stands up, pulling her with him. He takes her to the middle of the room, dancing with her as he sings to her. He pulls her to the air, dancing around some more. She lays her head on his shoulder, her arms around his neck. He lowers them back down, kissing her as they land. "Better?"

She smiles up at him. "Yes, love. Thank you. I'll use the washroom, then we can turn in."

He waits for her. As soon as she steps out, he scoops her up. She cries out, laughing. He kisses her. "Surprised?" he asks, walking her to the bed.

"Yes!"

He lays her down, laying with her and kissing her. "Ana, I love you. I have always loved you, and I always will."

"Oh, Rafe! I love you, too. I fought it in the beginning, trying to protect myself, my heart. I never should've done that!"

"You had every right to, everything you have survived. Just think, we'll get married in August and go on our honeymoon at our private cottage on the beach. How does that sound?"

"Like a dream come true." She looks up at him. "I'm sorry."

"For what?"

"That I didn't tell you sooner, about his camp. You were so concerned for me, begging me to open up, and I hid that. I had no right to!"

"Yes, Ana, you did. It was too much for you to handle. Once you were ready to talk about it, we did. Now we move on."

She closes her eyes at his words. *Like it's that easy. What does he know?* She takes a deep breath, thinking of dancing with him, being in the air in the cathedral. "Yes, we are. Goodnight, love."

"Goodnight, mia estrela. Sleep all night."

"Of course."

She turns on her side, thinking on his words. He pulls her against his chest, holding her tight, and drifts off to sleep. Lying there, she wishes it were so easy. That she could snap her fingers and be over everything she has gone through.

He really wants me to be past it, doesn't he? I think he is getting tired of my episodes, tired of dealing with me. He deserves better. He deserves to have me, free of my trauma. That's what he'll have. I won't let him see me hurting anymore.

It takes an hour before she finally falls asleep. Her nightmares come, opening up more of her past and showing her memories she never wanted to see.

Ana jerks awake, realizing Rafe's in the washroom. She lies back down, focusing on his love for her, on being excited about getting married. She refuses to let him feel what she is feeling, to feel her guilt or shame.

He returns to her, pulling the cover up and pulling her close. The moment he drifts back to sleep, she gently moves away, creating some distance. Overwhelmed by the memories, she closes her eyes to try and regain control.

When nothing helps, she goes into the washroom, closing and locking the door behind her. Sniffling, she grabs a towel and buries her face in it, trying to muffle her sobs.

"Ana, are you okay?"

She takes a drink of water while wiping away her tears. "Yes, love. I'll be right out."

"Okay."

She wets the towel and gently dries her face. With complete determination, she suppresses everything else and focuses solely on feeling love for him. Stepping outside, she notices him waiting for her. She grasps his hand, and they both go to bed. She watches him fall back to sleep, as she lies awake the rest of the night.

At seven, she gets up to request breakfast. Rafe is still sound asleep. She goes to the closet to get fresh clothes. After showering and drying, she looks up when he enters.

"Are you okay?" he asks, his brow furrowed.

"I'm fine," she says, smiling at him. "You were sleeping really hard. I didn't want to wake you. It's supposed to be our weekend to relax, right?"

"Still, I wish you woke me up. I don't like waking up in an empty bed."

"Oh, right! I forgot. I'm so sorry." She steps up, kissing him. "Breakfast will be here soon."

"All right."

She steps out of the washroom, going to the middle of the main chamber and expanding her wings. She furls and unfurls them, unable to believe how tight they are. Rafe steps up behind her and feels them.

"What's wrong? Why are they so tight today?"

"I must've overworked them yesterday."

"Ana, what's wrong?"

"What do you mean?"

"You sound different. Did you have an episode last night?"

"If I did, wouldn't I tell you?"

"No. Especially since you're avoiding the question. Why won't you tell me? Why are you hiding again?"

Her mouth opens in surprise. She turns away, hiding her tears. Fleeing the room, she races toward the battlement. He chases after her, but he can't maintain the same pace once she takes flight.

He flies around once again, scanning the skies, until he

looks down and finds her in the woods. He points her out to Roesh and Aylin. They land behind her. Rafe walks up, grabbing her hand and pulling her into his arms.

"Ana, don't ever do that again!" He feels her trembling, his arm soaking wet from her falling tears. "I'm not angry. I was so scared when you did that. What were you thinking, running off like that?" He pulls her closer, holding her tight. Her shame, anger, frustration are flowing into him. He replaces them with his love. "Ana?" he asks as she stops trembling. "If I let go, do you promise to stay and talk to me?"

"Yes," she whispers.

He releases her, waiting for her to explain. "Ana?"

She steps away, wrapping her arms around herself. "What do you care if I had an episode last night? Why does it matter to you?"

"Where is this coming from? I want to help you with them."

"I should be over it by now."

"Ana! I said that before I knew everything that happened. Even so, I never should've said it in the first place."

"I want to go back to our quarters. I need rest."

"Talk to me, please!" he begs.

"Let me have some breakfast and rest, then I swear to you, I will tell you everything."

He takes her hand, returning to their quarters. Breakfast is brought in. He watches her eat, wanting to ask but giving her space.

Returning to the closet, she puts on her black clothes and hoodie. She lies down on the ottoman and falls asleep. Standing in the doorway, Rafe watches her.

"Why are you hiding? Why now?" he asks, as he crawls onto the ottoman with her.

Chapter 35

Rafe is the first thing Ana sees when she wakes up. She withdraws quietly and makes her way to the chaise. Watching the fire, she pulls the blanket tighter around her. She remains still and doesn't look up as he sits beside her.

"Are you okay?" he asks, getting concerned when she says nothing. "Ana, please. I'm not angry about this morning. Why are you shutting me out now? What did I do wrong?" He watches her as her head goes down. "Please, mia estrela?"

She takes a breath, turning to him. "I've decided I'm going to handle this on my own. These are my episodes, my issues. There is no reason for you to feel them, for you to be burdened with caring for me."

"You aren't making any sense."

"I am. It's my issue, my condition. I will cope how I need to, and this is what I need. To deal with it alone."

"Are you breaking up with me?"

She scoffs. "That's really your biggest concern?"

"Look at me. Look me in the eyes and tell me this."

She meets his gaze, swallowing hard. "I love you. I'm not breaking up with you. I am simply letting you know that I can take care of myself."

"What happened?"

"Nothing," she says, looking down.

He shakes his head. "Will you stay here if I leave for a moment? I'll be right back, I promise."

"I'll stay."

He steps out, going to Evren's quarters, praying Kara is there. When she opens the door, he sighs in relief. "I need your help."

"What's wrong?"

"I don't know. Something has happened with Ana, and she is completely turning inward. I know we aren't supposed to push, but this is different."

Kara nods. "I'll talk to her."

They enter the quarters together. Rafe goes to the sofa, keeping his distance while watching them talk. Kara tries to comfort Ana, but instead she pulls away.

"Because he deserves better!" Ana cries out.

Rafe rushes to her, kneeling in front of her. "Better than what? Because I can assure you, there is no one better for me than you."

"Ana, you need to tell him."

"Kara—"

"He loves you so much. How can you even question that? He wants to help you, he wants to take care of you. Rafe isn't going to leave you, no matter what you tell him. The fact that he is here, right now, fighting for you instead of walking off angry, should tell you everything you need to know!"

She looks down at Rafe. "I did have an episode last night."

"Will you tell me about it?"

She looks at Kara, who nods. "I will. I was back in his camp, with that man on top of me. It triggered a memory of my foster father. I told you he broke my ribs when I was ten? That I told a teacher, and he was so angry?" Kara puts her hand on Ana's arm, reassuring her. "The night before, when he had come in, he was so drunk. He stripped me down, then climbed on top of me." She pushes down the tears threatening to escape. "He was… He was going to hurt me, but he passed out drunk instead. I managed to slip away, leaving him in my bed. I went to school and told someone, hoping it would all go away."

"Why didn't it?" he asks.

"She didn't call child protection like she was supposed to. She called him, instead. I didn't know that. I got off the bus, hoping to see cop cars. I was angry to see nothing. I went into the house, and he grabbed me by my backpack, knocking me to the ground. He hit me, breaking my ribs. He threw me onto the couch.

"As soon as he went to the bathroom, I managed to get his phone off the coffee table and call the police. I turned his phone off so they wouldn't call back. He was coming back to me when we heard the sirens. I went to the hospital and didn't see him again until the day he died."

"Ana, why are you hiding this? Why didn't you wake me, tell me what happened, and let me comfort you? I don't understand."

"We keep getting so close to my walls coming down. Then another pops up. It's not fair to you! It's why I want to work on it so you don't have to. I want to carry it myself."

"No, Ana, you don't. You said it, that I help you. My words, my love, my comfort, they mean so much when you are dealing with your episodes. I want to help you, I want to be here for you. Why don't you believe that?"

"Because I should be over it by now."

Rafe sucks in his breath, closing his eyes. "I am so sorry I ever said that. Please, please, stop hanging that over me! If I could take it back, if I could change it, I would. I never should've said those words to you."

"Why not? It's the truth."

"No, Ana, it most certainly is not! I would rather be without my wings than to have said that to you."

Kara takes Ana's hand. "Why do you think that? You are taking what he said out of context, twisting it to make you feel better about pushing him away. Even what he said, wasn't really that bad. He was right, too, wasn't he? What he said was that if you weren't hurt like that, you should be over it. You lied to him and me, denying what happened."

"Kara, please. It was too much for me!"

"I'm not mad you didn't tell us. I'm mad because you're turning inward, and I'm worried you're closing yourself off to us! Everything we've been through, everything he has done for you, why would you do that to him now?"

She looks at them both. "You really don't know, do you?"

"What?" Rafe asks. "Tell us."

She takes his hand, pulling him up to sit next to her. She traces her fingers along his hand and wrist. "I'm afraid."

"Of what?"

She looks at him, trying to keep his gaze. "I'm afraid of what other memories might still be hiding. I'm afraid of my own past. That if you help me bring down walls, we'll find something I don't want to find. Something bad enough you would leave me."

Kara and Rafe exchange a worried look. He turns back to Ana. "That will never happen! I have told you, nothing you tell me will make me think any differently about you. Whatever you have done, or has been done to you, whatever you've lived through, survived through, I am right here."

"How do you know? I'm still digging up my past. You don't know what's in there. I can't—"

"Shh," Kara says, pulling her into her arms. "Ana, Rafe means it when he tells you nothing you say or do will scare him away. I don't have what you guys do, but I can see and feel his love for you from over here! He will not leave you, he will not abandon you. Why do you think he will?"

"He told me he loved me, then he left."

"Ana, I didn't have a choice."

"I know that now. I didn't know it at the time. I was so worried, scared, angry, sad. I lied to you, to both of you."

"What do you mean?" Kara asks.

"I did try to kill myself, with the pills and vodka. After growing up alone, then finally finding someone who said they love me, just to lose them? It was too much. I couldn't bear it. I'm not saying this to make you feel guilty, Rafe. I don't blame you, but I want you to understand how badly it hurt when you left."

"But I didn't leave! I was pulled back here. I won't leave you, especially after all we've been through now. I thought I convinced you of that, in NightFall? Why do you doubt now?"

"Now we move on."

"What?" he asks.

"That's what you said last night, when we were talking about the camp."

"What?" Kara yells, getting to her feet. "Rafe, why would you say that?"

"Kara, wait. It's not how it sounds! She apologized for not telling me sooner. I meant that we move on from her hiding, not from what she endured at his camp."

"Really?" Ana asks, sitting up. "I thought—"

"Oh, mia estrela! No. I wouldn't say something that callous. I only meant I wasn't upset you hid it, not that you should be over it. I see now, how you take my words. I never meant it like that, I swear. I need to work on how I speak to you."

Ana stands up, wrapping the blanket around herself. She walks up to the fireplace, putting her hand on the mantle as she watches the flames. "It's me, too. How I take them, when I should know better." She looks at him. "I'm sorry. This was a misunderstanding, all my fault. If we talked, instead of me turning inward, this wouldn't have happened!" She hangs her head as the tears start to flow. "I'm so sorry. I've ruined our weekend!"

Rafe comes up behind her and holds her in a loving embrace. "You haven't ruined anything. You brought down one of your biggest walls yet. Don't you see that? Your strength, your resilience, everything about you is incredible. We're moving forward, getting closer to bringing them all down. Isn't that what you want?" He wipes her tears, looking at Kara.

"Everything he said is true," Kara assures her. "I'll go back to Evren. You two need your time together. We'll do breakfast tomorrow, that way I can catch you up before the briefing."

Ana walks to her and hugs her. "Thank you. And I'm so sorry."

"No, Ana. No apologies. You've done nothing wrong, because you thought you were trying to protect yourself. We understand now."

"I love you, Kara."

"Oh, sis!" She pulls her in tighter. "I love you, too. Now, rest today."

"We will," Rafe assures her.

"Evren and I will be next door, if you need anything. I mean that."

"Thank you."

Kara shoots her a smile then leaves. Ana turns to Rafe. "Are you okay now?" he asks, his voice thick with concern.

"I'm embarrassed with how I behaved."

"Why did you leave like that?"

"I needed space. I love you, but you don't give me a moment if I ask you to. I understand why you don't, but sometimes I am overwhelmed and need to collect myself."

"It's why I turn away, silently counting to ten and slowing down my racing heart. I understand why you would need that." He steps up to her, caressing her face gently.

"Are we okay?" she asks, looking up at him.

"Yes, mia estrela. We are."

She collapses into his arms, holding him tightly. "I'm so sorry! I know you'll say no apologies, but I do owe this. I owe you an apology for turning inward and leaving. I am truly sorry. Please, forgive me?"

"Ana, I already have. I told you, we're okay."

She pulls back, bringing her hand up and tracing along his jawline. "You really have worked on your anger, haven't you?"

"I have. I told you, I had to, for you. I want to be the man you deserve."

"You already are," she says, kissing him softly. "How can I make this up to you? What can I do?"

"Spend the day with me."

"That's what I want, more than anything."

"Let's get lunch brought in, then we can work on our office, if you want."

"I'll put in for it. I want to apologize to Roesh and Aylin, too. Please?"

"All right."

He watches her step out, realizing she's still in her hoodie. "Kara will kill me if anyone sees that!" He rushes over, seeing her talking to Roesh and Aylin. "Excuse me," he says, dragging her back in.

"Why did you do that?"

"You're in your hoodie," he explains, laughing. "Do you want Kara to murder us?" he asks, gently pulling it off her. "Get dressed. I'll see to lunch."

She goes to the closet, putting on black slacks and a pale blue shirt. She slips on her boots, loving the feel of them. She walks back out. "I need to finish talking to Roesh and Aylin."

They step out together. "Where to?" Roesh asks.

"No, Roesh. I wanted to apologize for this morning. I had a bad morning, and I'm sorry for what I put you both through."

"Majesty, you don't. We don't know everything, but we know you have been through so much to protect us and to protect your kingdom. It's all right."

"Are you okay now, Majesty?" Aylin asks.

"Yes, I am. Thank you. We're going to have lunch then go to our office."

"Yes, Majesty," Roesh says.

Rafe takes her back inside. "Are you sure you're okay?"

"Yes, love, I am. I wasn't thinking, stepping out. Good catch!"

He chuckles. "I'll get dressed."

As she sits on the chaise, she observes him entering the closet. The image of him sleeping there occupies her thoughts. Pulling up the blanket, she examines it closely.

"What's wrong?"

She looks up, seeing him dressed to match her. She smiles at him. "Thinking back, when this was where you slept. My 'assigned' guardian."

"That I was. I will always be your guardian."

"And I'll be yours," she replies. His eyes go wide. "What?"

"Even looking at you, seeing your wings, I forget that's what you are. I look at you and see my Crimson Queen."

"Rafe!"

He sits next to her, lacing her fingers with his. "Never had any idea that's who you were. I fell in love with Ana, the woman who stole my heart. Seeing you on the field, as your wings opened, I was so shocked. Even though I heard it all my life, I forgot about it, too. Like you. I was so stunned in the moment, I didn't know what I was seeing!"

"I think everyone was as surprised as I was. Watching wings of fire erupt from my back, to grow into these? I was horrified! I couldn't believe what happened. When I first came to, I prayed it was a nightmare, that I was in shock from my wounds. Standing up, feeling the weight of them, seeing them wrap around. It was almost more than I could bear!"

"I'm so sorry you had to go through that alone."

"I didn't, not really. The actual transformation, yes. Then you were with me through every step of the way." She kisses him. "Thank you for being there for me when I couldn't even do it myself."

"I will always be here for you. I wish you would believe that."

"I'm trying to. I swear I am. It's not you, either. How I am, how I think… it makes me doubt when I know I shouldn't."

Rafe gets up when the bell rings. He has food set up then walks back to her. He helps her to her feet, taking her to their table. "Ana, know this. I am always here. Whether you need to talk or have me hold you, all you have to do is let me know what you need."

"I know that. God, I know that. Thank you. I need to work on asking for help, on letting you in. I keep saying I will, but I get scared. I give in to the fear and make it so much worse than it needs to be."

"Ana, I will love you on your best days and your worst. I will love you when you are happy and when you are sad. I love you, every piece of you as you are. My love is unstoppable, unconditional, and unending."

"Rafe," she tries, as tears are falling down. He gently wipes them away, planting a soft kiss. "Oh, love. Thank you. I love you. I love you so much, I want to open myself to you. I want to stop hiding and let you in."

"So why don't you?"

She starts to get mad, until she sees the smile on his face. She punches his shoulder. "Jerk!"

"Ana!"

He pulls her from the chair, has her in the air and is planting kisses all over as she laughs, playfully pleading for him to stop. He pulls her to him, gently kissing her forehead.

"Oh, love. Thank you for being so wonderful with me."

"Ana, I meant it. You deserve to feel loved and cared for every second of every day. I never want you to feel alone or doubt my love for you."

"You do make me feel loved, all the time. I wish I could do the same for you."

"Ana, you do. You know you do." He kisses her as they lower back down. He laughs when she pulls away, flying up again.

"What? I know you want to see my wings. Do you deny it?"

"No, my Crimson Queen, I don't." She lowers back to him, hovering a moment as she kisses him. "I love when you do that!" he says as she lands on her feet. "It's beautiful to watch you."

"Thank you. Are we ready to work on our office?"

"Yes. I had our packages from NightFall taken there last night. Now, it's up to us to decide where to put things!"

"Is what I'm wearing okay?"

"Yes, Your Majesty."

"Guardian!" She laughs, as they step outside. She looks at Roesh. "Our office, please."

Roesh takes Aylin's hand, leading the way. Ana smiles at Rafe, seeing the look on his face, too. "They're so cute together!" she quietly gushes to him.

Rafe laughs, shaking his head. "Yes, they are."

Chapter 36

They arrive at Rafe's old quarters. Roesh steps in first. "It's a bit of a mess with everything. Are you sure you don't need help moving stuff?" he asks after he inspects inside.

"If we do, we'll come and get you. Thank you, though," Ana says as they enter. "Oh, I see what he means. They just kind of threw everything in, didn't they?"

"Let's start with the desks, since they are almost where we want them, anyway."

They move the desks where they want them, arranging them so when they sit, they will face each other. She helps him move the bookshelf to the opposite wall. They unroll the rug, laying it in the middle of the room. They finish with hanging the various art they had bought in NightFall.

"Well, what do you think?"

Ana looks around. "I am very happy with it. We have an office."

"With a bed," Rafe points out.

She looks up at him. "Really?"

"I'm teasing! I told you to rest and look at everything we did instead. Let's get cleaned up and ready for dinner."

She steps up, kissing him as her hand gently ruffles through his feathers. "Just cleaned up?"

"Ana, yes. We need to get clean."

"Hmm. Okay."

He takes her hand, smiling at her. They step out, telling Roesh they are returning to their quarters. She sees Aylin trying to look.

"Rafe, I think they would like to see our handiwork."

He opens the door. Roesh and Aylin step up, looking in. "Very nice office, Majesty," Aylin says.

"Thank you."

They return to their quarters. Rafe takes Ana to the closet, getting pajamas out. She goes to her dresser and gets out a pair of lacy undergarments. She slips them under her robe, carrying them to the washroom. Once inside, Rafe starts the water. She undresses and steps in, waiting for him. As soon as he's under the water, she grabs him and kisses him, hard and hungry.

"Please, love?"

He leans down, returning her kiss as his hand ruffles through her feathers. He plants his hand on the small of her back, smiling as the moan of pleasure escapes her lips. He pushes her to the back wall, holding her up. His hand works down her chest and stomach, stroking her desire as he moves up and down. She holds onto him, gripping him tight as her back crashes against the wall, crying out when she succumbs. She grabs his wrist, pulling his hand up and kissing it.

She pulls him to her, turning so he is against the wall, as her hand wraps around and gently strokes. As his pleasure washes into her, she collapses on him as he finishes. She looks up at him, kissing him.

"Thank you, love."

"We both needed that. Now, will you rest until we go to bed?"

She brings her hand up, caressing along his chest. "Hmm. Did you say bed?"

"Ana!" he cries out, grabbing her hands and pulling her to him. He kisses her hard. "We need to get cleaned up."

She doesn't argue, knowing he has yet to see what else she has planned. He watches her wash off, as she smiles back at him. She steps out and dries off, slipping on the undergarments. She puts on her robe and slippers, stepping out. She sits on the chaise, waiting for him.

As he's walking to her, he looks her up and down. "Are you feeling okay?"

She takes his hand and leads him to the bed. She slips off

the robe, smiling as he sucks in his breath. "Rafe, please."

"You are supposed to rest."

"I know. I thought maybe… um…" She takes a breath as he patiently waits. "I thought we could practice some more."

"Okay. Only for a minute."

"Thank you."

He places her on the mattress. "You're okay?"

"Yes. I want to try something different." She lays him down, then she climbs on top of him. She gently straddles him as she kisses him. "I think this will be less overwhelming for me, on our wedding night. How do you feel?" She smiles at him when he turns red. "Rafe, I'm sorry!"

He laughs. "Just like on the couch, huh?"

"Oh, love. Let me take care of this."

She unbuttons his pajama shirt, kissing along his chest. She works lower, when he pulls her to him and kisses him. "No, Ana."

"Why not?"

"I don't want to overwhelm you, not so close to bed. I'll be okay."

"Rafe, I swear to you I want to do this, too."

Only seeing her love and want reflecting in her eyes, he relents. "With your hands, mia estrela."

"Yes, love."

With a smile on her face, she assists him in taking off his pajamas. She wraps her hand around, teasing along. He trembles at her touch, his back arching. He moans when she slows down then speeds up, teasing him again. Her body quivers, responding to the pleasure she is giving him.

She nearly screams in delight when he finishes, as he grabs her to him and kisses her, all of his love and hunger consuming her lips. She lays on him, mirroring his breathing rhythm. Leaning on her elbow, she directs her gaze towards him.

"Not what I had planned!"

He laughs. "You have a handsome guy in your bed, what

did you think was going to happen?"

She returns the laughter, thinking of their office. "Right. I'll grab you a towel and get dressed."

She runs to the washroom, slipping on her pajamas and bringing him a towel. After helping him clean, she puts it in the hamper. She washes her hands, then opens the door, asking Aylin to please get them dinner. Returning to the bed, she finds Rafe still lying there.

"Are you all right?"

"I will be. Hmm, what you do to me!" He grabs her hand and pulls her on top of him. "I think that will be fine for the wedding night."

She looks at him, caressing his face and smiling at him. "As long as we're together, that's all I care about. Are you getting less nervous? Does this practice help?"

"It does. What about you?"

She chuckles. "You know me. I'm going to be nervous about every single thing! This is helping, though. I really think it's going to make it easier for us, having some idea of what's coming."

"You?" he asks.

"Rafe!" she says, falling off him with laughter. "Really?" She looks up as he climbs over her, kissing her gently. He pulls off when she tenses up. "I'm okay."

"No, I feel that. We will practice that early in the day, when you aren't so tired and overwhelmed."

"Thank you, love," she says, cupping his face and kissing him again. The bells rings. "Dinner is here!"

Rafe opens the door and helps them set up. He comes back, taking her hand and walking her to their table. She sits and eats with him.

"I'm happy to see you like this, but it worries me."

"What's below the surface?"

"Exactly."

"Except, now we know that can happen. I know to turn

to you, not to hide or run away if it does."

"Do you know that?"

She stares into his eyes, returning his intensity. "I truly do. No matter what happens, no matter how bad, I am to turn to you. Whether it's asking you to hold me or tell you everything."

"I want that. I really want that. You say you can't prove your love to me because you aren't ready to be with me? Prove it by showing me your soul. Expose me to your very core, everything you are."

"I will. No matter what."

He kisses her, finishing his meal. "Do you want to send dishes back and have dessert brought in?"

"That would be wonderful. Thank you." She stands up, helping him gather dishes. He steps out with them. She walks to the sofa, looking out at the rain. She takes his hand when he sits with her. "I hope it's not doing this Saturday for their wedding."

"I know. I'm sure Kara's worried enough."

"I wish she had let me help more. She was really quiet about everything. I don't know why."

"Ana, she knows you've had to deal with so much. From what I understand, it will be a very simple wedding with a small reception. It's not like she's having hundreds of guests and all of that."

"Oh, guests. We can start working on our guest list."

"We have an office."

She smiles at him. "Yes, we do. We'll work on wedding stuff in there, too. Believe me, I wish it could be us, our friends and a few guardians. Instead, I have to invite dignitaries, ambassadors, and other monarchs. Not a small, simple wedding. I shouldn't complain, though. At least we can get married, and we're getting married in the chapel we want."

Rafe goes over to get the dessert tray. He walks back, handing Ana her cocoa. She sets it on the table beside her, as he does the same. He puts the tray down between them. She eats a petit cake.

"And the cake! Oh, so much to do."

"Ana, we have months to plan. It's okay."

"We need to plan for the Rose Ball, too. Invitations should be sent out in the next week or two."

"You're really excited about this one, aren't you?"

"A ball in honor of my mother? Of course I am. I really wish I could've met her. I've only heard the kindest things said about her." She sees a look on Rafe's face. "What?"

"Hmm? Nothing."

"Rafe?"

"My father thought your mother was the most beautiful woman he'd ever seen. I won't say he was in love with her or anything like that, just that he admired her for her beauty and compassion."

"I wonder what he would've thought of me. Do you think he would've liked me? Would approve of our union?"

"Not at first, obviously. Not if he knew from the beginning. Once the treaty was passed, he would've been very open about you."

"When was the last time you saw your father?"

"He was with me when they removed my wings. I left almost immediately after. I promised him I would find you, that we would have peace."

"Then you kept your promise," she smiles at him.

"One of them."

"What do you mean?"

"I promised him I would tell him all about it when I got back."

"You still can. I'll go with you, to the Cathedral of the Dead."

"Your parents are there, too."

"Oh, right. Still, I will go with you. When you're ready."

"Why do we do this? It's so close to us going to bed, and we go from happy topics like weddings to something like death?" He looks over when Ana laughs. "What?"

"I mean, you're right. I don't know how we do that. Honestly, it's all tied together. My father was responsible for the death of yours. You knew my mother. I'm curious and ask because I never got to know them. I don't mean to do it before bed. It's just, we're sitting here talking. It came up. I'm sorry."

"It's all right. I worry over you, is all. I want you to have a good night. I know you didn't sleep last night. You need to rest. We have a full week ahead of us, getting ready for Kara and Evren's wedding, hosting her family."

"You're right. I'll use the washroom, and we can turn in. We can talk more in bed, of pleasant things."

"Okay."

She goes to the washroom then waits for him. He carries her to bed, holding her to his chest. She laces her fingers through his, holding his hand tightly.

"Ana? Are you okay?"

"I will be," she quietly says.

He holds her tight, feeling her fear and shame. "Oh, mia estrela. I'm right here, whatever you need."

"Please, please, don't let him hurt me this time!" she cries out, sobbing into his chest. Rafe holds her and reassures her as best he can, looking down when he realizes she's fallen asleep.

"I would give anything to take your pain, to stop it from happening in the first place. I'm so sorry I was too late. I was too late finding you on Earth, and I was too late to his camp."

"Hmm. Rafe, no. Not your fault," she mumbles, yawning. "I don't blame you. Please, don't blame yourself. I can't take your guilt."

He closes his eyes, quickly focusing. He'd forgotten she could feel that. Thinking of their kiss in the chapel, planning a wedding, getting married, brings a smile to his face. "I love you, my warrior queen. Sleep now."

He watches her fall back to sleep. He wants to stay awake all night, comforting her and reassuring her. Her exhaustion is too powerful, overtaking him. He falls asleep holding her tight.

Chapter 37

Thursday morning, Ana wakes up, looking at Rafe.

"Royse comes today." Her voice wavers with her nervousness.

"Ana, it's going to be okay. You reached out, got what you needed. If he starts anything, you'll quickly finish it."

"I hope so."

"Let's get cleaned up and dressed. Kara and Evren will bring breakfast shortly. They need you strong."

"You're right. It's their big day coming up. I'll be okay." She gets out of bed, stretching her wings and yawning. She sees the look on Rafe's face. "What?"

"That's the first time I've ever seen you do that."

"What? I stretch my wings every day."

"Not first thing." He stands up, kissing her forehead. "It's cute."

"Like you?"

He attacks her with gentle kisses. "I am not cute!"

She laughs, playfully fighting him off. "Thank you. I know the week started off a little rough, with everything Sunday. Your patience and love have helped me so much." She folds into his chest, holding him tightly. "I may need that again, worrying over this wedding."

"Whatever you need, I'm right here."

"Please help me not embarrass myself."

"Ana! You are the queen. You don't have to be so worried. Everything will go smoothly. You'll see."

She pulls back, looking up at him. "That's what I'm hoping. Now, about my wings? They did that on their own when I stretched. Is that normal?"

"It is."

"They'll move on their own like that?"

"If they're tight or need to stretch, they can. It's usually only first thing in the morning and doesn't happen very often. Did you have a bad night?"

"No, I promise I didn't. Might be because we didn't get to really stretch them yesterday."

"We will today, after breakfast."

"The morning briefing—"

"You need to stretch your wings. We have company coming after lunch, so if we don't this morning, we may not get a chance today."

"Okay."

Proceeding to the closet, she retrieves a selected gown. The sight makes her smile. She places it on the ottoman while grabbing new undergarments. They clean up in the shower. Drying off, she gets dressed in her undergarments and robe. She goes into the closet, slipping into the gown. She slips on her silver shoes and crown. Rafe comes in.

"Ana, is that one of yours?"

"It is."

"It's beautiful!"

"Thank you." She smiles at him, going to the mirror. The gown is sky blue, draped with white lace roses. Long tulle sleeves and a billowing skirt flowing down. She smiles at the sight. She looks up at Rafe. "Wings?"

"How did you know?"

She laughs as they open. "Well?"

"You know how beautiful you are, right?"

"Thank you, love."

She steps out as he finishes getting dressed. She smiles at the sight, his shirt the same color as her gown. They look up as Kara and Evren walk in, breakfast behind them.

"Royse will be here this afternoon. I'm hoping he truly is on his best behavior."

"Evren, it's okay. We'll deal with whatever happens. Just focus on what's coming Saturday. All right?"

"Yes, Ana. Thank you."

She looks at Kara. "Are you packed and ready for your honeymoon?"

"Pfft. You know me. I'll pack Saturday morning."

"Kara!"

"What? It's how I've always been. You know that." She laughs. "Knowing you, you'll probably be packed a month before!"

"I like to be prepared. Nothing wrong with that."

"I'm already packed," Evren boasts.

Ana and Kara laugh. "That's good, Evren. That's the smart way to do things." Ana laughs again when Kara sticks out her tongue. "Really, sis?"

"What?"

"Oh, we won't be at the briefing this morning. I need to stretch my wings, and we probably won't have a chance this afternoon, everything going on."

"Understandable. Do you want us to have lunch brought in here?"

"That would be fine. We'll plan for lunch here at eleven."

"All right. We'll take care of dishes and see you then. Are you going to fly in that gown?"

Ana laughs. "Yes, I am. I need to continue practicing in what I normally wear, to help it feel more natural."

"I'll take your word on that," Kara says, getting to her feet. She and Evren gather dishes and leave.

"Kellan and Erick are outside. Roesh and Aylin volunteered last weekend, so Melian gave them today through Sunday off."

"I'm glad to hear that. They need a break."

Rafe takes her hand, stepping out. Kellan and Erick come to attention. "Where to, Rafe?" Erick asks.

"Training center."

"Love, it's not raining out."

"Hmm. Promise you won't overdo it? We have a big weekend ahead."

"I promise."

"Change of plans, Erick. Our battlement."

"Yes, Rafe."

They escort them there, standing guard as Ana and Rafe go up. She steps into the center, opening and closing her wings. She laughs when he joins her. "Are you mocking me?"

"Me? Majesty, I would never!" he says, as his wings open and close with hers. "Why would you ever say that?"

Her head rolls back as laughter escapes her lips. Rafe smiles at the sight, thinking he hasn't seen her laugh like that in a long time. "What am I going to do with you?" she asks, taking to the sky.

"Ana!"

"What?" she playfully asks. "Catch me if you can."

"Ana!" he tries again, laughing as he chases her. "You are supposed to take it easy! We have company coming."

She flies over to him, taking him in her arms. "I know, but they need the exercise, too. I really don't want them to pop open, not in front of everyone!"

"I know you worry about that. We can practice a little more tonight, in our quarters. Keep working them throughout the day, all right?"

"Yes, love. Thank you." They lower back down, going into the hall. "Since we have a little time until lunch, could we stop by our office for a moment?"

"Of course." He smiles at Erick. "It's right over here. I'll lead."

They go to their office. Kellan steps in, checking the rooms. Rafe takes Ana inside. She goes to her desk, getting out her book of paper samples.

"We need to get our invites made up for the Rose Ball."

"Have you picked out what you want?"

"I think so." She brings them around to his desk. "I like this pale pink paper with the lace pattern. Any thoughts on font?" She shakes her head. "I'm sorry. You probably don't care—"

"Ana, it's our first ball that we are hosting. Of course, I care." He looks them over, pointing at a script font. "I think that will be fine."

"We'll get these taken care of and sent out. One less thing to deal with right now."

"We can deliver them to the scrivers now, if you want."

"Hmm. There's something else I want."

He looks up at her, smiling. He takes the book and places it back on her desk. He walks back over, clearing off his desk and sitting her on it. He steps up between her legs, kissing her hard. Her hand is ruffling through his feathers, as he grabs her by the back of her head, his lips devouring hers. He groans when there's a knock at the door. He steps back, going to open it as she rushes to put his things back on his desk. Kellan enters.

"What's wrong?" Rafe asks.

"My apologies. Evren's guests have arrived early. They are asking for an audience with the queen."

Ana takes a deep breath. "Then that's what they shall have. Where are we greeting them?"

"We set up the Lunala Ballroom to greet them. Evren made sure there is food and drink."

"Thank you, Kellan."

***

"It's going to be okay," Rafe assures her once they reach the ballroom.

"Yes, love."

They go inside as Kara and Evren arrive. They walk up to Royse and his entourage. He looks Ana up and down, not trying to hide his contempt.

"Majesty," he says, giving a half bow.

"Royse," she says, intentionally ignoring his title. "I hope your trip was not unpleasant." He towers over her, his hair white and flowing down his back. His eyes are piercing green, the same color as Evren's. He's dressed in white and silver robes.

"It was fine. Thank you for this… food," he says. He turns to Evren. "Well, hello, elletta. Long time, no see."

"Royse," she says. "How are you?"

"Tired. I'll be better once I've had a chance to rest and get some decent food in me."

"There is nothing wrong with this food. I picked it out myself."

"That explains it."

Ana bites her tongue, seeing the anger flash on Rafe's face. "Well, we can get you to your quarters, if you'd like to rest and freshen up," Ana offers.

"Yeah, later." He turns back to Evren. "So, where is your groom?"

Evren takes Kara's hand. "This is my bride," she proudly says.

"What? A human? Have you lost your mind?"

"She's not a human!" Evren exclaims. "She is an immortal, like me."

"She looks like a human. You really have no shame, do you? As if being a slave wasn't enough for you! Just because you managed to somehow climb into a higher status, doesn't make you any better than you were."

Ana walks up to him. "She earned her place. She didn't bribe or threaten anyone to get it. She has many friends in her court."

"Are you accusing me of something?" Royse asks.

"Of course not, *Lord* Royse. I was speaking of Evren. If you think it's against you, what does that say?"

"This does not concern you. Why don't you fly back to your little court?"

Rafe sees Ana's face turn red. He shoots Kara a look, seeing her smile at him, as she knows what's coming.

"Lord Royse, I am the Crimson Queen and will be crowned Empress over the Realms. I have authority to banish you from this realm, and I will happily message your king to tell him why," she says, as her wings expand open. "I laid down and died in battle protecting my people. If you think I will stand here and let you treat a good friend and trusted member of my court this way, you are sadly mistaken!"

His eyes go wide at the sight of her. "Majesty," he says, giving a full bow. "A thousand apologies. I must be more tired from travel than I realized."

"Apologize to Evren, and I will let her decide your fate."

He turns to her. "I'm sorry, elletta. I said I was coming in the spirit of peace, but I let my pride take over. I am truly sorry."

"Royse can stay, for now. As long as he behaves."

"Yes, Evren. You say the word, and I will take care of it."

"You truly are in the queen's inner circle. I didn't realize."

Evren looks behind him, seeing a female elf fixing a small plate of food. She has platinum hair in braids, wearing pink and white robes. "Royse, who is that?"

"Our sister."

"What?" Evren asks, shocked. "She said she wasn't coming!"

"She changed her mind."

"Adara?" Evren asks. She turns and looks at her. "You came?"

"Yes, sister. I have heard how well you are doing and wanted to see for myself. I must say, I never expected that you would be in such high regard with royalty."

"Evren has earned her place in my court. She is a good, well-trusted friend and companion. It is because of her I freed our slaves."

"High praise, Majesty," Adara says, bowing. "My apologies. I am Lady Adara of the Solstice Court."

"It is an honor to meet Evren's family. I apologize, as I did not know you were coming. We can have quarters arranged for you—"

"I'm not staying. I wanted to see her. Well, and if I'm being honest, you. After hearing of the Crimson Queen."

"Why aren't you staying?" Evren asks.

"I have no interest to. I wanted to see what you look like, see if you really were doing as well as I had heard."

"Adara, please stay. We have so much to catch up on."

She looks at Royse, who nods. "Fine. I'll stay."

"Thank you, sister," Evren says.

"I'll get quarters arranged," Rafe says, stepping out to the hallway. Ana takes his hand when he returns. He turns to Royse. "I apologize, as I did not introduce myself. I am Rafe."

Royse scoffs. "Why would I want to meet a lowly guardian?"

Before Ana can say anything, Evren walks up to him, her finger in his face. "He is betrothed to the queen and will be crowned as prince. You show him the respect he deserves, or I will take her up on her offer!"

Royse raises his hands, gesturing surrender. "Yes, elletta." He turns back to Rafe. "My apologies, Guardian."

"It's fine," Rafe says. "Eat and rest. I know the travel is hard."

"Thank you."

They look up as royal guards walk in. "We will escort you to your quarters, once you are ready."

"We'll go now. I do need to freshen up," Royse says.

"As do I," Adara agrees.

Rafe and Ana watch them leave. She turns to Evren. "Are you all right?"

"I'm fine, Ana. Thank you."

"What did Royse call you?"

"Oh, elletta. It means little elf. It's supposed to be a term of endearment, but I believe he uses it in jest."

"Evren, you don't have to put up with him."

"It's all right. I want to give him a chance. Kara and I discussed it, and if he is rude the whole time, we won't go to Vulcara. Not this trip, at least."

"Okay. If he or Adara get to be too much, please talk to me."

"Thanks, Ana. I appreciate your concern and everything you've said today."

"Evren, you know how much you mean to me. I'm grateful I can help, if you need me to."

"Yes, Ana. I'll let you know."

"So, what now? With Royse and Adara, I mean?"

"We'll have dinner with them in the dining hall. You and Rafe do not have to attend. Honestly, for tonight, it might be best if you didn't. So I can see how he truly acts."

"Understandable. We still need lunch."

"Have you ever had elvish food?" Evren asks.

"No, I can't say I have."

Evren takes her over, explaining the different foods. Ana and Rafe fix a plate and sit. She tries each piece, hoping not to gag or have any issues. She's relieved that the food is at least edible. Not nearly as good as vampyra cuisine, but she can stomach it.

"What do you think?" Evren asks.

Ana smiles at her. "It's good. Thank you." Her eyes meet Rafe's, but she fights back a laugh at the look on his face. She gives him a sympathetic look. They finish eating. "We are returning to our quarters. I need to rest after flying and meeting new people. Enjoy your dinner with family. We will see you both for breakfast in the morning, if you want."

"Yes," Kara says, "that will be fine. We'll see you then." She takes Evren's hand and leaves.

Rafe looks at Ana. "What's wrong?"

"Couldn't you hear the stress in Kara's voice?"

"No, I'm sorry."

She takes a breath. "I hope she's okay. She's so protective of Evren and seeing how she is already being treated. I don't want any incidents. She has enough to deal with, since her sister decided to crash the wedding."

"Honestly, I think she came to see you."

"The Crimson Queen of legend?"

"Exactly."

Ana yawns. "I do need to rest before dinner."

"Come along. We'll get changed and take a nap."

She takes his hand, stepping out into the hallway. Kellan and Erick escort them back. Kellan checks inside. Rafe takes Ana in after the quarters have been cleared. She removes her gown, putting it into the hamper. She picks out a nightgown, getting cleaned up and changed. She brushes her teeth, then steps out. She sits on the chaise, waiting for Rafe. He picks her up, carrying her to bed.

"I'm sorry."

"For what?"

"Being too tired to do anything."

"Ana, we knew this would probably happen. It's okay. Maybe we can have some time in the morning, depending on how you feel."

"You know, there is a chance I could be too tired on the night of our wedding. I hope not, but—"

"It'll be fine. We'll have all week in MorningStella."

"Thank you. I'm so scared I'm going to ruin it."

"Ana, I promise you, you won't ruin anything."

"Rafe, love, can I finish, please?"

"Yes, I'm sorry."

"It's okay. I'm so scared I'm going to ruin it, even though I know that's not the case. That you've told me, no matter what happens, everything will be okay. I'm trying to believe that."

"Please, do. It's the truth." He smiles at her as she grips his shirt. "Still holding on, huh? Always?"

"Forever," she replies. "I never want to be away from you again. My heart can't take it. Even thinking of it, makes me hurt."

"You won't be. I'm right here, not going anywhere." He kisses her forehead. "Get some rest."

"Yes, love."

Chapter 38

Rafe wakes up and checks the time. It's a little after three. He stretches and looks down, only to discover he's alone. "Ana?" he calls out. He checks the washroom and closet, only to be surprised they are both empty. Concentrating while he closes his eyes, he tries to feel for her.

Fear courses through him when he cannot sense her. He dresses before stepping out into the corridor. Kellan and Erick are not at their usual post. He goes next door to Kara and Evren's quarters, but no one answers. He runs to the Medical Center.

"Is Ana here?" he asks as Winslow steps out of his office.

"No. I haven't seen her."

"Shit!"

"Is she missing?"

"Yes. I have to notify Melian and Ramin."

He runs down to the barracks. Melian jumps to her feet at the sight of him.

"The queen is missing."

"We'll search the grounds for her."

Rafe runs back upstairs, going to their office. He checks inside, groaning in frustration that she isn't there. He's going back to their quarters when he sees Kara and Evren returning to theirs.

"Ana is missing!"

"What?" Kara says. "Where could she be?"

"We laid down to take a nap. I woke up, and she was gone. Along with Kellan and Erick."

"She wouldn't leave without telling you!" She looks at Evren. "We have to do something."

"Can you find her again? Like when Everard took her?"

They run inside his quarters. Kara goes to the drawer, getting out her engagement ring. She sits on the ottoman, performing her location spell. She closes her eyes, searching. She sees Ana lying in bed with Rafe, when a hand clamps over her mouth and drags her away. The vision goes dark.

"She was taken, but I don't know where!"

Evren joins. "I'll help."

They try again. Kara focuses, seeing Ana. She gasps at the sight. "She's in her father's quarters."

"That's where Royse is staying!" Evren exclaims.

Rafe grabs his sword, attaching it to his belt. They run to Caelum's chambers. He pounds on the door, breaking it open when no one answers. Ana is in purple magical bindings, lying unconscious on the floor. Rafe rushes to her, shocked to see the bruises on her face and legs.

"Freeze."

He looks up, a pistol at his temple. He slowly stands up, backing away. "Who are you?"

"I managed to get a place with Royse's entourage. We are fascinated with your Crimson Queen. I am under instruction to bring her back to my realm so we can study her."

"You aren't taking her anywhere!" Rafe declares. "Now, set her free before I kill you myself!"

"I have the upper hand here."

He looks at Evren when she moves suddenly, giving Rafe the chance to grab the pistol away. He pulls out his sword, battling Rafe. Ana comes to, looking up and seeing what's happening. She tries to get free of her bindings but is unable to. She gets to her feet, turning her wings to fire. She breaks free as the kidnapper charges at Rafe.

Unaware Ana had gotten to her feet, Rafe steps aside. He can only watch in horror as the kidnapper's blade goes into her stomach. She grabs his sword, pulling it out and stabbing him. She takes a breath as her wings return to their soft plumage. Rafe catches her.

Acknowledgements

Stephanie, my editor, who did an amazing job.

Kevin, my husband, who supports me and gives me unconditional love on this writing journey.

To my sister Lisa, for everything.

To my beta readers, thank you for your input.

To my followers on social media, who helped with cover adjustments and gave me support.

To my readers, thank you.

Thank you, God, for my love of writing, romance, and fantasy!

About the Author

A.R. Kaufer lives in Indiana with her husband and furbabies. When she's not playing video games or watching movies, she is reading or writing. She can be found on Twitter, TikTok, Instagram, Threads, BlueSky, and Pinterest, and she is happy to hear from her readers.

Author Photo By:
Kevin Kaufer